Lucky in Love

From the Portuguese series

MIGUEL TORGA
Tales and More Tales from the Mountain

JOSÉ RODRIGUES MIGUEIS
Happy Easter

JOSÉ SARAMAGO
Manual of Painting and Calligraphy

MIGUEL TORGA
The Creation of the World:
The First Day and the Second Day

EUGÉNIO LISBOA (editor)
The Anarchist Banker and other Portuguese Stories

Professor Pfiglzz and his Strange Companion

David Mourão Ferreira

LUCKY IN LOVE

translated by

CHRISTINE ROBINSON

CARCANET

in association with

CALOUSTE GULBENKIAN FOUNDATION

INSTITUTO CAMÕES

INSTITUTO PORTUGUÊS DO LIVRO E DAS BIBLIOTECAS

Um Amor Feliz by David Mourão Ferreira
was first published in Portugal in 1986
by Presença
This translation first published in Great Britain in 1999
by Carcanet Press Ltd
Conavon Court, 12–16 Blackfriars Street
Manchester M3 5BQ

This book belongs to the series *From the Portuguese*
published in Great Britain by Carcanet Press
in association with the Calouste Gulbenkian Foundation (UK),
with support from Instituto Português do Livro e das Bibliotecas
and Instituto Camões, and with the collaboration of Portugal 600

A CIP catalogue record for this book
is available from the British Library

ISBN 1 85754 388 2

The publisher acknowledges financial assistance
from the Arts Council of England

Set in 11/12pt Bembo
by XL Publishing Services, Lurley, Tiverton, Devon
Printed and bound in Great Britain
by Short Run Press, Exeter

I

She comes in, she lies down: there are times when these two actions happen in such quick succession it's as though the other, hesitant or blindly frenzied procedure doesn't take place, quite magical in its simplicity, whereby she first takes off her shoes, then discards her clothes.

Lying across the wide divan, in an almost panic-stricken expectancy of being worshipped, her arms suddenly assume the posture of two oblique branches. Slowly, she brings them together, until they are fully stretched out behind her; in the meantime, her legs have already begun to reproduce, in an inverted position, the same pattern of a letter.

To keep things simple, let's say that her name is Y. (And I find myself muttering: Why...?) Apart from neither wanting nor being able to mention her name, her name is what matters least of all; or what ought to matter least of all to us. Yet just by calling her Y she at once becomes different from who she is, from who I think she might be.

Bestowing this monogram immediately disguises her a little, concealing and diffusing her slightly, as though much of her face and hair are also partly veiled and intricately half-hidden by her vaporous, loose-knit white shawl, which she only ever wears over her naked shoulders. It makes matters worse: she then appears even more desirable to me.

The white shawl is her unfailing attire during our intimate ritual on winter days. She never forgets to bring it along, fluffily folded up in the bottom of her Hermès bag, buried under a jumble of beauty-cream tubs, hair-spray, a hair-brush, a bottle of perfume or eau-de-Cologne. I have suggested to her, on more than one occasion, that she should leave the shawl in one of those drawers in the dresser over by the entrance to this secret part of the atelier, yet she invariably ends up folding it up and spiriting it away in the bottom of her bag. She has often told me, however, that she never uses this shawl at home, and that neither her husband nor her daughter even know of its existence. Her father bought it for her in Rome, the last time they were both there, when she was still single.

As for her naked shoulders: when I mention her naked shoulders,

I am indeed thinking of the nakedness of all the rest.

I am stunned and awed every time I watch her enter the atelier, glowingly serene, like some goddess who only happens to be wearing clothes by mistake.

I delight in watching her rapid metamorphosis, soon after, on that divan over there or on this arm-chair here, into a provocative bacchante, almost scared of revealing this side of herself.

I experience a religious yet lucid ecstasy at being the one to bring about this metamorphosis, the one to participate actively in the liturgy of this passion.

I take pride, finally, after the climax, in being all the better able to contemplate the ravaged, somehow reborn, expanse of her body.

Yes, she is foreign. Or at least partly. On her father's side, she has a Portuguese great-grandfather and a Portuguese great-grandmother, who were both the product of the far-sighted bourgeoisie with a flair for business that was to become prominent during the Liberalist era. It was only during the final throes of the last war that this cosmopolitan branch of the family came back here to settle down again: Y was actually born in Portugal, and has spent most of her life in Portugal. Is she Scandinavian or Slav? British? German or American? It matters not.

Her husband, who also hails from foreign Northern shores, runs a few major businesses over here (properties in the Alentejo, a large factory on the outskirts of Lisbon), some of which have been in the hands of the family – her family – for three or four generations. Although they socialize mostly with other foreigners, they of course both speak quite good Portuguese. Especially her.

Is she beautiful? She is much, much more than beautiful. She is, rather, one of those women about whom other women, gulping gamely when they hear the old-fashioned term 'handsome' applied to her, cannot bring themselves to say much more than: 'It's a shame she's a little dull.' Or: 'What about that neck of hers... It won't hold out much longer. That's what usually happens with that kind of blonde.' Or even: 'When she was twenty, perhaps! You should have seen her when she was twenty!' And this last sanctimonious remark spurted from the fleshless lips of someone whom I still care for, yet when Y was twenty – and I should know! – was already beginning to look like the fifty-year-old woman she is today.

That's another thing, age. Her age should matter as little, or even less, than her name. But it does matter. Oh, how it matters!

When I was sixteen, I suffered dreadfully because of a moody, uninhibited Belgian girl who, with her family, had taken 'refuge' in Foz do Arelho, and who discovered, from one summer to the next, that she was in fact ten months older than me, which was all it took for her to start treating me like a kid, when we'd spent the previous summer among the steep rocks of a tiny, deserted beach, and she'd made me believe, intoxicatingly, that I was already quite a man. This retreat could be reached, with relative ease, at low tide, across the sand; then, as soon as the tide came in, we would be cut off, feeling free and safe, as if we were not of this world, or were at the dawning of the world. We would remain hidden from everyone for hours on end. As for my mother, she was aware of everything whilst pretending not to be, and during the first of those summers, she went no further than making fun of the Belgian girl, gritting her teeth whenever she said 'septante' instead of 'soixante-dix', and criticizing her from a distance, she would condemn the scantiness or garishness of her attire, exclaiming in private, as though in physical pain: 'What manners, Madonna mia! The likes of this have never been seen in this hotel before!' My stepfather, in turn, referred to my girlfriend as 'that wooden spoon'; he doubted that anyone with good taste 'could find that scarecrow attractive'. Yet the following summer, when they saw how wretched and alone I was, they were both more than willing to acknowledge the fact that the girl had changed, that she had even become 'gallant'.

Later, when I was twenty-four, I suffered embarrassments of a different magnitude, thanks to an entirely Portuguese platinum blonde, who was all eyes and mouth, all legs and chest, and who lived off a specialist in all things African. Her most persistent ambition was to appear on stage one day, in spite, she confessed with touching fortitude, of already being thirty-two years old. Hence my vexation: I thought of her as too 'old'. And one night, somewhere in the Bairro dos Actores, with the Africanist conveniently away in Africa, we had the most hellish row that lasted nearly until sunrise, after I chanced to find out – from the identity card left on top of her dressing-table (which she called a *psyché*) – that she was in fact thirty-six.

Oh, what tears the buxom blonde shed when she was faced with that damning piece of concrete evidence! Oh, how ashamed and reluctant I was from then on, even with the Africanist away in Africa, even to escort her to the cinema or to some local tea-house!

Having come to terms with the scandalous eight-year difference – what a huge gap! – it was such a cruel, indelible stigma to find out about those four extra miserable hundredths of a century!

Everything has to be paid for, often in the least expected way. Thirty-six is Y's age now. She was thirty-five when we first met. Twenty-one years younger than me. This time, if there was to be any vexation at all, it ought to be the other way round. Yet I do not feel vexed. Instead, I express something akin to arrogance on the outside and pride on the inside; but deep down, I feel quite uneasy and somewhat perplexed.

On the whole the predominant feeling is pride. Especially as it was she who... How shall I put it? As it was she who came to me, she who out of the blue... *chose* me. And in the least hypocritical manner possible; in the most simple and amazingly straightforward way.

As though pride matters to me! What does matter is the glorious fulfilment that Y has brought to my life at a time when I no longer expected anything from women, apart from those sudden outbursts of admiration with which they try to delude themselves or make themselves look good in the eyes of others. Not to mention the more or less venal favours they ask of me ('How about giving me one of those drawings?'; or, 'Some eau-de-Cologne would come in handy right now...'). Not to mention, either, those impersonal affairs that have no morning after or day before.

Many of the birds who came through this studio over the last few years did not cast even the shadow of their half-spread wings over these walls: with some, it was because they were only aiming as high as the divan; with others, it was because they were merely excited by the thought that it would be known, if only to themselves, that they had been through here; others probably also failed because they were only hoping, in passing through here, for a chance to escape from themselves; most of them, it must be said, were actually in too much of a hurry.

With Y, not only was she totally disinterested, but she also made the least concession possible to the hateful tyranny of Time.

Oh, that first morning when she walked in here! From then on, it was as though everything had been transfigured.

That divan, these plasters, these moulds, this arm-chair, these books, even that heater over there, even those easels on the side, those screens, those iron supports, and that dresser, and the mirror above the dresser, and this other mirror, running the breadth of the wall, all these things have taken on a different life, not quite because of a new light or a new atmosphere (these change each time she comes here), but because of a new correspondence between the different masses that seems suddenly to have been established for all time. Even the cleaning lady, who is as smooth and restless as a pebble in a waterfall, has never again dared, as she so often did before, to alter the position of this arm-chair or that divan, to slightly reposition one of the carpets, or even to point this monstrosity of a heater in any other direction.

While on the subject, I must just say this: on winter days, it is against the said monstrosity in particular that Y's white shawl stands out most of all.

II

I don't even know why I want to tell you, of all people, about this most ordinary, yet successful love affair.

That's a lie! Of course I do. As a matter of fact, it was you who, at the beginning of the year, told me something that I had never even thought about before. You confided in me some of the indispensable ingredients that make up the recipe for 'a successful love affair':

'Someone who's married… only with someone else who's married.'

Right from the start, from the very first time we met, even though you are younger than Y, a kind of complicity was established between you and me that we neither want, nor can allow, to go too far. But you must admit that it is quite fun, for both of us, to have this reticent pact of mutual support.

You wore an impeccably white shirt, with its collar pulled up over the back of your neck, and tight, dark-red velvet trousers, a chain bracelet of old-gold twisted round the fingers of your left hand, and your near-black hair was sensibly parted down the middle, only lightly waved either side of your forehead; you looked startled and wide-eyed from never having grown used to your contact lenses: indeed you appeared that night, from a distance, the living image of a chaste, well-behaved young girl who's been allowed to stay up as a treat to join the grown-ups' party. The contrast between all this and the conversation we were having, along with the clarity, maturity and capacity for shamelessness that your verses had revealed to me, was really quite disturbing. Which is why I was listening to you with rapt attention. Ten feet away from us, your green paediatrician and my mature paediatrician stood among four or five suitably assorted foreign paediatricians, and they must have thought we were trying to stare each other out.

(How will I be able to resist much longer the temptation of transcribing our dialogue that night? I have always enjoyed adding to the more than certain ephemerality of a conversation, the most probable ephemerality of its register.)

'Someone who's married,' you repeated, 'only with someone else who's married.' And that preferably one of them should be older. Preferably the man. Preferably even quite a bit older, little inclined to take new risks, especially capable of resisting the temptation of embarking on yet another extra-marital affair.

The reasoning seemed perfect to me. I was amazed I'd never thought about it myself: just like Columbus's egg.

That was it. As far as I could remember, the only serious problems I'd ever had until then were because of spinsters, widows or divorcées. To start with (or do I mean to end with?), there was the far-away instance of the ample Xô who, in a manner most Brazilian, incorporated the last two of these civil statuses, and who, in a manner no less Brazilian, passed herself off in Europe as the first. And remembering the distant image of the distant Xô (alive or dead, where exactly on this planet was she?), memories would jostle in my mind like a series of slides being shown too fast, of days on end spent in Rome, of small beaches on the outskirts of Amalfi, and Pompeii on the way back, then Rome again, and a furious argument in the quietness of the Via Giulia, and my extreme vexation by a fountain in the Piazza Navona…

'Have you noticed?' you asked me immediately afterwards. 'Have you noticed how we must look like a couple of drips amongst all these prominent names in Paediatrics?'

'That's how far our duty as scouts goes… A good deed two or three times a year.'

'Blessed meetings…'

'…during which we acquire a clear conscience!'

'They're worthwhile if only for that.'

'Especially, as far as I'm concerned, when I'm sure you're going to be there.'

'*Touchée.* Just as well you didn't say that smugly.'

'As if I could do such a thing! It's your paediatrician who is looking smug…'

'Seeing us behave so well?'

'And for looking good in the shadow of my paediatrician…'

'Ah, yes… God made them, God united them.'

'This time, I can assure you, my wife has at long last found the perfect assistant.'

'The assistant who assists.'

'The assistant who is assisted.'

'We're being rather naughty, wouldn't you say…? At least those two are pure.'

'There's no doubt about that. At least in the case of the one I know better.'

'That's nice of you…'

'And us?'

'What about us?'

'Aren't the two of us pure as well?'

'I think so. I just can't understand…'

'Probably because we belong to two different generations and have both made the same big mistake.'

'Do you think it takes a mistake to make one pure? What was our mistake, then?'

'That of thinking we would be protected from I don't know what, safe against I don't know what, simply by resorting to… very much married paediatricians.'

'You're right. As if one can be a prophet in one's own country!'

It was the closing dinner of yet another of those unavoidably unforgettable International Paediatrics Days that no one remembers any more. After the memorable session of fado singing for foreigners to listen to and then forget, for foreigners not to understand, for foreigners to be able to say that, yes, they had indeed found it entrancing, we had withdrawn somehow, on the top floor of that pseudocosmopolitan hotel, to that window from which Lisbon could barely be seen under a ragged cloak of fog: a grubby, eerie, crudely lit city, reeling under unemployment, with businesses and salaries in arrears.

We went on to say that your husband and my wife had been treating children for so long that they were probably, irrevocably, much more childish in some ways than we were. Of course, for them the greatest proof of our incurable childishness lies in the fact that you line up a few legions of words that they don't believe are verses (and that they accept even less as being poetry) and I still 'concoct' some bits and pieces that most people, including them, refuse to see as sculpture. (So do I. Even I sometimes have my doubts.)

Here's a curious fact: it wasn't even then – why not? – that I told you what I think – what for? – of your book of poems. All I did was to confirm that I did not like the title. But you cannot begin to imagine the reason why I so often (under the pretext of getting you a drink, an ashtray, a box of matches) kept staring at you from a distance, especially when your back was turned. The truth is, that also had something to do with your book. Let's proceed.

At any rate, what there is between you and me has nothing actually to do with your verses, nothing to do with my 'objects': I will never quite understand what you write, nor will you ever be interested (although you perhaps see me as some kind of sacred cow) in understanding the things I've made. Even less, surely, would you understand the things I would have liked to have made, and which I've been giving up on bit by bit.

Let's not be complacent: there's no point in fooling myself, because that's the way it is. The more the years go by, the more I am interested in finding, in real life, the so-called Beauty – with a capital B if possible – which I appear to scorn in nearly all the 'objects' that leave my hands. Or in finding, at least, the delight and fulfilment that the fruition of such Beauty ought to bring with it. Whether it does or not is another matter. I don't know if it is the same in your case, something similar, or something quite different. I would swear, nevertheless, that we both drift between what we are inside and what the age we live in expects us to make.

My 'objects'! I've thought about calling them *hobbyjects* before; I've wanted to call them *holyjects* before. My *marchand* in Lausanne, that spoilsport, turned up his nose at both those terms. But I cannot help seeing my 'objects' as something half way between a hobby and a religion. That's how I really see them, which of course does not prevent them being, for most people, rejects rather than objects, with blessed little fun about them, let alone holiness.

And then, as though this were not enough, there is that need for a kind of orgasm, a recurrent orgasm, that exists as much in the desire to play a few words off against each other, as it does in the fury of fusing or confusing a number of greatly diverse materials. Regarding the first of these tasks, I perhaps know a little more about it than you think I do.

Yes, we may indeed be children. But within the children that we are, we can never cease being horrifyingly adult. And I am always greatly dismayed by the wretched similarity between the word 'adult' and the word 'adultery'.

Adults, adulterers. How strange! Here are two words that never appear in the lyrics of fados. At least, not in any of those we'd just been listening to.

But without having to spell it out, the two of us realized there and then that we had practically the same vocation. And that, furthermore, there was not much likelihood of, or much to be gained by, our fulfilling it together just then. That, for the time being, we would prefer to exist in order to understand one another. Maybe even to help one another out, you with your intuition, and me with my experience. Or vice-versa.

'I've got it…'

'What?' I asked.

'Why we've suddenly gone quiet.'

'Well, why?'

I lit another of your long More cigarettes. And you carried on, after a first puff of smoke:

'You know why as well as I do. Because here we are, thinking about two other people… And longing to talk about them.'

'Could be.'

'But it's best not to say anything.'

'As you wish.'

'I've just one question to ask… May I?'

'Of course you may.'

'This person you're thinking about… Is she much younger than you?'

'By twenty years or so. Does it seem a lot to you? Does it seem too much?'

'No way. Not at all.'

'And in your case?'

'He's twenty years or so older than me.'

'That must be right, too.'

'Of course it is. I can assure you of that.'

'Has it been going on for long?'

'Over a year. How about you two?'

'Less. Quite a lot less.'

I'd only known Y for a month, if that.

III

I realize that throughout dinner (they had placed us at small adjacent tables but, fortunately, we ended up sitting almost opposite each other) I stared at her, I could hardly do anything but, and I did so so intensely that it would have been sheer impudence had she not been quite so beautiful. She must have taken it as a compliment, anyway; but something like a shadow of insecurity hovered over the barefaced simplicity with which she allowed herself to be watched.

Her eyes were huge, exceedingly well shaped; more than green, more than blue, they were almost beyond belief, bordering on the impossible. In those portfolios over there, I have dozens, perhaps even hundreds of drawings of Y's neck, Y's shoulders and bust, Y's arms, Y's entire body, some done with the model present, some sketched from memory. Only I have never dared to draw her face, much less her eyes.

And it was precisely those eyes of hers, seeming quite inaccessible to me, making her quite inaccessible to me, that gave me the nerve to look straight at her. But without the slightest intention – I swear! – of some day 'seducing' her or 'conquering' her (what loathsome words!), feeling only that emotional fervour – it, too, devoid of any intention of 'possession' (another loathsome word!) – that takes one's breath away when we are faced with a masterpiece – a masterpiece all the more surprising for being on loan to a mediocre, or even insignificant museum which we visit by chance, and where we are never likely to set foot again.

It was the first important dinner given by one of those Latin-American diplomatic couples who manage uncannily, six months after having got here, to become acquainted with all those people – and they believe *all* – they think are crucial to know in Lisbon. One of those couples who patiently put themselves to the trouble, week after week, of grouping these dummies into allegorical pairs, matrimonial or otherwise, so that they can best represent, I don't know, Politics and Literature, Diplomacy and Technology, Economy and Law, Music and Industry, Television, Transport, Tourism, Theatre, Bullfighting.

That night, if I'm not mistaken, my wife and I were symbolizing Medicine and Art: it was all too generic for us to symbolize, more specifically, Paediatrics and Sculpture. And when, at last, that somewhat 'Portuguesified' foreign couple arrived (who were also somewhat younger than most of those present), no one can have been left in any doubt: the husband might represent Finance, Agriculture or Foreign Investment, but as for the wife, she could only be there as the perfect representation of Beauty. There could have been no other strategic intention on behalf of the hosts.

When the time came for introductions, the appointed embodiment of Beauty (who, just because of that, was rubbing me up the wrong way) stood before my wife, smiling openly, in a way that quite disarmed me:

'Good evening, Doctor. Don't you remember me? You looked after my daughter when she was little... Vicky...'

'Ah! Yes, of course. I remember you very well.'

Then, when my wife asked after the child (who is not necessarily called Vicky), Vicky's mother raised her hand nearly level with her own forehead, in a gesture outlining in space the shape of a willowy young girl, and muttered through the same pretty, though slightly melancholy, smile:

'She's like this... About this big...'

Our hostess, who was watching the scene, baring her fangs, waited stolidly, with a patience worthy of an Inca or an Aztec, whilst the mother of the hypothetical Vicky provided my wife with additional information: the little girl was getting over her asthma; she was still at the French Lyçée; in two years time, she would be going to study in Switzerland; and they were, of course, still living in the same *quinta*[1] near Sintra.

Only then did I understand the Inca or Aztec patience of our hostess: she was not willing to let me be introduced by my wife, or merely as my wife's husband, both of which would result in openly damaging the allegorical nature of her party; and, as with all the other introductions, she made a point of following my name (after all, wasn't I there to represent Art?) with the required reference to my occupation as a sculptor. But, smiling all the time (ah, what a beautiful smile she had!), the mother of the purported child Vicky, in the almost veiled voice in which she always seemed to express herself, merely said, very softly:

'I have heard of you.'

At the same time, almost, her husband's handshake was casually formal, as was to be expected from his technocrat's spectacles; but he was also conventionally sporty, which suited his mid-winter suntanned skin.

Straight afterwards I lost sight of them; they were both swallowed up by the hubbub of introductions to other allegorical figures, clinking glasses, laughter, trays and conversations, while I found myself suddenly surrounded by walking allegories of Politics (a man), Music (a woman) and Diplomacy (somewhere in between) with whom I was expected to concur – none of them had any kind of opinion, although they all thought theirs was very different from everybody else's – about what our participation should be in the coming biennials of Caracas and Bogotá. Having reduced our non-existent disagreements to the convenient common denominators of yes-but-of-course, not-at-all, yes-yes-perhaps-why-not, Press and Literature then appeared (both women, and both ravaged ruins whom I'd known before when they were still in their monumental phase), anxiously beseeching me to tell them the story – to make a change from swallowing endless nauseating cocktails – that the latter had heard me tell, two weeks earlier, in the São Mamede Gallery, about the recent and simultaneous discovery of very rich oilfields in Jerónimos and Batalha, in the Temple of Diana and the monastery of Alcobaça, in the Torre de Belém and the convent of Tomar – an event that was obviously fictitious, but which did have, as far as I was concerned, the double advantage of solving the problems of our wretched economy, and also of greatly disconcerting the sterile minds of my colleagues, who were more and more concerned about saving our cultural heritage, but less and less able to contribute to it themselves.

I escaped as best I could from the clutches of the two fleshless, walking ruins, assuring them (a lie) that I was already writing this innocent little *art-fiction* tale as a sideline to my other work, and that I would have great pleasure in sending them, and only them, of course, a typewritten copy each, that they were to keep to themselves. (Another lie, of course: if I ever did get round to writing this little tale, how I'd like Literature to acknowledge it and Press to broadcast it! Deep down, I'm nothing more than a frustrated writer.)

In the meantime, the doors at the other end of the room were being opened and, already knowing which places they had been allocated, Literature and Press were among the first to rush around the six or seven tables that had been set in the adjoining room. As for me, I had forgotten to look at the seating plan in the hall, and with some difficulty I found myself walled in by an obese stage-manager (doubtlessly, she represented Theatre) and a rotund, but diminutive deputy (I never did find out whether she symbolized the whole Republican Assembly or simply Women's Rights). I found myself thanking the gods that I didn't have to spend too much time in conversation with them, as I neither knew them intimately enough, nor were they complete strangers to me. I found myself thanking the gods when the beautiful foreign (or almost foreign) lady with the eyes beyond compare sat down at the next table, almost opposite me, smiling at me as though we had known each other for ages, as though we had known each other for ever.

Even sitting down, she seemed taller than the two or three women, including Advertising, who were still milling around looking for their places.

Was it the candour of my harmless – or call it aesthetic – admiration that made her trust me straightaway? Or was it the apparent respectability of my greying mop of hair? Throughout dinner, both possibilities occurred to me: neither one nor the other was at all exciting. Better I should content myself with the lovely, unexpected spectacle before me, in itself more than enough compensation for all that tiresomely allegorical worldliness. As soon as the show was over, I would escape as fast as possible with my wife, far away from that sophisticated and noisy den full of civilized Amerindians. Too civilized by far, as far as I was concerned; or quite excessively un-Amerindian.

I had been immediately disgusted, in the hall, by the repulsive ornaments with which these poor first-class nomads, who actually looked so much more like gypsies, exuberantly indicated that Christmas was looming. Then in the living-room, the pseudo-Inca or pseudo-Aztec objects which the foolish women of Music, Press and Theatre had gone into ecstasies about, were only slightly less horrendous than the pseudo-canvases by pseudo-disciples of Kandinsky and Klein that our hosts had brought as mementoes and proof of their previous sojourn in a consulate in West Germany.

But when dinner was over and all the guests had flocked back into the living-room that housed said canvases and said objects, the beautiful semi-foreign lady with eyes more than green and more than blue, suddenly walked up from the back of the room, leaving behind her, with no great formality, the allegorical representatives of Politics and Economics who had flanked her throughout the meal, and strolled calmly towards me, smiling all the time, just to tell me, in her very low voice that was almost a murmur, with its slight accent, but with not the slightest interrogative inflexion:

'You realize I don't know any work you have done.' She corrected herself, 'Any of your work.' Then she added, 'It's my fault. I'm quite ignorant.'

Instead of asking her right there and then to visit my atelier (which I certainly would have done had she been merely pretty) or sanctimoniously trying to persuade her she wasn't ignorant (which I'm sure I would have done had she been a fool), I suddenly, as though I hadn't heard what I'd just heard, launched myself into a half-bitter, half-ironic attack on the artificial nature of such gatherings. That was the first time, when I talked to her, that I spoke out about all I had just discovered about allegories; and I must have done so with quite some animation: the presence of beautiful women, or even just pretty ones, still produces in me, in my gestures and in my words, a certain state of ebullience that my mother has always qualified as 'allergic' and that pedantic ladies call 'brilliant' – but that my paediatrician wife, much more soberly, merely refers to as 'clownesque'.

This time, it wasn't quite the same thing. It was something more spontaneous: it was a simple need to express what I was feeling just then; and to express it specifically to the only person there who seemed to me to be made of the stuff of gods and whom I considered also to be a complete human being.

In the meantime, we had sat down in a corner of the room, on two armchairs pulled up close together. Her gleaming knees, in spite of her dark blue stockings, were still obviously quite sun-tanned and gave off a shimmering glow as though from a half-hidden gas-fire.

In the corner almost opposite, talking with someone who was either Judiciary or Education, my wife stood stoically, in obedience to a theoretical slimming programme which never produced any visibly encouraging results, and she glanced at me complacently every now and then, more like a nurse than a paediatrician, thus keeping an eye on my behaviour with the splendid borrowed toy I was playing with. At times she would even smile, proud, I am sure, to see me so well-behaved. Looking less tall than she once had, but still quite imposing nevertheless, and with her hip measurements three times what they were when we got married thirty years ago, she looked more solid and trustworthy than all, or nearly all, the puppets that surrounded us. At the other end of the room, Y's husband was chatting to Diplomacy, and he kept his back perfunctorily turned towards us.

And somehow or other, we sailed off into a conversation about travelling.

All things considered, the Italy that Y knows like the back of her hand has little to do with the Italy on whose footpaths I destroyed the soles of many shoes, and where I nearly destroyed other things too. All things considered, the States that she visits often do not have much in common with the States that I barely know. But what did surprise me was the extremely sensitive and kind concern with which she listened to me. And we both agreed on the main point: talking of large cities, we could only consider living for any length of time in Rome or in New York.

Rome? Yes, indeed, I thought to myself. Despite the screams of indignation, in purest Brazilian vernacular, that probably still resound, even today, off the many walls in the Via Giulia; in spite of that time it was so hard to walk past a fountain in the Piazza Navona... Ah, only someone with these eyes that are more than green, more than blue, could ever, for once and for all, sweep away from those places, and from my memory, the recriminating image of those other eyes that were clear too, but clearly not at peace.

'Especially in Rome...' Y added. 'In Rome... for ever.'

But I felt it would be ridiculous to say the same back to her, as my 'for ever' would surely have a narrower scope.

IV

Then came Christmas; and at that time you published your first book of poems. It was just the day before Christmas Eve that I came across the copy you sent me – just for me – with the necessary sibylline dedication.

Why is it only now, on the eve of yet another Christmas, with your book here to hand again and having re-read it several times, that I feel the need once again to tell you what I already wanted to tell you back then? It's nothing new to you that I do not particularly like the title you gave it: it seems unduly provocative on the one hand and, on the other, unfairly limiting, as though the only value your verses have is their sterile daring to shake middle-class values. The middle-class nowadays barely exists; and where it does exist, it is shocked by nothing: not by what the church still forbids, nor by what can now be found in sex-shops.

Who are you trying to shock, apart from your husband perhaps, when you compare yourself (page 23) 'to the Earth who masturbates / beneath the rain', or (page 58) 'to the beach that comes with the Sun / while the Sea comes with the Moon'? Whose sensitive soul, apart perhaps from the one referred to just now, do you think you offend when you confess (page 81) that you lack the experience 'of being like a boat / on the high seas, / pierced all at once / by three masts'? And whose defunct sense of propriety do you think you offend when you sprinkle your verses with numerous anatomical terms that nowadays every primary schoolchild already knows?

Regarding some of the longer poems, I sometimes regret that they are quite so long; if I knew about poetry, I'd be able to tell you why. But, going back to the others, there is at least one – which I think lies half way between those that are just provocative and those that are somewhat more than provocative – that makes me feel both slightly frustrated and yet fascinated, disturbingly fascinated. It's the one over which you placed an epigraph by Vinícius de Moraes:[2]

> *I thought the clouds were happy not to have a womb,*
> *until they gave me grief for not having buttocks.*
> *I do not mean to say by this*

that they do not very often have
the shape of a womb,
the bulkiness of buttocks.

I also know some women,
equipped with wombs and buttocks,
who are nothing more than clouds.

Of all this, the most ugly
is just the word buttocks.

Just the word.

I speak for myself, and of myself, of course.

Do you know what I felt like as soon as I read these lines for the first time? No, I am not going to tell you. But I longed, right then, for one of those paediatric meetings that would inevitably bring us together. Unfortunately it didn't happen. However strange or paradoxical it may seem, Paediatrics also takes a break over Christmas.

And I found out, afterwards, that you had gone to the Douro, to your in-laws'. And my wife, having promised herself a new and even stricter slimming diet after the 'holidays', gave in to the numerous temptations of *broas* and *filhózes*, *bolo rei* and *rabanadas*, *doces de chila* and *lampreias de ovos*,[3] first, ever solicitous, at my mother's, in the so-called 'home' that had taken her in, visiting her twice during this period, then, more often than that, calling on three surviving aunts, who all still had good teeth and in whose old houses – in the Lapa, the Amoreiras and Estrela respectively – she generously gave of herself, in a praiseworthy, once-a-year effort to show the Senior Citizens the same care that she gives rather more assiduously to the Juniors. But this didn't stop her from poring long into the night over thick reports and learned articles from the many societies of Paediatrics. As for me, I still had to finish a complicated commission for my hatchet man in Lausanne before the end of the year.

It was a strange week, that one between Christmas and the New Year, when some days I would stay shut up in here for over twelve hours at a time, when two different images constantly danced before my eyes, not to distract me from my work, but rather to provide me with stimulating company while I worked, like two different promises of two different kinds of happiness, both just as inaccessible, both just as unlikely. One of these images was the eyes of that foreign, or half-foreign woman, whom I had met the week before. The other – forgive me! – was your buttocks.

That poem of yours (see what poetry can do!) had made me realize, amongst other things, why you so consistently wear those very tight trousers, or those very narrow skirts that emphasize even more that successful part of your anatomy of which you are so justifiably proud. And I can still see myself over there, on the other side of the atelier, hammering furiously against some resounding, misshapen objects that had less and less to do with me, or concentrating on the flame of my blow-lamp to lick some of their more enigmatic surfaces into shape, and the only way of discharging the extreme stress of all that activity was for me to mutter out loud to myself: 'Oh, you goddess!' At other times, I would cry out: 'Oh, you whore!'

Of the near-foreigner, I saw only the eyes. Of you, I saw merely your buttocks. But do not be shocked and do not let it go to your head, thinking that either of these exclamations was directed specifically at you. What provoked me was my repeated and confused craving for a goddess that was a whore, and a whore that was a goddess. And I couldn't even remember your face (only your buttocks!); and I couldn't even remember her body (only her eyes!); and I couldn't have given a damn about whatever else was going on in the world; and all that work bored me, overwhelmed me and excited me; and I would promise myself that, in the next few months or even for the whole of the coming year, I'd take a long holiday under the sign of flowing buttocks and huge eyes – a holiday so long I wouldn't even mind if it turned out to be my last.

Then, exhausted but exulting at the prospect of a truly sabbatical year, I would come over here and stretch myself out on this divan. Exhausted, I would pick up your book: what a ghastly cover! It was the ghastly cover of a beginner's book. (Why didn't you ask me for advice? Or at least for a suggestion?) I would try not to read the buttocks poem; but I kept going back and glancing over it again and again. Then I would linger, mostly, over the texts that I still linger over today.

Shall I tell you which ones I like best? Shall I only now tell you which? What's in it for me? What's in it for you? When I am praised for some piece that I made a year before, only sometimes do I feel vaguely envious of the person who made it. Or else – and this happens more frequently – I merely feel sorry for him. In either case, the person in question has very little to do with me now.

Nevertheless, I shall tell you that I do particularly enjoy the poem in which you say:

It's on the front page today of all the newspapers that have never existed,
it was talked about today on all the televisions and in all the supermarkets,
that today was used as an escudo[+] *(because the Dollar is very dear)*
for all the refugees from the planet Venus
and for all the naked people born under the sign of Sagittarius
the poignant account of the amorous space-suits.

There is yet another poem, but it's shorter this time and quite different (the critics will probably tell you, if they have not done so already, that it is not a good idea to do things that are quite so different; send them packing) and I would like to record it here, in order to enjoy it all the more:

I live (naked) on a planet
where no one knows nowadays
how to feed watches
or how to wind up the leopards.

I live (shit!) on a planet
where no one knows nowadays
who it was who scrapped free time
who it was who lost the key.

Anyway (but I don't know why), the poem that moved me most, deep inside, was another one from the same series, and it's even shorter still:

Do not ask the reason
for this three-tear hat.

I removed it from the head
of that statue of Beauty

where it has always
never been.

It must be the mingling of the words 'tear', 'statue' and 'Beauty'. Or else it's the contradictory juxtaposition of 'always' and 'never'. All I know is this: every time I read this poem, I stopped thinking of your buttocks. All I could think of were Y's eyes.

V

You can imagine my surprise when, on one of the very first days of the year, I found a small calling-card on the floor in the hall of the studio; it had obviously been pushed under the door, and it read as follows:

I cannot understand you not having a phone in your atelier. But it would be hard for me not to speak to you again. Then came three words that had been crossed out, but were still quite easy to read: *I would love*... Then a bit further on: *I would ask you therefore for* (sic) *to phone me on*... There followed a phone-number, preceded by the code for the Sintra area. By way of signature, there was simply an initial (which, of course, was not Y). Finally, a bit lower down, it said: *It's always better in the morning.*

It was nearly ten o'clock in the morning. The calling-card was made of an excellent granular Wathman paper, of the kind that is hardly found in Portugal anymore; she must have brought it the day before, or even the day before that, as I hadn't been there for two days. And I sat on the edge of the divan, I don't know for how long, holding the card between my fingers as though trying to hold on to the words it contained (the truth is that I memorized them straightaway), mindlessly fascinated by the handwriting that was jaunty, yet at the same time sober, almost timid in some of its details, and I marvelled at its impetuous fs, with their long up-strokes and even lengthier down-strokes, so characteristic of someone who is used to travelling the world.

I had not even got round to shrugging my duffle-coat off my back. But an inner, almost imperceptible, tremor made me think it was cold. I automatically moved closer to the heater, certain that I'd already lit it; a few minutes later, once I realized my mistake, I did in fact light it. Then I stood up, and leaning on the top of the dresser over there, I wrote down the phone-number (which I had already learned off by heart) on another piece of paper, where I wrote its seven numbers in a vertical line, from top to bottom, first of all in a straight line, then following different styles of subtle curves, as though trying, through these patterns, to evoke, to summon, to reproduce, the outline of a person. I was carried away by this absurd activity, in an exultant but almost painful way, to a distant incident of my childhood, of which only I know the secret. In the end, I placed the card in one of those portfolios (it's still there), my fingertips delighting for one last time in the roughly soft texture of the card.

I looked at my watch: it was nearly a quarter past ten. And suddenly, my whole being rebelled against the stupidity of wasting time like that; I rushed to the door and yanked it open, went out, crossed the Praça at a near run, without even noticing the light rain that had started to fall.

I now remember walking past the oncoming figure of a mature but still attractive figure of a cold, shivering woman – in a light-grey raincoat, with an astrakhan collar and hood of a darker grey – who smiled at me from a distance as though she knew me, at the same time giving me the strange impression that she did not want to be seen by anyone else. When she walked past me, she smiled even more broadly, dipped her umbrella, and that's when I realized it was drizzling.

On the other side of the Praça, after the tram-lines, I found the phone in one of the *pastelarias*[5] was out of order. In the other, there were only an old man serving at the bar and a youth waiting at the tables; and what with collecting coins from their trays and taking coins from the till, it took such a long time that it felt like an eternity before they found a sufficient number of coins to give me change.

But, soon after twelve o'clock, Y was outlined for the first time against the doorway over there.

For a moment, just a brief moment, we stood facing each other without knowing what to say.

On the phone as well, the same thing had happened to us on and off. Then we had listened to our halting respiration, imagining that we were trying – whereabouts in space? – to tune in to each other's rhythm. This had then been followed by a torrent of sentences that we'd been unable to finish.

'It seemed to me so awful if…' 'Me too. It's just that I don't…' 'It's just thinking that… that perhaps… we might never again…' 'That's just what I thought, but…' 'I don't even understand how I was able to…' 'Don't say that. All that matters is that…'

We were feeling so ridiculous that, all of a sudden, we burst out laughing.

'And when do you think…'

At last we managed our only complete sentences:

'When can we see each other?'

'Today. Today would be all right. Right now even. I was just about to leave to Lisbon.' She corrected herself: 'For Lisbon.'

I take her hands and pull her gently towards me. The shoes that she is wearing today make her a fraction taller than me; but at once our faces snuggle up to each other. Then she moves away; and, looking straight at me, she mumbles:

'It wasn't because of this. No, it wasn't because of this. I think it wasn't because of this.' Then a little furrow of doubt creases her brow: 'Is that how you say it? Or is it, for this?'

'It depends. It doesn't matter.'

Then we are kissing each other. And not just with our mouths: with our fingers as well with which we lightly trace the bulge of each other's forehead, the contours of each other's eyes, the outline of each other's ears, the thickness of each other's hair. It's as though we are no more than a blind man and a blind woman, who have known each other for a long time but have been separated for years, who can still barely believe the miracle of finding each other again. Blindly, with our eyes closed, each propping up the other, we drag each other, or allow ourselves to be led, from the doorway over to the foot of the divan over there. Then, without bending over, using just the pressure of one heel against the other, she frees herself from her shoes. Yes, now we are both exactly the same height.

'It wasn't because of this. It wasn't just because of this. I am so afraid of becoming for you... Of being for you...' She hesitated over the choice of word; then she plucked up her courage, and using the definite article: '...the disappointment.' Her huge eyes expressed both a childish terror and an adult curiosity: 'You are going to have to... learn me everything.' She corrected herself: 'Teach me everything.'

Within seconds we were naked. I didn't have to work too hard for the first obstacles to be overcome, for the last veils to fall. But her haste was more like that of someone, on a scorching afternoon, getting undressed to take a cold shower or to rest in the folds of a crisply clean sheet.

From then on, all she did bore the mark of a timid voracity, an eager inexperience, as well as a kind of touchingly impetuous assiduity. She didn't balk at a single suggestion I made; there was no request, no impulse, however unusual for a first encounter, that she did not try to respond to, in a genuine, or apparently genuine, mixture of goodwill and inexperience.

'From books,' she replied. 'From a book,' she specified. She was saying that it was through a book that she had become acquainted with many things.

'And apart from those books? Apart from that book?'

She was still on her knees in front of me; but she straightened up and closed her eyes, shaking her head in negation:

'No. This is my first time... Nearly all of this is.'

What flicker of disbelief was she able to discern in me, that she even sensed it with her eyes closed?

'I know you don't believe me,' she murmured. Even more faintly, she added: 'But it's true.'

There was something moving in her hieratic posture, with her head thrown back, her hands gripping my knees, her eyes and mouth pursed rather than simply closed. The glow from the heater, rising from near the floor two or three feet behind her, made it look as though she was hovering in an aura of smouldering unreality. I smoothed her hair and bent over to whisper in one of her ears:

'And what about at home? Not even at home?'

Her eyes shot open, in an expression of sheer horror:

'No, no! Never. Neither this, nor...'

Still on her knees, still with her hands firmly on my knees, still with her face turned towards me, without warning, she burst into tears, sobbing and shaking as though they were coming from deep down inside; and her eyes widened in alarm, more blue now than green, with fine traces of red. Finally, in a still lower voice, almost a murmur, she begged me not to ask any more questions.

On that day, on another day of that same week, on three days of the following week, throughout the whole first month, her progress in terms of voluptuous pleasure and erotic self-confidence filled me with pride and delight – as well as leaving me more and more confused and disbelieving.

It was from the second week on that she started bringing her white cashmere shawl, with its intricate loose stitch that looks like the tracery of sea-spray. During our encounters, when I go into the other room to get some sandwiches, savoury pies, cold meats, petit-fours, ice for the whisky, or occasionally a bottle of champagne, I come back in here to find her with her shawl round her shoulders.

And the shawl, whose provenance she later told me about, invariably takes me back to that night when we first met.

'Rome,' I say to her then.

'Forever,' she answers, smiling.

Oh! How far we have come since that dinner in the Amerindian's home!

Without our realizing it, the rooms had gradually emptied of all those allegories that had been inhabiting them. Y's husband, over in a corner, hid his embarrassment at having been left alone – alternately taking his glasses off, then putting them back on again – by redoubling his apparent interest in a succession of pseudo-Inca and pseudo-Aztec objects. Coming from the opposite corner, her shabby mink coat thrown over her shoulders, my wife stood three feet in front of us:

'I have said good-bye to our hosts. I don't know if you…'

In the end, the four of us left together. We said our last good-byes near our car.

'Remember me to Vicky,' said my wife. As they moved away, she added: 'I'm sure she no longer remembers me.'

Neither Y nor her husband will have heard that comment. And my paediatrician had another remark for my ears only; as soon as we got into the car, out of the corner of her mouth, she asked:

'Interesting woman, was she?'

'Who?'

'Who do you think?!'

'Oh!'

Then, settling heavily into the car-seat, she added:

'What about when she was twenty! You should have seen her when she was twenty!'

VI

What about you, when you were twenty?

You were dark-haired, well-bred, irreverent and headstrong, a diligent young medical student, still unaware you were destined for the philanthropic heights of Paediatrics, yet already by then afraid, not to say terrified, of the way I spoke, behaved, even dressed; you considered the old ruin of the Belas Artes[6] as a kind of sordid annex of hell and seldom dared to meet up with me in the Chiado at lunch time, but not once were you bold enough to enter the narrow *leitaria*,[7] opposite the Rua Ivens, where my friends from the Belas Artes and I believed ourselves to be the greatest bohemians in the world, the fiercest enemies of established order, simply because we washed down our *pasteis de bacalhau*[8] with glasses of white wine in the middle of the rowdiest discussions. When you were twenty, you would zigzag across the Rua Garrett, from one corner of the Rua Ivens to the other, always hoping that I would see you from inside the *leitaria*, and come at once to find you, and drag you away from that neighbourhood of perdition, up the Chiado, across the Largo de Camões, down the Calçada do Combro, to the Avenida das Cortes, where you would have lunch with your grandmother three times a week. (But we had to make sure that your aunts or even the cook or the maid didn't see you in such strange company.) When you were twenty, you had already duly assimilated hundreds and hundreds of pages of Testut's Anatomy into your grey matter, yet you forbade me touching you above the knee on those occasions, on spring or summer afternoons, when you would rashly agree to meet me up in the dome of the Estrela basilica (we had to go in and climb up separately because of the warder; oh, how many hundreds of steps for the mere half-dozen fleet caresses on those few inches of your skin!); or that even more infrequent event, when you would agree to sneak off with me, at dusk, into some doorway of some street in the Lapa, where you would give me the supreme reward of a kiss that wouldn't even last ten seconds, with infinitesimally open lips, your fists clenched up against my shoulders, your knees quaking in fear of the ignominy of a door opening perchance inside the building and people hurling profanities down at us.

That's when you were twenty. Then you were twenty-two, already so radically free of the hang-ups of two years earlier that, during the summer holidays at Foz do Arelho, you even graciously conceded, more than once, my request to see you completely naked, inside the only assembled canvas tent, facing the sea; there we would arrive breathlessly, early in the morning, each coming from a different direction, two hours earlier than your aunts (I had to set off towards the lagoon, giving everyone the impression that I'd come straight from the village to the beach), but what moments those were – oh, what fabulous moments! – burning with fever yet shivering with cold in the invariably misty morning, standing, completely naked, flustered, elated, side by side, facing each other, once even both lying on the damp sand almost one on top of the other, and your mouth would twist, your eyes would widen, your thighs tighten around my hand, you were no longer afraid of moaning gently at times, and I would marvel proudly, fascinated and bewildered, yet at the same time almost terrified, at so suddenly discovering that you too throbbed, and that it was not only the others, venal or otherwise, well-versed and greatly experienced, who held the monopoly on pleasure between their thighs.

When you were twenty, and then twenty-two, you already looked back with nostalgia to when you'd been eighteen, barely aware of what was waiting for you: that whole stupid treadmill of exam after exam, tests and more tests, whole series of competitive entrance exams, symposiums and conferences, that you needed to tread in order to hoist yourself up to the pinnacles of Paediatrics, gradually swapping your ephemeral tawny-skinned ebullience for that shrivelled olive complexion, not to mention your secretly giving up on the idea of ever having children, either through fear of the father they would have, or so you could better fulfil your mission as a mother to other people's children, mother to your pupils, to your assistants, to your own husband – and how worried, distressed and afraid you were going to be while he drifted wherever his ever-changing whim took him, wavering between his inclination to sculpt and his penchant for writing; and while he went abroad to Italy (another whim?), just as easily sending you three SOS telegrams in one day as going seven weeks without telling you where and how he was; and until, most importantly, he met his providential *marchand* in Lausanne, who was also to be closely associated with one of your colleagues in Paediatrics, that *marchand* who has been sucking him dry like a leech, but who very shrewdly indeed managed to establish him first abroad, and only then here in Portugal.

Finally, when you were twenty-four, you were still not aware of any of this six months before our wedding. You had already qualified in medicine; I had finally ditched my course at the Belas Artes, and was doing a period of in-house training for some weekly publication which would only ever run to eighteen issues. We both reluctantly agreed to accept financial help to start with from your grandmother and my mother, from your aunts and from my stepfather, all of whom were busy plotting and sorting everything out behind our backs. And I found no better time than this to tell you, one afternoon, about every sordid little detail of my miserable adventure with that pathetic platinum blonde, who said her name was Lídia, but who was really called Laurentina!

You had seen her for yourself a couple of times, and both those times your suspicions had been aroused. What you didn't realize was that whenever this frightful, showy creature turned up to the matinées at the Condes or the São Luíz, it was on purpose, after having previously arranged it with me, as there had been no other way to satisfy poor Lídia's – I mean Laurentina's – natural curiosity: she so wanted to see, at least from a distance, the girl from such good stock (and already qualified in medicine!) that I was soon going to marry.

'It's only curiosity, honest. I don't have anything against the girl. On the contrary. Your life is one thing, mine is another. And don't worry, I won't even look at you...' But at the matinée at the Condes, you straightaway said, 'That person seems to be making fierce eyes at you.' And two weeks later, in the foyer of the São Luíz, you exclaimed, 'There she is again! She can't take her eyes off you... God forgive me, but she looks just like a child-eater.'

'Yes, that's the one,' I confessed, weeks later, in the evening, in a *pastelaria* in the Calçada da Estrela. How amazingly torn I was between the noble honesty of that confession and the perverse delight of hurting you, between the selfishness of easing my conscience and the even greater selfishness of also showing you that I wasn't short of women! I led you to believe that it was all over; that it had only been a fleeting adventure; that I had always been ashamed (and this was no lie) of the fact that she was much 'older' than me. (I only mentioned the eight year difference, though I did already know by then it was twelve.) And, worst of all, that night, and the next, and the ones after, I didn't stop going to the Bairro dos Actores, to the house of the pseudo-Lídia who was entirely Laurentina. The Africanist was still in Africa; and he required her platinum presence in Africa very soon, not caring at all whether her name was Lídia or Laurentina. Wasn't I going to be married very soon? I had to have my final fling.

Why didn't you guess, if only then, what it was I was *not* saying, namely that I knew for certain I would never change? Darkness had fallen quietly over our recess in the *pasteleria* in the Calçada da Estrela. You stroked my hair gently; then you went on and brushed away the black curls that dangled over my forehead; and finally your hand slid down my face, once, twice, three times, as though I were a sick child. I am sure that was the exact moment you decided to specialize in Paediatrics.

No; even if you were still twenty years old, even if you were once again twenty-four, it would still be useless telling you about what is happening to me now. But how I'd like to ask you, if I met you again when you were just twenty-five and married to me – how I'd like to ask you how quickly or not you found out about certain things.

Ah! yes... Now I remember: you found out quickly. But you soon forgot.

VII

Beauty; simplicity; sensitivity; sensuality; intelligence. An intelligence deeper and sharper than her reserve might seem to indicate. But are these not too many predicates? Too many gifts celebrating the beginning of winter?

Of course, it's not the existence of these or other attributes that really matters: what does matter is our own certainty or delusion regarding their reality. And what is for sure is that no other woman, before I met Y, seemed to me so beautiful and simple, so sensitively intelligent and intelligently sensual.

There is a sound track that accompanies all this: the volume, tone and pitch of her voice, all in shades of sepia, with its irresistible tendency to whisper, murmur, confide, confess, often hovering over the indistinct borders between silence and speech. When I am with her, I am frequently suspicious and fearful that I am going deaf. Maybe I am.

There are still other gifts, other prodigies: her relative availability; the amazing fact that, especially at ordinary times and within the limits we establish beforehand, we can always agree on the days and times that suit us best. And then there's her dignity whenever she reveals the slightest detail about herself: a dignity that has nothing to do with that atrocious social class she belongs to. And there's that quiet sadness with which she often speaks of her father; and the colourful way she sometimes fleetingly remembers her childhood, most of it spent on a big *herdade*[9] in the Alentejo; or, in an even more elusive manner, her teenage years shared between the French Lyçée in Lisbon and a convent school in England. And then there's her well-bred soul, little inclined to malicious gossip and unkind thoughts. (She has few friends in Portugal.) And there's her radiant, innate politeness.

Could there be any more precious materials with which to build and cement a relationship between two people? Or with which to maintain, most importantly, the balance of that fragile yet armour-plated, aerial yet subterranean structure that an illicit liaison always is?

Beyond the confines of this atelier – whose skylights open onto the heavens, whose great windows open onto the river, but which also provides a private hideaway, as though buried in the bowels of the earth – the world was covered by a kind of greyness for nearly the whole winter – and I couldn't say if it was a mild one or a severe one – and the whole, equally colourless spring.

I was only vaguely aware of what was going on in the outside world during this time: new muddy rivers of old words; more bombs exploding, more crimes being committed; new plots, new crises, new clashes and battles in many areas of the planet; and everywhere, to a certain extent, both on and around our own doorstep, right under the noses of those pompous, lethally farcical, and more or less disastrous organizations that call themselves national governments, the world watched as some impostor or other stepped down in favour of another impostor – perhaps even a lesser impostor! – or, as so often happens, the world watched the fall of some lesser impostor in favour of some new and more experienced impostor. But however much my attention was drawn to all this stuff leaping out at me from the headlines of newspapers (which I make a habit of hardly ever reading) or from the glass screen of a television set (which I avoid watching for health reasons), all this belonged hopelessly to a discoloured world to which I had long refused to belong and where, more importantly, there could be no place for Y's eyes, nor her voice, nor her gestures, nor her body.

We went on meeting here, always from around midday to about four in the afternoon, two or three times a week. During those months of winter and spring, I would draw most of those many, intricate curtains, close that door to the more extensive 'workshop' area of the atelier, light the heater, in short get everything ready for Y's arrival, and I would generally sit in this very armchair, waiting for her, trying not to get too impatient.

It was during this time that I took up the habit, some mornings, of jotting down some of the events of the previous day, or the day before that, writing down certain scenes, remarks, retorts or scraps of conversation. Right at the beginning of the year, I brought from home one of those pretentious diaries advertising pharmaceutical products which my wife is flooded with over Christmas and that we then have the greatest difficulties in getting rid of. Many of them end up crackling delightfully in the fireplace of our house in Monte Estoril once the first chills of October set in. This one still hadn't succumbed to the flames and is still of some use to me nowadays. But each time I look through it, searching for some detail captured almost red-handed at the time, what amazes me most is that I am still almost physically aware of the state of anxiety in which I jotted down many of those notes; and am almost eerily aware of Y's presence still – her words, her reserve, her gestures, even perhaps her silences and her skin – amongst the eulogies of new milk formulae for children and the no less milky pictures of the Madonna with Child, taken from totally innocent paintings (innocent in terms of their future in advertising) by Giotto and Fra Angelico, Schongauer and Grünewald, but most by Murillo and Raffaello. What is most worrying is that, in some of those over-sensitive pictures, I can even see – and this is absurd – the material representation of the anxiety I felt on many of those mornings.

Although I never doubted Y's punctuality (another of her virtues), and however much I tried to remain calm or use the time to read a book, sketch, make notes, that diary was never really any great help. I would get up every three minutes or so, crouch down by the heater over there to adjust its heat, go inside over there to see if there was enough ice in the freezer, and return finally to this recess to check if the cleaning lady (who always comes every other day, towards the end of the afternoon) had hoovered the carpets properly, replaced the water or the flowers in the vase, and changed the linen on the divan.

At last Y would arrive, and suddenly summer would burst into this room, a balmy summer of late August, beginning of September. Beyond that door, the gloominess outside would deepen at once. My wife was plunged in gloominess, she remained an untouchable shadow, an untouched shadow; as for Y's husband, he remained an untouchable shadow also – and, it seemed, untouched and fortunately, untouching too.

Sometimes, on quite a few occasions during those first few months, we politely enquired after them, telling each other about their respective occupations, their respective states of mind and states of health; our interest always arose from a mixture of fraternal warmth and paternal or daughterly interest which, in different circumstances, with other women, I would have thought impossible, not to say ridiculous, an expression of scorn at the most. But this way we had of talking about them originated really in the extreme respect with which Y invariably referred to her husband and also the admiration which she invariably expressed when talking about my wife. ('Oh! She was so good with Vicky! She always got it right! Always!') Only I don't know if we did this because of a lack of guilt or if we did this for a lack of guilt. The ambiguity between 'for' and 'because' was a permanent feature of Y's idiomatic uncertainty.

Every so often, she would just about bring herself to ask, in a smiling, yet subdued whisper, the embarrassing question:

'We are not doing them any harm, are we?'

It was also hard to decide if she said this for peace of mind or because she was at peace with herself.

And as for me? I was so much at peace with myself that I attached no importance at all to the fact that one day, after leaving the atelier in the evening, I found a piece of paper, folded in two, firmly jammed under one of the windscreen-wipers of my car.

A ticket for careless parking? Far too fancy here in the Praça. It was just an inane and abstruse message. The text went as follows: 'It's not too late to avoid a scandal. Stop playing with fire. This is a friendly warning.'

The handwriting was round and shoddy, probably that of a pubescent schoolchild or someone who had left school at eleven,[10] and it was in marked contrast with the obvious power in the conciseness of the words. This is probably why I decided to put the piece of paper in my pocket. But then I thought that the person who'd written it had simply put it on the wrong car.

It was not a carnival caper. Carnival had long gone.

VIII

At Easter, my mother took to her bed with pneumonia. I never did visit her, not even once. But I found out over the phone and through my wife that it was nothing very serious: her tough constitution, having survived nearly eighty years without coming into contact with antibiotics very often, reacted well to her new-found exposure to them.

I realized, again round about that time, that the country was once more on the verge of bankruptcy. A good friend of mine, Nyasa, who was an anarchist by nature, sent me a flowery postcard with views of Papua New Guinea and postmarked Restauradores, assuring me that it was not yet anything to write home about.

The woman who has been doing the cleaning in the ateliers for the past twenty years bumped into me one day, I think it was on Good Friday afternoon and, with all the impudence of someone who was ready for a longer chat, she fired at me: 'Hey, Mestre! What's with the new bird? There have been such comings and goings… Not that I've seen who it is, I swear I haven't, but I bet you anything you like that it's been the same lady for quite a while now, because this nose of mine, Mestre, this nose of mine is never wrong!' To shut her up, I stuffed a note into her claws: 'Here, take this for your sugared almonds.'[11] Then I gave her another; but this one was given for the special intention of the tottering state of the country and my mother's recovery.

And during that Eastertide, with unusual regularity, the image of a vast, glassed-in terrace kept on recurring.

A large terrace bathed in sunshine even when its many intricate curtains were drawn. The floor was covered in white tiles, the chairs were made of wicker; there were flower-pots, and a brand new tricycle which I was not in the least bit interested in.

What I had learnt to like, sitting on the floor or in Tá's arms on sunny days like this, was drawing numbers and letters, numbers especially, preferably in a long row going down.

A 2, then an 8… Tá would insist on drawing them first; then she would place them side by side and urge me to do the same: 'Say it then: twenty-eight… That's your mother's age.' Then she would draw a 6; and she would add unnecessarily: 'That's your age.'

I thought the 28 was fun, with the 2 just like the neck of the swan I had seen in the Jardim da Estrela, and the 8 reminding me of that fluffy teddy that I myself had eviscerated but without which I refused to go to sleep. On the other hand, the 6 usually only ever looked like the small pretentious oval mirror with a curved silver handle, that had recently appeared, amongst other knick-knacks, on my mother's dressing-table. The best bit, when all was said and done, was scrawling a great big 2, then a great big 8, either far apart from each other or, as Tá wanted, right next to each other, so long as afterwards the tiny 6 could hide inside one of the holes of the 8, reduced almost to nothing.

It was only Tá who, at that time, still fiercely wanted me to remember my father: 'You do remember. So keep on remembering. Why shouldn't you remember? In his white uniform, here on the terrace, not even three years ago, it was, teaching you to ride that other tricycle...' She would shower me with other details: 'It was long after we came to this house... From that other one, in Pedrouços, where you were born; that's the one your father liked. It's hardly surprising you don't remember it.' She whispered all this to me countless times, when there was no one else about on the terrace, as though it were a secret that only concerned the two of us. 'But watch it... Don't go telling your mother that I've been talking to you about these things.'

As for me, all I could remember, or thought I could remember, was a shining white uniform; and in order not to annoy Tá, I assumed that the white uniform was my father's. It was only much later on, little by little, again through Tá, that I found out about the rest: the white uniform belonged to the Navy but had ended up being defeated on dry land, after an uprising around the beginning of the 1930s; unfortunately, on a corner of the Largo do Rato, a misfired bullet made a direct hit. Life went on, though, as if the white uniform had no age.

The only precise ages I was aware of were mine and my mother's. But I do remember the last day I ever amused myself drawing those figures.

I had been dressed up in my Sunday best, that morning, as though I were going to a party. Tá, hidden away in the kitchen, surrounded by more white overalls than I had ever seen before, seemed incapable of coming near me. But there were other hands closing in on me, other mouths slobbering over me; and, equally syrupy, there were other voices that stopped me from sitting comfortably on the tiles of the terrace. I pretended not to understand, I stood my ground; finally I was given some blank sheets of paper, and my colouring pencils.

Then my mother emerged, dressed in pale colours, green or blue, with a wide-brimmed hat flapping on top of her fair hair. She pulled me towards a chair, glancing at the numbers I had been drawing; and in her strange voice, she suddenly started saying even stranger things: 'Ah, Mummy's age… You see? Mummy's growing old. Mummy needs someone to look after her. You also like being looked after by Mummy, don't you? There has to be someone to look after us.' That didn't seem to make any sense, as it was mainly Tá who looked after me. But I do not know if that was why I started to protest quietly, in a sleepy outburst, demanding that Tá, and only Tá, should bring me some new colouring pencils.

That's when, her naked arm brushing against my neck, my mother asked me: 'Wouldn't you like to begin calling Dr — "Father"?'

Simpering faces started milling around us, some more hideous than others,

Dr — strutted out of the gloom of the dining-room into the dazzling brightness of the terrace. He wore an oddly-shaped black jacket, striped trousers, very pointed varnished shoes, and his thin greasy hair was pulled back between his ears. He sat next to me on a wicker chair, which immediately creaked as though on the verge of tears. Clumsily, he pulled me up on to his lap; the chair creaked even louder.

In the meantime, the dining-room was filling with other grown-ups, with other dark suits, other pale dresses, other large hats with huge rims, nearly all stuck through with pins that glinted in the light. From inside there was a growing and unfamiliar sound of tinkling glasses; from inside billowed out ever thicker clouds of smoke.

Many photographs were being taken of the doctor and my mother. The doctor wanted me to be in one of the pictures too. But it wasn't easy, as I refused to open my eyes.

This doctor was not like the other doctor who came to see me at home when I had a temperature; this one spoke only to my mother, never calling for a spoon to flatten my tongue with, never making me open my mouth and say 'Ah…!'; he never placed on my chest a disc of very cold metal that hung from a string that split in two up to his ears; and neither did my mother or Tá ever give him a roll of cotton wool and a bottle of spirits for him to rub his hands with afterwards.

Of course, neither the spoon nor the disc were very pleasant objects; even the smell of the spirits made me queasy. But because of these things, I always knew for sure that he really was the doctor. Not like this one: this one sweated a lot and never looked me straight in the eye. That's probably why, right from the start, I took an immediate dislike to the tricycle he'd given me.

Many years later, I find myself on yet another terrace. And Tá is white-haired, all shrivelled up, almost translucent, lying between the whiteness of two sheets, framed by the whiteness of a hospital bed. I have been coming to see her every Saturday for over two years, here in the very clean and plain sanatorium in Parede dedicated to the treatment of bone disease.

I sense that today will be the last day I see her: I am leaving for Italy next week; I do not know how long I will stay there, nor do I want to. My stepfather – who never even drank – has been snatched away by an apparently uncontrollable cirrhosis.

'God rest his soul,' says Tá. 'He wasn't that bad a person, really.'

She then says, without a single trace of reproach – her voice rather like that of someone who merely accepts the inevitable – that, for the past few months, they have stopped taking her up to the solarium on a 'trolley'; but to give them their due, whenever there is any sun, they still bring her bed here to the terrace.

I am sitting as usual on an uncomfortable chair that is also made of metal and spotless white enamel. On my right I can see Tá's white hair; in front, I can see the white crests of the spring tide. But the rumble of the traffic on the Marginal drowns out the sound of the living waters against the rocks.

And Tá mentions my stepfather again:

'I just cannot help thinking that he was not the right man for your mother.'

IX

'Back at home, how long is it since…?'

Her abrupt, convulsive crying started again; or, at least, in her very quiet voice, her hands clenched, she pleaded with me again not to ask questions on that subject. Until one afternoon, closing her eyes, she suddenly hissed through gritted teeth:

'Over three years.'

Then she started shaking violently, as if suffering from an attack of malaria. She asked me to cover her with the sheet, then with the blanket; and finally she asked me to bring her white shawl from the bottom of her Hermès bag. Only then did she calm down. A while later, propped up on the divan, with her white shawl over her shoulders and the rest of her covered by the sheet and blanket, she said:

'Never again. Don't ever ask me again. He is so kind! So kind! He loves me so much! It was me who… Right from the beginning. When we first got married. He was always for me… the disappointment.' And she used the definite article, as she always did, as she still does today.

I hugged her shoulders through her shawl. It was stupid, but at that point, I wished my hands had been the ones that had bought it for her. However, all I said was 'Rome' – as usual by now, when it came to her shawl – but also, this time, to see if it would cheer her up. But instead of playing the game, instead of replying 'For ever' as she always did, with her eyes at that moment more green than blue staring alternately at me and her shawl, Y merely proffered this simple piece of information:

'It was in a boutique in the Via Condotti.'

How many, many boutiques on the Via Condotti have I gone into, walked out of, then gone into again, always trailing behind the comet that bore the name of Xô? There were times – and these were the only moments of respite she would allow me – when I would take refuge in one of the many *salotti* of the Antico Caffè Greco, waiting for her to fish me out again. And she would turn up, a few minutes later, just when I'd settled down to enjoy an espresso or a cappuccino, overloaded with parcels, and would immediately submerge the circular top of one of the little Empire tables or the dark-red velvet-upholstered bench with these parcels, which she would start unwrapping at once, pulling at strings, ripping paper, opening bags, ferreting out the 'trifles' and the 'madnesses' she had bought:

'Just look... Isn't this madness?'

And she would show me beach towels, beach gowns, beach shoes, beach trousers, beach shirts – all indispensable 'madnesses' for the great madness of our going to Amalfi for three weeks.

Once, to the great amazement of an old man at the next table who was reading *Il Tempo*, she tried on a minute bikini over the dress she was wearing whilst standing in the middle of the room:

'Isn't it cute? So teeny... But I'll fit into it, I swear.' And in reply to a question from me, she replied: 'Yes, it was impulsive. But I'm no good at sums... I am still waiting for all that money from Rio, as well you know.'

How strange: only now did I feel like doing sums; other sums. Y was sixteen last time she was in Rome with her father, and it was precisely at that time that I first met Xô there.

'In a boutique,' Y repeated, 'almost opposite that very old café... you know?'

Then, crossing her shawl over her chest, she added:

'Promise. Never again. Never ask me again. It must be my fault. It was at first, that's for sure. When I got married, I was still very... How do you say? Very distressed by my father's death. Only later, quite a bit later, did I begin to feel... to feel that my body existed.'

Unexpectedly, with the glorious shamelessness that so often transfigured her, she freed herself from her shawl, brought her legs up, pushed the sheet and blanket off with her feet, and looked for a moment at her completely naked body:

'It does exist. It's no longer what it has been. But it's mine. And it's large. I cannot throw it away.'

Following this, we shared a desperate surrender, an abandoned passion, such as we'd never known before. In the end, when it was all over, we were both lying down, fused to one another, with our secretions binding us to each other more than ever before, and I felt myself falling heavily down one of those slippery tunnels of sleep where certain images and visions of whose origins we are totally unaware are projected with photographic clarity, before we reach, right at the bottom, the murky waters of the unconscious.

At that moment, crushed by the weight of my body, in a fainter and more drawling voice than usual, an almost obscenely drowsy Y whispered:

'Oh!... My wingless horse!'

I lifted myself up a little, bewildered and speechless. Without opening her eyes, she then said:

'A while ago it seemed you had wings.'

A few seconds beforehand (and this is what I found most uncanny), I'd just had a vision of a wild stampede of horses running free. I told her this there and then. And, shuddering, Y said:

'That's what I was *seeing* too...'

At the same time, the bottom of the well was still drawing me down, dragging me down deeper and deeper. On its walls was now projected the image of a large country house, with two turrets, a large courtyard, a smaller one – almost a cloister – everything looking austere and yet full of light and movement.

As though hypnotized, I started to describe this house to Y, or tried to: it was a house I was sure I had never seen, but whose slightest detail I could see clearly in my mind's eye.

'How many floors?' she asked. 'Two?'

'Yes.'

'With shutters on every window?'

'Yes.'

'Painted green?'

'Yes.'

'With one turret higher than the other?'

'Yes.'

'With a pond in the middle of the courtyard?'

'Yes.'

'And in the middle of the pond?'

'A... a kind of fountain.'

'In the shape of what?'

'In the shape of a bowl.'

'A bowl of stone?'

'Yes.'

'In marble?'

'Yes.'

'Pink?'

'Yes. Pink.'

And shuddering once again under the solid weight of my body, Y exclaimed:

'That *was* our house in the Alentejo. *Was*. It's no longer like that. It's been completely altered since my father's death.'

It may seem strange, it may seem stupid. But it was from then on that I became convinced that I would find it very difficult to hide some of my most secret thoughts from Y.

X

You too spoke to me of your father one day; your endearing seriousness quite surprised me. Perhaps it was due to the fact that I'd never known my father; perhaps it was because my mother had never made much of an effort to 'know' me – when in fact there was a time you could have been a kind of daughter to me.

Regarding your father, you mentioned how much you regret only having grown to like him when it was too late. The strange thing was that we had that conversation during the time – about six months ago, towards the end of spring – when Y too started talking more often to me about her own father. The big difference was that Y never says 'regrets': the most she does is to say she feels sorry.

It would hardly be worth mentioning anything, anything at all, about that conversation of ours and what happened between us – and it was so little! – afterwards, if it weren't for something you couldn't have known about then; or especially if it weren't for this need I feel at the beginning of yet another winter, to keep coming here, two or three days a week, usually between twelve and four o'clock in the afternoon, always sitting in this same armchair, always with the diary to hand to write down what's happened to me throughout this past year. Which is not a lot. Successful love affairs have no story to tell.

Besides, maybe you have different memories from mine about that conversation of ours. Maybe one day we will be able to share and enjoy them, alone, at our leisure, in a way we have never yet been able to.

It happened towards the end of the World Year of the Child, when that huge Canadian was here, who was as big as a disused battleship, apparently a respected authority in Child Psychology, and to whom my wife and your husband had to give due assistance whilst the man was in our territorial waters. Once again, the two of us were in tow. And I greatly admired your duplicity when you suggested to our paediatricians that, instead of the inevitable dinner in a fado restaurant, we should, instead, take the 'battleship' that Saturday to a musical in the Parque Mayer. Of course our lumbering Canadian enjoyed the show even less than he would have enjoyed the fados. But still, it was a change for you; or rather, for us. And of course it was a good way for us to see that irreverent farce about Lisbon politics that so many people had been telling us about. But we never did get round to discussing whether it was good, bad or simply the same as all the rest.

All I remember about the show is a very emaciated chorus-line girl who seemed more lively and impulsive than her companions, whose hair was obviously dyed blonde yet made her look like a natural blonde, whose fiercely light-coloured eyes (were they green? were they blue?) I found quite unsettling – for all these reasons, they kept reminding me of what I still think Xô looked like. Unless it was my unconscious getting even by finding her double in the Parque Mayer.

Necessity made us have dinner in a hurry (we were going to the first showing), and we ate in the least gruesome snack-bar your husband could find, and even that was nothing much. (There had been a function dinner two days earlier in a proper restaurant.) We decided – at the Canadian's own suggestion – to eat at the counter; and we found ourselves sitting next to each other, as we were expected to, or as we contrived to, whilst the Canadian, on your left and on my wife's right (who, in turn, was on your husband's right), spent the whole time with his back mostly turned to us, being understandably attracted by the dazzling lights from the other two vessels of Science.

That was when you mentioned your father. How horrified he would have been to eat under such conditions! What an unfailing instinct he'd had to unearth, in Lisbon or in the countryside, in Spain or in France, those pleasant, cosy little restaurants that were so conducive to the enjoyment of what he called a 'good post-prandial conversation'! How bracing it was to listen to him, how exhilarating it was to travel with him!

You made a slight gaffe after that: having told you that I did indeed remember your father very well, you asked me if he and I had been at the Belas Artes together.

'No, my dear friend. When I started at the Belas Artes, your father was already quite a well-known architect.'

And then, without being unduly disconcerted, you replied:

'Of course… Do forgive me. It's just that I always see my father as he was towards the end. Which is what you're like now, really.'

Was this another gaffe? But you rested your fingers on mine, squeezing my fingers with yours. There could have been no better consolation prize; in gastronomic terms, it could be said to have been the *pièce de résistance* of the whole dinner.

Half an hour later, in the theatre, within the narrow confines of the box they had packed us in, you made a point of allowing our paediatricians, as escorts to the psychologist, to sit in front and whisper alternately to him, unveiling the transcendent mysteries of this show that expressed so well the quintessence of Lisbon. Behind them, sometimes sitting, sometimes standing, we frequently repeated, in the most spontaneous way, the hand-touching that had first taken place under the counter of the snack-bar. At one point (when we were seated), neither your hands nor mine could refrain from going a little further.

During the intermission, as the Canadian's parched throat demanded a ginger ale, we all went down to the ground-floor. Then you rummaged in your handbag and in your jacket pockets, realized you had left your cigarettes upstairs, refused one of my Gauloises and assured me you couldn't do without one of your Mores. Naturally, I offered to go with you to find them. While we were going up the stairs, all it took was an exchange of glances for you to confirm that this was no more than a ruse; and for me to intimate that I approved and was grateful.

But, once back inside the box, you merely confirmed – by taking one of my hands and putting it in your blazer pocket – that the packet of Mores had been there all the time.

With the all the lights on in the auditorium, providing no propitious hideaway, the box was now as exposed as a small stage. We went out again into the corridor, somewhat unsteady and disconcerted; and yet firmly intent on... we didn't quite know what.

Ahead, a little beyond the top of the stairs, behind a curtain that was not fully drawn, was a very large window frame. We walked towards it without a word, in tacit and mutual accord, trying to kid ourselves we weren't walking too quickly. We both looked round to see if there was any lurking danger: apart from the usher arguing, down the end, with the female toilet-attendant, there was a downy-lipped youth, bashfully scurrying down the stairs at the side of a portly woman with unfashionable platinum-blonde hair. Looking as cool as possible (or so we thought), we vanished behind the curtain as though we were highly interested in what could be seen outside the window.

How long did we stay there? A minute and a half? One minute? Perhaps not even as long as that. Just long enough to lean against each other unsteadily, to embrace each other eagerly, to plunge finally with our eyes wide open into a single kiss that wasn't so much long as duly savoured. The flashing lights of an advertisement outside made your contact lenses sparkle with bright intensity. Suddenly, we thought we heard steps.

'That's enough,' you said.

And moments later, as we were going down the stairs, you said in an objectively detached manner:

'That was nice.'

Then, stopping suddenly on the last few steps, you broke one of your long cigarettes in two, threw one half on the floor and lit up the other half with the filtered tip, and said:

'That was nice. But we needn't kid ourselves.'

Meanwhile, my wife and your husband came towards us, ushering the Canadian battleship with solicitude, and berthed next to us. Now that the small squadron was reassembled, new ephemeral combinations occurred between its members: you were steaming ahead and probably felt duty-bound to lend your support occasionally to the two vessels with the widest berths; and your husband, as formal as ever, drifted unexpectedly leeward, in an eloquent invitation to cruise away gently. Once we had sailed off, there he was, very tall and thin, slightly bent, gathering up his courage to say to me:

'One day, if you wouldn't mind, I'd like to talk to you...' After a brief hesitation, he added: '...about my wife.'

I could swear I didn't even bat an eyelid. It was just as well, though, that your husband added hastily:

'About the book she's had published.'

'Oh! With the greatest of pleasure...'

The greatest of pleasures, however, was having just realized that there is always a slight difference between thinking that one is not betraying one's emotions – and being sure of being in the clear.

'With the greatest of pleasure,' I repeated. 'Only I'm not too sure if my opinion...'

And at that moment, the bell rang, indicating the end of the intermission.

During the second half of the show, you and I were again relegated to the darkest part of the box, and almost throughout we held hands, palm against palm, without linking fingers, without going beyond a vaguely séance-like contact, as though by so doing we were attempting to invoke – someone whom you were missing, or someone whom I was missing.

In the end – do you remember? – I asked you all to go on ahead to my house in your Fiat. I would join you later. And it was indeed, like I said, to see if I could find my old friend Nyasa in the Parque Meyer; or at least to get some news of him. But even the Parque Meyer didn't look like the Parque Meyer anymore. Oh, how humiliating it was that no one was able to tell me the whereabouts of Nyasa, the former prelate of the community! However, on my way out, I did come face to face with the now un-made-up features of the skinny chorus girl who had reminded me of Xô, and who didn't look like Xô after all.

Two days later, first thing in the morning, your husband rang me to apologize for having 'disturbed' me (that's the word he used), stating most politely that he didn't even know why he'd done so, that what he had said was 'of no consequence'. And that same day – a Monday – was the first time Y arrived rather late at the atelier.

XI

I had been waiting for over half an hour, and I was beginning to worry. So I went over to the other side of the atelier, to one of the windows overlooking the Praça, to watch for Y's car from behind the curtains.

I had only rarely done that before, I don't know whether it was so that I could answer the unmistakably discreet rapping of her knuckles that much more quickly, or whether it was to take even greater delight in having her within reach of my arms the moment she appeared. I knew, nevertheless, that for the last six months or so, Y usually left her car in the corner of the Praça nearest the river, which is the one that can be seen most easily from these windows. And, indeed, a bluish Italian coupé – it was Y's – was parked there, forty or fifty yards from my observation post.

The car appeared at first to be empty. Where could Y have got to? Was she already on her way here, making her way behind the other ateliers? Or had she gone to buy something from one of the shops on the opposite side of the Praça?

On this morning in the middle of June, the sun was almost at its zenith but its rays were still slanting (even though the clock showed that it had gone half past twelve), making the glass of the windows a bit hazy, which did not exactly make it easy for me to see things very clearly, especially from that distance. But in the end I managed to make out a mass of shimmering fair hair in the car, leaning slightly over the steering-wheel.

The left side of the car, three-quarters turned away from me, its bonnet almost completely hidden by the sunroof, was the side I could see the best. But, as I said, conditions for seeing her were far from ideal. There might even have been someone to Y's right, someone she might be chatting to – who on earth could it be? – but who remained hidden both by her hair and by the headrest of her seat. However, the complete stillness of her hair made me think that, no, that couldn't be it, and I found this even more intriguing.

I must have spent a good ten minutes trying to discover more, trying to understand what was going on. How long had the car been there? Another suspicion arose suddenly in my mind – what if Y wasn't feeling well? – and only then did I think of rushing up to her, and who knows, perhaps helping her. But just at that moment, her mass of loose fair hair stirred. Immediately afterwards, Y got out of the car; and slowly collected her handbag and her Hermès bag from the rear seat; and even more slowly, she bent over to lock the door after slamming it shut.

Still very slowly, she put her keys in the little handbag which she then flung over her left shoulder (where it dangled from its chain), she picked up the Hermès bag in her right hand – it looked heavier than usual – and instead of crossing the Praça diagonally, as might have been expected if she was to walk round the block of ateliers and come to my front door, she went off instead along the embankment by the river, treading heavily, taking deep breaths and stopping every now and then, as though it wasn't just her bag that was weighing her down, but as though the land and the proximity of the sea were also weighting her steps, as though even the sun in the sky had thrown over her shoulders an invisible mantle of fatigue, not to say anguish.

She was wearing a very plain blue or green dress, apparently made from a kind of silk jersey, with a flared skirt a little below the knee swinging with each step, that underlined nonetheless her solemn and poignant stride and, made her look, on that sunny morning, like a dejected goddess on a ceremonial walk.

Suddenly, she came to a halt. I felt at that moment that she was capable of doing something unexpected or even desperate. In the end, all she did was to go back to her car, still walking just as slowly but with a somewhat more resolute air about her. Reaching the car, she removed from her bag a large item that could have been a record carrier or a photograph album, and put it on the front seat – or rather, from the way she leaned over, under the front seat. Finally, still moving very slowly, with what seemed like great weariness, she again slammed the door, locked it, going through all the same little gestures as before, again in slow motion, with a scrupulous exactness and an almost fanatical precision, and at last she walked diagonally across the Praça.

It was at that point that she walked past another woman, not as tall as her, but pleasant to look at, well-heeled, well-dressed, and probably leaving one of the other ateliers. After walking past Y and staring at her intensely, she turned her head slightly to look back towards the window where I was standing. Neither her face nor her looks were unfamiliar to me – she seemed delightful and disarming, but unusually so. Because of the sun's position, it was highly unlikely that she could see me anyway.

Then I too moved slowly, back into the room, having made up my mind, I don't know why, not to say anything about what I'd just seen. But I did notice that the flowers in the vase were beginning to let off a nauseating smell of decomposition. I threw them away at once, just as the cleaning lady should have done the day before, or the day before that: it was imperative that Y should not notice such a smell when she came in.

Although I was now certain of her imminent arrival, I remember waiting with a growing, inexplicable anxiety for her knuckles to rap lightly against the other side of the door. But, after waiting for several minutes, instead I heard a sharp slap on the door, followed by the sound of nails scratching the wood.

XII

But the Y who stands before me is exactly the same luminous Y as she has always been when she comes, with her eyes more blue today than green – her dress is blue after all – and as always, she is surprised and grateful for the delight with which I always greet her; as always, she touchingly responds to the way my eyes always delve into hers, the way my arms always hug her shoulders, the way I always embrace her when I first greet her by tenderly engulfing her between her shoulders and my chest.

She has just, as always, dropped her Hermès bag and allowed it to fall, as always, right by our feet, and I have just, as always, taken my right hand from her left shoulder for a second to make sure, as always, that the door right behind her, which I'd merely pushed to when she came in, is indeed duly shut. Only then, apologetically brushing her brow, does she contritely apologize – 'I don't know how it happened' – referring to her being nearly an hour late today; and this time, unlike the others, she turns ever so slightly away from the kiss I try to give her, saying that her mouth feels dry, she is thirsty and desperately needs a drink of something.

'What of?' I ask her.

'Anything. Anything nice and cold.'

I rush over to the fridge to get a bottle of champagne. (I had decided yesterday, or the day before, that it would be champagne today.) But, irritatingly, I cannot open the bottle as quickly as usual; the liquid gushes out faster than usual; and although I know I have already put two glasses on the little table by the divan, I run to the cupboard to get another, just in case the champagne carries on frothing, so that Y will not have to wait any longer.

I find her back here, standing barefoot in front of the dressing-table mirror. I notice that she has left her shoes over by the door; that she has abandoned her bag on the armchair; that her tights are hanging from the arm of the chair; and that she has already spilt all, or nearly all, the contents of her bag on top of the dressing-table: tubs of beauty cream, a hairbrush, hairspray, a bottle of eau-de-Cologne. However, I don't know whether or not her shawl is at the bottom of the bag. She still had it with her last week, even though the weather was already getting warmer by then. And there's something else I haven't done today, for the first time ever, which is to light the heater. I can only conclude (why the hell should it worry me?) that things between us have entered a new phase.

'Oh, thank you,' murmurs Y, without looking at me, unable to pretend any longer that she cannot see the glass I have lifted up to her chin. But, taking it, she merely wets her lips. 'I wasn't thirsty after all. I was probably just feeling tired. It's this sun, all this sun all of a sudden...'

Her face is very near the mirror; looking at herself, her face turns hard and pitiless, an expression that I've never seen on her before. With two fingers of each hand, she now pulls up the corners of her mouth and the corners of her eyes as though trying to iron out some possible wrinkles, which seem to me to be more hypothetical than real. Then, all of a sudden, she picks up the glass she'd put on top of the dresser, and drains it in one go.

'More. More, please.'

I immediately do as she wants (why the devil is my hand shaking?), but this time she sips at the champagne slowly, at the same time she stops looking at herself in the mirror and slowly turns her whole body round until she is facing me whilst, no less slowly her lips, her eyes – I would almost say her hair as well – light up with her gentle smile of radiant kindness:

'How old is that girlfriend of yours?'

'What? Which girlfriend?'

Y's smile grows more disarming; the tone of her voice grows sweeter:

'The one who published a book a while back. The one who is married to your wife's assistant. And the one who... You're the one who told me... the one you like to talk to so much. How old is she?'

'I don't know. She's probably around your age.'

'No, no,' Y protests with unexpected heat. 'She must be much younger.'

'But does it matter?'

'Not at all. I was just wondering.'

Automatically she unscrews her little bottle of eau-de-Cologne, shakes a few drops onto the tips of her fingers, her fingers then stroke her neck, then the back of her ears. 'Two days ago, at the house of some friends of ours, there was a lot of talk about her husband. They spoke very highly of him. They said he is very competent, that his career is already very… Never mind! I can't remember how to say it. And he's probably not even thirty yet.'

'Oh, isn't he? Well he looks it. But then again, I've never asked to see his birth certificate.' And I add: 'Neither of theirs.'

Then, as though she hasn't even heard me, after a pause during which she carefully screwed the lid back on her bottle, Y says:

'There were also some people who had read her book. But who hadn't understood a thing. Or thought it best not to understand. I can't remember exactly what they said now.'

She picks up her glass again and holds it out for me to fill again. This time, however, she doesn't even put it to her lips and places it at once on the dressing-table. And she casually takes a few steps between the dressing-table and the divan and back again, before muttering, with forced volubility:

'Right, I've made up my mind. This year I shall not wear my bikini anymore. Just as well that swimming-costumes are back in.'

Then, coming nearer the arm-chair, she deftly pulls the zip of her dress down her back, letting it drop off her shoulders, over her hips, down her legs until it is no more than a miserable rag around her feet. And she is wearing a bikini.

Then she gestures imperiously for me not to move:

'Now… now for most important bit.'

All of a sudden she yanks a white swimsuit out of her bag and places it in front of her so as to completely cover the bikini:

'Do you blame me? Do you blame me?'

And then she suddenly runs off towards the divan, flings herself face down on it and, hurling the white swimsuit onto the floor, she exclaims,

'Oh, why? Why? Why couldn't you have known me when I was younger?'

XIII

'But this is absurd. This is quite absurd. Can't you see that it ought to be the other way round? It would make sense the other way round. I am the one who ought to be sorry (but I'm not even sure I am) that I didn't know you when I… when I was younger. Why should you, of all people, turn this into some kind of problem?'

Illogical in their excessive beauty, Y's eyes persist in not accepting the logic of what I am saying. I whisper these words to her as my mouth travels from her shoulder blades to the back of her neck, and from the back of her neck to her ear lobe. It is nearly a month since the day she arrived so late, bringing the white swimsuit with her in the Hermès bag instead of her white shawl. Here on this divan, we have just been the caverns and muffled cries of the same flooded sands; the roots, branches, leaves and fruits of the same horizontal tree.

We are both standing naked in front of that huge mirror that covers the width of the wall; and I am completely hidden behind her body, showing her in this way that only her body is worthy of being reflected. I cup her breasts and fondle them, first one then the other, in the palm of my right hand, whilst the fingers of my left hand stroke her neck, her shoulder, her waist, her stomach, the fascinating swell of her thighs, imploring her, through these caresses, to be proud indeed of such clean lines, of such slim and well-proportioned forms. But she has eyes only for the reflection of my half-hidden face in the mirror. In the end, the one time she allows her eyes to follow the journey of my fingers, she says:

'I know. I am very thin.' Then, closing her eyes, she adds: 'That's why my chest… that's why my chest is no longer what it used to be.'

How can I convince her she is wrong? How can I convince her she is at the height of her physical splendour? And to think this is happening to me, who is twenty-one years older than her and a wreck, a crumbling wreck! But in a flash I understand something I hadn't understood until now: it is her insecurity and not only her beauty that deeply disturbs me; and it is this insecurity that is making her more daring as days go by, as though trying to *compensate for herself* or *compensate me*, inventing everything day by day, reinventing everything, adhering to everything, exceeding everything, each time that on this divan (more and more often, I must say) we once again become the flooded sands and the horizontal tree.

Roots, branches, leaves, fruits. And the cavern; and the cries. This time we didn't even try to reach the divan. In front of the mirror, the small rectangle of that carpet was enough for us. And I don't really know how we manage, afterwards, to hoist ourselves onto the armchair. But we are much more awake than we thought: we feel as light, serene, weightless and clear-headed as after a storm.

'Those drawings of yours,' said Y. 'May I see those drawings of yours again?'

She goes over to get them herself from one of those portfolios. Then, kneeling at my feet, she passes them up to me, one by one, from the floor to my lap, and, one by one, first on the floor and then on my lap, she looks, not for the first time, at those hasty sketches that 'represent' her. But, in her concentration, her expression betrays not the slightest interest in the 'model': without touching the paper, her fingers closely follow the imprint of certain lines, the wonder of certain curves, as though merely carrying out a kind of expertly rigorous inspection:

'Do you know? I like these drawings of yours much more than... than the rest. Than the sculptures. The sculptures... can I go on?'

'Do.'

'The sculptures, to my mind (but I am quite ignorant, as you well know) are very... very sophisticated. The drawings aren't. These drawings are like when you... when you enter me. And when...'

She adds the rest in an even more muffled voice, her eyes staring at mine, and her cheek bones and lips and neck muscles strain upwards towards me like the corolla, the calyx and the peduncle of a single flower. She says:

'But it's not because it's me or because you think it's me... *who* is in these drawings. I'm sorry... this is hard to explain.'

I stroke her hair with one hand; I lift her chin with the other; and I assure her that, on the contrary, she explained it very well. Gaining in confidence, she then asks me if I have one of those older sculptures in the atelier, from when I was in Italy, and that I have indeed mentioned to her before in connection with those drawings. I tell her I don't. But I do know of one that is being exhibited right now in a gallery in the Campo Grande. I look at my watch: it is twenty past three. 'Shall we go and see it?'

Y's first reaction is one of sheer enthusiasm. We would go separately, just as a precaution, in our own separate cars. It is hardly likely we shall meet anyone who knows her.

'What about someone who knows you?' she asked. 'Don't you think it could be… unpleasant for you?'

'Unpleasant?' I assume she means 'dangerous'. 'Not at all! That's ludicrous!'

Then, smiling again, she suggests that we rest for just a few minutes longer on the divan before we get dressed.

I quickly put the drawings back in their portfolio. I go to the fridge to get a few more ice cubes and another bottle of sparkling mineral water. I come back to find her lying down; and I even think she may have gone to sleep. She hasn't: she has merely closed her eyes. Without even opening them, she lifts the corner of the sheet with her left hand in a silent invitation for me to lie down next to her.

'Do you know what?' she says as soon as I lie down. This is the question with which she usually starts our heavier, more difficult conversations. 'Do you know what? A while back, a few weeks ago, I brought you a photograph album with pictures of my father. For you to look at. But then I thought better of it. And I took the album back to the car.'

'I know. That was the day you came very late.'

'It was,' she affirms, not in the least surprised. 'I thought it would be better… And I didn't want you to see… To see what I was like when I was single. Nor to see my mother when she was my age now. That's when she… when she left my father. She was much younger then… much, much younger than I am today. That's why. I didn't want you to see it. Sorry.'

All this is said with an obvious effort, with her eyes closed throughout. When she's done, she suddenly raises her hands to her ears, as though trying to stop me from criticizing her. But I merely go on stroking her, almost sleepily, while an extreme languor overcomes us both. I don't even feel like reminding her that we'll have to choose between going to the gallery and giving in to this drowsiness. It is more than drowsiness, more than torpor, and we suddenly fall asleep.

And we are woken up, I don't know how long afterwards (an hour and a half, two hours?) by the sound of a key noisily unlocking the front door.

'What is it? Who is it?' asks Y anxiously, waking up with a start and snuggling up closer to me.

'It must be Floripes. It can only be Floripes.'

'Who?'

'The cleaning woman.' And I shout out, 'Floripes? One moment Floripes!'

The door, pushed open with caution, creaked a little. It could only have been open a crack.

'Yes, Mestre. It's me.'

'Would you mind coming back in half an hour?'

'Certainly, Mestre. I understand. Don't worry. But look, Mestre, if possible... I'd like to have a little word with you today.'

'OK, Floripes. I'll wait for you.'

As soon as the door closes, we both jump up at the same time. Then, before Y starts to dress, I give her a brief description of Floripes, her full name being Floripes-with-a-resonant-O, born and bred in Moimenta da Beira, but a resident of the Bairro da Alcântara in Lisbon since the age of fifteen.

XIV

'You must forgive me, Mestre. It's nothing to do with me, what you get up to, I know only too well what artists are like, I've been working that many years in these ateliers, but I've been meaning to have a word with you for quite some time now. I hope you won't take it the wrong way, Mestre, but it's for your own good, you know, you're not a youngster any more, Mestre, but sometimes people think they're stronger than they are, they believe that youth lasts for ever, but it's all an illusion, and then when it comes to health, it's gone before you know it.

'I shouldn't have to tell you this, after all there're enough mirrors here, and in your house too no doubt, Mestre, and even your lady wife or your friends must have told you that you're looking pretty awful. Just the other day my daughter said to me that you looked quite down in the mouth, Mestre, when you went to the salon where she works now and, to tell the truth, I wish it was a ladies' hairdressers', it would be more proper, really, but it's hard to get a job nowadays, and no one can afford to be choosy. I think you have been a client there for quite some time, Mestre, and of course you would not have recognized her, because you haven't seen her since she was at the Ferreira Borges.[12] Only she gave up on her studies afterwards, it was such a shame, but it was her fault, she's been shy ever since, and the other day, the twit, she wasn't even capable of telling you who she was, Mestre, as if it was such a dreadful thing to do. But as soon as she got home – and I don't mean to scare you – she told me straightaway that you were all worn out, as pale as anything and with shadows under your eyes as dark as I don't know what.

'It's hardly surprising, I thought to myself, but believe me, Mestre, on my daughter's happiness, on my granddaughter's health, I swear that not a single word has passed my lips. I thought to myself, I must admit, because no one knows better than me, I'm not trying to flatter myself, what a coming and going of ladies there's been in this atelier – oh Mestre, Mestre, if that divan could speak, there would be such an uproar from the womenfolk that they'd hear it on the Outra Banda![13] But for the past few months I know jolly well that it's always been the same woman, my nose never lets me down about these things and she must be really classy, she must, because everything always smells so nice and is left so tidy, I must say, apart from that filthy eye-liner on the pillows, it's a real pain to take it off afterwards, and I think there's even been some crying going on, but I don't know, Mestre, forgive me, if it's you who upsets her or if it's the lady, and I say this, but don't take me wrong, Mestre, if it's the lady who's one of those who always cries for more.

'Luckily, your wife never comes here, so she doesn't, and that's what you call luck, Mestre, and I even think she does it on purpose, that she only pretends not to understand, there's a real lady for you, you wouldn't expect any different, and I cannot forget, so I can't, I cannot forget what she did for my daughter, as her doctor, and she always looked after her so well, when she was a kiddie, and she had measles, then it was scarlet fever and those swellings that came up in her neck, and even afterwards, when she was at the Ferreira Borges, that time she caught brucellosis all because of those cheeses my mother-in-law brought from her village, and nobody else had been able to find out what it was. If it was up to me, and it's not that long ago that I was saying this to my son-in-law, I'd have already taken my granddaughter to her by now, up to the hospital or even to her surgery, and I know the good doctor, she would have willingly seen her, but my son-in-law says no, no, because he also has a lot of faith in the doctor who looked after that other child of his he had by his first wife, poor thing, the one who died when the child had just started to crawl, she was even friends with my daughter, anyway these things happen.

'Now it's really lucky that your doctor wife never comes here, it really, really is, and let's hope she never gets to hear about anything, what does she need to know about anything for? It's not like the wife of one of your colleagues, say no more, in one of the ateliers near here, almost next door, who actually pays to find out everything, and there's always someone who lets on, and she always turns up when she senses someone else is coming, and once she even took a gun to her husband's head and tried to make him do to the other woman, in front of her, what he hadn't done at home for ages. That would have been something else, but what he did do was even worse, something so gross there was no point in taking the sheet home afterwards or pouring a whole bottle of perfume all over the place because I can tell that smell's still there, this nose of mine, ah, this nose of mine never lets me down.

'It must be said, Mestre, that there's never been that kind of scandal in your atelier, and that's another thing that can be said for you and for your lady wife, nothing less could be expected, your wife being a doctor and all. But you're doing your health in, Mestre, so you are, and you can be sure that they won't kill you, but they'll wear you out, and don't forget you're still lucky enough to have your mother alive, and that's a blessing that not everyone your age can boast about, and just you tell me, what need is there, now that her life is nearly over, to cause her even more grief? I know it's nothing to do with me what you get up to, Mestre, I know what artists are like, and forgive me, Mestre, but I've been meaning to tell you this for a good few months now, because since the New Year there's been so much changing of linen, it's silly, there's so much washing and ironing like there hasn't been for ages, and you know, Mestre, everything's getting more and more expensive, it can't get much worse, there's the water, the electric, the washing powder, public transport, and I can just imagine how much those bottles of champagne and whisky must cost, and all those nibbles you've always got in your fridge now, Mestre, starting with those really expensive little black beads, at least, my daughter says they're very expensive, and God help us, they even stink of rotting fish.

'Forgive me, Mestre, but I have to get this off my chest, it's only by talking things through that one can make sense of things, after all we've known each other for long enough by now, and I'm so worn out at times, my varicose veins play me up something rotten, my back doesn't half give me what for, and last year my holidays were ruined, because my son-in-law had the bright idea that we should go camping, but I've said I'm not going this year, I can't stand tents, and unless we rent a little house, and we've already seen one near Peniche, that's it, they can count me out, that's for sure! Trouble is the house isn't exactly free, that would be the day, and we do have six mouths to feed after all and there are two, poor little things, that do nothing but eat, the others all have to help and because my daughter's only been in her job for two months, she'll have to come and go every day, and it's such an expense, even with a pass, the cost of a coach, it's no joke...

'Oh Mestre, for heaven's sake! I wasn't telling you all this just for you to go and...

'Heavens, God forbid, there's no need to be in that much of a hurry! I only wanted you to think about it, Mestre, to be thinking about it, you might not even have enough...

'Enough, that's enough. I mean, these three notes will take care just fine of what we've been talking about... We won't mention it again and that settles that... As I said, the holidays are in August and then, come September, we'll think about what to do next.

'But, you do understand, this isn't why I wanted us to have this little talk. On my daughter's happiness, on my granddaughter's health, it was only to say how awful you've been looking. And I didn't mean to scare you, or even stick my nose in your life, Mestre, I know what artists are like and you're the only one who knows, Mestre, you're the only one who knows how far you can go, you're the one only who knows how strong you are, the only one who knows what to do for the best.

'Now promise me you're not going to worry about all this, it's not worth it and, after all, my daughter hasn't seen you for many years, all she said was that she thought you looked quite worn out, and all I said was, "so he should!", and I can't understand how come they haven't worn him to a frazzle yet.

'But there you go Mestre, I'll be on my way now, and just you pretend I never said a thing. If it makes you happy, and if you think it's worth all the trouble, then enjoy it while you can, because life's too short.

'There was this lady whose house I did, and I mean lady, but she ended up doing drugs, poor thing, but she was quite right when she said that, because life isn't a bed of roses, we actually have to hop into bed as much as possible, to sleep or whatever, you know what I mean, and make the most of it.'

XV

And all at once plausible reality drops upon me.[14]
And [I] savour in the cigarette release from any thought
I follow the trail of smoke like a route of my own
And enjoy, for one sensitive and fitting moment,
Release from all speculations
And the awareness that metaphysics is a consequence of feeling out of sorts.
Then I sink into my chair
And carry on smoking.
As long as Destiny allows me, I shall carry on smoking.
(If I married my washerwoman's daughter
Perhaps I would be happy.)
This settled, I get up from the chair. I go to the window.[15]

You must meet Floripes. (Floripes, and Nyasa too; but Nyasa's case is much more serious.) When you hear Floripes (or Nyasa), you at once feel the need to read, or reread – as a complement – something equally substantial.

I'm not joking. Even in Floripes's case. That time I opened *Poemas* by Álvaro de Campos, at random, and I've just told you what happened to me afterwards. But I was far from knowing, at the time, what the early evening of that day held in store for me. I have kept it to myself until now, on purpose – so that I could tell it to you at this point.

It was hot, very hot. I felt like going for a drive along the Marginal[16] to see if I could find a quiet place by the sea where I could drink a nice, ice-cold lager. A little before Monte Estoril (where my wife and I had already settled in for the summer), I found more or less what I was looking for: a quiet esplanade, at the back of a small beach, with a café where only four or five tables were occupied, leaving a recess at the rear that was completely unoccupied.

I headed straight for the recess. But next to the table where I sat down, there was another table which, although vacant at that point, had on it two unfinished drinks, a pair of sunglasses, a copy of *JL*[17] folded in half, and on the newspaper a closed book, and on top of the book a packet of More cigarettes. The glasses obviously belonged to a woman.

It wasn't hard to deduce, looking down at the now nearly deserted beach, that all this stuff belonged to the only couple there, who sat on the sand, facing the sea with their backs turned to the esplanade, supremely unaware of the world about them. Which was not a lot: some rowdy young boys playing round the bare framework of a tent, under the brooding watchfulness of three matronly ladies.

As for the couple, even seen from the back, there was an obvious contrast between the two: from the petulant outline of her shoulder-blades and her neck emerging from a casual strapless blouse, even from the swaying rhythm of her hair on her neck, it could be assumed that she was very much younger than him; as for the man, he was almost completely bald on top, and from the curve of his back, in spite of the sporty shirt he was wearing, it was obvious that there was a clear generation gap between them. Were they father and daughter? No way! Unless they were openly incestuous: she rested her head on his shoulder with languid abandon, and waited beseechingly for him to kiss her on the mouth. And then, when he did, she displayed a touching modesty by raising one of her hands in futile defence to cover their faces.

Every now and then, without looking at her, he would hug her round the shoulders with a solicitude that was either demanding or desperate; at other times, he would place his arm over her shoulders as though trying to enfold her inside an invisible shawl. Then they would both sit somewhat stiffly, most probably with their eyes lost on the horizon; and I could swear that's when they were feeling overwhelmed by the prospect of having to part shortly, perhaps it was the looming spectre of forthcoming holidays which they couldn't take at the same time or during which they would each have to go their own separate ways.

Unless I was projecting onto them the spectre that was haunting me: over the last few weeks, with Y, we had only touched very lightly on that same question. And not always in a very peaceful manner. Once – on the most recent occasion – the only reason I didn't lose my temper with Y for her constant indecision was because it was the day we were celebrating her birthday.

Ah! Under the sign of Cancer lies the beginning of summer… an ungrateful stage in the development of any love affair; a test that is all the more gruelling in the case of a clandestine relationship. All things considered, it wasn't just to do with this spectre in particular:

it was also to do with the temptation to experience in broad daylight what had until then only been experienced in darkness.

I didn't even notice the girl getting up. Still facing the sea, she is now standing two or three steps in front of the place where the man is still sitting. Below her strapless blouse she is wearing a very tight pair of blue jeans, but it is more because of the skittish way she shakes her black or nearly-black mane that I at once associate the person modelling those blue jeans with the owner of the packet of Mores on the table next to mine. When she then turns round, signalling to her companion to get up as well, I am certain that the girl is in fact you.

Your friend has finally stood up as well. But he still has his back turned towards the place where I am sitting; putting your hand on his shoulder, then sliding it down his arm and forearm, finally squeezing his wrist, you seem to be trying to convince him that you should both go into the sea. It so happens that the tide has reached its lowest ebb; the beach is so vast, it is almost unreal; at that moment, both your fluid, narrow shadows are reflected on the mirror-like surface of the wet sand that prolongs the beach. But, faced with the pools of water that have been left behind, he hesitates: that's when he stands sideways on, pulling a pipe out of his trouser pocket, followed by a box of matches. I don't need more than that to recognize, at last, who it is.

So this is your friend! Your so-called older friend. The one whom you seem to miss even during those rare moments when we talk to each other. And why, for what, have you kept this secret so jealously from me? Of course you're aware, and always have been, that he and I have known each other for years; and although we have never particularly felt for each other what might be called admiration or affection, neither have we ever had any real cause to hate each other.

We must be about the same age. I was at the Belas Artes when he was reading literature; we met up quite often just after the war, during our adolescent political meetings that were at times pathetic, at others ridiculous, and which, I believe, neither of us took too seriously. From then on we would vaguely acknowledge each other from a distance, discreetly, as though we had at that time both caught a strange virus of convenient furtiveness. Then I travelled abroad for a few years, mainly through Italy. By the time I came back, he'd already had some of his books published, and the newspapers were already carrying his photo (whilst I was quite unknown at the time), and he had already assiduously begun making appearances on television, forever hanging onto his pipe, which seemed to go down well with certain perverse young girls and certain innocent young ladies, but which had the irritating knack – and I don't know why (and please note that I wasn't the only man this happened to) – of making my blood boil. Perhaps he too objected to my dishevelled mop of hair, which was in full glory at the time, or to the garishness of my jumpers and duffle-coats. The truth is that, from then on, our greetings became even more evasive.

Later, through foul means or fair pillow-talk (or is it the other way round?), I came to realize that we had been hunting (poor hunted hunters!) in almost overlapping hunting grounds. I remember, for instance, a desperate vixen who made us believe, one after the other, that she was about to succumb once we'd caught her: she enacted a sham suicide in front of me that she'd already enacted three times in front of him. I also remember a bewildered doe, still quite young, who one day made blindly for my hideout, but I stupidly, perhaps kindly, spared her, whereas he, on the other hand, appears to have caught her in his snare and sacrificed her. These are the kind of incidents, in short, that do not exactly contribute to a great friendship between two men once they have found out about them.

And there were times, you must forgive me, when I felt that your friend co-operated too closely with the newspapers, presided over too many conferences, took part in too many debates, too many round-tables, giving too much the impression that he had a finger in every pie – I don't know if these were alibis or a means of providing alibis for all his women. There would follow quieter or less wanton periods: then we would resume our not always clandestine greetings.

After 25 April,[18] it fell to his lot, as the expression goes, to take on a few political responsibilities (didn't everyone? but who took them seriously?) and, what with my anarchic temperament, I found it hard to forgive him for hanging around strutting young peacocks and mixing with a motley of failures, high-flyers and charlatans, whom we had known for nearly thirty years, since our youth, and who even then couldn't be taken seriously, and that he really should have seen through much better than me. One day, in the name of a member of this group, in fact the most puffed-up one – whose pretentious taste in artistic matters has always provoked in me an explosive mixture of nausea and laughter – he even went as far as inviting me to some 'official' lunch or dinner, which was to bring together the cream of the Portuguese intelligentsia, and which I had, of course, the greatest pleasure in not attending. During that period, if we happened to see each other at some private viewing or embassy do (I'm no saint either, I too have my weaknesses), we would immediately become quite invisible to each other.

Now, at the bottom of the beach, he has lit his ever-present pipe while, leaning on his shoulder again, you try to take off your shoes, and it's plain to see your companion is not going to venture any further onto the wet sand. He will probably turn at some point and come back up here, either alone or with you: in either case, we'll find ourselves face to face once more, and there will be no point in keeping up our parody of invisibility, let alone the longstanding 'clandestinity' of our relationship. Apart from that, he knows that I know you. And he will soon realize that I saw the two of you together – and *the way* I saw you together. But I don't feel like leaving my beer half way through. Not in the least. The best thing to do then will be to play it by ear.

I stretch my fingers towards the table you will return to; I push your packet of cigarettes away from its place; finally I pick up the book and put it on my table with the utmost nonchalance. It is an anthology of contemporary Spanish poetry: nearly half way through, there is a little bookmark between two pages; on one of them, the odd-numbered one, some verses have been underlined in pencil.

Underlined by whom? By you? By him? There's no clue either way. Never mind. I am sure that you were both reading them today. And these verses speak to me too.

Fortunately, I have a Biro on me. But no paper. The anthology's dust cover, if torn carefully, will do fine. With the manual dexterity that the gods have endowed me with, I do this in the twinkling of an eye.

In the meantime, down below, something strange is going on between the two of you. Your friend remains standing in the same place as before, holding your shoes in his left hand, while you walk on over the wet sand and then, still in your blouse and jeans, you resolutely walk into the water. As soon as the gentle waves reach your waist, you begin to swim – in that endearing dog-paddle adopted by women, even if they are good swimmers, a mixture of caution and skill, when they try not to wet their hair. And your friend, on land, is waving repeatedly at you with his pipe (you can't even see him), more than likely trying to get you to return to shore.

As for me, I transcribed all the verses that were underlined in the book onto that emergency piece of paper (I still carry it on me today):

> *Um plazo fijo tuvo*
> *Nuestro conocimiento y trato, como todo*
> *En la vida, y un dia, uno cualquiera,*
> *Sin causa ni pretexto aparente,*
> *Nos dejamos de ver. Lo presentiste?*
> *Yo sí, que siempre estuve presentiéndolo.*[19]

Only then do I look for the author's name: it's Luis Cernuda. The name seems familiar – unless I am confusing it with Neruda – but (I must confess my ignorance) I am sure that I have never read an entire book by either of them, just as I have never read an entire book by your friend. I could have sworn, however, that it was he who underlined those verses. And they were obviously meant to be read to you.

What possessed you to go for a swim dressed in your clothes? That's a whim that even Xô, even with me, never indulged in! How many other whims of yours will your friend have put up with? How many more will he put up with when he knows, when he senses, that your 'relationship and agreement' will not disobey the rule and will inevitably have a 'fixed term'?

To tell the truth, I already suspected that your friend was somewhat burdened with certain troubles of his own... I believe he is on his second or third marriage, that he has children, that he may even have grandchildren; and he's put on weight, he's going bald. Do people ever learn? Or do we only see the mote in our neighbour's eye? I am getting older and older; and yet...

I put the book back on the table next to me. I try to leave everything as it was. Come to think of it, it would be better if the two of you didn't see me here. Better that he, especially, should not realize that I have been watching you both from here.

But I suddenly know for sure that, from now on, whenever I bump into him on an opening night of some exhibition, or at a do in some embassy or other, that I shall be speaking to him in quite a different manner.

XVI

'We received our invitation yesterday.'

'Ours arrived today. And my wife thinks we should go. I'm the one who...'

'It's the same at home... But we have that wedding to go to on the same day.'

'Oh, no! If you're not going, I'm not in the least bit interested in going either. I'm not at all thrilled at the prospect of seeing those two cockatoos again. If you were there, of course... it would make all the difference. Besides, I am indebted to them for... for having met you at their house.'

'Come off it... If I hadn't called round and left you my card... you probably wouldn't even recognize my face by now.'

'Yes I would. Of course I would. I would remember your face, your voice, your eyes, your knees...'

At that moment, out of all Y's body – her extensive, exhausted, expurgated body – I find myself stroking her knees. After the new depths to which we have just descended – or to which we have just soared – what explanation can there be for our having drifted so smoothly onto the subject of that invitation with which those Latin-American diplomats have reminded us of their existence?

The truth is that they recently bought one of my pieces; and that I hastened to sell it directly to them – somewhat clandestinely, without my *marchand* knowing – so as to make up, to a certain extent, for the effects of inflation and a few necessities for my 'sabbatical' year. And talk about selling my soul to the devil! I even went as far as scratching off the date at the bottom of that object which I'm not too pleased with (I wish even my signature wasn't on it!) and which the well-to-do Amerindians not only delighted in buying, but even decided to place with great pomp and circumstance right in the middle of the garden of their horrendous villa in the Restelo, where they settled after Easter after leaving the flat in Estrela where they had first pitched camp. This time round we have been invited to a party in this same garden, with a barbecue on one side and a swimming-pool on the other: it's to take place next Saturday, on the last day of July, from twelve o'clock onwards; they say that it will be quite informal; they recommend bringing swimming costumes.

'At home...' Y repeats. 'My husband also thinks we should go. Apparently they've been really good to him. It seems they've done some important business with the factory. They've placed a large order, for this year already...'

It was the first time I had ever heard her refer to such matters.

'Is that why you're going?'

'That's not what I said. I don't even know if we can go. We have that wedding to go to on the same day. Unless we leave a bit early... But it would definitely not be until mid-afternoon.'

More abruptly than I would have liked, I remove my hands from her knees. I also stand up too abruptly. I am now standing next to the divan, pouring out another three fingers of whisky into an almost empty tumbler.

'Aren't you drinking too much?' asks Y, very gently, as though immediately embarrassed at having asked the question.

'I think we need to clear the air,' I answer, swigging my drink without having bothered to add water or ice. 'Unless I am very much mistaken, I can only conclude that... when it comes to me, when there's the slightest chance of our seeing each other, and you make this quite obvious, you won't make the slightest effort to turn up. Now then: it's all very well for me to say that I am indebted to those Incas, or Aztecs, or whatever the hell they are. But that still wouldn't be a good enough reason for me to consider going back to see them. I'd only go if I could be sure you'd be there. Sure of seeing you there, in broad daylight... in the sun. This may seem ridiculous, but at the end of the day, when all is said and done, this is the big difference between you and me. You are quite satisfied with our meeting here like this. I am not.'

'Oh, I'm sorry!... I thought you liked it too...'

'Pardon?'

'That you liked it too... my coming here whenever I can.'

'That's not what I'm talking about. I didn't say I don't like it. Quite the opposite. But I would like to see you in different circumstances.' I take another slug of my drink. 'Or do you think I can't see what's going on? How you always wriggle out of things? How many times have I suggested to you that we go out to lunch to some quiet restaurant, at least occasionally? Or meet in a museum, an exhibition, as though by accident, as though it were the most natural thing in the world...? Or even on a beach. Why not on a beach? All we'd need to do is plan how to do it. We'd hardly be likely to come across anyone we know…'

I am now by the dresser, pointedly turning my back to Y; and my battered image reflected in the mirror makes me realize how incoherently and illogically I've been talking and, at the same time, reminds me insidiously of some of the things Floripes said… That was all I needed: to be on the defensive right at the beginning of this absurd argument! Then I drop into this armchair, holding my glass in my fingertips, annoyed with myself, avoiding looking at Y's great and splendid body, stretched out on the divan, unyielding as a recumbent statue, vulnerable as a sailing-boat with its sails down and, worse still, run aground on a sandbank.

'And that's not all,' I hear myself exclaim, even though I know it would be better if I didn't say another word. 'How many times have I brought up the question of our holidays? When will I know if you are going to the Algarve or not, if you're going to Switzerland or not…?'

How far had we got? The fortnight they were going to spend in their villa in Vale do Lobo was sometimes planned for the middle of August, sometimes for the end. There were also plans for spending a few days at a childhood friend's near Saint Moritz (where she'd go alone, or alone with Vicky) which had been pencilled in for various dates throughout September and, subsequently, I had contemplated going to Italy or even to Switzerland during that time, so that we might meet up in Rome or Lausanne – even if only for a week, three days or one night.

I charge ahead:

'Unless… Unless you can't bear the thought of our meetings… even if it's somewhere no one knows us at all.'

Without a word, without looking my way at all, Y slowly gets up; and as she stands there, with her beautiful profile clearly outlined against the whiteness of the wall, I feel as though she might fly away at any moment, vanish into the skies and disappear for ever from the heaven of my days. Or maybe she is standing like that, waiting a little bit longer, to show me just how foolish I'm being with the Present and with the present of her presence, by tormenting her, tormenting myself, with derisory details of Past and Future.

I want to run up to her, grab her by the waist and by the knees, force her back again on the divan, and fill her ears with a renewed act of thanksgiving. But this armchair seems to be holding me down to the basest part of me; although my glass is empty, it feels heavy in my hands and I hold on to it as though it's a lead weight.

'While we're at it...' I persist, 'there is one more thing...' I take a deep breath, hoping perhaps to stop from saying what I was about to say, or perhaps for Y to stop me with a single gesture. 'A little over a week ago, after you'd been looking at my sketches... do you remember? Do you think I don't know what was going on? We had agreed to go the gallery, to see that sculpture and at the last minute, you... At the last minute, you were ashamed of being seen with me.'

As though someone had slapped her across the face, she turns her head towards me, just her head, and looks me in the eye.

'I was, yes...' she admits then in a quiet whisper. 'Yes, I was. But it's not what you're thinking. It's not that at all.' And raising her voice a little, she says: 'If it had been five years ago, if it had been two years ago, even if it had been when we first met... I know I wasn't then what I am now.'

'What? What? What are you on about?'

She sits on the divan, sideways again, showing me her profile, again not looking at me:

'You're the one who pretends you can't see. And I know you mean well. You do it just for I lack confidence...' She corrected herself: 'Because I lack confidence.' And she went on, talking faster as she went: 'But one thing I do know... I do know that I have aged a few years over the past few months. It's my fault. I thought it would all be much easier. Or that I would be stronger. That I could deal with an affair, how do you say... That I even had the right to have an affair... and that it would be no more than an affair. But all this, here, the two of us, and everything that's going on at home, and things can never be the same at home any more, and living just for the days I come here to see you... All this has turned out to be more than I thought.' Turning round to stare at me again, she tries to smile: 'It's no big deal, anyway... I've just let myself go a little, that's all. But the truth is. I'm no longer so... How do you say? I am no longer so... presentable. No; I'm not ashamed of being seen with you. It's the other way round. It's entirely the other way round. It is you who deserves, for so many reasons, to be seen with someone who... someone like... See? I'm not even being modest... with someone who is perhaps more like how I used to be.'

Faced with the conviction and the relative ease with which she has just spoken (I don't think I'd ever heard her speak for so long at a stretch), there is no point whatsoever in responding with logical arguments. I remain seated, but after putting down my glass, I merely say:

'Very well then. In that case, there is only one thing to do... something I have been meaning to suggest to you for a while now. It's the only solution, at least so it seems to me, it's the only way for you to stop feeling so... torn, if I can call it that. It's not something to be undertaken lightly, of course. But as far as I'm concerned, I have no doubts whatsoever. And you can take the whole of August, or even the whole of the summer holidays, to make up your mind.'

Only then do I get up. However, instead of going up to her, as perhaps she was hoping I would and as I so much wanted deep down to do, I go back to the dresser again; and there I stand, between the dresser and this armchair, carrying on with what it is I have to say:

'I don't like big speeches. And I'd like to make this sound as simple as possible.' I am still looking at her profile: I notice she has gone very pale and that her eyelashes, her eyelids and her bottom lip are quivering ever so slightly. 'There is only one thing, I believe, though this is not the only consideration, that can help you... stop having all these doubts about yourself. The thing to do... The thing to do is for us to live together.'

I feel as though I've delivered this speech with all the wrong intonations. I haven't been feeling too good of late: two new bits of paper have been put under my windscreen wiper – on afternoons, as it so happens, when Y did not come to Lisbon – but I didn't know whether I should tell her about them or not. Something was said in one of those papers ('Watch it, you're the wrong age to be getting up to mischief') that no longer makes me think this is just a mistake; I'm beginning to think it's a foolish and tasteless prank. It's probably best not to say anything at all about the matter.

I rest my hands on top of the dresser behind me. I can see Y's profile, and her eyelashes, her eyelids and her bottom lip have suddenly stopped quivering. Her posture has suddenly become quite hieratic, she is so still that she no longer looks as though she's about to fly away and disappear any minute now, as I had feared before, but as though she has turned to stone and will stay there until the end of time, to overwhelm me with the vision of her presence. Of her presence – but not her existence.

XVII

You, Xô, you existed. What I did doubt, even when you were with me, was your presence.

You, Ana Dora Q. – branded forever on my olfactory memory as Inodora – you too existed, although you were always so reclusive and so ascetically odourless, through your submissive capitulation to the gentleman from the perfume industry who was in his sixties when he married you, after replying to a lonely heart ad, and you were in your thirties, still innocent or at least so it seemed, a man who, in spite of the branch of industry in which he flourished, declared himself allergic to all perfumes, including, in particular, the very ones he made.

You, Elvira de V. e S., you existed, in spite of the gulfs of absence you periodically disappeared into and from where you would emerge with your hair striped with new highlights, with a renewed anger against your mother and your sister, with amazingly confused stories, always propelling me into your friends' beds, always assuring me that you were not jealous, and that you wouldn't even mind 'watching' or – and why not? – even 'participating', but then, as soon as one of them merely pulled back the sheets, you would immediately go off on a stretcher to the nearest clinic and undergo yet another sleep cure.

You, Isabelinha P. M. de B., the imaginary militant and martyr of a multitude of mythically extremist movements, you existed – and how! – in spite of the necessary scarcity of the few spare minutes between meetings when you did 'surrender' – if such a ridiculous verb actually means anything.

You, Octaviana T., immoderate and illiterate collector of innumerable free History of Art courses, willing galley-slave of galleries, tireless pilgrim to any workshop on ceramics, screen printing, jewellery making, poker-work, weaving or fabric printing, uneducated holder of doctorates in various decorative arts and of rival schools of flower arrangement, you existed, exuberantly, within and without all this, although your bird-like flightiness and your painstaking ineptitude in all these things never helped you realize, oh eternal fifty-year-old child, that in order to fulfil yourself as a creator of Beauty and for the whole universe around you to be touched by Beauty, all that was needed was the incomparable twitters of your multiple orgasms.

You, last of all, Ursula von W., whom I shall always call the *Corps Diplomatique*, not only because that was the corps that your diplomatic husband belonged to, but mostly because of the creative, physical talent your *corps* displayed for all kinds of pacts and treaties, agreements and conventions, sublime bluffs and subtle commitments – oh, you generous and elusive creature, how you existed!

Ana Dora, Elvira, Isabelinha, Octaviana, Ursula: it was indeed on purpose that, as the more visible symbols of some of the many women I've known, I aligned you in this elementary succession of vowels – the guileless A, E, I, O, U of the poor student that I am, a contrite yet incorrigible recidivist, the dunce who never goes beyond the first page of his very first textbook.

But you, Xô, you're the one, some twenty years ago, who became the great touchstone, the terrible illustration of my singular behaviour with women that 'exist' and women, on the other hand, who are merely 'present'. I don't know why, but I've never been able to imagine going through the rest of my life with the first kind.

And here you have, Xô, after all these years, the reason, or one of the reasons, why I so cowardly beat the retreat when we arrived back in Rome, after those wonderful three weeks in Amalfi.

Hadn't we firmly agreed, after all those Camparis we had at dusk at the open-air table in front of the steps of the Duomo, that you wouldn't return to Rio, nor I to Lisbon, and that Rome would somehow, from now on, be the eternal city of our love, the holy see of our future life together?

But you existed, in your twenty-fourth year, in the intensely secure knowledge that you stood to inherit one of the greatest fortunes in Brazil and that you were a celestial body that could include in its orbit all the satellites it wanted to, and that you could treat yourself to the luxury of starting a brand new life in Europe, with only a passing thought, if that, for the after-effects of your two marriages – the first was still being annulled in the Roman Curia when your husband committed suicide (he was a young man from São Paulo, from a very good family, nevertheless) and the second marriage (to a great brute of a Texan who'd been a war hero in Korea) culminated in an even more scandalous divorce. It was none of this, I swear, that worried me: I was much more worried about the meteoric pace at which you lived your life.

Only I cannot forgive myself for the pathetic way I tried to blame it on not being able to leave my wife. Of all the stupid excuses I could have used – can you imagine! – I had to go and say it was because *we had no children*!

'What? What rubbish are you talking about? All you want is to be her little boy forever.'

In the quiet of that evening in the Via Giulia, your huge and scornful burst of laughter – a single, two-toned peal: crystal-clear to start with, then turning stony-hard – was more insulting than the way you started screaming immediately afterwards, inserting at regular intervals, like a slogan, this expression of grating pity: 'You're such a fool! You're such a fool!' Every time you uttered these words, chin up and head flung back, the stony whiteness of your too healthy teeth would flash at me intolerably. Finally, turning your back on me ('I never want to set eyes on you ever again!'), you took off, shaken but standing tall, under an arch round the nearest street corner.

But that same night – because I had been witless enough, at the beginning of our conversation, to tell you I was meeting someone on the Tre Scalini esplanade, a lady recently arrived from Portugal – you sought me out on the Piazza Navona, standing shamelessly in front of the table where I was sipping a *grappa* and where a portly lady of about my age – but who already back then looked older than me – was attacking *con brio* a monumental and intricately designed mound of ice-cream.

'Please excuse me, Madam, but I must have a little word with him...'

I stood up at once, murmuring discreetly to my table companion: 'She's one of my colleagues. I'll be right back.'

And I went off by your side, my head politely inclined towards you, pretending I was listening to your every word, although you said not a thing and merely escorted me, as it were, to the centre of the piazza, among the tourists, the hippies and other such buffoons, up to the fountain closest to the Pamphili Palace, which is where the Brazilian Embassy is situated. It was only when we reached the edge of the fountain that you came to a stop and deliberately said to me:

'Do you see those two great big men at the Embassy door? All I have to do is raise my hand once more just like this, and they will come straight over and thrash you to pieces. But I don't think it will be necessary, do you? All I want is to tell you what a bastard you are. A bastard, do you hear me? And I know full well who it is you were sitting with… Go back. Go back to her. Go back to your wife. Back to your mummy.'

Again you turned your back on me, as you had already done earlier that afternoon in the Via Giulia; but this time there was no abruptness, just a discreet wave of your left hand – the gesture of someone throwing over their shoulders less than a handful of ashes.

I never saw you again, and I never did find out how it was that you found out – probably after our conversation on the Via Giulia – that it was indeed my wife who had arrived in Rome the day before, after having had no news from me for over seven weeks; and after having bombarded a resounding Roman address that was no longer mine with telegrams from Lisbon; after having phoned either the Consulate or one of the two buildings of the Portuguese embassy in Rome every three days, then every two days, then every single day, always in vain, without anyone in Rome able, or willing, to tell her where the hell I'd vanished to.

She was here in Lisbon, throughout a scorching month of July, completely worn out by yet another of her countless exams and, with her clinician's pragmatism, she decided that desperate ends required desperate measures; pawning some family jewellery and valiantly driving off, one sweltering morning in August, in her second-hand Dauphine which wasn't yet paid for in full but was already beginning to fall apart, she managed, all alone, in less than three days, to cross the rocky lands and pine forests of Portugal, the sprawling plains and distant towns of Northern Spain, the whole of the South of France, crawling as it was with holiday-makers, then the bends and the tunnels, more tunnels and more bends, of the Italian Riviera.

It was the middle of the night when she arrived in Rome, where she had never set foot before, and which she felt she 'knew' a little from the dozen or so films she had seen belonging to the good phase of Italian neo-realism, from the few vague references I made in one or other of my exciting letters, and most of all, from the detailed, often repeated 'descriptions' by the most unmarried and sterile of her venerable aunts, the one who belonged to the Mothers' Guild, and who had been to Rome on a pilgrimage once during the glorious age of Mussolini. With such a wealth of information, it was hardly surprising that my wife should land, that night, in a dismal and squalid *albergo* in the Via Cavour.

It was too late even to try and find me at the address with the resounding name. The next day, in the morning, she started off with the Consulate. And she arrived there just at the right time, or just at the wrong time, for them to tell her straightaway that I had indeed turned up again: I had been away from Rome, in the area of Naples, in Amalfi and Pompeii; but that I'd phoned the day before saying that I would be coming back the following day, perhaps that very morning, to pick up my mail from the Consulate.

Reassured by this news, she waited stolidly around the entrance to the building until four o'clock in the afternoon, having had nothing to eat or drink all day apart from the miserable brioche and watery *caffè latte* she'd had for breakfast. When I saw the state she was in, and realizing what she'd been through, I thanked various gods that I had only arranged to meet Xô in the Via Giulia at around seven thirty that evening. The most important thing to do just then was to take my wife to some pizzeria that might still be open, move her out of that awful hotel where she'd left her luggage, to one that was less gloomy and less dodgy – and to find, amidst all these mundane activities, the best way of telling her of more serious matters, of much more important decisions.

Oh! If only she had uttered the slightest word of criticism, I would immediately have found the courage to start telling her. But not once did she enquire about the reason for my silence; she was almost making fun of herself for having been at all worried in the first place; she swore she'd never before seen me looking quite so sun-tanned and quite so well; and, as though talking about someone else's sporting achievements, she related in detail the different stages of her journey, her lack of sleep, the meals she had eaten, the speeds she had averaged in the dilapidated Dauphine, from the banks of the Tagus all the way to the banks of the Tiber. She wasn't in the least bit interested to know what I'd been doing in Amalfi; she wasn't in the least bit bothered about why, and with what money, I was indulging in such a long holiday, when I had actually written to her in June saying I'd be back in Lisbon at the beginning of July.

'Now that we're both here…' she suggested, finally, 'why don't we stay for another week?' She was looking around her (we were walking up the Via del Babuíno, towards the Piazza di Spagna) at the red and ochre of the façades, the green of the shutters, and the attics covered in multiple variations of other greens. Taking my arm, she added: 'Have you noticed...? We've been married ten years and this is the first time we've been abroad together.'

There was no bitterness in the way she acknowledged this fact; there was no trace of petulance in her suggestion: all there was, or so it seemed to me, was a circuitous way of letting me know that she did not 'exist', but was 'present'; and would remain so for as long as I wished.

Unless, as I see it now, being 'present' in this way is actually, for some women, the only way of truly 'existing'. It's all a matter of terminology; everything is as arbitrary as the world itself, as are the standards we set for it, as are the criteria that we judge it by.

In any case, when I say 'present' with reference to my wife, and when I say 'present' with reference to Y, I am of course being as imprecise as when I say 'light' with reference to a lamp and when I say 'light' with reference to a star.

Y was still there, I don't know how many minutes or how many centuries later, sitting on the edge of the divan, frighteningly still and tensely silent. In the end, I found myself almost shouting:

'Did you hear me? Did you hear what I said? The only thing to do is for us to live together.'

She then turned her head towards me, without quite facing me, as though she didn't really know where she was, as though she too had just returned from far away – and had just realized that she was back where she had started.

Then she got up, picked up her clothes that were strewn over the arms of this armchair and the back of that chair; and still without a word, she began to get dressed. As I continued to lean against the dresser, she walked over to the other mirror, fully dressed now, to freshen up, somewhat more quickly than usual, brushing her hair, touching up her eyelids, lightly painting her lips, rubbing a little cream into her cheeks and on her forehead. Only then – while putting away her tubs, bottles and brushes in her Hermès bag – did she finally whisper to me, between two sighs:

'I'll do what I can... I'll do what I can to turn up on Saturday.'

It took me a while to realize she was referring to the Amerindians' party.

XVIII

The party? It was dreadful. Worse than that: it was rubbish. (Forgive me using the 'rubbish' word, nowadays only 'crap' is acceptable.)

I felt more embarrassed being there than if I'd been caught out, like some idiot, by the most basic joke ever played by a practical joker. However (and this may interest you), I did end up with a better opinion of your friend – who so often enjoyed such foolishness – when I happened to find out that he too had been invited, but had backed out, at the last minute, from parading his pipe around the place.

It was Press who told me this, not the one who was at the dinner where I met Y and whom I mentioned to you before (though she was there too), but another, more mature one, whom I shall refer to from now on as Press 2 – and who turned out to be, for most of that awkward situation, the best company I kept.

In reality, both Presses would not have been enough to 'cover', even if they'd wanted to, the socio-political transcendence of the event – seeing that in and around the edges of the amazing swimming-pool, no less than one junior minister, two private secretaries, five or six cabinet ministers and other secondary (or tertiary) figures, wearing at least three different 'party hats', were exhibiting their bodies on that afternoon towards the end of July, in this year without grace nineteen eighty something. So, from a pseudo-left that kept winking at an apparently 'civilized' right-wing (cross-eyed since birth, anyway), to an extreme right-wing pretending for the time being to have dropped its obsession with the goose-step, there were a good number of representatives from the three 'big' parties who had their elbows and buttocks firmly ensconced in the Republican Assembly. Not to mention a number of exuberant and unenterprising entrepreneurs, a few self-important television puppets, some unimportant technocrats with no techno or cracy, and other hangers-on who made obscure and dubious livings.

Seeing all these people, it was immediately obvious what the practical considerations had been for our Inca or Aztec hosts when selecting the present company: it was no longer, as at the beginning of winter, a mundane, allegorical group of people; instead, in most cases, their guests now offered the promise, the prospect or the guarantee of safe wheeler-dealing under cover, naturally, of accommodating diplomatic immunity.

From the world of so-called 'culture', apart from me – poor me! I only made out two plodding bureaucrats: an ex-dauber and an ex-scribbler – the first was tallish, as melancholy and obtuse as the Pink Panther; the second had a ruddy complexion, was restlessly sedate, a meddlesome mythomaniac, a tiny Speedy Gonzalez intent on eating his way, with equal voracity, through second-hand volumes of little merit and the pieces of cake provided by Public Administration. Both had become justifiably famous in their respective fields, for never having shone with the slightest spark of talent, for having excelled at spreading apocalyptic rumours, for going around kow-towing to the whole motley set of new ministers and for having known how to raise themselves, through such virtuous behaviour, to the position of very general directors of organizations that did not exist or organizations that served no purpose.

This time, there was no Theatre, or Music, or Cinema, or Literature. (As for Art: there was me. Out of purely commercial considerations.) But, as I said, Press was reinforced by another representative, also female, although in this case – just as in mine – our hosts had missed their target: this Press 2, as physically robust as Press 1 was skinny, enjoyed the reputation and prerogative of not being easy to get on with, of having an unrestrained hand and using outspoken language – unless purists cowardly prefer language to be made up of traditional clichés.

There were other women, or people who might look like women to less demanding tastes: the most legitimate wives of some of the above-mentioned boors – nearly all of them flabby, insipid, fat-bottomed, sunburnt, short-legged, with overflowing hips – but also other colourfully self-important women, slimmer on the whole, claiming to be both sexy and efficient, haughtily introduced as secretaries and personal assistants to private secretaries or attachés of this, that or the other, some of whom were present at the party, some of whom were not, all of whom were non-existent.

As soon as I arrived, and because it was so hot, I took advantage of the oversized hip-bath and unwisely had a little swim in the polluted waters of that family-sized bidet. Afterwards, I retreated lazily to a point half way between the barbecue and the swimming-pool, and stretched out on the most unobtrusive deckchair in the welcome shade of the leafy weeping willows.

The not inconsiderable inconvenience of that particular spot was that it presented me with the house's pretentious back porch, a frightful architectural mixture between a small colonial mansion façade and a typically Portuguese family vault in the Alto de São João cemetery. To make matters worse, between the porch and me stood the ominous object that the Latin-Amerindians, in appalling bad taste, had bought from me a few weeks earlier.

Only then did I realize that I should have called it 'Monstrosity', as it reminded me, especially from the angle at which I was sitting, of the ancient heater in my atelier. But at the same time I was beginning to think that my concrete and stone mound of crap (there's that 'crap' again, to show I can keep up to date) would always and anywhere be worthier than most of all the perfumed human crap around me. I do have to admit that, in this particular case, I did not offload my merchandise in the cleanest of ways. But it was assembled, nevertheless, applying my mind and my nails; I did not use it in any way to guarantee for anyone the imminent salvation of our Country, even less that of the whole of humanity; and if it didn't leave my hands looking exactly as I would have liked it to, I take comfort in the knowledge that such failures, or even greater ones, were necessary for me to be able to scatter throughout this world a dozen or more other objects – *hobbyjects*? *holyjects*? – that have not yet put me to shame – and before which, during their existence, or subsidence, some people might show some interest, might feel some impact, some amazement, a doubt, a shudder, a mere shiver up the spine or, at the very least, express a slight interest, not quite in the eccentric person who produced them, but in the strange and simple fact that such eccentric people do exist.

Duly clad in her bikini (how wholesomely indifferent she was to her forty-odd-year-old cellulite!), Press 2 came just in time to wrench me from my mental turmoil of self-satisfaction. She had tempted me from a distance with a gin and tonic and a ham sandwich. She had helped herself to another Bloody Mary and she came to lie down on her tummy next to my deckchair, asking me straight out:

'Did you see that? Did you hear that?'

I had seen it; and I had heard it. The scene which was too

ridiculous even to be repeated here, had taken place on the edge of the pool, between the foolish junior minister with his great big teeth and greasy mop of hair, and a member of his cabinet.

Speedy Gonzalez was making his way towards both of them just then, coming from the other side of the pool, leaning forwards, with his revealing swimming trunks billowing in a great flurry of inquisitiveness. In another group, sheltering under a large sunshade, was my wife, all trussed up in an old, over-decorous bathing costume that must have once been navy blue, listening with professional composure to two of the most insipid ladies there – and either I was very much mistaken, or they were both shamelessly availing themselves of the opportunity for free consultations for their respective offspring. Then the Pink Panther, who was known for being stingy and for having fathered a large number of children, also entered the improvised consulting-room. He stayed there for a good half hour, going on at length, more than likely, about his large family, discussing a veritable catalogue of choice ailments. From the gestures he was making, with his hand moving up at regular intervals in ever greater steps from the ground, it was clear that his report was rigorously following the ascending ages of his brood.

In the meantime, on the opposite side of the pool, there was a great commotion: two of the more self-important women had spectacularly removed their bikini tops. In turn, their audacity provoked a contagious shiver of excited open-mindedness. Girdled, after an Inca or Aztec fashion, in a multicoloured bathing costume with oblique stripes that made her look as though she was at the same time naked and wearing her ribbons, our hostess promptly left the barbecue area to come a bit closer and start a red-faced but appreciative fingertip applause for the civilized daring of the topless duet.

Encouraged by such examples and by such reactions, Press 1 – who had just come over, dripping wet, to cadge a cigarette off me – decided that she too would expose the two folds of discoloured skin that adorned her stunted chest. She was not brave enough, however, to remain standing, as the other two had, and she came to lie down next to Press 2, who at once growled at her:

'You slut, you! People will say I was stuck between two blokes, at the very least...'

But Press 1 was the first to underline these words with a cheerfully uninhibited chuckle. From then on, she monopolized the conversation, telling jokes, revealing scandals, hinting at intrigues, foretelling dangers, foreseeing calamities until, finally, running out of subjects of conversation, she told us of something that only she knew about – for the love of God, we were not to repeat this to anyone! – namely the more than definite existence of vast oilfields in the regions between Alcobaça and Tomar, including the town of Batalha; and even, so it seemed, right under the ancient monuments; and that, naturally, the government was aware of this but was nevertheless reluctant to allow the first drillings to take place (because of the monuments, of course), in spite of great pressure from the Americans.

'It's not only that,' I replied seriously. 'What the Americans are trying to do is to pull down the monuments stone by stone in order to rebuild them in the States.' In a conspiratorial aside, I added: 'I have this on good authority, too.'

In spite of the apparent sobriety of my words, there must have been a short circuit in Press 1's mind. She quickly stood up, covered up the folds of skin on her chest, muttering something about having had too much sun; her cheeks were indeed at least as fiery as the four or five Bloody Marys her friend – who in the meantime had fallen asleep – had imbibed so far.

I took the opportunity to go over to the barbecue and help myself to some obscure burnt bits of some kind of shrivelled meat that tasted of nothing except piripiri.[20] As for the wine, either it had been in the sun for far too long, or else it was truly bad wine, but I had such heartburn after the first gulp that I was forced to stick to gin and tonic.

When I returned, disgruntled, to my chair, and looked again at those half-baked oligarchs, who ate and drank so heartily, their avid throats so full of shady deals of make or break, trafficking in territory or terrorism, it occurred to me that it was not by chance that, in Portuguese, the words 'power' (*poder*) and 'putrid' (*podre*) are spelt fatefully with the same letters. I believe this is the only language in the world where this happens.

On the other hand, one only had to look at that techno-caste of high-flyers, with their slick hair and their well-trimmed beards, those overly-smug jackasses dripping Piz Buin and clichés, all those power pups stripping the bones of an already boneless country, delightedly involved in corrupt community campaigns or grumbling governmental guerrilla-warfare, to realize at once that those hollow minds had never thought, imagined or suspected that only Love is at the centre of the World.

As for Woman – never a queen, much less a goddess to them – they merely banished her to the outskirts of their lives; there, she was seen as a store, an inn, a service station, a springboard, at best an amusement park. That she could be, on the other hand, the centre of centres, the pivot of life, the gateway to heaven or hell, the key to everything, the redemption of nothing – that's something that would have been quite incomprehensible to those testicles with no soul, those souls with no testicles.

Was I being unfair? Probably.

First thing that morning, my wife had told me about some silly phone calls to our house: always when I was out; always the same, conveniently garrulous, female voice, speaking from somewhere where someone seemed to be whispering to her what to say. But, seemingly, she never even mentioned my name, nor even my wife's name: she merely said a single sentence over and over again, something along the lines of 'Tell your husband not to play with fire'. It was enough for nearly everyone to appear hateful to me.

It had gone six o'clock in the evening and, as the minutes ticked by, the fact that Y hadn't turned up yet became more and more unbearable.

XIX

Suddenly, I started thinking about Ursula von W. whom I hadn't heard from for over three years and whose husband, having been promoted to minister or councillor, I can't remember which, should by now be holding the position of ambassador (and was she with him?) in some bustling, bewildering capital city in the Third World, perhaps even in Latin America, or in the actual native country of my Amerindian hosts, who knows?

I imagined her in a pretentious little garden like this one, complete with swimming-pool and barbecue as well, probably adorned by now with a sculpture by some local artist, and perhaps at this very moment (taking into account the time differences) hosting a reception at least as tedious as the reception I was at now.

Ah! What would Ursula be like right now, in the tropics of her thirty-six or thirty-seven years of age, after transplanting her somewhat thickset, smiling Bavarian prettiness to the actual tropics, with her many freckles, her sardonic nature, her black hair and green-speckled eyes? She would certainly be in contact by now with the relatively dull intelligentsia of the area, and the newly accredited plenipotentiary of her body more than her heart would doubtlessly be a sculptor, a painter, a musician or a poet – seeing that her inclinations tended toward these types, and that only these (as opposed the 'career' ones!) had her husband's – albeit tacit – approval. With her current *chargé d'affaires intimes*, there would be a repetition to a certain extent of what had happened with me – and which, according to her uninhibited disclosures, was little more than a Latin edition or variation of previous involvements with a Swedish painter, a Nipponese novelist and a Czech composer. It was none of this that disconcerted me or worried me unduly: it was just the fact that such similar pretences at love can so easily be found in such widespread parts of the world; and that, in spite of the differences in longitude and latitude, these pretences unfurl in such analogous stage-settings of stereotypical worldliness.

Faced with examples such as these, my love for Y suddenly acquired a more luminous gleam, something akin to a dimension of the absolute. She was right after all, even if for reasons other than those she had given me, in having stubbornly avoided our being seen out together in public up until now: what was happening between us was incompatible with masquerades, with the kind of monkey business typical of this social circle which was, to a certain extent, common to both of us.

But I would have found it hard, that afternoon, to be denied her presence.

My wife had already waved at me on two occasions, insistently, not very discreetly, meaning, or so I thought, that we had fulfilled our obligation and could leave as soon as I was ready. The second time, she even put her hand to her throat, as though trying to make me understand she'd had enough. It wasn't one of her usual gestures. I pretended not to understand.

The most important amongst all the important people there had started to leave, followed of course by the not-so-important who thought this would make them seem important too. In return, as though rounded up at the last minute to fill in the gaps these people left behind, men formally dressed and women wrapped in muslins started filling the garden: after greeting the masters of the house, they slipped gleefully through a kind of trapdoor into the cellar, which had been converted into a changing-room, only to emerge a few minutes later in their swimming attire, obviously quite eager to splash about in the more than questionable waters of the questionable pool. But in the pool that was by now almost in the shade, in a flurry of hysterical screams, two opposing teams of upstarts were attempting to play a game of water-polo with a gaudy plastic ball.

Press 2, having just woken up (because of the hysterical screams) enlightened me about the formal ties and the muslins which, turning up in pairs like this, must be returning from the glamorous wedding that had taken place that day between the daughter of a socialist councillor and the son of one of Salazar's ex-ministers. Rumour had it, she added, that one of them was filthy rich and the other penniless; trouble was, after so many Bloody Marys, she wasn't quite sure, just then, about which one was Job and which one Onassis. I thought it was quite irrelevant to know which way round was right, as it was obviously arbitrary. What I was pretty sure of, however, was that it was the same wedding that Y had gone to, as the mere existence of a Portuguese Onassis, be he an active councillor or a recycled ex-minister, would have justified the need for Y's husband to be at the ceremony. And what I was also pretty sure about was that Y would soon be turning up.

That was enough for the upstarts' carryings-on not to get on my nerves quite so much; and for me to not to feel too neglected when Press 2 suddenly disappeared.

Among the women who had just arrived and stepped out of their muslins, there was one who had the fetching looks of an end-of-season, bargain-basement mermaid; the front of her swimsuit had a series of different coloured concentric circles on it, making her look rather like a fancy shooting target on legs.

Greeting everyone around her, she waved at me immediately, frantically signalling that she had recognized me straightaway; and she kept on waving as she moved towards me, as though I was to be the highlight of her round of greetings. As she came towards me, I noticed that most of the people she was greeting were finding it hard to recognize her straightaway. Smiling all the time, she recited her own name – a single name that from a distance sounded like Ana or as though it ended in *ana* – and to show she didn't hold it against these forgetful people, she made sweet, comforting sounds such as, 'Never mind', 'It really doesn't matter', 'It's hardly surprising, it was such a long time ago.'

Her pleasing eyes, neither glowing nor glowering, were strangely familiar to me, as were her unusually perfect nose, her gentle, prettily oval face, her dark-skinned, maturely svelte yet still ebullient figure. When she was two steps away from my deckchair, I knew it would be terribly unkind and unforgivably rude for me to add to that sea of people with bad memories. But all it took, when I stood up, was the comforting gift of two resounding kisses and an unmistakable twitter reminiscent of her other kind of twittering, for me at once to exclaim:

'Octaviana!'

I hadn't seen her for about a year and a half. It was long enough, however, not only to have nearly forgotten her face, but also to forget how easily forgettable her face was. According to what I was told once by one of the many teachers of History of Art whose classes she had beatifically attended, she was in fact, heaven knows why, one of the least 'mnemogenic' creatures he had ever known. Added to this lack of 'mnemogeny' (a word entirely of that master's fabrication) was the difficulty everyone had in remembering her name, which was either completely forgotten, or twisted into versions of Victoriana, Valeriana, Vitorina or even Vicência. She took comfort for all these shortcomings, with cheerful courage and good nature, from the enduring hope, if not knowledge, that her tapestries, her jewellery, her trinkets, her ceramics would, once seen, never be forgotten by whoever saw them. The trouble was that that 'once seen' very rarely happened.

Dragging a short metal stool next to my deckchair, and alighting on it with the grace of a seagull ('No, no, thank you. I'd rather sit lower down like this, truly...'), it so happened that she immediately asked me ('You won't forget, will you?') to go and visit the new gallery in the Travessa das Chagas ('It's on the fifth floor, you know. It's a shame there's no lift...') to see an exhibition of her work and the work of three of her friends ('They're only just starting, but...') and where, by strange coincidence, her most recent tapestries happened to be on public display ('They're all small ones, of course... The novelty lies in the technique, and I can assure you that...') along with some ceramics and pieces of jewellery she had made recently.

But I was dying to ask her, only I didn't know how to, if she had seen anyone at the wedding she had just come from who had anything remotely resembling Y's build, figure, bearing, face or eyes. At the same time, concerning Octaviana ('You rogue! You've forgotten that I prefer to be called Vana...'), my whole being was tortured by this totally misplaced walking case of extreme goodwill, when with no effort at all – or only very little – she could have been so much happier and occasionally made someone else happy too, through her incomparable twitters, which, when all was said and done, were something of hers that could never be forgotten.

Her husband corresponded perfectly in every way to what other men's wives refer to as 'good looking' and 'well turned-out', and apart from being quite a bit younger than Octaviana herself ('Sorry! Vana...'), he was enduringly besotted by all that emerged from those hands so gifted in the lesser arts; and he was assuredly one of the few people in the world who would not forget her face or mispronounce her name. There he was, four-fifths of his body covered in hair – two-thirds eyebrows to one third of forehead – standing like a domesticated gorilla at the edge of the swimming-pool and greeting me from afar with as much affection as respect, obviously delighted at the extraordinary fact that someone was actually paying attention to what his wife was saying. Then I felt like shouting at him, 'Hello, Esteves',[21] even though his name was Tavares or Torres or Tovar or Teixeira, just to see if, as a result of that call, the world would appear to me 'without ideal or hope' – and if it would make the head of the household smile at all.

But it was only too clear, knowing Vana, that her husband was not enough for her as a critic or as an audience; and although he was probably satisfactory in every other way, it was only in order to raise herself in the opinion of others that she had been revealing for so long and to so many, not as an end but as a means in itself, the secret melodies that emerged from that body of hers whose exact worth she so carelessly ignored.

By then, she had moved on from the subject of the collective exhibition to tell me of another exhibition – a big, individual exhibition of her best works – that she intended putting together in October or November. It was seven fifteen, and still there was no sign of Y, and I was suddenly overcome by an overwhelming pity for the poor, keen and headstrong Vana, and was assailed, too, by the insidious suspicion that my case was probably no different from hers, that I too was probably doing no more than overloading the world with perfectly useless objects and that in fact I had had nothing more than a similar, parallel vocation to that of my generous interlocutor. But how can one sail through life without the gravest doubts about the said vocation?

Oh! If only I could know for sure, amongst other occasional noisy tributes (to mention only these), that I hadn't been lied to too much by Xô's raucous screams, Vana's own twitters, Ursula's measured groans, Elvira's sleepy moans, Ana Dora's gentle gurgling, Isabelinha's single, unchanging roar! Oh, yes! And long before all these – jumping backwards over I don't know how many others, to reach a period in my life, way back, which now seems as distant and as hazy as the deepest Middle Ages – the shrill, off-key warbles of Lídia-alias-Laurentina, the platinum blonde, and even further back still, in the soft yet cruel light of the dawning of the world, as a result of equally elementary stimulation, the squeals of the unhinged Belgian girl (her name was Liliane) who, in 1940, had come tumbling out of the Nazi occupation to the Atlantic shores of Foz do Arelho and would swap me the very next summer for a Jewish tennis player from Poland who had also come seeking refuge, and who was ten years older and ten centimetres taller than me!

Just a moment! I must add that I was still growing up then. Or, in other words, I was generally aware of the idea of Space, but barely aware of the infinite dimensions of Time.

XX

Seven forty-two, seven forty-three, the afternoon heat is not abating – it's been almost as hot throughout the whole day – but the evening is creeping up behind my back, still sheltered as I am beneath the increasingly sentimental willows. The concrete and stone Monstrosity is immersed in a purplish gloaming, as though waiting for someone to light it. Only the brazenly pretentious back porch is still sparkling in a splash of declining sunshine.

Seven forty-four, and there's Y's husband, emerging from the back porch. Yet another 'good-looking' and 'well turned-out' man: I recognize him straightaway from his suntan and his technocrat's spectacles; but at once I am almost certain that he has come alone after all – and I suspect he will even make a point of apologizing for his wife's absence. Our host has run up to greet him on the step below the one he stopped on. They remain there for a few moments, chatting; I presume they must be talking about what I suspected.

Straight afterwards, our hostess – still naked and beribboned in her stripy swimming-costume – rolls up suddenly from the back of the porch, coming from inside the house, allowing someone much taller to precede her – and who nevertheless takes a moment or two before standing out clearly against the doorway. It is Y.

After having waited for her for so long, I have managed, after all, to forget to prepare the slightest kind of strategy that would draw us together as soon as she appeared and bring us face to face in the quickest and most natural way in the world. Standing twelve or fifteen yards away from where I am, she has spotted me too; and she too seems to hesitate, not knowing either what would be the shortest and safest way to obliterate, as if by chance, the distance between us.

There is something else that must be worrying her right now: the fact that, because so many pairs of eyes have converged on her – and that most people are mostly undressed – she appears scandalously, even indecently, overdressed in the sober elegance of a sheath of pure silk or jersey crêpe, I can't tell which, draped around her, with a short jacket of the same material, in a deep Mediterranean blue with black polka dots.

As Y comes down the steps, the shade climbs up her dress and, for just a second, the last beams of the sunny day linger on her face alone and sparkle right in her eyes.

Next to me – either because she too felt attracted by that flash in Y's eyes, or because she merely noticed me watching it – my friend Vana raises herself a little from her stool, touches my elbow and asks, in a muffled twitter:

'Who is she? Do you know who she is? She was at the wedding, too... But no one knew who she was.'

I try to answer her as casually as possible:

'She's a foreigner, I think. Or half-foreign. My wife and I have met her before... Right here in the Incas' house, as a matter of fact.'

'The what house?'

'The Incas' house, or the Aztecs', or whatever they are. Our hosts. Towards the end of last year. When they still lived in Estrela. If I'm not mistaken, my wife already knew her before then.'

And in the meantime, it was towards her that Y made her way. She must have thought (as indeed she did, as I found out afterwards) that it would be the easiest way for me to then go and say hello. But it wasn't at all. Not once during the whole day had I been near my wife; to do so now would make it really badly obvious. Unless I went up to her to say it was time to go now. (Time to go now? Now that Y was here?)

'That's funny!' Vana exclaims 'I hadn't seen your wife. I'll have to go and talk to her in a minute. I hope she doesn't think that...'

'No, she won't think anything... Don't worry.'

What does worry me is that everything is becoming more complicated. Y's husband, not having recognized me or pretending he hasn't, is selectively shaking hands with others – half a dozen if that – who are also wearing highly technocratic spectacles. Which I am not. And, to make matters worse, he has already walked past Vana and me, and his fleeting glance at Vana (it had to happen, there had to be an exception) betrayed the merest flicker of recognition. But, as for me, nothing. Was he expecting me to...? That would have been too much. I wouldn't. No way.

And, too late, I suddenly understand, from the casual way he has been going around shaking hands, that he must be intent on keeping this purely courtesy visit as short as possible: a visit, in short, of someone who had turned up merely to say why they hadn't been able to turn up. He is soon talking to our host again and, side by side, they go up to Y who is still chatting to my wife. A light but imperative touch on the arm of one woman; to the other, he proffers a deep, formal bow, followed by a kiss on her hand.

Just now, seen from the side, Y looks like a nebulous divinity waiting to find out if the dying day will see the increase or the demise of her powers. Again it seems as though she doesn't exist; but is merely present.

'Foreign, did you say?' asks Vana. Then with frank admiration, she adds: 'She is so beautiful! And what a figure!'

Just as they are about to leave (her husband's hand again possessively supporting her forearm), Y looks towards me and, pretending to have only then spotted me, attempts a smile, the sketchy outline of a greeting. She is trying so hard to be natural that it all seems quite touching.

'She's beautiful. She really is beautiful,' Vana mumbles again, while Y, with her back to us, by her husband's side and escorted by our hosts, walks up the stairs of the porch.

Out of mere courtesy, the sun bestows a last few disdainful favours on the top part of the dreadful villa; but it is obviously only intent on illuminating the last truly blue patches of sky.

Then, getting up at last from her little stool, nudging my elbow with hers and pointing her *retroussé* nose towards the door through which Y has just disappeared, Vana puts on what she must consider her most intelligent smile and whispers meaningfully:

'I understand. I understand perfectly well why you're so fascinated.' She removes her elbow for a moment, then she nudges me again: 'I've only just remembered! I have seen *her* a couple of times before. Once, going into your atelier. Another time, on her way out.' Then she joins her hands in front of her face pinches her nose with her thumbs as if to straighten it out, and says: 'You know very well you can trust me. With anything you want. Anything, you hear? There's no point our having secrets from one another. You can work out for yourself *who* it was I had gone to see… in an atelier right next to yours.' She lowered her hands in the meantime, entwining her fingers at the point where her cleavage started showing above her swimsuit, adding: 'I know that I can trust you too. I might even need to… You never know. *His* wife (as well you must know…) is a beast… The scenes I've had with her! I'm sick of all the trouble I get from that bitch. Who knows, one of these days, if she keeps this up, I might need to go to your atelier…

and ask for political asylum!' She underlines her felicitous choice of words (that are probably not hers) with a twittering peal of laughter; but she at once resumes the more serious guise she probably thinks serious matters should be discussed under: 'About your friend... Will you promise? Will you promise not to get cross if I tell you something?' Without the slightest interest, I merely nod my head twice to give her my promise. And, pretending to shudder, Vana says: 'She's beautiful. She's really beautiful. But she looks like Death.'

No, I have no doubts about how much I can trust Vana. It's just that I find those last few words of hers somewhat annoying, even though I'm sure she's just trying to be clever. Indeed, it is with equal volubility that she adds:

'What can I be thinking of? I almost forgot... I must go over and speak to your wife.'

Oh, you daft idiot! Why now? Why only now? Three minutes earlier, as a pretext for keeping you company, or at least with the worthy intent of telling my wife who you are (as if she'd recognize you!), I could then have gone up with you, and at least been able to touch Y's hand. It would have been one way to keep up appearances. But only then did I come up with that as a plan.

Stretching her swimsuit out, as though trying to make her shapeless figure more tempting to anyone who might be in any way interested, Vana repeats:

'I hope your wife won't think that I... It's just like I said... If I haven't spoken to her yet, it's only because I hadn't seen her before.'

I surprise myself by answering her back, almost insolently:

'Really? But she's quite obvious, don't you think?'

There is not the slightest sarcasm in my words. They are merely (perhaps as a revenge for having been forsaken) a flash of pride, a reply to a challenge. Perhaps they mean to express my awareness, or my relief, that my wife, as opposed to Vana and all the other people there, is nothing if not a solid reality.

XXI

Stay here, on the veranda, drinking another whisky, smoking another cigarette. '*As long as Destiny allows me, I shall carry on smoking.*'

Pretend today isn't Sunday. Pretend I will not have to wait until tomorrow to see Y again.

Digest, with great resignation, the lunch (lunch?) that I swallowed in great haste in the arcades in Estoril: a mixture of squidgy rubber and chopped up sinew streaked with blood, bearing the pompous pseudonym of 'hamburger'.

Have another go at my headstrong wife: see if I can get her to call the doctor after all.

No more rushing to answer the phone. To shatter my hopes, all it took was your phone call just now, so formal yet so full of 'doublicity': 'Just to see how you *both* were... Just to talk to *the two of you* before going on holiday.' I felt at once that your paediatrician must have been hovering in the background.

Throw myself, in free-fall, onto a plain.

Go up to my wife and tell her once again that just staying in bed is probably not the best thing to do.

Give in, until then, to this drowsy exercise of parading mirages, goals, dreams, plans, wishful thoughts and conflicting desires.

Wander off, right now, my arm round Y's waist, down a street in Rome, preferably down the Via Giulia; leisurely kiss her in the shade of an arch; without telling her of Xô.

Climb all alone up the dome of Estrela.

Decide once and for all to visit that model senior citizens' home where my mother has been vegetating, rotting and surviving for the past two years; but without in any way letting her find out that I am the one paying for most of her expenses.

Place a notice on the door of my atelier, saying: 'Closed for Stocktaking'. Meander down the Avenida da Liberdade with an identical notice hanging round my neck.

Forget the Vanas and the Ursulas of this world, forget that Xô ever existed, that Lídia existed, that Liliane existed. Forget even that my wife exists.

Find out, as best I can, regardless of her stubborn need to appear strong at all times, what kind of pains she was having yesterday (in her back? down her arm?) by the side of the Amerindians' pool. (And to think I misinterpreted the meaning of her semaphore.)

Not worry too much about the fact that my bank balance is going down at an alarming rate.

Drive a bulldozer over the Amerindians' property: ruthlessly pulverize the Monstrosity they bought off me. See if I'm lucky enough, while I'm at it, to accidentally crush some (literally) crappy career politician who stayed behind to devour the leftovers.

Go to Amalfi for a really long stay, hopefully until the end of my days, with Y; without telling her of Xô there either.

Tell our innocent paediatricians to their faces, once and for all, that I don't give a damn about the worldliness of Paediatrics.

Suggest to you that we must go for a drink, for two drinks, for ten drinks, and then decide what to do afterwards.

Go back at least thirty years for the sole purpose of calling my stepfather a fool; or, especially, to call myself a fool, for having always considered the man a fool yet having called him father for as long as he lived.

Go back instead to a much more recent past: six, five, three months ago. And again see Y's eyes floating, shadowless, above the cloud of her white shawl.

Accept Isabelinha P. M. de B.'s next request to sign a petition against everything and everybody.

See if I can work out who is the son (or daughter?) of a bitch who has recently been placing those idiotic pieces of paper under my windscreen-wiper (or getting someone else to put them there) and making those no less idiotic phone calls to my home (or getting someone else to make them).

Get round, one of these days, to looking up my old friend Nyasa – one of the few trustworthy people I have ever met in this garden of buggers on this buggered-up shore.

Listen, non-stop, with Y, to all the songs by Dolores Duran, Elis Regina, Gal Costa, Clara Nunes and Maria Bethânia; without telling her of Xô then either.

Agree with my mother about everything when I go and see her: she has really only ever had my sister (my half-sister); she has really only ever been able to count on her, always so attentive and generous – in spite of my brother-in-law (my half-brother-in-law) being as stingy as ever, however much money he makes.

Demand that the minister for culture grant Floripes the Order of Santiago with Sword; and, for Nyasa, as he is an atheist, at least the Order of Christ.[22]

Applaud my wife enthusiastically whenever she calls me a clown; phone Inodora and ask her if she still thinks I'm 'cute'; reread some of the letters from Elvira de V. e S. where she calls me in turn 'genius', 'impostor', 'god', 'barbarian', 'warlock', 'sadist'; and also something like 'soul of my genitals' or 'genitals of my soul', but I can't really remember which. (The order of the words was quite arbitrary.)

Find out, while on the subject, what you're like in bed. Meet your friend afterwards and, depending on the outcome of the experiment, look at him with envy or pity, with scorn or reverence.

Compile with great care, in readiness for a great exhibition at the Gulbenkian, the complete catalogue of all the sculptures that I haven't done yet, and never shall.

Say to Y right now: 'Living together? Look, I was only joking when I said that.' And say to her also: 'Go on, then, answer me! I've never been so serious in my life.'

Ask your friend right now, through you of course, for a fitting preface to the catalogue of my great exhibition. Assure you that he is the best person to do so, because I think he knows even less about sculpture than I do about poetry.

Drink just one more whisky, smoke just one more cigarette.

Go upstairs in a minute to see if my wife needs anything; and try and talk her into finally calling for the doctor.

Have a private consultation, as soon as possible, with the greatest specialist there is (if there is one) in complaints due to the coming (the climax?) of the male menopause.

Have another consultation, before that, with a reputable astrologer; and ask straight out what the hell chance there is between a Cancer with Scorpio in her ascendant (Y) and a Taurus with Pisces in his ascendant (me).

Carry on pretending today isn't Sunday.

And drop down right now by parachute, by parachute or by helicopter, onto the roof, the patio, the garden of Y's house – not the house she's in now, but the other one, the one where she spent her childhood, in the Alentejo.

Discover that I hadn't yet met Xô by then; but that, on the other hand, I had met, and was indeed already married to, my wife.

XXII

It was a little after six in the morning. I woke up in what is known as a state of grace: my head was clear, my eyes were in focus, my nerves and muscles were in working order, my arteries were unclogged. I felt as though I had neither drunk nor smoked the night before. It was as if the sea and the sky – one almost invisible, the other already blue – had also, under the cover of darkness, washed the face and cleansed the lungs of Earth itself.

Even my wife, when she came down from her room after seven, told me she felt very much better: no sign of the pains in her arm; nothing but a little twinge above her breastbone. (Oh, it was above her breastbone, was it? I thought she'd been complaining about her back.)

At half past eight I was already in Lisbon. Leaving the Marginal after Algès, I drove aimlessly down the narrow streets of Pedrouços that have obstinately survived – either through instinct or amnesia – in the outskirts of the city and of the century itself. There was one little street that decided to welcome me that morning with a refreshing simplicity; it was modestly quiet, the same tea or tea-rose colour as someone stepping out of a bath. It was called Largo da Princesa ('Princess Square') and I felt like calling it Largo da Deusa ('Goddess Square'). There was a fountain nearby, and though it was quite dry, it seemed to me to recover, there and then, its long lost *joie de vivre*.

I returned to the little street to confirm the fleeting impression I'd had of it a few minutes before. There was no doubt whatsoever: the sober, two-floored building where I've been told I was born was in good shape, almost unbelievably well preserved.

It was barely nine o'clock when I rushed to the bank; I was pleasantly surprised to find out that, after they'd sent me my last statement, an unexpected transfer had been made from Lausanne into my account. This ensured the continuation of my sabbatical year. And it even meant that any future expenses could be met.

I popped into the Lisbon house to fetch the post: there were half a dozen invitations to four exhibitions (there are always some galleries that send me duplicates; heavens, these people don't even take a break in summer!), and among them was the one that referred to the exhibition by Vana and her three friends. As for the rest, it was all good for the bin, apart from a parcel from Lausanne with a long letter from my tenacious henchman (all I saw was another SOS: more objects! more objects! I must remember all my commitments) and the this year's fat May edition of *Das Kuntswerk*, from Düsseldorf, which contained an article on some of my work (a few coloured reproductions that could just as easily have been in black and white); luckily there was a typewritten supplement at the back with a delicious translation of the article into French.

Then, although I still had another two hours to wait for Y to come, I went back to the atelier, intent on wading religiously through what the learned German scholar (her name was Gretta Hörstel; what a glorious name!) had found out about me, especially about what she called my 'communication breakdown' phase. As the pictures immediately showed, it was based mainly on a series of compositions I had put together in the mid-seventies, entitled *Le Couple*, *La Famille*, *Table Ronde*, *Conseil d'Administration*. She admitted to not being able to discover the whereabouts of *Table Ronde*, and merely reproduced bits of information and opinions she'd found here and there. (A few acknowledgements followed.)

What all those pieces of mine had in common (and here comes the 'communication breakdown'!) was the fact that they were all made up of mainly grotesque metal figures, slightly larger than life, invariably seated around simulated stone tables – invariably with their backs to one another. Had I heeded, when I should have, the commercial flair of my *marchand* (or his name isn't David O. Steiner), I would still be producing, one after the other, similarly inspired sculptures (did I say inspired?), in ever larger groups, of course, around ever larger tables; and by now my CV would boast – instead of my *hobbyject*, *holyject* and any other reject phase – huge, massive compositions that would probably be entitled *Le Gouvernement*, *Le Parlement*, *Le Parti*, who knows, perhaps *La Patrie* and even *L'Humanité*.

From the four that I did complete (and even those were probably three too many), I was glad to discover that *Le Couple* – the only one I was actually proud of – was carefully looked after, in Santa Margherita Ligure, in the leafy garden of a wealthy old Scottish pederast; there was no trace of *La Famille*; *Table Ronde* (but who the hell owned it?) had roamed around various cultural centres in sedate Norway; as for *Conseil d'Administration* – comprising thirteen figures and originally called *La Cène* ('The Last Supper': Steiner was all for it at first, but then he got cold feet) – it still graced the campus of Greenwich University, in San Pablo, New Mexico, and had been targeted by two different groups of vandals, one linked with the new American rightwing, the other linked with nothing at all apart, perhaps, from an equally fraudulent leftwing.

But the most newsworthy item presented by the Teutonic specialist of *Das Kunstwerk* concerned the recent purchase of both *Le Couple* and *La Famille* by a foundation based in the French Riviera. The learned Frau or Fräulein Hörstel had gone there specifically to photograph them. *Table Ronde*, poorly reproduced from what must have been a very poor reproduction to start with, was just about acceptable, placed as it was in a green field, as the representation of a picnic scene where everyone was suddenly at odds with each other. The faithful reproductions of *Conseil d'Administration* (with obvious traces of the aforementioned acts of vandalism) had been taken by an American colleague of Hörstel's, a lecturer in History of Modern Art at another university in the state of New Mexico who was, to the great benefit of contemporary art, also a keen photographer. (There followed more acknowledgements; there were many references to the main works of the distinguished master; his medals, two silver and four bronze, and the nine distinctions he obtained in various local competitions of photographic art were reverently mentioned.)

Only then did I carefully read Steiner's letter; and only then did I understand the reason for the transfer of monies that had already been credited to my account. In plain terms, it was *my* cut from the share *we* made – Steiner *dixit* – according to some law he invoked, when *Le Couple* and *La Famille* were acquired.

Little did I know that these two institutions, which I have held in so little respect, would end up being quite so profitable.

When – just before twelve – I hear fingers rapping on the other side of the door, I find myself not rushing to the door as usual but, instead, being painfully slow in getting out of this armchair.

I pick up the magazine that I'd put down on the dresser and turn again to the pages with pictures of *Le Couple* and *La Famille*, and leave it casually opened on the divan. It suddenly seems vital that, as soon as she comes in, Y's gaze should be immediately drawn to this shameless display of my paltry past accomplishments and the paltry reactions they are still provoking nowadays (oh, how titillating to have one's name mentioned abroad!), as though either of these, or even both, might influence her final decision, in a few minutes' time, concerning what I suggested to her a week ago. Unless (oh, Narcissus!) I just want to show her my worth. Neither of these two possibilities is greatly approved of by the little integrity I have left in the inner tribunal of my conscience. I even think I can hear my wife's merciless and pitiless voice calling me a clown. But what I can in fact hear is drumming once again on the wooden door: although light, it is more insistent and more impatient this time round.

I end up displaying the whole magazine on top of the divan. I run to unlock the door: it's Vana.

XXIII

'Please forgive me,' she mumbles, smiling, not daring to come in (that's all I need), using her most breezy vocal register. With indolent mischief, she goes on: 'I was just passing by... You already know why... You already know where...' Then, suddenly making it sound as though she is merely passing on a message, she adds: 'So I took the opportunity to come and tell you that we found out only yesterday that the gallery will have to be closed until Wednesday. Burst water pipes... Even the neighbours have been complaining. The houses are so old, you see. God, the stink, you can't begin to imagine! And as it's five floors up... I thought I'd better warn you.'

I merely grunt a most polite, 'Thank you', but still I don't ask her in. Instead I almost bar her access, half filling the doorway.

'Oh, don't tell me I'm interrupting...' (The corners of her mouth hesitate between a repentant pout and a mischievous grin.)

'As it so happens...' I answer. That does the trick: ambiguity always works against people like Vana.

'I'm so sorry, do forgive me!' Before turning back, stifling a twitter – perhaps the first one of the day – she puts two fingers to her lips, then brushes the corner of my mouth with them. 'Forgive me! Goodbye!' But she comes back to whisper to me conspiratorially: 'Do you know what? You can congratulate me... The beast is fortunately in the Algarve.'

'Ah! The beast is on holiday...'

'That's it, that's it.' And off she goes, so gratefully pleased with my comment that I suspect she will use it as her own from now on.

With the door ajar, I watch her disappear at last, back right. Straight after that – it's twelve o'clock precisely – Y appears slowly, front left. In a flash I realize that it was Vana whose path Y had crossed, a few months earlier, that day when she was so late in arriving. Suddenly, because of how relatively slowly I see Y coming towards me, I am superstitiously afraid that today also the atmosphere between these walls will be charged with electricity.

How foolish to be superstitious. How groundless was my fear. She crosses the few yards that separate us now with a smile on her face; and still smiling, without her usual precautions, she kisses me straightaway, resting her head on my shoulder before I have even closed the door. Then, searching my eyes, looking like someone seeking forgiveness for some unknown misdemeanour, she almost spelt out the following words: 'I could not have done anything else.'

I realize at once that she is referring to our unsuccessful encounter at the Amerindians' two days earlier.

'Of course you couldn't. Nor could I. There's nothing else we could have done.'

I stroke her hair, then her brow; I kiss her between the eyebrows, on her two worry lines which then disappear. Meanwhile, in her usual way, by pressing her heels together, she has already taken off her shoes. In sharp contrast with this lack of inhibition, she asks me shyly:

'Could you get me a glass of water? Plain water. Just water. As cold as possible.'

When I return from inside with two glasses in one hand and half a bottle of water in the other, she is standing over here, completely naked, with her back to the divan. Still smiling, she exclaims:

'Oh, you came back too soon! I wanted to give you a surprise.'

Only then do I notice, hanging from her left hand, a long, white item of clothing that is so lacy it is almost ethereal: it is a nightdress which she slips on over her head and which clings to her from above her breasts down to her ankles. As for me, I've just finished pouring water into one of the glasses, then into the other (I'm thirsty too) and I put them on the dresser. But I don't even have time to get rid of the bottle, so quickly does Y come up to me, hold onto me and slither down me; and, half kneeling, half sitting – or should I say both leaning on me and sitting on her haunches – she suddenly grasps my only free hand and takes it to her mouth, not quite to kiss it, but to press it very gently against her lips. Then she starts talking, quietly but clearly, as though wanting to be heard through my hand:

'I've been rather stupid, haven't I? *Très sotte*, I know. Sometimes I don't understand, I can't understand, what's happening to me. When I'm away from you... I have oh, so many things to tell you! But there's no time, there's never any time.' And without pausing to catch her breath, as though it all held together, she says: 'You know, I came to Lisbon really early today. I didn't come by car. It wouldn't start. I gave up straightaway. My husband was about to go out too, so I came with him as far as the factory. Then I took a taxi (they called one for me) and I looked at a few boutiques, first in the Bairro Azul, then over towards the Rua Castilho, then back again to the Bairro Azul. But I didn't want to turn up here today, I couldn't turn up here, without bringing this nightdress with me today.'

I have already put the bottle down on the top of the dresser. My fingers are now free of the bottle and I run them through her hair that is more lively, wild and curly than usual.

'You must think I'm mad... Never mind. That doesn't matter.' Taking a deep breath, she goes on: 'This nightdress... It isn't quite the one I wanted. But it can stay here, I'm going to leave it here. I want to wear it for the first time for you, with you. I want to sleep in it often. Next to you. Here. Here, for the time being.' And taking a deep breath, she continues: 'You must give me time. What you want is the same as what I want. But it isn't easy. We can't rush into it just any old how simply because we want to.'

Without knowing how I go there, I too am now sitting on the floor – or at least, I'm kneeling down – next to Y. And with her eyes staring into my eyes, enormously close to mine, she talks on with my hand still against her mouth:

'The other day... remember? What I found hard, what baffled me... was that you spoke to me so angrily. As though you were trying to punish me. I know you didn't mean it. But it seemed like a punishment.'

The armchair, the mirror. The nightdress is quickly flung off, then put back on again; later it is discarded again like a useless rag; finally it is folded and put away with the utmost care, in the second drawer of the dresser there.

In the meantime, there's the divan, with its cover pulled back, the sheets crumpled. Fruit and water, water and fruit; fruit on its own, water on its own, alternating throughout the day. At around six in the evening, we wearily yet willingly go through our chores, straightening up the sheets, tucking them in, putting the cover back on, going inside to wash our plates and glasses up, leaving everything more or less tidy – as though we didn't need Floripes after all. Perhaps it is a kind of 'rehearsal' to prove to ourselves that, if we needed to, we'd be able to lead a more simple way of life, to do without some of the help and comforts we still enjoyed.

Before all this, however, when she first went up to the divan, Y noticed the photographs of *Le Couple* and *La Famille* and, paying no attention to the captions, much less to whose name was in those captions, she exclaimed spontaneously:

'How strange! *Quelle idée plutôt macabre*!'

Even today I have to agree that those photographs taken by Frau or Fräulein Hörstel are particularly good at bringing out (a lighting effect? a matter of perspective?) the relentlessly weird, even morbid, way those figures – two figures, obviously, in the case of the first one; four figures, less obviously, in the second – have their backs turned not only to each other, but also to the actual tables. The refusal of all of them to communicate with each other was indeed radical; and their refusal went as far as excluding the very objects that could have brought them together.

Later, when she found out that they were my creations, Y became interested in finding out more about them; her interest was keen, unqualified and good-natured – all that was lacking was the actual approval of her senses. She made several shrewd remarks to start with: she saw at once the resemblance between the woman in *Le Couple* and the mother in *La Famille*, who were both stocky, stolid, trustworthy in spite of holding themselves so stiffly; she had also noticed the resemblance between the man in the first group and the son in the other one, who is patently the elder son of this second couple: they both have the same mop of tousled hair, suggested by an identical tangle of steel wire, as though the second man were no more than an earlier version of the first as a young man; finally, the repulsive appearance of the head of the family in *La Famille* whose head is, meaningfully, no more than a huge hole partially covered by a very thin, shiny metal plaque, which could be interpreted as a sign of baldness or, more seriously, as a frightening insufficiency of grey matter. But what really shocked her in the second group was the complete lack of 'family likeness' between the figures, especially between the two younger members of the 'family' group – the two 'siblings' as it were – where the boy was already an adolescent seemingly engaged in open warfare with the world, and the girl was still a little child, not just waifish but actually wizened, shrewdly aloof, precociously enigmatic.

'Strange', 'curious', 'interesting' were the adjectives she restricted herself to (and not always in Portuguese), only to end up by saying:

'Do you know what? I still prefer your drawings.'

For the first time ever, we leave the atelier together: it is half past six in the evening. For the first time ever, I take her by car back to near her *quinta*.

During most of the drive, she rests her head on my shoulder. And during most of the drive, following her directions, we go down minor roads that I hadn't used for many years: we pass ancient manors that are still somewhat grand, their derelict gateways leading to an infinite nothingness, their ancient walls covered in ivy and Virginia creeper, standing up heroically to the impinging vulgarity of pretentiously common housing estates, shacks and workshops that are cropping up all around the properties.

Finally, a few hundred yards or so away from her *quinta*, after zigzagging steeply, we stop half-way down the road to look, among the planes and the lemon trees, at the back of the house, two gabled rooftops, a corner of the cobbled yard, the blue gash of the inevitable swimming-pool, nearly the whole of the also inevitable tennis court. There, right now, two girls are brandishing their tennis rackets; one of them is Vicky.

'Her father can't be home yet,' says Y. 'Just as well.'

In the car, we kiss again; unhurriedly. Then, still taking her time, she reaches over for her Hermès bag on the back seat, insisting once more that I should not get out ('It's safer that way...'), suggesting I should only phone her the day after next.

'Not tomorrow. Tomorrow, as I've told you already, I am either going to the Alentejo (but coming home at night) or else I am going to spend the whole day with Vicky at Praia Grande.'

Then she gets out of the car, making her way slowly round it, and sets off down a twisting path that will enable her, as she had explained to me earlier, to reach the entrance to the *quinta* easily, as though it were the most natural thing in the world, without even being seen from the tennis court.

However, her flimsy, bright green dress is unlike any of the other greens that surround her; rather, it blends in with all the other greens as though it were just the green that was missing. She is walking down the path with such surefooted agility in her white court shoes that it's as though the path were made of hard-packed earth rather than gravel.

I wonder if she will at least pause for a moment when she reaches the bottom, at the last bend, by the first plane-trees and where, for a few moments, no one would be able to see her from inside the house or from its surroundings. And, as though she hears me, she not only stops there, but she turns round quickly – looking back up towards me – her face is already tiny from this distance, and her eyes seek mine, and her bare arm waves at me.

Then I switch on the engine; then, straight after, the radio. An old Sinatra song is playing: *You make me feel so young.*

XXIV

Taurus, with Pisces in the ascendant. Cancer, with Scorpio in the ascendant.

See what I have been reduced to: slipping out at nightfall – as boldly as my self-consciousness would allow me – into the antiseptic bookshop of one of those elegantly tasteless shopping centres that have sprouted up all over Lisbon lately; then, boldly going over to the shelves in the corner which I know hold – quite rightly housed next to other such frivolity – treatises, guides, abstracts and handbooks, all on astrology. At the counter at the other end was a lone shop assistant, a pretty girl who was minding her own business, and had the angelic look of someone who would prefer to be eating chocolates (‘*eat some chocolates, child! eat some chocolates!*’[23]) to the tedium of selling books. Between her and me there was just one other customer, facing away from me and half hidden by a revolving bookcase.

I didn't have any trouble carrying out my deceitful and humiliating task with the greatest impunity: all I had to do was to reopen a handbook chosen beforehand to the pages I'd chosen earlier; all I had to do was scrape my Biro on a piece of paper brought for that purpose. I shall spare you the ordeal of having to read the whole of what the (two) authors of the aforementioned handbook thought about people born under the sign of Taurus with Pisces in the ascendant. It was a trite list of clichés: *makes friends easily*; *ability to create climates* (?); *love of the arts, of nature and of pleasure, but* (sic) *not greatly materialistic*; and so on and so forth. All this leading to this following conclusion: *Attracted to Virgos*. How out of touch can this book be? Not only are there no virgins left in the world nowadays, but my wife is a Virgo.

However, on the subject of my very own Cancerian with Scorpio in her ascendant, the two astrological stars had excelled themselves and were bang on, or so I believe. Based on what you already know, see how appropriate this is: *extremely sensitive and intuitive, verging on the psychic. Has premonitory dreams and hunches; highly anxious. Powerfully charismatic charm. A love of travelling, of escape... to wherever it may be. In childhood, sudden events or separated parents. Prone to depression when cannot deal with reality.* Most importantly, it concluded: *Attracted to Taureans.*

At the same time as I was writing down these clairvoyant words, inwardly rejoicing, I kept wondering about the other solitary customer who was hanging about, seeing something strange or even suspicious in his behaviour whenever I looked towards him. Still with his back to me, and I think still without having noticed me, he began frantically searching and feeling along the shelves of another mobile bookcase. He was tall, thin, too well-dressed for the weather and for the times. The curvature of his spine expressed a tension suspiciously characteristic – in a bookshop of this nature, both selective and progressive *ma non troppo* – either of a modestly ambitious amateur or a misdirected scholar. And even when he stretched up to look at the top shelves, his curvature remained.

After thoroughly inspecting the second shelf, he scrutinizes the titles behind the glass doors of a fixed bookcase and finally (almost on all fours by now) he searches the books lined up underneath a long shelf. I watch him as, still crouching, he removes three, four, five identically sized books that he clumsily stuffs under his left armpit. One of the books slips from under the sleeve of his suit (made of good, heavy dark-grey material) and as he goes to pick it up, he turns three-quarters towards me and I make out the broad, bulging forehead of an ex-child prodigy; the baldness worthy of a future professor; the straight nose of the fanatical disciplinarian; the hollow cheeks of a strict puritan; the sharp slit of an almost lipless mouth: as you have probably realized by now, if I haven't done too bad a job in describing him, it was the highly moral profile of your paediatric husband.

Something stops me from revealing my presence straightaway, as though I've been contaminated – these things are catching – by the furtiveness of his behaviour. Even so, after I see and hear him get up, I go up to him. (Sound of creaking joints.) I follow closely two steps behind, while he makes his way quickly over to the counter where he deposits the five books he's just dug out. Then I realize what the books are; and I clearly hear the shop assistant ask him:

'Are they gifts?'

A little breathless, your husband's terse reply:

'No, no. Don't bother gift-wrapping them. A carrier bag will do. They can all go in together.'

But, forgetting her lack of chocolates and smiling in a way she probably hadn't done since last weekend, the young assistant apologizes for not having any bags at the moment, then expertly pulls out from under the counter a grimy sheet of brown wrapping paper.

'Fine, fine,' your husband exclaims in a cutting voice that I would never have thought him capable of. Then, more gently, he adds: 'That'll do just fine. It's even too nice.'

At the same time his fingers nervously flick the booklets, one by one. Only then does he hand them to the girl, one by one, in cold, almost brutal sequence, as though he'd rather see them destroyed than wrapped up nicely.

Five times he repeated these movements. Five times; as you probably guessed, those were five copies of your book of poetry.

'Fancy seeing you here!' But I only fire these words, point-blank, once the books are duly wrapped and your husband is being given the change from the two notes he'd thrown onto the counter. Before he can pull himself together, I add: 'I thought *the two of you* were on holidays. Your wife phoned me at home a couple of days ago, and I thought…'

No, no. Not yet. That is: yes and no. He said you were actually already on holiday, that you had accepted an invitation (he made it quite clear: 'from a girlfriend') to spend a week to ten days at the most in the south of Spain. As for him… not yet… Right now, he had a few things to sort out first.

He is almost stuttering; his hands are shaking visibly; he tries to moisten his non-existent lips with the tip of his tongue; a few beads of sweat appear on his forehead. But, mixed with all this, it seems almost as though my being there has actually taken a weight off his chest.

Acting as though I too am looking for a book, and pretending I haven't noticed your spouse's strange and conflicting agitation, I turn a little on my heels so as to stand at his side rather than face him. I almost turn my back completely to him; and thus, talking continuously, I tow him away from the dry dock of the counter towards another quayside, or rather a kind of marina: in other words, towards the top of another shelf where another half-dozen books have been berthed under the heading of 'new arrivals', and which have probably just arrived from the shipyard. But I do so with such a lack of skill that (talk of the devil) we both happen to land in front of half a dozen copies, in a tidy, even untouched, pile of a new edition or a new book by none other than your friend. My immediate reaction (I agree it was stupid) is to pick up the top book in order to turn it around as discreetly as possible. The medicine is worse than the cure: covering the whole of the back dust-cover, the sophisticated portrait of its author, pipe and all, stares straight up at us.

After the initial embarrassment, or near embarrassment, I am almost amused by the appearance of this new character. Here, merely in the form of a picture. But where was he, at this very moment, in actual flesh and blood (surely more flesh than blood right now)? Unless I was much mistaken, he was more than likely in the south of Spain, wasn't he? Or perhaps anywhere else that the south of Spain was being used for merely as an alibi or a hasty metaphor.

It's obvious, however, that neither the pipe nor the middle-aged man that are staring up at us from that photograph is saying anything personal, at least at this point (just as well!), to your husband's scientific intellect; your husband was far from associating, with any degree of certainty, the shadow cast by the pipe and any shadow that might have come between the two of you. Everything leads me to believe that he is being tormented by other, lesser shadows right now: had I or had I not seen the books he'd had wrapped; if I had, was it worth his being the first to broach the subject, making up some kind of excuse; finally, would he have to put up with me for much longer, especially as I started, surprisingly, to tell him how pleased I was to see him and how much I'd like to have a chat with him. Was I being deceitful? No, I wasn't. I was merely being excessively good-willed. I even end up making a suggestion:

'How about going for a drink? There's a bar round here, on the floor above, that's not too bad at all…'

Although he mutters noble excuses, among which 'alcohol at this time of day? no way!', I trot your husband off through a maze of quiet passages and staircases. At last I find the familiar, dark-slatted storm-doors, which commendably imitate, on the scale of a local *leitaria*, the entrance to a saloon bar in the Far West.

There are only half a dozen tables inside. They are all unoccupied. At one of these tables – ah, yes, the one at the back – I once had the brilliant idea of introducing the complacent Inodora to Elvira de V. e S.; in terms of a *serenata a tre*, although it led to nothing, it went better than similar ones we'd had with Elvira's own friends.

But why should I pretend to remember Ana Dora, to remember Elvira, or claim perversely that this table still means something to me, when all I can think about is where it is – the Alentejo? Praia Grande? – that my Cancerian with Scorpio in her ascendant has spent her day today?

XXV

In the meantime, it's towards this table that your paediatrician and I make our way. And surprisingly, we each indulge in our one seasonal treat: reconsidering what he had first wanted, he decides to order a vermouth; as for me, contrary to my faithful habits, I settle for a sparkling mineral water.

With some difficulty, while he gradually unwinds, I get him to talk about his progress with his doctoral thesis; about the invaluable support my wife is giving him; about the bucolic mediocrity of the little village in the Douro where he was born; about the economic shrewdness of his no less bucolic parents; about his hopes of being released from teaching the following academic year; about how one of his uncles (a deputy of the Social Democratic Party) helped him to set up his consulting rooms and another uncle (regional leader of the Socialist Party) to buy a new Fiat; about the possibility, at long last, of getting a grant for postgraduate studies in the United States.

Then (after a second vermouth) it's your husband's turn to enquire tersely – a mere formality – about my own work.

'Are you getting many orders? Are you working on anything at the moment?'

'Nothing. Nothing at all, lately. *Dolce far niente*. Closed for stock-taking.' I add: 'Luckily that's all it is. There are so many problems out there…'

Only then (still on the same glass of mineral water) did I start telling him, in greatest confidence, about a friend of mine, someone who is my age, almost a brother to me, and in such a state over an awkward situation that he has me quite worried:

'Money problems?'

'Worse than that…'

'Is he ill? Does he have some kind of illness?'

'Yes and no.'

'What do you mean?'

'Yes and no… He is in love. Can you imagine! He is in love…'

'Ah!…' Then, after an awkward silence, adding: 'Is he an artist too?'

'Yes and no. He's a writer. He's a writer in his spare time.'

'What about her?'

'She's younger than him. Quite a bit younger. That's where all the trouble begins…'

I go into details. I say that my friend has got it into his head to leave his wife (a fine woman, also a friend of mine); and that he is trying to persuade the *other* woman to leave her husband. To start afresh, as he puts it… Oh, the fool is walking around on cloud nine! You should hear him. It's heartbreaking. It's hard to believe he is quite in his right mind. If I am to believe all the secrets he throws at me, he's at long last found the pearl of all pearls, the most wonderful creature in creation. My fear (although he doesn't mention this) is that he may be overdoing it. In more ways than one. Hence my concern. And, to top it all, I'm fully aware of my share of responsibility in all this: in the beginning I 'gave my blessing', so to speak, to the whole thing; I've lent them my atelier; it is in my atelier that the two of them get together.

'Of all places for this to happen! Right there, within those walls that have a lot to tell, a great deal to tell, and I'm sorry if you find this shocking, but they were in no way expecting things to get so serious! If they both settled for a straightforward affair, what the hell! I am no saint, nor have I ever been… But I never went beyond certain limits.'

At last, I ask your paediatrician the questions I wanted to ask him: could it be possible, given my friend's age, that there could be a psychic reason for this? Or perhaps physiological? What exactly is this male menopause all about? Should I advise him or even talk him into seeing a doctor?

'I know this isn't your speciality. Quite the opposite, in fact… But I should like to hear your opinion.'

Our clinician avoids the question, blushing furiously. (Even though he had not gone beyond his second vermouth.) Then, as I persist, he cautiously puts forward the considerate possibility of arteriosclerosis. In any case, yes, there is indeed much to be said for my friend seeing a specialist. Or, to start off with, just going to his GP.

I feel like asking for another sparkling mineral water. But your husband is already getting up, putting his parcel of books under his arm, saying that it's getting late, that he's expected for dinner at one of his uncles. (The Socialist? The Social Democrat? Who knows…) I point to the parcel, as though I have only just noticed it. I lightly touch one of the blunt edges of the darkly wrapped parallelepiped:

'Ah! Holiday reading...? I see you've done well. I haven't been at all lucky... I didn't find a single book I was interested in downstairs. The truth is I look through most of the stuff that gets published and I find I understand less and less of what is written nowadays.' I am tempted to add (but I don't): 'Perhaps this too is the effect of arteriosclerosis.'

A barman answers my signal. Your husband tries to put his free hand into his coat pocket; that would be going a bit too far, so I insist that he must not deprive me of the pleasure of settling the bill:

'Don't even think of it! I'm the one who invited you.'

Then, while the barman is getting my change, I again touch the parcel that your husband is now holding under his other arm:

'I bet you're going to make the most of your wife's absence... You're going to indulge in an orgy of reading and solitary reflection. No poetry, I bet... I must say that poetry has never done much for me either. But I've always liked novels. The ones with characters in. The ones that make you feel as though time is passing by. In which stories are told, proper stories. Even if they are stories where nothing happens... But where we always expect something to happen. Do you think there are still novels like that? Nowadays, I find almost everything so incredibly boring. Of course, I'm a layman... One of these days I'll consult your wife. She ought to know about these things.'

We walk towards the dark slats of the storm-door.

'This is what you might call,' I add, 'a deluge of consultations.'

Your paediatrician stopped short, looking very serious, even sombre, interrupting his opening of the storm-doors:

'Talking about consultations... I've been thinking that I ought to tell you... I think it's best if I do.' A brief, apologetic pause ensued. Then he added: 'I think... I think your wife has not been very well at all. But today I did manage to convince her to go for an electrocardiogram in the morning.'

XXVI

My first reaction: 'It's probably nothing; it can't be anything too serious.' My second: 'What if it is?' (Whoa there!) My third: 'And to think your aunts are still in such good health!'

Oh, those aunts of yours! It took me ages – I'd say nearly forty years – to disentangle them from one another. The three of them are equally magnificent and well-built: one belongs to the Mothers' Guild, one belongs to the Concert Society and one is a brigadier's widow. The first and the third, in particular, seemed quite interchangeable to me. Probably even the deceased brigadier got them muddled up every now and then. (How lucky for the one from the Mothers' Guild!) After all, the three of them were probably no more than the three sides of a triangle – fortunately equilateral – that contained the living memories of your mother's virtues after her premature death (when you were twelve) from a galloping consumption that might at least have had the good grace to wait for the discovery of antibiotics. On the other hand, although the three of them remained adamantly barren (and the first two fanatically unmarried), they continually gave birth to the mythical image of their own parents, who were born in Lisbon to traders from good bourgeois stock (confectionery on one side, fashion and dress-making on the other); both parents were sadly felled in their late fifties, yet still the patriarch and matriarch grew and flourished day by day through their own saintly offshoots, who kept alive the endless memories that they alone had of their parents. You, however, not only became the daughter of each and of none of the aunts, but at the same time, you symmetrically took the place of the sainted mother they so missed.

As for me, they strongly resisted me at first. Overcoming their downright disappointment at my not becoming the desired father substitute they'd equally longed for, they finally adopted me as a kind of half-brother who had been indecently late in arriving; not only that, but I was also the incorrigible black sheep of the family, as I was not at all impressed by the domestic glories of their clan. I must say that I reacted to them at first with the suppressed rage of someone who cannot help feeling like an outsider, and with the wary mistrust of someone who feels out of place for having come into the world too late. Hence my disinclination to distinguish them from one another; or my unconscious desire to perceive them as a whole. It was a good way of making them seem more vulnerable.

What a relief it was to put down to optical illusion the three extraordinarily similar versions of each other I sometimes saw when they were all together! It was asking for trouble to enquire of the brigadier's widow if she knew whether or not Rubinstein or Menuhin were definitely coming to Lisbon; or to ask the Mothers' Guild about the post held in India by the martial husband she'd never had; or when talking to the Concert Society, to be eloquently disparaging of the awards given to large families. There would at once be an incredible uproar; misunderstandings and embarrassing situations would ensue, which could not always be explained away and smoothed over, however tactful you were in your role of caring mother.

That's what it was all about; it still is: you're a mother. You learnt how to be a mother from living with your aunts. It is with them that you began the apprenticeship of what you were to become to me and to all your students, your patients and assistants.

Even in your father's case, as well I know, no sooner was he widowed than you lavished maternal care and support on him for as long as you could; but your father soon chose to look for these in mature and accommodating women; he went as far as marrying one of them five years later, when he was almost *in extremis*, between two severe heart attacks that happened almost one after the other.

With my mother, the second time she was widowed, you once again became all maternal in many different ways, without ever wanting to understand (although I did warn you) that my mother has never needed any kind of mother and that she has always held firm to the conviction that the universe only began with her. This has never been at odds with the fact that she has always expected – and probably still does to this day – that the Dogma of the Infallibility of Mothers will one day be proclaimed *urbi et orbi*. But it would apply to her only: no sharing, no competition. In the same way as there is only one Pope.

On the other hand, and I'm sure it's because you never had any real children of your own, you would gladly see the feminine hemisphere of Mother Earth transformed into a huge International

Association for Fallible (yet obstinately understanding) Mothers.

I don't know if this rising fog is coming from inside the car or from the outside, as I drive along the Marginal after nine at night, on my way to Monte Estoril, with a strange weight in my stomach (do I mean stomach?) in spite of all the sparkling mineral water I've just drunk to lift it.

In spite of this fog, I can see clearly in my mind's eye that clearest of all mornings during that summer when the sea and the lagoon at Foz do Arelho shimmered so brightly. News was spreading that an atomic bomb had been dropped on Japan, and that this time the war would end once and for all. Starting and ending with me, almost no one seemed to know exactly what the bomb was all about. As far as I was concerned, I saw it as a tight bundle of small rockets with their heads facing downwards, and in these heads would be an atom of something or other. Of course I didn't dare share this glorious, well-thought-out idea with my female companion of that summer; she was Belgian like Liliane, not as wild as Liliane, not as pretty as Liliane, and she was already the fourth or fifth fainter version of Liliane in as many wartime summer holidays. As for Liliane herself, and her impertinent Polish tennis player, I had seen neither hair nor hide of them for at least three dismal Augusts. And this makeshift Liliane wouldn't have the foggiest notion what the atomic bomb was all about either.

We were both stretched out on the hot sand, drying ourselves off in the sun, a few feet from the water's edge, speaking French and trying to appear knowledgeable about the catastrophic words we couldn't understand and that had spouted, that morning, from the lips of the more informed holidaymakers. One of them was, of course, my encyclopaedic stepfather, who had posted himself on the hotel terrace, his bald pate in the shade, holding discussions with two or three learned asses, busily comparing the previous day's editions of *A Voz*, the *Diário da Manhã* and the *Diário de Notícias*.

It was then that you emerged from the sea, water streaming down your body, far from your aunts' watchful eyes, and you suddenly came towards where the two of us were lying side by side, me and that colourless counterfeit Liliane whom luck had thrown my way that summer. Just half an hour earlier, you and I had walked past each other, exchanging our brief, daily greeting of, 'Hello, good morning!' But now you were coming towards us with a disgruntled frown furrowing your brow, a mocking sneer on your lips – and you simply came up to me, with the sun blazing down on your soaking-wet hair, and simply sprinkled my chest with the water dripping from your hands and your arms. You then shook both your arms and both your hands over me, in a sudden rush of spite or revenge. Just before running off, you wrung out the skirt of your bathing costume over my shoulders. Your mouth was open in an attempt at a smile, but your eyes and your frown expressed a fury that was quite uncalled for. 'You idiot!' I shouted. 'You're the idiot, and always will be!' And you ran off up the beach.

We had known each other since we were small; we had played together until we were eleven or twelve years of age, on the edge of the lagoon, with other kids our age. Then there came a summer when you didn't turn up; neither you nor your family came to the house with the horizontal blue stripes and its single floor (the windows remained closed throughout), a house that had always marked the dividing line, as it were, between the beach – with its hotels, holiday villas, two or three 'mansions' belonging to families from Lisbon – and the town, that comprised only the local peoples' homes or houses, many of which were rented out for the season to others who lived in neighbouring towns, or even further afield.

When you came back the following year, having shot up like anything and keeping to yourself, the haughty, well-built women that came with you were no longer four in number, but three, though they still all looked the same; but although they were fewer in number, it seemed to me that they were more careful of you and you of them. In the meantime, those who belonged to our age-group had begun splitting into the 'town group' and the 'beach group'. I belonged to the latter, but you didn't belong to either. You only 'belonged' to your aunts, unless it was they who 'belonged' to you. 'Hello, good morning', 'Hello, good evening'. And we hadn't gone beyond this kind of greeting for the past five years.

As for the gentleman with a straw hat who only used to come at weekends (he used to hire a flat-bottomed boat to take your white Panama and the ladies' four parasols out across the lagoon on Sunday mornings), he turned up bare-headed that summer, wearing a grey suit, a black tie and sun glasses. I cannot remember if the regularity of his comings and goings remained the same as before, but he did stop turning up altogether during subsequent summers.

My stepfather and I came across him, later on, during the war, coming out of a bar in the Restauradores in the company of a huge, brash peroxide blonde, with a pair of silver foxes flung across her shoulders; and my stepfather stared only at the foxes, clearly pretending he hadn't seen the man, let alone recognized him.

'You're the idiot, and always will be!'

The next few mornings, I didn't even see you on the beach. But several days later (three, according to you), as it was cinema night in Caldas, we went there and came back– from Foz to Caldas, then from Caldas to Foz – travelling together in the same unsteady coach. Did I say together? That's just a figure of speech. I was with my usual gang of friends, making a terrible racket as always in the back of the old coach; as usual, you were there with your aunts, one to port, two to starboard, and you all sat quite demurely, not to say stiffly, on the first two seats in the coach.

On the way there, it was still daylight and, seen from where I was seated right at the back, your dark hair glinted at times with the coppery sparkle of the ripe red grapes that hung from vines along the way.

The film showing that night, or so you've assured me since, starred Ava Gardner; also, a film has never depressed you quite as much as that one did that night. You had gone to the balcony, I had gone to the back rows of the stalls; we didn't even see each other during the intervals. On the way out, you walked past me, indifferently – 'Hello, good evening' – but, going against what had already been arranged, I decided not to go to the casino with the rest of the gang. Thinking about it, it was highly unlikely that we would get a lift back; and suddenly I really did not feel like walking the five miles back with my friends, as we had done so often before, at three o'clock in the morning. 'But what if the Belgian girl is at the Casino?' one of the others asked. 'You dance with her,' I replied. He answered: 'Thanks, mate. Thanks, but I'll pass.'

A few moments later, I emerged onto the rectangular square where they sold fruit in the mornings, now fully illuminated yet still full of bustle, the cafés full of foreigners (although fewer than in previous years), and I saw the four of you forming a solid block in the midst of half a dozen individuals waiting near the fire station for the coach.

Ever since we'd been using it, the coach always arrived at around twelve forty; but it only left at ten past one, on the dot – it was the last one of the day. While waiting for half an hour with both its doors ajar, the old heap welcomed into its gloomy interior those who had been waiting for it and those who arrived in dribs and drabs to catch it. Not a single light would be on inside. People yawned; springs creaked; sounds of quiet talking. When the night was particularly humid, people's breath would steam up the windows. Apart from the lamplight in the square, there was no other light except for the flash of matches being struck and the glow from people's cigarette ends here and there in the conspiratorial gloom, to which one's eyes soon grew accustomed.

This time, the night was not humid. The four of you had already been waiting in the bus for nearly half an hour. As for me, I didn't go inside like everyone else, but stayed outside on the pavement, pretending to be waiting for someone, but in fact relishing the puzzled and exasperated glances you couldn't help throwing my way from inside the rattletrap, peering over the shoulder of one of your aunts – the large one who had settled herself portside near the window and who was beginning to nod off, revealing, in her dignified drowsiness, a fine sense of rhythm. She must have been the Concert Society member.

What I was also trying to do, out of the corner of my eye, as though noticing such details for the first time, was to admire the perfect outline of your neck as it emerged from the woolly cardigan you had flung over your shoulders, the intelligence of your wide forehead, and this new mobility of your dark eyes whose usual scornful expression had completely disappeared. At the very last minute, I pretended to give up on the idea of getting on the coach, but just as it started moving off, I jumped in through the back door, which was fortunately still open. Then, crouching low, I slipped into the shadow of the back seat; and there I stayed throughout the entire journey, keeping out of sight as best I could.

Finally, I devised a plan for getting off at the same stop as you – two stops before the end of the route to the hotel – without your realizing it; or so that you would only realize I was there when you reached your house (which is what happened); I knew you'd be the last one in, and from the other side of the road I threw a small fistful of gravel at your feet. They scrunched on the ground just as if someone was walking right behind you. Even before you turned round, I knew you wouldn't be able to conceal your surprise. You did, however, have the presence of mind to pull the door to a little, after calling out to those inside the house: 'You go on in. Don't worry. I'll be right there. I've got a stone stuck in my shoe.' Then, crossing the road, I asked: 'Do you still take me for an idiot?' You took a deep breath, and said: 'Perhaps not quite. You're getting better... But do go away.' I am two steps away from you: 'What about tomorrow. Can we talk tomorrow?' All you say is: 'That's what we're doing now. This is already tomorrow.' You turn round; you go back indoors; you close the door ever so carefully behind you.

Then I crossed the road again; and I waited for I don't know how long behind some bushes, watching as flickers of light between the blue stripes of the plain façade gradually lit up four of the six equally narrow windows, three either side of the front door

Only later did I find out that that you and your aunts, however close, have always been particularly respectful of each other's privacy – and still are today. Which is why they still live (how dreadfully shocking in these days of housing shortages!) in three different, yet very similar flats, in the Lapa, Estrela and the Amoreiras.

Which is why we too, very early on, decided to sleep in separate rooms.

That night, once the four lights had gone out (paraffin lamps flickering through the cracks in the wooden shutters), how I wondered about which one of the four would be the first to light up again... It was the one that had gone out last. Just as I'd expected, it was the light in your bedroom. You confirmed that the next day. It was still on at half past three in the morning.

Should I have thrown a few more fistfuls of gravel against your windowpane? Or at least brushed against your window with a twig? I did think about other ways of letting you know I was there. But I also thought you might not forgive me. That was all that held me back. Now we will never know whether or not it was the right thing to do.

At one point, I heard an alarming clatter of voices and footsteps coming from town. It was more than likely the semi-civilized troglodytes of my gang on their way back from the Casino in Caldas. They must not find me there, for obvious reasons. Far better to jump over the ditch, set out across the fields all the way to the lagoon, then get to the beach that way.

I know I reached the shore and stood before the sea as though it were the first time the sea and I'd had anything special to say to each other. I didn't in the least feel like crossing (how many billions of grains of sand would I have to tread on?) the hundred yards or less that separated me from the hotel.

I am back in my car, in the little street in Monte Estoril where it used to be pleasant to live, and a hundred yards or less is the distance that separates me from our house.

There is one light on, in one single window: it's your bedroom window.

Listen to me: for a long time yet, that light must always be the first to go on, and the last to be switched off. Even if I should stop living here. Even if our life is turned upside down.

Believe me when I say that it is not for your sake that I want this, nor is it for mine. I don't care if you don't believe me. I don't care if you call me a clown. I am in fact only thinking of your aunts.

XXVII

You and your friend. Me and Y. We are standing on the long, deserted platform of a dismal underground station. In front of us, the opposite platform is crawling with people: they are horrendous people, atrociously noisy and all formally dressed. I feel quite sick at the thought that I have already met some of those crafty bespectacled eyes, those self-confident mouths, those puffed-up faces, those ravenous teeth: I have seen them either at the Aztecs' (I suddenly know for sure that they are Aztecs), in the news on the telly or on the front pages of the papers.

We are in pairs, the two of you and the two of us, at either end of the same platform with no one in between. But you wave at me from the other end, while your friend is carefully lighting his pipe. Y catches sight of you waving in the distance, and, with an impenetrable look, she says:

'How can I ever trust you?'

Then, to reassure her, I pretend to agree with her about the dubious good taste of wearing such tight jeans.

All at once, I don't know how, the four of us are standing unbelievably close to each other. So close in fact that you manage to whisper something in my ear without Y noticing:

'Look who's waiting for you over there…'

You point discreetly to a trap-door behind us on the platform itself: and you're in there too, six feet down, on top of a box of sand. You are wearing just a light, strapless blouse; you are quite naked from the waist down.

Yet at the same time you are still at my side, still wearing those really tight jeans. I can no longer see Y, I no longer know where your friend has got to.

And there before us, without stopping, an empty carriage, all lit up from inside, rolls endlessly past us.

Suddenly, there is not a living soul left on the platform opposite us. On that side and on this side, there is now an identical, absolute silence.

Then another carriage rolls past, as slow and as endless as the first, also enchantingly lit up from within. But this time, there are two passengers on board, on a twin seat, back to back: it's you and your friend. Then follows a slow succession of many, many empty seats. Finally, there's Y, standing near the last window, her huge eyes that are greener than green, bluer than blue, staring out of that receeding rectangle of glass.

'They were huge. That's what I remember most of all: your eyes... They were huge.'

'And before that?'

'Before that is irrelevant. A load of nonsense.'

'But why is it irrelevant?'

'Call it some kind of superstition.' Looking straight into her eyes, I repeated: 'They were huge. Just as they are now.'

It was the first time I had seen her at that time of day, not at dusk, nor under the electric light of my atelier, but in the fullness of broad daylight. When she had told me that morning on the phone that we would be able to meet that afternoon somewhere near the *quinta*, a little higher up the road from where I had dropped her off two days earlier, I could hardly believe it was true, I could hardly believe it would happen.

I left the car at the top of the hill, where the road suddenly became little more than a track. From that hilltop in the shape of an up-ended half of an orange, with a fragrant gum-tree behind me, I could see a strip of sea to my right, a terrace of lemon trees in front of me, and finally, on the left, the entangled place where two heavily wooded valleys converged.

We had been walking side by side for nearly an hour, beneath the scorching heat of the sun, following the same footpath: on one side, conifers and eucalyptus trees scaled almost vertically up the side of one of the hills that lead to the Capuchin monastery; on the other side, amongst the water tanks and cedar-wood nurseries, on two or three descending levels, a motionless ballet of apple trees, orange trees and lemon trees brought to mind the decorations on some of the frescoes in Pompeii.

She had been very keen, I don't know why, for us to stop for a while by an old fountain, clearly inscribed with the precise date, 1754. The year after that was the year of the earthquake,[24] and it wasn't hard to imagine the terrible fate that befell the many, or rather the few, who had drunk at the fountain for just one or two summers before. Where would Y and I be in one or two years' time?

She was wearing a kind of jump suit that day; it was quite plain, sleeveless, made of white linen streaked with pink like some types of marble, slightly crinkly yet smooth to the touch: it was like a reproduction, in material, of that Wathman card on which she had written me that note eight months earlier. Never before – not even on the coldest winter days – had I ever seen her wearing anything except a skirt; but those trousers elongated her body, without clinging to her thighs or the calves of her legs, and were yet another way I'd never seen before, of her appearing naked while still fully dressed.

We hadn't bumped into anyone, we hadn't seen a single soul. But we were still uneasy in each other's company, almost like two strangers, as though nature mistrusted us, or we mistrusted nature, and as if, instead of bringing us together, it was pushing us apart. The stifling heat – at five o'clock in the afternoon – didn't allow for conversation, let alone intimacy. Several times I felt the urge to tell her what I'd found out the day before about my wife's state of health, and to relate the brief, inconclusive conversation that I had tried to have with her when I got home. The feeling never lasted very long.

In the meantime, we had changed direction. Y pushed open a rotting, rickety wooden gate. From two footpaths that opened up before us, she chose, not the one that went back up into another pine forest, but the one that snaked downwards, through lines of dried bracken and fading hydrangeas, towards the second valley that we had seen from afar.

'Yes,' she explained. 'We're back inside the *quinta* here.' Then, as though apologizing for the semi-wilderness of the place, she added: 'We haven't had the time or the patience to do anything decent to this area.'

Then, rounding a bend, I suddenly noticed a house that was obviously uninhabited; clinging to the land, it was the colour of earth and blended in with the soil. Although not a single windowpane was missing from the sash windows, the façade seemed to have been eroded by a ruthless skin disease; and from beneath the tiles on the roof sprouted tufts of dried grass, like hairs from the nostrils of a row of old men. The main door bore only the faintest traces of paint, and the little that remained was faded and cracked; there was also a large oblong hole where the lock had once been: you had to put your hand in through it in order to release a rusty wire. Y performed this operation quite expertly, and afterwards restored the wire to its previous position.

Inside, there was nothing more than half a dozen agricultural implements, a bag of cement, a broken-down fridge, a disembowelled wardrobe, a battered kitchen table: all this was scattered throughout three or four tiny rooms. Another, larger room, better preserved than the others, was almost completely bare, with two closed windows overlooking the valley. There was nothing in the room apart from a round raffia mat.

Y and I had still barely touched each other; we hadn't even kissed yet. But all at once, we suddenly came alive, or perhaps died, in each other's arms; and I am pulling her zipper down between her breasts to the end of her abdomen. She frees her shoulders from the top half of her jump suit; it slithers down her body, with only a slight hitch round her hips and again round her knees, and it falls like a cloud or a stone in a tangle around her feet. Then her body is stark naked, surprisingly naked, giving me the sudden and absurd illusion that I have only just finished carving it.

Ah! If only I had been born one hundred years or more before... How thrilled I would have been at creating such a sculpture! Had I perhaps created it in a previous existence which I can no longer recall? Or was this moment a rehearsal, a foresight, perhaps even a promise, of what is yet to be when I am reincarnated in a few hundred or thousand years' time? Unless this is the only 'creative' peak the gods have decided to allow me... And why should this not be the case, as indeed the illusion of 'creating' is never more than the pursuit of, or encounter with, what has already been 'created'?

Indeed, in the light of eternity, there cannot be much difference between a living being and a statue, between a piece of linen and a block of stone. And the few minutes we spent there were touched, somehow, by the awesome radiance of eternity. I believe that, even without mentioning it, this had just then been revealed to us both.

To tell the truth, I even found myself at that point (forgive me, my brother, my master, my forefather, my patron!) wishing that I were some kind of Pygmalion in reverse. So that I might change into a statue the actual body that my fingers were now moulding as though it were indeed a statue... but not so that she could appear in some gallery or museum. Not at all! With each passing day, I am increasingly dismayed at the foolish ignorance with which we revere 'art', the way we degrade the cult of 'culture'... Where would this statue end up, then? Perhaps it would be placed in a shrine in

Purgatory, or in a loggia in Paradise... Perhaps, a bit more down-to-earth, in the shrine of the Universe itself, where the magic function of what is beautiful, of what deserves to last, can be miraculously reclaimed.

This was all nonsense, of course. A mixture of nonsense and rhetoric. But not even my awareness of such foolishness could in any way affect the gestures of adoration with which I tried to give a definite shape to that hair, those eyelids, that neck, those shoulder blades. Around her feet, the linen jump suit was crumpled and shapeless, looking more and more like a block of marble – from which her whole body might have emerged. It was almost becoming an obsession.

Y was reacting to my caresses, so different from any before, with a grateful passivity that completely transfigured her. Slowly, still without a word, as though obeying orders or instructions that were beyond us, she started to raise both her arms obliquely in the air, high above her head, so that she was half way between the outline of a tree and the symbol for an unknown quantity. All this with her eyes shut, while at last I came to realize that beneath the wonder of her eyelids, her eyes were not just a wealth of colour, but also of shape and volume. It seemed to me they ought to survive a little longer, even if only for a very short time. And thus I was reassured once and for all about the essential primacy of sculpture over painting – which, deep down, I had never really stopped believing.

The Sun was beating down on the raffia mat; you could tell it was brand new.

A disturbing smell of fruit exuded from the walls, from the floor, perhaps even from the mat itself.

A bird sang. Then another; this one was much closer.

As we knelt down, we could see nothing through the windows except for two little patches of blue sky. Each one had a line through the middle.

And Y was not a statue. Nor had she come to me that afternoon, with nothing on beneath her linen jump suit, to be worshipped as though she were only a statue.

Half an hour later, she cried out in a hoarse voice:

'I need you. I need you in order to live.'

It was a most intimate moment: this was the first time she'd ever used the *tu* form with me.

XXVIII

'Well? How was the ECG?'

'Well I've had it done.'

'And?'

'There's nothing to worry about.'

'Nothing at all?'

'No more no less than was to be expected. Only I can't assure you...'

'Assure me of what?'

'Of having the same heart I did when I was twenty.'

'And why not?'

'Because when I was twenty, I never had an ECG.'

'Maybe you did...'

'What do you mean?'

'Maybe you had one, and you just can't remember any more.'

'No. I'm sure I didn't.'

'Be that as it may, that's not the one that matters.'

'Of course it isn't. Especially as it didn't happen.'

'It's this one I'd like to know about...'

'I've told you already. It was as expected. As can be expected from the heart of someone my age.'

'Our age. Someone our age.'

'All right, then... But you don't have quite the same problem as me; I have the heart of an overweight person. Maybe this time I'll go on a proper diet.'

'I hope you do. It's about time you did. At least make the best of the summer holidays.'

'Yes, so must you.'

'Me? What for?'

'You need to go on a diet in the other direction. You're as thin as a rake.'

'So I've been told. I mean, that I am too thin... It's the first time it's been put quite like that.'

'It's only a figure of speech. Don't let it get to you.'

'No. No, I won't.'

'And as for the holiday bit...'

'I know, I don't have holidays, I am permanently on holiday. As long as Destiny allows me, I shall remain permanently on holiday.'

'It's not that. There's something I'd like to ask you. If you don't mind...'

'Of course I don't mind.'

'Did I dream it, or did you really tell me, a while back, that you intended to go to Italy this summer?'

'Me? I might have. I might have said something like that.'

'Are you still going?'

'I don't know yet.'

'And if you do... Will you be going on your own?'

'I should be. Why?'

'Nothing! Forgive me for asking. I'm not being nosy or anything. It's just...'

'Just what?'

'It's just that I also need to know what to do. I don't know whether to go to that conference or not.'

'Which one?'

'The one in Oslo. I don't really feel like going to Norway. I'll probably give up on the idea. Especially as I've been promising my aunts, for the past year or so, to take them back to Foz do Arelho for a few days.'

'I don't think much of your choice of holiday spot. That place is turning into a real dump.'

'So it seems. But still, they're longing to go back.'

'I don't think much of that either'

'As for me, can you imagine? I've been longing to go back to Italy.'

'That's more understandable.'

'Do you realize how many years it is since we were both there?'

'Quite a few, I'd say.'

'It's coming up to twenty years.'

'Already?'

'That's right. It will be twenty years ago in a few days' time. Since then, we've never actually been back together.'

'No, we haven't. But we've been to lots of other places.'

'Some places. Yes, indeed we have. But I'm talking about Italy. That was the first time we were both together abroad.'

'You may be right.'

'As it so happens, that was the time I most enjoyed Rome.'

'As it so happens? Just like that? Is it really so hard to acknowledge the expertise of your tourist guide?'

'It's not hard at all. If it makes you happy, I do acknowledge… that it had a lot to do with it.'

'Your tourist guide thanks you.'

'Just last night I was dreaming of a piazza, fountains, a huge church… It must have been the Piazza Navona.'

'Maybe it was.'

'We were both sitting in the esplanade…'

'Which we did. More than once.'

'On the very first night.'

'I think so.'

'Only, in the dream, you suddenly disappeared. It was as though the ground had swallowed you up.'

'I hope you weren't too worried.'

'Not at all.'

'Good. You must have thought that I had gone to catch the underground.'

'I don't think there were any underground trains in Rome when we were there.'

'You're right. And the one they have now doesn't go that way in any case.'

'You're the one who mentioned the underground.'

'Only to see if it would give your dream some kind of logic.'

'And who says I need logic in my dreams?'

'You need logic in everything.'

'Not in my dreams, I don't.'

'I'm sorry. I meant well. Or maybe I was trying to understand… this mysterious thing of my disappearing into the ground.'

'Oh! So it's actually you who needs logic…'

'So it would seem. At least when it comes to dreams.'

'See how different we are.'

'Or how well we complement each other.'

'You're right. You have to go on a diet to put on weight, whereas I have to go on a diet to lose weight.'

'That reminds me… Where are we having dinner tonight? Should you care to know, I'm actually quite hungry.'

'I've already had dinner. I didn't know what time you were coming home. But it wasn't just that. I decided to start that diet today.'

'In that case, I'll…'

'If you want to start today as well, and seeing how hungry you are, I wouldn't recommend eating what's in the fridge.'

'That's what I was going to say. In that case, if you will forgive me for being so cruel, I'll treat myself to a banquet in some restaurant in Cascais.'

'I forgive you.'

'But I mustn't be long. It's later than I thought.'

'Are you going out in those trousers? Don't tell me you're going out in those trousers...'

'And what's the matter with these trousers?'

'They're covered in stains.'

'So they are... I hadn't noticed.'

'And besides, they're all creased. They look as though you've been on your knees fulfilling a promise to Our Lady.'

'You're wrong. I was...'

'I'm not trying to find out where you've been.'

'But I want to tell you. I went for a walk. For a stroll in the countryside.'

'How sweet. How bucolic.'

'And I also went to see some marble... round Sintra way.'

'That's it then. You must have been crawling round the marble.'

'I cannot deny that possibility.'

'And did you find anything interesting?'

'I did.'

'Better still. But it's not just earth or marble or marble dust, it looks like bits of plaster...your trousers are covered in stains.'

'Really? And I thought you'd finished with your inquisition! What a truly scientific mind...'

'Purely scientific. But I also take pleasure in seeing that you are well turned out. If you must know...'

'If you say so...'

'Turn towards the light... It's just that a moment ago it seemed to me there were some oil stains too.'

'Oil stains?'

'There. On the side. On both sides.'

'Oh! Yes... So there are. It would have to happen... The blasted wheel! Let me tell you about it.'

'There's no need. If I were you, I'd keep my excuses and give them to the dry-cleaners.'

'Who said anything about excuses?'

'I thought they were.'

'Well, you thought wrong. I'm just telling you what happened. And I think it even includes someone you know...'

'Oh, yes?'

'It's just that I had to change a tyre...'

'I can see the connexion between the tyre and the oil. But as for someone I might know, I honestly...'

'Wait. I'll come to that. On the way back...'

'On the way back? On the way back from where?'

'From the marble.'

'I'd forgotten about the marble. Sorry.'

'So, on the way back, between Sintra and Colares, I pulled over at one point to go and look at the scenery below... When I got back to the car, bang! One of the tyres was flat!'

'It happens.'

'But wait, that's not all. What really got to me was this young horse-rider who came by. He was rather trendy, wearing trainers and a Pancaldi shirt, behaving quite as though he was lord of all he surveyed... He was the one who pointed out the state of the tyre as soon as he saw me.'

'That was kind of him, if nothing else...'

'But he said it in such a way! You know, really snootily, with a foreign accent, he took his glasses off, then put them back on again, he was so infuriating, all I wanted to do was punch him in the face...'

'And is this monster the person I might have known? I can't imagine who that could have been...'

'I'm coming to that. I could have sworn, I really could have sworn, that it was the husband of that tall, rather pretty girl with green eyes, well, greenish-blue eyes, that we've met a couple of times at the Aztecs' house...'

'I know. I see who you mean. I can understand that you should remember her in particular. She's the mother of... Well, how silly! I can't remember the little girl's name.'

'That's it. That's the one. She's the mother of a child you used to look after. They live around there, don't they?'

'I think so. I've only been there once or twice. And that was a few years back.'

'That's him. That's who it was. But, you know, he may not be a fool, but he knows very well how to act like one. What do you think of him?'

'Me? Nothing.'

'Nothing?'

'Or the same as you: it's his wife who is really interesting.'

'I'm talking about him. And I haven't told you everything... He then stood a few yards back, taking his glasses off, then putting them back on again, his arms folded... All this while I was wrestling with the jack, unscrewing the bolts, then screwing them back on again, taking one wheel off, then putting the new one on... As for him, if he was who we think he was, he didn't recognize me, or he pretended he didn't, and he watched from high up on his horse like a complete idiot, as though he was controlling me, it even seemed he was trying to hurry me along to get me out of there...'

'He probably thought you were prowling around his door because of that wife of his...'

'That's what I thought he might be thinking too. And I can tell that you're probably thinking the same thing as well... Heavens! Seeing how beautiful she is, I don't know how to thank the two of you for your flattery.'

'There's no need. Now go and get changed. Soon you won't get dinner anywhere.'

'How about you?'

'I've told you, I've had dinner already. I can even tell you what I had, without being cruel: yoghurt and apple. To be more precise, two yoghurts and two apples.'

'I wasn't meaning dinner. What are you going to do now?'

'I'm going to bed.'

'Isn't it a bit early?'

'I'm tired. We haven't talked this long for ages.'

'Is that it?'

'Is that what?'

'Is that the only reason you feel so tired?'

'What other reason do you think there could be?'

'I don't know! Correct me if I'm wrong, but you haven't told me anything about the ECG.'

'Didn't I? Don't be silly! I told you all there was to tell.'

XXIX

No, her husband hadn't mentioned anything to her; I must be imagining it; but he probably hadn't even recognized me. But it was just as well that we had gone our separate ways, at her suggestion, once we reached the little wooden gate.

Her voice was so confident over the phone that I was quite reassured. Tomorrow? Of course she would. Of course she'd come and meet me in Lisbon. At midday. At midday, on the dot, in the atelier.

We were separated by just over twenty-four hours – almost twenty-six in fact. First things first, how was I going to occupy the rest of the morning?

A few low clouds were threatening rain and scurried across the August sky, the kind of clouds that are out of synch with the calendar and never really know what they're about. Perhaps it was a good day after all to go and visit my mother.

But it wouldn't be very wise to turn up empty-handed: perhaps I should buy her some marrons glacés to delight her palate, or a new recording of some opera to charm her ears.

Coming from the Marginal, I drove up Avenida da Índia, along Avenida 24 de Julho, and down Avenida das Cortes, which is now called something else. Then I went up Calçada do Combo, along three sides of Largo do Camões, and I was just getting ready to slip down the Chiado towards the Ferrari Café and the Valentim de Carvalho record shop, when some traffic signs I always forget about forced me to turn right. I ended up parking the car between the front of the São Carlos[25] and the building where someone who is much talked about nowadays was born (oh church bell in my village![26]), but whom I'm only interested in as he became the partner of the engineer, Álvaro de Campos. Then, a little further up, I suddenly caught sight of Nyasa.

I would have had trouble recognizing him straightaway if it were not the way he had, when greeting his friends, of slowly raising both his enormous hands a little above shoulder level, then waving them in two symmetrical question marks either side of him. He was emaciated, his features drawn, with only his eyes, his eyebrows and his moustache standing out from his yellow skin pulled so very taut over the sharply jutting bones of his face. One could almost say of his once heavy-set body that the walls had all gone but the scaffolding remained: it was as though he had decided to play a trick on people who might see him by pretending to be dressed up as a corpse. In reply to my shocked expression, which I was not able to hide, he attempted an impudent smile:

'As you can see. I've lost five and a half stone. It was six, but that was too much. Now I'm just about right: quite handsome, wouldn't you say?'

Nyasa! I never did find out why we've been calling him this ever since the Belas Artes. He was already a veteran when I went there, he was a veteran among veterans by the time I left; he's from the riverbanks of the Ribatejo, he has never set foot in Africa, nor seen any other river apart from the Tagus: for over forty years, he has limited himself to living exclusively between the Parque Mayer and the Cais do Sodré. 'Any further north,' he would say, 'any further north, bollocks, don't even think it, that's still Visigoth territory. But to the south, blimey, beware, that's Saracen territory.'

When he was young, very young, he had belonged to a group of grapplers.[27] Then, according to him, he got fed up with having to travel, between April and October, round to all the bull-rings in the provinces; even going to Algés or Campo Pequeno hurt him as though he were exiled each time. 'If only someone had had the bright idea of changing the Rossio into a bullfighting-ring! This way, I'm not interested... Do you know what? Another missed vocation.'

As for his other vocation, his true and unique vocation, the one that has provided him with a living with many ups and downs, he would rather not talk about it. It's as though he was weighed down by his amazingly confident ability to create an illusion of life with half a dozen strokes, to suggest unexpected volumes with a few scrawls, most of all to fill in with colourful contrasts vast expanses of cardboard or canvas. He was an expert at painting scenery; and he always tried to surround himself with as little help as possible, aiming to design and execute nearly everything by himself from beginning to end.

He was the idol, the protégé, the companion, the defender of successive generations of actresses and chorus girls, and every so often, he would expound his ideas on women with sober or intemperate *bonhomie*, depending on how many glasses of *ginjinha* and *genebra*[28] (which he liked to alternate meticulously) he had drunk: 'Let me tell you how it is. They were born to suck us dry. We always have to give them something: either sex or money or a beating.' But sometimes, under the mellowing influence of one *ginjinha* too many, he would hurriedly amend this simplistic view: 'Pay no attention. I'm just winding you up. There are also those who only need a kind word, a little display of affection.' Then, more thoughtfully, digging his enormous thumb-nail into his brow, he would add: 'I don't know! Perhaps they all need that. And that's what we least think of.'

There was a golden period of his life: he unexpectedly got an order, some twenty years ago, for the São Carlos. For two consecutive seasons, with this as a pretext and his ability to organize all the workers, the order allowed him not only to be totally at ease moving around the Theatre, but also to establish there, during the quiet hours of the day, the headquarters and fixed moorings for his amorous dalliances: 'You can't beat it as a call house... Who really annoy me are the show-offs who only want to be consumed in the best seats or in the dress boxes. The good sports don't mind if we do it in the gods. And for some of these, I swear, unless it's really impossible, I always reserve the presidential box. You should see them, their legs spread apart, slapping on top of those furnishings, or wiping themselves afterwards on those drapes... I'll say no more: but that's what you really call the banquet of the gods!'

He was big and tall, with broad shoulders, his hair always in mutiny or in flight, his eyebrows always wiggling, his goggle-eyes one minute the picture of innocence, the next sparkling with mischief; and beneath the pelmet of his great whiskers, his large yet delicate lips were less exuberant when eating – wink, wink! – than when talking, smoking, drinking or laughing. He was an A1 mate and he baled me out during a rough patch three or four years after my marriage, four or five years before I set off for Italy: when he saw the hot waters I was in, he broke his self-imposed rules of sailing solo, allowing me to help produce the scenery for a couple of reviews that were quite a success, and for one operetta that was a complete flop.

Every now and then, he would get the urge, as he would say, to paint 'something more serious, with more substance'. Only once however, towards the end of the forties, did he ever hold a solo exhibition, in a certain milliner's in the Travessa de São Domingo which had gone bankrupt and was being sublet. It might not have been the greatest artistic event, but it was quite a spectacle. He had only two write-ups, he sold only two paintings; most of the others he either gave away or destroyed, after discouraging the rare, prospective buyers any way he possibly could, either by escorting them out of the door with impassive politeness ('Please excuse us, gentleman, but we are closing down for repairs'), or by assuring them, with even more laid-back solemnity, that certain paintings carried contagious diseases, that others gave off the evil eye or induced bad habits, that others, finally, had been painted with explosive materials: 'It's the latest thing! There is nothing like it in the world of revolutionary art. This goes straight to the client's home, and a few days later... bang! It explodes. It obliterates everything around it. Of course, it can only be recommended to people with a great sense of self-sacrifice. You, sir, you look as if you fit the bill...' Stabbing threateningly with his finger as though pressing on a doorbell, he prodded the Legion badge[29] the poor wretch was wearing on his lapel. 'Take the painting on trust, it's to die for...'

In the olden days, no sooner were the farcical, so-called free elections announced and the stranglehold of censure loosened a little, than Nyasa threw himself into the fray, in an outpouring of satirical cartoons and fierce caricatures, making himself heard during rallies, going to stuffy meetings presided over by geriatrics or apprentice geriatrics, only to end up, invariably, by saying: 'I've been taken for a ride again. What those shit-heads want is to rule the roost. I'll only be happy when all those roosters have flown the coop.'

But where Nyasa was at his best, where he always found, lost and rediscovered his vigour ('Ah, split beaver!') was in the multiple, mobile world of womankind.. He had always grouped them into 'show-offs' and 'good sports': sometimes it even seemed as though he alternated them, as he did his *ginjinhas* and *genebras*.

'Fortunately, there are always good sports just around the corner. Trouble is, the more the show-offs show off, the more pretentious they are, and they can only turn on us if we ignore quite how pretentious they are.' Indeed, only the show-offs who made his life hell also gave him his zest for life. However hard the good sports tried to act like show-offs (out of scorn or spite), the show-offs always had the upper hand when they calculatedly became good sports: Nyasa always fell for that one; he'd be completely fooled.

With the good sports, there'd be displays of affection, quiet lunches, an exchange of gifts, gentle naps with fingers entwined, repeated glances at the time mingled with stifled yawns. For the show-offs, there was no present good enough, no supper or dinner that could satisfy them: everything was an excuse for big scenes, screaming nights, sleepless dawns, and then, hey presto!, long mornings of reconciliation merging blindly with the afternoons. Frequently, however, these reconciliations were only illusory; then Nyasa, beside himself, would go out of his way to be unfaithful to the show-off in question with the first good sport he came across. 'The hair of a kitten to cure the bite of a bitch.' But the treatment was not always successful; sometimes this quickly come-by good sport turned out to be a new show-off in disguise; and the same hellish cycle would start all over again.

'One of those! It would have to happen to me! I'll be damned if I ever fall for that one again!' Two weeks or so of abstinence would ensue. During those days, Nyasa would age a few years, the tips of his unkempt moustache would droop, his eyebrows snarl, his feet drag like two lead weights from the Parque Mayer to the Cais do Sodré, passing necessarily through the Chiado. A drink of *genebra* here; a glass of *ginjinha* there; in between, he would sing in a disconsolate voice tunes from old musicals as though they were extracts from operas or arias from old operas rewritten for musicals. Then, from one minute to the next, with a good sport on land, a show-off at sea, Nyasa would once more start sailing full steam ahead.

The last time we had seen each other, over a year ago, he weighed well over 14 stone and had in tow a diminutive, eccentric-looking redhead, half punk and half brazen, who kept tugging at his jacket: 'Look, the shoe shop will be closed by the time we get there! Look, I must buy those sandals today!' She didn't give us time to exchange more than a few words.

This morning, however, reduced to a mere shadow of his former self, Nyasa seemed to have a large slice of Eternity at his disposal. He dragged his feet, but without discouragement, as though he might even be enjoying the feel, through his espadrilles, of the flagstones underfoot.

We went into a couple of bars and a couple of bookshops; we walked round the statue of Camões a couple of times; and we ended up sadly chewing things over in the foul-smelling atmosphere of the Brasileira, remembering days gone by when we paid twenty or so times less for two minute steaks like the ones we were eating.

'Did you receive the postcard I sent you a couple of months ago?'

'I did, but…'

'But you're a bastard and never replied to it. I wasn't expecting an answer. It was just to let you know that neither me nor the country had been scuttled yet. Can you believe that there were rumours going round, at the same time, concerning the two of us? Me and the Country. But they were false rumours. Fortunately for me. Unfortunately for the Country.'

'Another drink?'

'Not right now. Just a *ginjinha* as usual.'

Half an hour later, slowly led by Nyasa, we were at the bottom of Rua Ivens, in the Largo da Biblioteca Pública, which nowadays bears a more pompous and academic name.[30]

We come to a pretty row of yellow-fronted houses, and go up to a large gateway in the middle; from there we can now see the twin turrets of the Terreiro do Paço, a broad expanse of smooth river, the ogee arch of the Rua Augusta, the façade and battlements of the See that appears laboriously made of golden sand. But we turned our backs on all that and stand facing the old wreck of the Belas Artes, now more derelict than ever.

'Shall we sit on one of those benches?' Nyasa asked, hastily adding: 'Not that I'm tired. On the contrary. I feel quite sturdy. Handsome, but sturdy.'

The clouds must have gone off somewhere else to bask in the sun that morning. It is sunny and we sit in the sun. Around the bust of the worthy Valmor, a few pigeons lazily peck the ground, waiting for rewards, or at least hand-outs. That's what Nyasa suggested. Only then did I dare ask him what he meant by that story about his being scuttled along with the Country. But Nyasa pretended not to hear my question. He chose instead to confide in me about other things:

'Do you know something, I've got it in my head again to paint something more serious, with more substance. It's probably rubbish, but I do have a painting put aside for you. I want you to have it.' Then, putting his head back and looking at the sun, with his eyes half-closed, he adds: 'This has done me good, you know. To tell the truth I've had a rotten few months. I'm all right now. I'm sturdier now. But they wanted to do me in at the beginning of the year. I was even admitted into hospital, can you imagine? They said I had some sort of crap in my left lung that they wanted to operate on. The usual carry-on... When I'd known perfectly well for the past few months that what I had was some filthy virus. You can imagine the obscene gesture I threw their way! Operate on me? There wasn't a single nurse worth the trouble... One of the female doctors was a bit of all right, but she was one hell of a show-off. What were they on about, cancer? When I even put on weight while I was in hospital! When I even did them the favour of giving up smoking! I told them all to go and get lost... I did all I could to be discharged, I came out, I started painting like a man possessed, and it worked wonders. Now I take that much more pleasure in everything I see.'

A sapless pair of sweethearts had just got up from the bench next to ours; another equally stocky and insipid pair were already making their way to the same bench.

'Argh!' he groaned, as though actually in pain. 'What ugly people!'

But just then a long-legged woman sashayed past us; she was rather pretty in a dishevelled sort of way, and was certainly more a show-off than a good sport, if her arrogant, light-coloured eyes were anything to go by; right behind her followed a hunk whose face we were fortunate enough not to see, carrying a toddler (one and half, two years old?) of dazzling, angelic beauty. Then Nyasa muttered:

'There are always some women and some children that make up for the rest... Especially children. Children have the advantage of being beautiful for a shorter time. And they don't drive us mad just because they're cute.'

We took leave of each other at around five o'clock. I offered to drop him off, wherever he wanted. He declined:

'No, no, I'm not even going to tell you where I'm going. It's my secret... And I'd rather walk, anyway.'

He raised his two enormous hands just above shoulder level; then he waved them in two symmetrical question marks either side of him:

'See you, lad. And remember, I mean it: that painting is going to turn up at your front door...'

Lad! No one in the whole world will ever call me that again.

It was too late to go and visit my mother, and too early to go back to Monte Estoril. The alternative was to go to the Lisbon house and see if there was any post.

There was. Piles of it! Without mentioning the usual triviality – mostly invitations, leaflets and begging letters – my eyes caught sight of some verses, typewritten and unsigned, that only you could have written.

They were entitled 'The Summer, this Summer'. They came in a magnificent envelope from Italy, stamped in Venice. But on a separate sheet of paper, also typewritten, were the two indications of time and place: July, Lisbon. I thus concluded that, in terms of actual content, the verses were already out of date; or that the circumstances that had given rise to them had been miraculously overcome.

Another considerable feat was your display of ubiquity: you were in the south of Spain, according to your husband; and at the same time, so it seemed, you were also in Venice.

Peace on earth to men of goodwill! Glory in the highest to the powers of poetry!

XXX

The morning never asks
for more than a pair of sandals;
but the night before
keeps its tights on.
I am not surprised at the bad taste
with which Life clothes herself,
if the mornings and nights
fade away far from you.

It is only late afternoon
that I come barefooted to you.
Only then do you allow
my circus act to begin:
I kneel with my mouth
on the core of your body,
to control with my lips
the burning flame of a candle.

You swear that in my arms
you find the height of Summer;
that the pulse of Eternity
is measured in seconds;
that you get drunk on shadow
much more than on light;
that chances excite you,
but the future not much.

You describe Venice to me
in this room that is leased
with no door to the stairs
nor view on the river.
You despise brutes
for we are ruled by brutes,
but you do not know what direction
you will give to your life.

You are a vital constituent
of eighty commissions,
all of them indeed
of a cultural nature.
You never have the nerve
deliberately to say no
and to spend with me at least
a few more minutes of your time.

In the meantime you confess
that, for you, the Sun
is now the pseudonym
for a dying star;
that the turmoil of waters
is stilled in the blood;
and that ever since childhood
you have planned to run away.

Who you plan to run with today
is a thing you do not always reveal:
you have developed the caution,
worthy of a diplomat,
of leaving me in doubt.
That's how you feel
how I follow your trail
while walking in darkness.

The Nation does not thrill you,
the State even less:
but already for them both
you have accomplished so much.
I fear that in my case
the opposite will happen:
you will not lift a finger
for the woman you love.

Look how faithless I am,
how unscrupulous too,
when you have already promised
to write the preface
of my next book of poems;
apart from hitting the jackpot,
once the days begin to shorten,
they'll make the evenings last longer.

Your sense of practicality
will force your confrontation
with our two horoscopes.
For now, you are happy
to see, in the Universe,
a tentative copy
of the various hemispheres
that exist on my body.

You count my orgasms
in order to be sure
that a quarter of a century
is nothing between us.
I collect your semen,
as though trying to gather
the irrefutable proof
that you belong only to me.

I pretend to believe in the premiss
that I'll go with you one day to Venice;
Actually I'd be content
if we went only to Óbidos.
I do not mean Óbidos precisely:
What I mean is the Moon,
to make it easier for you
to say it cannot be done.

There are other acts
in the Circus of Gentle Derision:
we could reduce the World
to barely ten square yards;
we could say 'See you soon',
knowing the phone
can be of no use
to meet my need of you.

Do not worry that I might take
you away from your duties;
even less put an end
to what is meant by a home.
I ask you only to bring
Venice as close as can be
to this craving I have
of being your gondola.

Of being your gondola
not only on late afternoons,
but every now and then
during the night-time as well.
Then I would awaken
truly barefooted,
without feeling on my legs
the shadow of my tights.

This cannot go on.
I feel like telling you
that I wish you'd commit
at least a single transgression;
that I'd rather you throttle me
instead of embrace me;
that calling this Summer
is probably wrong.

But I swear to limit myself
to asking you to amend
some verses a bit further back
that I'm sure must be wrong.
I know how able you are
in matters of metre.
I know you will suggest
that it be all put into octets.

I shall kneel with my mouth
at the core of your body:
some verses will emerge,
far more yours than mine,
because of the effect
of the semen I collect.
You will hammer out the beat
on the bumps of my spine.

That will be the moment
we will be at our closest
to the canals of Venice,
to the gondolas of the night,
to those instances of flight
when you never took off.
I might convince myself
that this means Summer indeed.

To ask for more would be too much.
Venice, however,
survives without us being there;
without my ever having been there,
which is even worse.
Rest your hands
on my head.
Right now you exist.

XXXI

So your friend is also one of those people who is always plotting his escape! Between him and me there is therefore an endearing affinity, which we could never have suspected.

In my case, it was a defect, a flaw of obscure origin; a perversion I've had to live with since childhood; a kind of masturbation that coexisted to a certain extent with the joys of the real thing, but that fortunately managed to replace and survive the practice of the real thing.

For almost six years I boarded at the Colégio Militar (from which I was in due course expelled) and hardly a month, or even a week, went by without my dreaming of putting one of my amazing plans into action. It was the same during the first years of my marriage: these at least culminated in my departure to Italy. But even when on holiday – from school or from my marriage – I would often fall prey to those tempting bad habits.

Before getting married, long before knowing who my bride was to be, the best time during the holidays for putting these plans into action was generally the first two weeks in September, after we returned from Foz do Arelho. My mother and stepfather would leave at that point to take the waters, without me and without Tá: just the two of them, taking with them as extra luggage (half-bored or half board) the insipid and insidious girl they had laboriously produced together. Back at the Lisbon house, which Tá returned to with me, Tá's duties were first of all to see that I behaved well and then, assisted by the cook and the daily, to preside over the great operation of the autumn 'spring-cleaning': the curtains and drapes were thoroughly washed with potash; carpets, rugs and runners were beaten sadistically; winter clothes were aired, with mothballs and lavender sachets liberally redistributed; furniture, doors and floors were waxed, silver and glassware polished, not to mention the furious whirlwind of scrubbing and cleaning that had earlier overturned the kitchen area, the pantry and the two *marquises*.[31]

One year (I must have been fourteen or fifteen), Mrs Zolda,[32] the sewing woman, was there as well to deal with the more urgent jobs in her field. Mrs Zolda was about thirty years old, but her body was ageless, her features were somewhat unprepossessing, except for her lively though tormented, dark eyes. She had many attributes that filled me with respectful awe: she was a spiritualist; a divorced woman; a vegetarian. I had known her before to allow me surreptitiously to cover her mouth in avid kisses, to touch the firmness of her solid thighs, to squeeze the soft perkiness of her proud breasts: she in turn would reward me with rushed hand jobs that never quite went all the way. But that autumn she took the initiative of going quite a bit further: while the other three were barricaded somewhere between the kitchen and the pantry, she gave me my marching orders to hurry across the bedroom that my mother shared with my stepfather, and meet her in their private bathroom. I found her casually exposing herself, completely undressed from the waist down, with her hands covering her face and lying on her back between the toilet and the bath. She had taken the commendable and tasteful precaution, beforehand, of placing one of my stepfather's dressing-gowns, carefully folded, under her bottom. Then it all happened so fast, in such an aseptic, soundless, mechanical and nebulous manner, that we might as well have been a pair of extraterrestrial beings. During the days that followed, the battle of the mighty 'spring-clean' spread further afield; and Mrs Zolda made it her business to find other entrenchments for our other form of hygiene: the last one took place on the terrace, which had long since been glassed-in, but still held the wicker chairs that creaked at every opportunity. On some afternoons, the positions we adopted were imaginatively different. Yet, with remarkable consistency, Mrs Zolda proved herself to be particularly adept with her hands. She claimed it was safer; but somehow I knew that it was mainly a vocational bent. Beyond the windows of the *marquise* were the dockyards, boats, cranes, the hills on the Other Side, a long stretch of the Tagus up to the tower of the Bugio. If I remember correctly, that must have been the only September in all those years that I didn't frighten Tá half to death by pretending to run away.

Everything had to be 'as clean as a whistle' (the cook's words) and worthy of my mother and stepfather's return home (I'd be off to boarding school!), but the more the mighty cleaning operation progressed, the more I'd been consumed, in previous years, by the desire that they should not find me at home on their return; and that, too late, they would be filled with anguish when faced with the incontrovertible fact that I had run away, disappeared, even perhaps been killed. This last possibility always unnerved me a little; but it in no way spoiled the delighted excitement I felt at other images, with their necessary ingredients of both farce and tragedy: there was nothing more pathetic or more farcical than associating my mother's highly unlikely distress with my stepfather's hopeless gesture of still smoothing back the hair on his head when he had already been totally bald for so long.

Yet it was always Tá who suffered the most from this dreadful prank I wanted to play on them and that they never even got to hear about. All I needed, really, was just for someone to 'know' about it and to 'take it seriously', so that I too could actually believe in what I was planning to do. It was too bad that that person had to be Tá. However many times the scene was re-enacted, she would always look on, petrified, crying her eyes out, while I went through the same motions as always to make ready for my escape, from stuffing all sorts of clothes into an old suitcase that had belonged to my father (I never did use a suitcase that belonged to my boarding-school 'trousseau'), to leaving by the back stairs (why always the back stairs?), swearing that no one would ever set eyes on me again.

Then would follow three or four hours of aimless wandering along the streets that led down to the river: I would stop in front of eating-houses and dubious restaurants, I would look at the menus in their windows, I would work out how much money I would need to get by – if Tá would lend it to me – and to survive alone for a year, a month, even a week. The trouble was that I always forgot to ask Tá for money before I left.

Later on, I would stroll sombrely through the stinking maze of the docks, weighed down by the heavy suitcase that, paradoxically, through a playful trick of levitation, added greatly to my feelings of freedom and elation. What if I offered to work as a mere cabin boy on that cargo ship that was about to leave? What if I sneaked on board this other ship where there was no one to be seen on deck, and left as a clandestine passenger? My mind was full of the bad films they showed at the Politeama and the Odeon; half of me believed such enterprises could succeed but, lazier and wiser, the other half refused to take them at all seriously.

I would then make my way back home, and Tá would be so happy her streaming tears would dry up. 'You're such a whelp,' she would say. 'You're a right whelp!' She would raise her arm to ruffle my hair affectionately, without realizing how well this name fitted me – like a glove! – in its picturesque and rarely used meaning of young dog, the young version of the despicable man I was to become. She must have brought this kind of word with her from her remote village in deepest Alentejo, along with the flower-painted chest where she still kept some of her things and her rambling, ancestral wisdom made up of proverbs, songs, legends and tales of *malteses* and *ganhões*.[33]

While we're on the subject, here's another of Tá's amazing peculiarities: the dreams she used to have, the dreams she told me about. I have never heard of anyone having such delightfully incoherent dreams: 'I woke up in the middle of such a strange dream this morning!... My stepmother was coming right at me, all mealy-mouthed and sweet as pie, but I knew what she really wanted was to wallop me, then in the twinkling of an eye, she turned into a spinning-top, I started to play with it just like that (something she never used to let me do, that's a boys' game, she'd say), and didn't it go and land right by the pig we'd been keeping since Easter, and, scrunch!, into the pig's jaws it went, and it even got stuck in the pig's gullet!' Another time: 'You won't believe what I dreamt about last night!... I was riding on a little jug on my way to Serpa, when my stepmother (she's been dead for years, but she was no saint, God rest her soul!) came and overtook me, riding a huge pitcher, and she got to Serpa long before me!'

So have I, Tá. I too have spent most of my life dreaming of running away, I'm not sure where to exactly, usually astride objects – *hobbyjects*? *holyjects*? – that are even more unlikely than your innocent little jug. And when I wake up from these dreams, how can I deny that I'm the greatest, most incorrigible bastard?

But I believed that, since Xô, I was on my way to a complete cure. Which is why I was all the more disconcerted by what was happening now with Y. Have I gone back to being an adolescent without the acne? Am I miraculously back on the threshold of adulthood? Or is this merely sclerosis, even the onset of senility, to use your husband's indirect diagnosis? Perhaps it was just the healthy desire (was it not legitimate?) to drastically shake up my life before people started calling me venerable or damnable, a precursor or a has-been; before they turn me into an institution or a sacrificial goat complete with the latest trimmings of recollections, misdemeanours, conventions, witticisms, bowings-and-scrapings, accolades and knocks. Most of all, before what was happening to Nyasa and perhaps even to my wife happened to me – the first already a dying wreck, the second, at best, having to slow down greatly from now on. The time had come for the Big Leap, to carry through the Great Escape.

It was good to see beyond the perfidy of your verses that someone my age – and certainly more conventional than me – had been brave enough to actually run away, however briefly or spasmodically, something that neither you nor I had thought him capable of. It would be unfair if I couldn't do the same. Especially if I couldn't do the same in collusion with Y.

All the women I've known in over forty years have been no more than caricatures, sketches at best, of what had become a perfect portrait: the best in them was no more than loose stones of some kind of puzzle that I've only just finished putting together.

But the incredibly white nightdress that Y had bought recently, having now become the unfailing attire – or talisman – during our encounters, had also become a subconscious excuse for me not to insist too much on our plans for living together, and first of all 'running away' together. Oh, how conditioned we are by objects! Especially when we allow them to be filled with symbolic values.

I was thinking all this over, more or less, that Friday morning (it was Friday) while making my way here to wait for Y to arrive.

There was not a cloud in the sky, which seemed to have recovered from the chaos of the night before. It was a little past eleven when I parked my car. A lumbering cargo ship was heaving on the river, near the bridge, striving for the day it would be decommissioned. Nearer the docks, idle seagulls pecked at the dirty water.

As soon as I entered the atelier, I spotted a piece of paper on the floor under the door, bearing Y's scrawl:

'*Do not wait for me. Do not worry. I ask you just for* (sic) *to phone me before twelve. I will explain then. I swear, nothing to worry about. Lots and lots of kisses. You know I cannot live without you. Do not forget to phone. Forgive this paper.*'

Instead of the excellent Wathman she had used before, these words were written on a page torn out of a pocket diary. It was dated November of last year: a time, therefore, when we hadn't yet met.

What now? It was gone a quarter past eleven. On the other side of the Praça, beyond the tramlines, one of the two *pastelarias* was closed for staff holidays; the phone in the other one, the one from which I had phoned Y at home for the first time, seemed to be keeping a vow of silence and holding a hunger strike in its refusal either to emit a single sound, or to consume a single coin. Then it was gone half past eleven. The only solution: go back to the car and find a public telephone a little further afield.

But, lo and behold, when I got back to the car, there was another anonymous and repulsive note waiting for me, stuck under the windscreen-wiper as usual (this was certainly the morning for notes). It was less threatening than usual, and all it said was: 'Don't think you're clever. Nor that everyone else is a fool.' The writing was rounded and revealed a minimal IQ, with capitals and lower case letters all the same size, and it was exactly the same writing as the other notes, and the contents were exactly comparable in terms of terse conciseness.

Although my initial reaction was to rip it to bits, I ended up putting it in a compartment of my wallet to join all the others I had received.

XXXII

My hands were in the hands of a sullen Rucha; my feet were in the huge hands of senhor José; as for my head, it was being prodded by the strong, efficient fingers of a girl who seemed fragile in every other way and who had washed my hair two or three times before. It was most enjoyable, after the five hellish days just gone, to surrender like this to so many hands.

But the only truly soothing ones belonged to the girl who was washing my hair. Her height was above average, yet she wasn't actually tall; although her skin wasn't quite fair, she couldn't be called dark; she was more willowy than thin, her eyes were narrow and slanted, enigmatic as usually only eastern eyes can be; and I decided there and then that the term 'geisha' would suit her quite well.

In the meantime, the proprietor of the salon, the quivering Palminha[34] – my regular barber for over thirty years – kept an eye on each successive phase of the operation, first telling the girl which shampoo to use on my hair, then pointing out the areas on my scalp that were in need of firmer massaging. But when for a moment she caught him off guard, she managed to whisper in my ear:

'You're very tense today... Try and relax a little.'

That's what I'd been needing someone to say to me for the past five days; especially with such spontaneous concern. And just for that, I felt a bit hard done by that soon it would be Palminha, and not her, who'd have the job of cutting my mop of hair.

As soon as I'd come in, I had caught sight, at the far end, of a low-flying cloud of bleached hair floating above the profile of a new manicurist with long eyelashes and a turned-up nose: I suspected at once that she must be Floripes's daughter and, as I couldn't be bothered with introductions and idle chit-chat, I willingly accepted that Rucha should do my hands, although I usually found her perpetual look of a retired, hypochondriac chorus-girl somewhat trying on my nerves. But that afternoon, Rucha seemed quieter than usual, perhaps because, deep down, she was grateful that I had so eagerly accepted her services, or perhaps because she'd been mysteriously infected by the comforting influence of the girl who was washing my hair.

'Hey!' growled Palminha with obvious impatience. 'That's

enough water, my girl… Really! Just dry the hair now…'

How impertinent Palminha has become! And how he's prospered since the death of the elder Palma! It all started (in the late 1950s) with a little bit of refurbishment: whatever it was, it was enough for the ancient Barbearia Palma, near the Largo do Rato, to cease to exist and be replaced in a flourish of chrome by the Palm Beach Salon, Gentlemen's Hairdresser. Later on (towards the middle of the following decade), the place underwent vast expansion, not only through the opportune acquisition of the haberdasher's next door (what a bargain!), but also through the daringly difficult excavation of the basement; it was honoured, then, with its first illuminated sign and a new christening ceremony: it was renamed Palm's, Salon de Coiffeur. Finally (during the first half of the 1970s or, to be more precise, in the summer of 1973), following good returns from the buying and selling of shares (it was almost as if a branch of the stock market had been opened there), new capital was invested, all the equipment updated and the number of personnel significantly increased; from then on, although it was still called Palm's (with modernized font), it bore the sober subtitle of 'Hairdresser' (in English), elegantly followed by 'Men's Hair Stylist' (again in English) in smaller letters. How pedantic of Palminha, with his cocky sixty years of age! As if I didn't know he'd been wearing a wig for the past fifteen years!

What was the point indulging in these sarcastic thoughts about the restless and ridiculous Palminha – who, if nothing else, was a competent professional, a devoted monogamous husband, an intrepid go-getter on his way up – when all I wanted to think about was Y?

On Friday of the week before, from ten to twelve until past midnight, all my attempts at phoning her house had been fruitless: I kept getting the same irritating tones, engaged or out of order, and the operator kept telling me different things. The next day, at around eight o'clock, I managed to get through: this time a halting voice with a strong Alentejo accent ('This is one of the maids!') informed me that, yes, sir, the phone had been out of sorts the day before, but it was better now and, yes, sir, that the masters and their daughter as well had left the day before. She wasn't allowed to say where it was they'd gone, and even if she was, she didn't know. ''Scuse me, please, but the milk's coming to the boil,' she said, adding: 'I'm off as well, to my village, soon, with my husband,' and so they still had to close up the house. As to when they'd be back, she replied: 'How'm I supposed to know? All I know is that we're coming back on the fifteenth of September.'

Two hours later, with no explanation – having merely had the courtesy to suggest to my wife, why the heck didn't she take the opportunity to go and stay with her aunts in Foz do Arelho – I recklessly set off in the car towards the Algarve. Vale do Lobo... wasn't that where 'they' had a house? But, once I'd got as far as Grândola, I was filled with doubts, unsure as to whether the house was in Vale do Lobo or in Vila Lara. What a strange phenomenon, that I should remember so few specific details about Y's family life! As though all that mattered to me was where and when she was present for *me*! As though it was me after all who subconsciously erased the unmistakable evidence that she existed away from me!

Besides, in my claudicating mind, Vale do Lobo and Vila Lara, along with another three or four tourist compounds of a similar nature, belonged to the same, muddled magma of enviable abominations or abject fairylands – depending on the time of day, the phase of the moon, the season of the year, my gut-feeling, and the feelings of other, relatively more noble organs of my body. And the most important of these is the mellow rook that has fluttered in my ribcage for the past fifty years and seemed ready to break free, during the drive under a blazing sun that seemed to be taking forever to cover the distance between Ourique and São Bartolomeu de Messines. Just before Ourique, the name of a village, Torre Vã ('Vain Tower'), seemed to stand for exactly what I had been, what I had done, what I was trying to do right there and then.

I arrived in Vale do Lobo towards the middle of the afternoon, after taking countless wrong turnings and getting quite lost (after all that, I was confusing it with the Balaia compound), and my crazy lack of planning in going there hit me squarely for the first time. What was I looking for? Y's whereabouts? Was I going to snatch her away from her husband? If so, with or without creating a scandal? By force? By force of arguments? If so, which ones?

For now, I needed only to know where she was. At least to see her. And, if possible, to talk to her.

But there was no way of finding out – either through her husband's name or her own maiden name – if they had a house there or not. When they saw the dreadful state I was in, the more co-operative people I spoke to sent me quietly packing, as though I were some kind of carpet salesman; the less affable would shake their heads in various languages, probably seeing in me some kind of terrorist or a potential abuser of fair and tender children.

Perhaps my search might be more successful the following day after I'd tidied myself up a bit? But I found it rather hard to find somewhere to spend the night, which was not surprising, as the coastline of the Algarve that I'd seen so far appeared to be completely submerged beneath horrendous waves of an amphibious fauna, simmering with brilliant shoals of holiday-makers. Luckily, in the sixth or seventh hotel I stopped at, one of the receptionists seemed to know me, to remember me (I at once pretended to remember her too: oh, that's right, that inn in Lagos, how many years ago now?) and was fortunately able to fit me in, as it was just for the one night – 'Aren't you the lucky one?' – in the room that had been inexplicably and hurriedly vacated at lunchtime by a Danish couple who, it later transpired, were supposedly being sought by Interpol.

The room looked out onto the beach or, to be more precise, onto the caterpillar-shaped swimming-pool that stretched in the glow of a night light between the beach and the back of the hotel. At around midnight, two great sylphs, obviously of Germanic origin, were still wading about with ponderous determination. Earlier, glowing softly, the tipsy crescent of the waning moon had risen over Spain, resembling a drunkard's drawing of a heaving ship.

At three o'clock in the morning, with sleep still eluding me, I was still sitting outside, on one of the chairs on the veranda. And suddenly, on the veranda next to mine – next to mine, yet angled in a complicated way, so that the privacy of both might appear to be respected – there emerged the unexpected outline of a superb young mestiza, very tall, with greenish eyes, wearing a clinging yellow sarong tied above her breasts, her shoulders bare, her profile clearly outlined against the light from her bedroom, her eyes lost in the almost total darkness of the sea. I don't know how long she stood there, motionless, as though I didn't exist. In the breathless silence, she was a blend between an exotic plant and a tame wild animal on the lookout, able to communicate only with the sea and the night. She seemed to have stumbled into the wrong bedroom, the wrong hotel, the wrong beach, the wrong country, the wrong continent. Perhaps even the wrong planet. And I couldn't resist seeing her as a negative print of the image of Y herself.

The girl who had washed my hair came up to me at one point,

with her cute geisha looks, to ask if I should like some coffee, water, or some other drink, such as gin or whisky: she was also in charge of these things now. And, straight after, making the most of the fact that Palminha had been called away to the phone, she added:

'Forgive me for speaking my mind, but it seems to me that water would be best for you right now.'

'You're right, water. Make it still water, then.'

'And wouldn't you like to try that thing over there, afterwards? I don't know if it does any good, but some people say it does. Hasn't senhor Palma told you yet? It's our latest gadget.'

She was pointing to a metallic chair like mine, some three yards in front of us, but it was shaped differently and had leather trims.

'You plug it in and it starts vibrating. It seems it's good for relaxing the nerves.'

Palminha, in the meantime, had come back from the phone and was obviously delighted with the girl's suggestion, so he went into all the technical details, scientific explanations and financial considerations: it had, after all, involved quite an expense, but one must keep oneself up to date in order to serve one's clientele properly, especially as equipment like this (but not quite as good as this) could already be found in some of the barber-shops in the new shopping centres. He said the word 'barber-shops' with contempt – it was a word he no longer used for his own 'salon' – as though the word derived, not from *barba*, but from *barbaria*.

As for me, I promised the geisha that when I'd finished, I would go and try the vibrating chair.

Not that my life had been lacking in 'vibrations' these past few days. All day Sunday was spent travelling between Faro and Albufeira – and later, out of desperation, between Portimão and Tavira – and could not have been more frenzied. These exertions came to absolutely nothing: both Y's name and her husband's were completely unknown amongst the so-called jet-set in the tourists' realm of the Algarve. And this, in spite of my having worn, since first thing in the morning, the most discreetly European sports shirt, chinos and tennis shoes that I owned. It was late at night by the time I set off back for Lisbon. Everything went quite well until I reached Lisbon itself; but on the Marginal, on my way to Monte Estoril, I was so tired that I was almost driving in my sleep. The next morning, surprised at seeing me back, my wife remarked:

'You weren't gone long. With all the luggage you took, I thought you wouldn't be back before Christmas.'

'How about you? Did you go to Foz do Arelho after all? When did you get back?'

'Over thirty years ago.'

As soon as I'd had breakfast, I got myself ready to set off on the required, thorough scouting expedition around the neighbourhood. Shouldn't I have started there in the first place?

First, I went to Y's house: it certainly looked closed from the outside and quite uninhabited inside. Both entrances displayed metal plaques, which I could have sworn had not been there on either occasion when I'd been there before, informing that the property was alarmed against burglars and under the care of a named security company.

The next thing to do was to find out where Y's husband's factory was located (even regarding this, the information I'd retained was skimpy and incomplete) and to go there straightaway, whatever the risks such mad behaviour entailed, and at least find out the destination of such a precipitous departure. In the end, it wasn't too hard to find the factory; and it was easier still to get repeated confirmation – from the doorman all the way up to one of the foremen – that the boss was indeed away. However, no one could tell me where he'd gone. Unless his secretary knew.

I asked to see her, on the pretext of an urgent matter. I was presented with a sullen, broad-shouldered woman in her early fifties, wearing a suspicious pair of dark glasses beneath her thinning crop of salt-and-pepper hair. She looked me up and down as though I were some kind of escaped convict or police officer in disguise:

'Who are you?' Even without her guttural accent, she could have passed for the daughter of some worthy concentration-camp guard. 'Please tell me your name.'

I gave her the first name that came to mind:

'Nyasa.'

'Pardon?'

Of course that was foolish of me: only a man like Nyasa could get away with having a nickname like that for a surname. But I stuck to it and tried to be a bit more specific:

'Nyasa. Joaquim Nyasa.'

'Can you prove this? Do you have a card?'

No; as it so happened, I didn't. But all I wanted was to know where her boss was. I added:

'And his family. If they are in this country or abroad.'

These additions, far from making things easier for me, seemed to cause the battle-axe's dark glasses to steam up with even more suspicion.

'I regret. We are forbidden to tell. We can only tell people we know. We have our orders.'

Tersely, she dismissed me. No luck there. More than anything else, I found it was the atmosphere of the factory itself that made me feel uncomfortable: it was both antiseptic and sticky, exuding efficiency, exactness, monotony and concealed horror. It was hard to believe Y lived mostly off the continuous production of those inhuman machines.

People we know? Eureka! The Amerindians... They ought to be good for something.

I rushed first to the atelier in case there was a new message waiting for me there. It would be highly unlikely: and indeed, there was no sign of one. Then, plucking up heart and putting on a brave face, off I went to rap on the door of the horrendous villa in the Restelo. No, no, what a shame, they're not in; but madam should be back soon, she's just gone down to the beach with the ambassador's wife; sir is out for lunch, but he said he'd be at the chancellery all afternoon.

A diplomatic luncheon, especially a Latin-American one, would not be over before four o'clock: an opportune moment for me to gather strength too, and find a good restaurant where I could recover, not only from my recent exertions, but also from the concoctions I had hastily swallowed down in the Algarve the night before. At ten past four, I presented myself at the chancellery; and the counsellor, returning punctually at five, saw me straightaway at five past five. He must have thought I'd come to negotiate the sale of another work of art, for he hesitated between appearing eager and wary, cautious and flattered: he'd been the one to come after me for the Monstrosity, so I had to take judicious advantage of my relative position of strength. I allowed him to persevere in his misinterpretation for a good few minutes; only then did I broach the subject. I'd had enough time to prepare my spiel down to the slightest detail:

'Can you believe it? I'm here, in the greatest secrecy, because of that friend of yours...' I mentioned Y's husband's name, and this had the immediate effect of deflating him, or so it seemed at first, but I later realized he was actually deeply perturbed.

But on I went, stressing the fact that it was quite simple, really:

a friend of mine who was also an extremely close friend of the husband's (I subtly insinuated that I might be talking about a woman) needed to get in touch with him urgently; but this person had found out that they'd unexpectedly gone abroad; and at the factory, only people he knew and who identified themselves as such (which would be out of the question in this particular case...) would be told by the secretary where her boss was. Would *mi caro consejero* happen by any chance to know where they were? Or, which might be asking a little too much, would he mind just ringing the secretary of *su amigo*? She could not refuse to give *mi caro consejero* the required information.

The more I developed this tortuous argument, the more nervously did *mi caro consejero* fiddle about with either the ashtray that lay between us or the collar and lapel of the jacket he was wearing, and from which he appeared to be brushing off an imaginary and inopportune insect. Then, standing up, he asked whether it was just him, or was it indeed too hot, and he went to check if the air-conditioning was working properly. Finally, sitting down solemnly in the far armchair, he began telling me that he would have had *mucho, muchíssimo gusto* in being of assistance – to both me and to the other *persona* – but unfortunately, he did not know where or how to reach *el señor ingeniero* (it was complete news to him that he'd gone away) *ni tampoco* was he in any position even to phone the factory because of events *muy recientes*. This, he added, because an argument *aburrido* had occurred between the factory and '*un organismo estatal de mi país*'. It was nothing, he added, that in any way diminished *su personal afecto por el ingeniero*, but in the diplomatic world, things are *lo que son*, and a distinction has to be made between personal sentiment and official sensibilities, and who knows, perhaps in a few weeks, or even a few days, it would all have blown over, and then he would have the *grandíssimo gusto* in being of service; in the meantime, would I like to have *una copa* with him (it's been so hot these past few days!), and so on and so forth.

All that was left for me to do – which I did the following day – was to attempt the Alentejo, just in case there was the slightest chance that, in spite of the heat, Y, her husband and her daughter had gone there for a break.

But in the Alentejo, as all I had was the most tenuous of clues, namely that the house was situated somewhere between Estremoz and Vila Viçosa, it was rather like looking for a needle in the proverbial haystack: between Vila Viçosa and Estremoz, with a longer stopover in Borba, whenever I mentioned their names and surname to anyone, their faces would crease in amazement and surprise, beads of sweat dripping freely down the deep furrows on their brows. I began to think it would be easier to get a satisfactory reply from the huge, recently dug-up lumps of stone that were piled along the side of many of the roads. I hadn't chased that kind of 'quarry' for years! And at dusk, I felt a painful stab of regret at having so soon lost patience with the taming of those blocks of marble, those fabulous prehistoric beasts, at having succumbed so timidly and so soon, as had so many others, to the ignominious seduction of less noble materials whose very vulgarity made them more fashionable.

I spent the night in Estremoz. In the morning, I raided the neighbourhood again and made further enquiries in the town itself: all in vain. Not even the old barber who had hailed me from the doorway of his little shop ('Hey, my friend, won't you come in? Your hair could do with a bit of a trim...') was able to give me a good lead to follow, although from what he said in the ten minutes we stood chatting under the sun, he seemed to be well up to date with all the local gossip. As for the shocking state of my hair, he was quite right: so much so that I'd already decided that, on my return to Lisbon that very afternoon, I would subject myself to the shearing expertise of Palminha, hairdresser and men's hair stylist.

After checking the car's fuel level, I sat down on the esplanade at a café: just for a sandwich and beer. The broad expanse of the Rossio was spread out before me, totally exposed to the baking sun. It was past midday; the other tables emptied gradually, one by one. It seemed as though the city itself was emptying. Most of it, that is, with the exception of the drowsy waiter who had served me and was taking his time in bringing me the bill.

Not a single leaf stirred in the acacia-trees. Everything seemed to be waiting for something unexpected to happen. A cricket began to chirp, alone and insistent. Not enough, however, to interfere with the beauty of that great space and stillness.

'Well, Mestre?' (Mestre? I'd never before had the honour of being addressed as such in that salon.) 'Would you still care for a little relaxation?'

She was waiting for me by the chair that promised so much delight, the new and magical piece of equipment, bestower of pleasure, that Palminha had just installed in his model salon. But the corners of her slanted eyes twinkled fittingly in a barely perceptible smile of derision; when I went to sit down, she muttered an aside:

'I don't guarantee anything... But I'm sure it can't do any harm.'

She was an amusing little creature, this apprentice geisha, with her blend of seriousness and fun, of submission and mischief, of good manners and cheek, of devil-may-care yet nobody's fool. It was clear that she was conscientiously ensuring that Palminha only saw her sweeter side (all orange, no lemon); but when it came to other people – at least me at that point – she didn't mind showing she could and would also be acidic. Sweet and sour: taking into account the shape of her eyes, this was probably the term, from oriental cuisine, that described her the best.

With due care and attention, she had plugged the chair in; then, standing in front of me, with no less care or attention, but without dispelling that smile that twinkled in the corners of her eyes (and her mouth), she seemed to be watching my face, and indeed my whole body, for the unlikely miracle of a complete transfiguration. I was utterly sceptical, and merely allowed myself to be lulled by the gentle bouncing that would probably have been a curious new experience for someone who had not, as I had, spent the last one hundred and twenty hours enduring the thrill of some of the Portuguese roads. But in the end I tried to reassure her with obviously fake gravity:

'That was excellent! I must go and congratulate senhor Palma. And you too. That was, indeed, superb.'

Then, when I discretely slipped a few notes into the pocket of her orange overall, I asked her what her name was.

'Itszu,' is what I heard.

'Pardon?' Could she possibly be Japanese after all? Or from somewhere else in the Far East? 'Pardon?'

Then, enunciating more clearly and lowering her voice as though telling me a secret, she repeated:

'It's Zu.' Then, even more quietly, she added: 'Floripes's daughter.'

XXXIII

'Do you remember when I toyed with the idea of buying or leasing a *monte*[35] in the Alentejo?'

'I do. It was after you came back from Italy. At that time, all you could talk about was the marble in Vila Viçosa. You were going to show the world that it was just as good as Carrara marble.'

'And so it is. At least for the most part. Did you know I was there four or five days ago?'

'Really? In Carrara?'

'No, of course not. In Vila Viçosa.'

'Ah! Were you still looking for marble?'

'Something like that.'

It didn't seem kind or timely to tell my wife at that point that my unfulfilled longing for a *monte* in the Alentejo had been rekindled. Even less to tell her right now that I thought it would be an ideal place for me and Y to go and live for a few months every year. It was too soon to tell her of such plans: everything in its own time; let time take it's course.

'King! Another king!' she exclaimed triumphantly. 'With this new king you don't stand a chance!'

Resigned, I pushed the board away, while she tallied her victories:

'Out of four games, you only won once.'

We had brought the little card-table out onto the veranda. For the past three days, in the evening, we had gone through the same ritual. But it was only the day before that she had made the comment in a tone not so much sardonic as diagnostic: 'You're staying in rather a lot.' What harm was there in 'rehearsing' for a few days, with a head-start of ten or fifteen years, the kind of couple we might have become if I hadn't met Y?

I still had no news of her, of course, nor was there any hope of getting any. In the meantime, the anxiety of the first few hours and the frenzy of my thoughts had gradually been replaced by a strange phase of almost passive acceptance or numb expectancy. This was probably caused in part by the mild sedative I took every day in the morning and at night (half a tablet each time) and also by not exactly the tedious routine of our early evenings, but rather the soothing effect of the 'conversations' I could see myself, with an almost hallucinatory clarity, *perhaps* having with my wife sooner or later.

All I had to do was to bring up the subject of Y, trying just to describe her without identifying her, and my perceptive paediatrician would slap her forehead and exclaim:

'Oh, I know! You mean that little girl's mother...? That child I looked after? The one who lives near Sintra?'

'Yes, that's the one,' I'd confess, like I did on that other distant afternoon, in the *pastelaria* in the Calçada da Estrela, about Lídia-alias-Laurentina, but this time I wouldn't feel the slightest shame or the slightest regret, but instead, the modest pride of a veteran who is still able to collect enviable trophies. Not that I expected hearty congratulations from my wife... All I needed was a flicker of understanding – the kind of understanding that certain amazing feats occasionally demand – to then tell her everything or, if not everything, at least the why and wherefore of my present gloom. I would even show her – why not? – the piece of paper I'd received over a week before; and then perhaps, with her inflexible logic, my wife would indeed be able to help me *see* what I wanted to see in that piece of paper whenever I looked at it:

'Look, here... See, there's nothing to be alarmed about. "Do not worry", she says here. A little further on, she says again, "I swear, nothing to worry about". So it must be something unexpected but not necessarily serious. Besides, whatever it was, it didn't stop her from going into Lisbon specifically to do all she could to try and find you. That was very thoughtful of her. You're the one who started rushing about in a panic, literally, dashing off to the Algarve and then to the Alentejo. When all is said and done, all you wanted was to punish yourself in some absurd way for not having spoken to her. Look at it this way: all that stopped you from speaking to her were a few technical problems...'

Oh, it would do me such a lot of good to hear her talk like that, so sensibly, in the considered voice of Science and Reason, as though cheering up one of her young patients, or at least a father, when discussing the result of an X-ray or some other obscure test! So why didn't I start telling her about Y? Was I afraid of hurting her? Was I worried that she might still be a little emotionally attached to me in spite of our convenient, long-standing agreement to lead physically separate lives? Or was I instead deeply afraid at the thought that I no longer mattered to her, even emotionally? Or else was it simply that I was epidermically scared of the icy scorn she so often poured over me?

But during the slow unfolding of those evening games of draughts, I could picture other, more nebulous scenes – I don't know whether before or behind my very eyes. This one, for example: that it was my wife who suddenly started telling me she was in love with a Mr X (why not Y?); that the man had disappeared into thin air under such and such circumstances: she therefore wanted to know what I – as a friend – thought about the last note he left for her... Although I invariably 'saw' Mr X (or Y) as having the ruddy face of the Canadian psychologist who was around towards the end of the International Year of the Child, and although the mere fact of 'seeing' him filled me with amused sympathy and all the goodwill in this world and the next, the truth is that I didn't 'see' *me* or 'hear' *me* saying anything at all to my wife. So much so that I kept pinching myself *in mente* at the same time as goading myself again *in mente*, more or less as follows: 'Come on, you fool! Speak, you cretin! Prove once and for all that you know how to behave like a civilized husband!' That would be the day! Mum's the word!

With my head crowded with ideas such as these, it was hardly surprising that I kept losing at draughts.

'As long as you don't mind cold meats and scrambled eggs,' my wife had said, after I'd told her I intended to stay at home that night too. As it was Sunday, we were deprived of Sofia's usual culinary assistance, which was no problem as far as my wife was concerned, especially as she was heroically persevering in her simple diet of yoghurt and apples. 'But if you'd rather go to a restaurant...'

'No, no, I'm quite happy with cold meats.'

There was no hurry either: before having anything to eat, I wanted to watch the news.

That's right: another visible change in my habits was not only to have succumbed to the weakness of buying all the morning papers, but also to have sunk so low that I was now watching the news on television with religious discipline; all this, as may be obvious, was a kind of personal exorcism so that I would *not* find out in the newspapers or on the television – fingers crossed, touch wood, hope for the best! – about any foreigners residing in Portugal who'd been involved in an accident or in any of the more spectacular disasters that were happening throughout the world. I even felt – how childish and morbid of me! – that such horrendous events would only occur if I didn't keep myself abreast of all the other calamities.

Such as the ones on the news that night, and which were no laughing matter: first, there was a grey-haired, puffed-up politician (ugh, what a boor!) tritely extolling the dignity of the State, disgracefully tripping up every three sentences or so over the agreements of predicates and their subjects; then, sucking on the shortest, stubbiest pipe ever, it was the turn of a bigwig from the Finance Ministry, looking much like a warmed-up Salazar, denouncing the insanity and lack of patriotic feeling in those who think life is nothing but one long party; a little later, an authority from Public Works or the Ministry of Social Equipment was promising that by 1990 we would have many millions of centimetres more motorway. In the meantime, the sixty-four radiant teeth of the duty newsreader had made radiant appearances to radiantly announce the news of renewed slaughter in Chad, Lebanon, Iran, Iraq, South Africa and various Central American countries. When expecting to be shown unradiant pictures from some or all of these countries, idyllic scenes from the Minho would appear instead, touched up with Robbialac,[36] showing the *Tour du Portugal à bicyclette*. At that point, through whatever meaningful association of ideas, it was the turn of a civilian of military bearing, wearing a striped suit, striped shirt and striped tie who had the audacity to draw the line at the possibility of shortening military service in the near future. As there was an apparent lack of other equally exciting news, there followed another generous batch of short interviews: one with the learned Speedy Gonzalez, boldly predicting the imminent victory of the Portuguese over the Castilians in the battle of Aljubarrota; another with an outraged, genteel woman with dark shadows under her eyes (oh, I could have sworn I'd seen those lips before, in a softer and less puritanical pose) taking an arrogant stance against the possible decriminalization of abortion; another, with a high-ranking detective inspector who joyfully announced – after admitting that there's (*sic*) already been more bank robberies during the first half of this year than in the whole of the past year – that an important network of currency trafficking, in which members of the diplomatic corps accredited to Lisbon were allegedly implicated, had been discovered and was about to be dismantled; and finally, ye gods in heaven!, there was an interview with the genial Vana and her three girlfriends, on the subject of their joint exhibition, but Vana alone took the opportunity of twittering to the whole country, in six seconds flat, about the tapestries made by all four of them. ('The novelty lies in the technique, and I can assure you of that'). To finish it all off, there were yet more variegated pictures of the Minho and the *Tour du Portugal à bicyclette*; and this time, there was only the occasional reappearance of the newsreader's radiant teeth, now drastically reduced in number to conform with regulation issue. Finally, there followed the usual guesstimates of the weather forecast: continuing hot weather; clear skies; slight drop in temperature at night; morning mists north of Cabo Carvoeiro; otherwise, no change.

Fortunately, it was only when the news faded away (indeed, how could I miss such a precious radioscopy of Portugal during this first half of the 1980s?) that the phone started to ring faintly from the other side of the house.

It was you. Good timing, you. Ringing up to enquire about 'us'. Had we had our holiday. Oh, not yet? When would we be going away? Nothing planned? Probably best that way: holidays in August were usually a bore.

'Was yours?' I asked.

'No, not mine. Mine was wonderful. It was the exception to the rule. It was so good that it didn't matter about the overcrowding and the temperature. Overcrowding, from the tourists. The temperature, scorching…'

I realized that you must be alone at home; or at least that your paediatrician was not stuck to your side. Mine, on the other hand, was prowling around somewhere.

'Yes, well… Your husband told me you were in the south of Spain.'

'That's right: in Venice. It was fascinating, in spite of the heat.'

'Did you only stay in Seville?'

'Yes, only in Venice. It was far too good. Now it's going to be really hard for him and for me not to be together twenty-four hours a day.'

'I'm sure. I can understand that very well.'

In a flash, I could clearly see (wasn't I imaginative, these days?) you and your friend walking through the *calli* and the *campi* that were off the beaten track, only going late at the night to the Piazza di San Marco or the Piazzetta to avoid embarrassing compatriots who might have known him or known you and your husband, and then returning, romantically entwined, first down the Mercerie and the Calle Larga, then through the intricate maze of dark alleys, steps, bridges and tunnels, all the way to the discreet little hotel, conveniently far from the town centre, where finally, thankfully, you would have been heedless enough to share a room *con letto matrimoniale*. Unbearably hot during the day, the *stanza* would include the inevitable window with its wrought-iron balcony, or even narrow veranda, overlooking the tepid darkness of one of the more isolated canals, the incessant whispering of the water lapping against wooden stakes, the bilge of a disused gondola, the stonework of a flight of steps or a crumbling wall. The two of you may never again nod off, sleep and wake up to the sound of that music which is both enchanted and enchanting in its simplicity, its essence and its primitiveness; but you will never again be able to be together any more, be it where it may – in bed, on the beach, in an armchair, a pine forest, a bench, on the floor – without the sound of that music secretly awakening the rhythms of passion and desire that keep you two together.

'Did you receive the poems I sent you? They weren't even poems: just a bunch of verses…?'

'Yes, I did. I enjoyed them very much. You have no idea.'

The strangest part of speaking to you and imagining you in Venice (lucky for your friend, *beato lui*!) was that, with magical precision, I could *see* the outline of your clinging jeans; but instead of your face, all I could see was the almost oriental face of Zu, or Itszu. By the way (merely out of professional interest): what would Itszu be like dressed in equally tight jeans? That was one of the many mysteries that the ample overall she wore had not allowed me to explore.

It was only after your phone call, when I was telling my wife about how I'd met Zu again, that I asked my wife if she still remembered Floripes's daughter.

'Very much so. She had these eyes… You even used to call her Chinky. I used to refer to her as Little China Girl…'

'You've always been kinder than me.'

'I remember how you used to tell me that you suspected that Floripes had gone off with one of those Chinese men that used to sell ties in the streets of Lisbon…'

'They've all gone now.'

'Yes, they have. Or else they're the same ones who started opening restaurants all over the place.'

Chinky! No, it wasn't that name that jerked my memory but, rather, Little China Girl… Suddenly I remembered the little girl – she must have been nine or ten – skipping along by her mother's side, one foot over the other, on the edge between the pavement and one of the flower-beds on the Praça. And, when her mother had asked my permission to show her the atelier, how well I remember her fright, her panic, her terror, her near-hysteria when she saw the monsters I was working on!

But, on Wednesday, after having identified herself to me in Palminha's barber-shop, she had found an opportunity in which to tell me, in a whisper, of her unusual aspirations:

'Oh, how I'd like to "poise" for you one day, Mestre!... I'd really love to have one of your drawings! Even if it was just the one...'

'Really? We'll have do something about it then, won't we?'

To make up for the cold meats (which were not only shrivelled up but congealed as well), I entertained myself afterwards by flicking through a picture-book of Egon Schiele's work and listening to some excerpts from Carl Orff's *Aphrodite's Triumph*. It was a little after ten at night when my wife went up to her bedroom. Before going, she asked me (how many years since she'd last bothered?) if there was anything I needed. It would have been unnecessarily cruel to tell her the one thing I really needed was to be left alone.

I picked up a note pad and found myself scribbling down a few snatches of sentences: 'She comes in, she lies down: there are times when these two actions happen in such quick succession...'; 'Her eyes were huge, exceedingly well shaped, more than green, more than blue...'; 'Beauty; sensuality; sensitivity; intelligence...'; 'The white shawl is her unfailing attire during our intimate ritual on winter days...'

At the same time, I was thinking that my body has always had a short memory. Of other bodies, once they've gone, it remembers their perfidy, not their perfection, the moments of explosion rather than the hours of fulfilment. But with Y everything was happening differently: I was choked at the thought of her spontaneous gestures, made in almost slow-motion; not only my throat, but my every pore would suddenly constrict at the unexpected recollection of the lingering games her fingers played on my skin, the enthralling, circuitous wanderings of her mouth over my body, the many deep marks her skin had left all over mine, inside as well as out. For the first time ever, I could feel my body secretly groaning, howling in silence, longing desperately for someone else's body.

I switched the television back on: it was probably time for the last news of the day. It was later than that: the news was nearly over.

They were just running through the summaries again, repeating the gems spoken – grammatical mistakes and all – by the semi-head or vice-head of the detective force; but they cautiously added to his words those of a spokesman for the Ministry of Foreign Affairs (oh, oh, it was that man at the Aztecs' first reception who 'represented' Diplomacy) regarding the alleged involvement of members of the diplomatic corps in currency trafficking: he said it would be premature right now, at this stage of the investigations, to take an official stance regarding this matter. Really? Either I was very much mistaken or *mi caro consejero* was very much part of the gang.

The phone rang again, this time before the end of the news. It was the international service notifying me there would be a call for me from London the next day, after two p.m. That's all I needed! It would probably be my *marchand*, that hyperactive, pain in the neck of a Steiner who was always gadding about Europe, plaguing me for I don't know which overdue pieces!

Unless... No; better not to even think it; it would be too good to be true.

XXXIV

London? But why London? London had never been mentioned when we'd been planning our holidays and travels. Switzerland had; so had the Algarve. Ah! An urgent case... With whose partner...? Yes. Yes, I see; partner of... and Vicky's godfather. To the heart? They did a bypass? But everything's OK now? In Surrey, with Vicky? With her godfather's wife? Of course, to keep her company...

The connection was so bad that I had to keep repeating almost everything that Y said so that it could make sense. Everything? No, only later would she tell me everything. And after all that, the most important bit: she was coming back Thursday night, only for a few days, but on Friday, dead on twelve o'clock, she would come to the atelier. That's right, Friday; Saturday as well, and Sunday too. Only if I wanted her to, that is. (Of course I wanted her to!)

'If you only knew how much I need you!'

These words, or similar ones, were repeated several times on both ends of the line.

My wife had made an excellent decision in going to Lisbon first thing in the morning; the absence of Sofia was also most opportune: she had plodded off after giving me my lunch. Thus, at 14.42 GMT, I had been able to answer the phone in the quiet of an underwater grave. I felt as giddy as if I'd just come up from a deepwater dive, I felt as comforted as if I'd just received some holy sacrament; these two feelings still mingled inside me half an hour later, as I drove down the motorway towards Lisbon. And in this frame of mind, I was overcome by a somewhat idiotic desire to do a whole string of good deeds. I would go and visit my mother that very afternoon.

But on the way there, and because Rucha had left an irritating hangnail on one of my nails, I first of all went over to Palminha's shining grotto. A slight setback: it was still closed. Of course it was: it only opened again at four o'clock, and it was still barely half past three.

I was just about to leave when I saw Zu coming towards me on the opposite pavement, walking very slowly, head high, eating an ice-cream. She was wearing a loose yellow dress, which vaguely resembled a kimono and, from the fingers of her left hand, she was swinging a small leather bag. If Nyasa had seen her last week in Palma's shop and then come across her in the light of day on this almost deserted avenida, he might have hastily come to the conclusion that, although she was still a good sport, it would not be beyond her, sooner or later, to turn into a show-off. I would say, instead, that all she wanted to achieve by walking with her head held high like that, was to conveniently distance herself from the possible advances of three or four louts in shirtsleeves, very much the local Fittipaldis, with their lust on full throttle, leaning lazily against the door of a car showroom and making loud and bawdy remarks about the way she was sucking her ice-cream.

'Zu!' I shouted, hooting to help her locate the four-wheeled Rossinante who was coming to her rescue with her unexpected knight-errant. This could turn out to be my first good deed of the day.

'Oh, Mestre, you might not believe this, but I've been thinking of you all morning.'

In a succession of quick dashes, she'd run across the avenida, walked nimbly round the back of the car, and was now leaning over through the right-hand car window. But in her haste, her ice-cream cone had split in her fingers, dripping chocolate and vanilla all over a conspicuous area of her yellow dress, between her waist and her chest.

'Damn! It would happen with this dress!' Two tiny, sorrowful tears broke through the straining dams of both her eyes.

'Come on in... Let's see if the *pastelaria* up there can take that off with warm water.'

I don't know how it happened, but twenty minutes later we had firmly agreed that, the following day, Zu would come to the atelier at lunch time to 'poise' for me, as she was fond of saying. Also, after overcoming her feeble protestations that were a mere formality, she had stuffed a cheque signed by me into her handbag, in a more or less symbolic gesture towards getting her a new dress. The one she was wearing had to go to the dry-cleaner's: then we'd see.

'Oh, Mestre, thank you so much... I always knew you were a darling!'

She even tried to brush the palm of my hand with the kind of tiny, soft, silent, fleeting kiss that one could imagine a geisha giving.

The trouble with good deeds is that they are very quick to self-perpetuate: the single one I had wanted to perform for Zu – rescuing her from being assaulted by the Fittipaldis – had engendered two more. What further opportunities for the exercise of my noble intentions did the afternoon hold in store for me?

The model nursing-home to which my mother had withdrawn two years ago was exactly as I'd imagined it, a blend of spa residence and country hospital, suitably transferred to the vicinities of Avenida de Roma. I found a withered, anxious-looking, seventy-year-old woman on my side of the white reception desk, trying with great difficulty to extract two obstinate knitting-needles stuck at the bottom of her knitting-bag. I didn't have time to ask myself whether she was a resident or a member of staff, for as soon as she saw me, she completely lost interest in the recalcitrant needles, and addressed me as her doctor:

'Have you seen my daughter-in-law anywhere, doctor? She was due here at three o'clock, and now it's nearly half past four! I don't even know whether I should wait here or if I'd be better off going back to my room. You can tell me what to do, you're the doctor. The same thing happened last week: she said yes, she'd come and see me, then she didn't come and, like a fool, I waited for her up in my room all afternoon. I never did like liars very much! You know very well, doctor, that it's not because of what she's done to my son that I'm saying this. It's just that she's a liar! That's all. I don't say a word about any of the other business. I know my son doesn't like it, so that's that. I know they put me in here to stop me seeing what was going on, and no one will ever make me believe otherwise.'

She took a deep breath. She looked very smart, in a sober dark-grey dress with white collar and cuffs, half way between a maid's uniform and the discreet habit of a lay sister; she smelled endearingly of lavender; she clutched my sleeve with her small, arthritic hand; there was no point in my trying to tell her she must be mistaking me for someone else, because she then stood on tiptoes to make it easier for me to hear the rest of her disclosures:

'Would you believe it, doctor... But this is for your ears only, mind... Would you believe it that she's run away from home three times now? She's mad. Completely mad. And my son always goes and brings her back. Then she's very shrewd, when he drags her into the house, she pretends she doesn't want to come in, she's probably afraid I might say what I think. As though I'd go and say anything! Apart from anything else, I wouldn't want to trouble my son. And as for him, poor thing, he just tries to make a big joke of it all, calling her his "little tearaway"... Just like that: "Get in, you little tearaway... You're worse than a child!" But with such sadness deep down, that only I can tell! She comes across as quite insipid, but she's a shrewd liar. I never did understand what my son saw in her... God forgive me, and you too, doctor, but sometimes I think the girl's forever on heat!'

Even these last few words were uttered with an infinite sadness.

In the meantime, a storm-door flew open and an old man with rosy cheeks and a mane of snowy-white hair came up to us; in his deep baritone voice, he announced triumphantly:

'Two more! I've painted two more pictures this morning: one marine and one still-life. The marine is delightful. It even makes you feel like going to the seaside. If you like, I'd be delighted, you can come up to my rooms and see them...'

And off he goes, obviously delighted with the message he's just given us, when through the same storm-door now emerges a young woman (who has probably never been truly young), with a solid and authoritarian homeliness that is generally only found in certain so-called good families and who, to all intents and purposes, seems to be looking for the buoyant artist:

'Senhor Pulido! Senhor Pulido! The carpet in your bedroom is all covered in paint again! The poor maids are at their wits' end!'

Senhor Pulido did not hear her, having already escaped onto the landing next to the reception room. Only then did the bristly, inquisitorial, homely young woman, who had never been truly young, appear to notice my presence. The poignant, wizened seventy-year-old clutched one of the woman's sleeves with her other hand, and with sadness confided:

'Do you know, dona Mercês, I was just telling the doctor here those things about my daughter-in-law.'

'What's this all about?' dona Mercês asks indignantly, with the stentorian voice of someone speaking to the deaf. 'Can't you see that this gentleman is not the doctor? It's not even the right day of the week for the doctor to be here.'

The old woman let go of both our arms, stepped back and looked first at dona Mercês, then at me:

'Oh, isn't he? But he looked just like him!' Then, picking up her bag with the unmoveable knitting-needles from near the counter, she added: 'You're right. It isn't him. That's funny! He looked just like the doctor just now.'

Only then did I introduce myself to dona Mercês and ask about seeing my mother. Dona Mercês's homeliness abated somewhat, her manner improved greatly; but it was nevertheless with some trepidation that she asked me:

'Did you tell her you were coming? I'm sure you know what your mother's like far better than I do. She's a real lady. In all things. But she does have her ways.... And she's fiercely protective of her peace and quiet and all her creature comforts... She even expects her own daughter to let her know when she's coming. Her daughter! How silly of me! I mean your sister... I'm so sorry but I wasn't making the connection between the two of you... Unless I'm much mistaken, you don't look very much like each other.'

'No, we don't.'

'But I do know who you are... Who doesn't? Your mother talks a lot about you. Always with great affection. And a lot of pride. She admires you very much. It's such a pleasure to listen to her! I have never had the honour of meeting you when you've been here before.'

'No, you haven't.'

'Now, if you wouldn't mind, please step into this little waiting-room, and I'll order you some coffee, just while I go and speak to your mother to tell her you're here and see if there's anything she needs first. She'll want to straighten her hair (she still takes such good care of that lovely hair of hers!) and she'll probably want to change her clothes. I'm not saying this because she's your mother, but to tell the truth we don't have anyone else here who is quite as *soignée*... After all, we do have a little bit of everything here. Just like abroad... This equality thing is all very well, and of course I'm not against it, not at all, but there are always some who come from the top and others who cannot get up from the bottom... Here, we cannot help but reflect this, starting with the different kinds of rooms available. Your mother's, as I'm sure you've noticed, if only by how much they cost, are certainly the best in the whole house. But I'm not too pleased with this little waiting-room. We've already decided to have the walls painted a softer shade, come October... Do sit down, do sit down. Please sit down. And please forgive the muddle with that woman on your way in just now. She's not a bad sort, far from it, but her atherosclerosis is quite advanced and the poor thing, well, she's not one of those who comes from the top... Now, then, please sit down. I'll tell them to bring you some coffee straightaway.'

'Please don't trouble yourself. Thank you very much, anyway, but I'd rather not have any coffee.'

'As you wish. But please make yourself at home. Really. See you in a tick.'

Phew, what a character! She spoke like a machine-gun. Was she the poor relation of some wealthy family? Or even a noble family, unless the signet ring glinting on one of her fingers was borrowed and worn out of sheer snobbery? And what exactly was her job here? Owner, manager, secretary, director or housekeeper? Whatever she was, she couldn't help being like this little waiting-room that wasn't to her taste – and that, however soft its new shade, would never look like anything other than a morbid chapel of rest.

But what was really on my mind, after hearing the beautiful baritone of senhor Pulido's voice, was the fact that I had completely forgotten to bring my mother a present, such as a new recording of some opera or, at least, a selection of favourite arias.

A few minutes later, with all the majesty of the great soprano that she never became (because of her marriage to my father? because of having me?), my mother made her entrance, followed by dona Mercês. When I first saw her, my heart missed a beat: when Y grows old, she could end up looking just like her. Or else, in her old age, my mother's features were becoming strangely softer, leading to this unexpected comparison, this aberrant impression.

'Figlio!' she exclaimed.

Ah! She would go to her grave without losing the accent of the little girl born in Bergamo in 1905 – who, some twenty years later in Genoa, met a romantic second lieutenant in the great and glorious Portuguese navy. As a child, what amazed me most was the fact that she couldn't even pronounce my name properly. How about Y? Would she ever be able to pronounce my name properly? All because of the damned nasal diphthong at the end of my name, which caused many an obstacle, in the beginning, to the relative 'internationalization' of what I call 'my pieces'. (As for Vana, she already calls hers: 'My work'.)

'You're looking very well, Mother!'

'Do you think so? Really?' There was a note of something like pleading in her voice, which, as far as I could remember, had never been known to plead before. She turned a little towards dona Mercês who was blissfully witnessing the scene: 'Only because I've known since this morning that my *figlio* was coming to see me this afternoon. Isn't that right, dona Mercês? Isn't that what I said earlier on? I even changed my dress after lunch.'

She was wearing a navy-blue linen suit which emphasized the bluish whiteness of her hair and – it was hard to tell which – the green or the blue of her eyes. She moved now with a stiff and stately dignity.

'I know you've been talking to dona Mercês. She's my guardian angel, in here, this lady is... Outside, it's you... And your wife, of course.' There was the slightest hesitation before she added drily: 'And your sister. Your sister too.'

'So many angels, Mother!'

'Thank goodness. And that's not to mention those who are in heaven. Those who have already gone to heaven. You know who I mean...' She rested her hand lightly on one of my shoulders, then on the other, in a vague gesture that was half way between a caress and a blessing; 'They loved you very much. They both did.'

It was the first time that she'd referred so clearly to both my father and my stepfather in the same breath. I was completely dumbfounded: everything was going contrary to what I'd expected. And once dona Mercês had left us alone, there were even more reasons to be amazed: it was like a bolt from the blue, not one that knocked me over, but one that lifted me higher and higher.

Leaning on my arm with a gentleness and trust that I'd never have thought her capable of, my mother asked me:

'Would you mind coming upstairs with me? I'd like to show you some things you haven't seen yet: I've moved things around since your last visit...'

'Since my last visit? But, Mother, I...'

When I saw the complete certainty that was written all over her face, how could I possibly tell her that I had never once been to see her there?

'What is it, *figlio*?'

'Nothing, Mother.'

'If you don't have time... I understand.'

'No, it's not that. Let's go.'

Was she deceiving me? Was she deceiving herself? Or did she honestly think I'd been before? I needed to be clear on that, but it didn't look as though it would be an easy thing to ascertain.

The rooms she occupied were on the first floor of the building: a reasonably large bedroom, with an adjoining private bathroom, and a small, crowded living-room as one went in. I had already been told by my wife that the terms of her tenancy allowed her to bring to this 'home' some of her own furniture, as well as personal belongings, of course, and which she would have been loathe to leave behind. This gave me the feeling that I was indeed familiar with everything in there – from the *chaise longue*, the pier-glass and the D. José chairs that cluttered the living-room, to the D. Maria bed and dresser that dominated the bedroom – and for a moment I almost thought she was right, and that I had been there before. But I hadn't; I knew perfectly well that it was just a momentary illusion.

'You've seen this record player already... It's the one your wife gave me for Easter. It's much easier to manage than the other one, the one I brought from home. Sitting over here' (she pointed to the *chaise longue*) 'I have listened to all of Verdi's operas again. As far as I'm concerned, he's still the greatest.' Then, walking over to another corner of the room, she continued: 'This bookcase is new. New in here. You do remember it, don't you?'

It was an English polished-walnut bookcase, that Tá had always said belonged to my father, dating back to his bachelor days; it was now filled with soberly bound books from the beginning of the century, mostly by Italian authors: D'Annunzio, Serao, Fogazzaro, Pascoli, Verga.

'This is my little corner of Italy.' As I picked up a book by D'Annunzio, she said: 'Did you know I spoke a couple of times with Duse – Eleanora Duse. And I saw D'Annunzio, I'm not sure how many times, but that was always from a distance, in Milan, Venice, Bergamo, Lake Garda...' Why was my mother only now telling me these things? Still leaning on my arm, she then led me towards the pier-glass, saying: 'Last time, I didn't have this portrait here... Nor that photograph.'

She pointed to a portrait of my father in his white uniform, standing next to what must have been the gate to the old arsenal, and a photographic reproduction, that I didn't even know existed, of my sculpture, *La Famille*.

'Where did you get that, Mother?'

'It's a secret. I cannot possibly tell you.'

She went on talking and smiling with a gentleness that was almost frightening, especially as I'd always known her to be either distant or unfriendly, lost in the inaccessible backstage scenery of the operas she had never been allowed to sing.

'You have to tell me, Mother. I lost track of this sculpture years ago.'

'I can't, *figlio*. There are other things I know too...' With the air of a sorceress or a fortune-teller, she carefully pulled me down next her, onto the *chaise longue* where she had just sat down: 'I know of a very beautiful woman, a very strange woman, whom you're very fond of right now... It's your life, *figlio*. But I would ask you one thing: try not to hurt your wife.' Then, brushing my forehead with a kiss, she added: 'That's all. I shan't say another word on the subject.'

She then went into the bedroom to fetch an old photograph album: there were photos of her, before she got married; of her with my father; of the two of them with me. No; when she was young, she looked nothing like Y at the same age.

'I know I've never shown you these photographs. I'm going to leave them to you. But for now... I want them here with me. I spend hours and hours looking at them.'

After a while, we went down to the ground floor for tea. At another table, senhor Pulido was enjoying a cold drink and he greeted us boisterously.

'What a buffoon!' my mother muttered between her teeth; and only in the sharpness of that remark did I recognize my mother for the first time that afternoon. However, she did add: 'But he does have rather a nice voice.'

All of a sudden, I felt someone behind me and before I even had time to turn around, two hands covered my eyes, while a twittering voice teased me playfully:

'Guess... Guess who it is.'

Those twitters! Of course, it couldn't be anyone else but Vana. It was beginning to feel like persecution. I was surprised at first when I noticed that she and my mother knew each other, but it wasn't really that surprising; I also realized my mother wasn't too pleased I'd noticed.

'Who has such a beautiful mother, then, you arrogant thing, you? I only found out the other day... But since then we've already had a couple of really interesting chats, you wouldn't believe it! Oh, you're so lucky to have such a darling mother!'

With these and other flattering remarks, Vana ran her fingers through my hair and tugged one of my ears. Only then did I notice the obscure presence, a little behind us, of the wizened old woman with the knitting-needles. I watched her shaking her head, her lips pursed and her eyes sad.

'Oh!' exclaimed Vana. 'How silly of me! I haven't yet introduced you to my mother-in-law...'

'We've already met,' the woman said, without moving or coming forward.

'I was just on my way out,' Vana explained. 'But when I saw the two of you together, I couldn't resist it!' Suddenly, as though unable to hold back any longer, anxiously watching my eyes, she asked: 'Did you see me on television yesterday?'

'Oh, were you on television? I never watch television.'

'Oh, what a shame!'

'I – I saw you,' muttered my mother, separating each word clearly, in the same voice she had just used to qualify senhor Pulido.

But it was my reaction that Vana had wanted. Which is probably why, when it was time to go, she was far less gushing than she'd been when she arrived. In the meantime, her mother-in-law had gone to sit at another table. We overheard Vana telling her crossly:

'Well, Mother, I'll see you next week.'

The old woman replied: 'Goodbye, child. God be with you. Don't get lost on your way home.'

XXXV

It was unbelievable; but there could be no doubt about it: someone must have followed me; or someone knew where I'd be. There: in the 'home' which I'd just left. For the first time ever, the car had not been near the atelier when one of those repulsive pieces of paper had been placed under my windscreen-wiper. It was more elaborate than some of the previous ones ('Beware! He who breeds and foments disgrace will die in disgrace') and, although the handwriting was as rounded as ever, and some of the letters had been pusillanimously left unfinished, it was even more childish than before. This confirmed my belief regarding these messages, that the brain who had thought them up and the hand that had written them did not belong to the same person.

Why deny it? Of course I thought of Vana; but only briefly. I couldn't imagine her having such a warped mind; nor – to be fair – that she had such bad handwriting. And, besides, people who are forever on heat don't usually resort to such flaming tactics.

To hell with the mystery of the pieces of paper! I felt like a man with a new heart, as though it was I (God preserve me!) who had undergone the bypass operation. I mustn't exaggerate: who at least had a pacemaker fitted... And only then did I remember a stupid dream I'd had the night before.

I'm in my wife's consulting room where I haven't actually set foot for I don't know how many years. Floripes opens the door, all dressed in white. (A receptionist, no less! Holidays, my foot: what she wanted was to go up in the world...) But what possessed my wife (or was it Floripes?) to bring over the divan from my atelier? 'Oh, if that divan could speak!' And Floripes lets out an insolent burst of laughter. But my wife's assistant stands up suddenly from behind the ottoman (that's not an ottoman at all, that's the divan from my atelier), he drops an armful of books and starts kicking them about, and there he is, standing in front of me, shaking me by the shoulders, shrieking: 'The poor aunts! The doctor's poor, poor aunts! It's them I feel sorry for!'

Oh, to hell with dreams! I should be savouring Y's phone call and the news of her being in Lisbon in four days' time (less than four) and, on top of that, there's this suffused, almost eerie feeling of well-being I've had ever since meeting up with my mother again. I remember as a teenager having read – I could swear it was by a Brazilian author – something along the lines of: the existence of mothers is a serious matter. Mine had always seemed like the past that I wanted to renounce. But, that afternoon, I came to realize for the first time that she could also become the possible image of a conceivable future: in another twenty years, perhaps less, I too would be confined to 'my little corner of Italy', not the one of the 1910s or 1920s as in her case, but the one of the 1970s, obviously, one equally condemned to sink into oblivion with whoever had experienced it.

But why talk about problematic, more or less distant, futures? My real future was going to happen next Friday: I will expect Y, spot on twelve o'clock; I will take her in my arms with the same delight as always; I will feel her feet wriggle loose from her shoes as usual, with the pressure of one heel against the other; and finally, we will both be exactly the same height.

Oh! To think there were another four days to go! How could I cross that arid succession of deserts that were Tuesday, Wednesday and Thursday, without noticing them too much? And to think that just a few hours before I had stupidly given in to Zu's inane desire to 'poise' for me! At the time, it had seemed like as good a way as any, or perhaps better than any, of filling at least two of the ninety or so hours that separated me from Y. Now, instead, as I drove along the Avenida de Roma (oh, the coarseness of Lisbon toponyms: fancy naming such a dreary thoroughfare after Rome!), it seemed to me a gratuitous sacrifice, not to say a useless sacrilege, to spend around two hours the following day with someone else, in a space that, through some kind of divine right, now actually belonged to Y alone. This might sound ridiculous. But why should I care about being ridiculous?

'Poise' for me! There is no way of removing ideas of such sweet innocence from little heads like Zu's... And it was precisely Zu's little head that I was going to attempt to draw with practised sufferance the following day and, afterwards, seeing it gave her so much pleasure, I would offer her one of my most kitsch and conventional drawings.

One important thing while on the subject: I mustn't forget that I promised I would fetch her first, at two o'clock, not at Palm's

Hairdresser's, but at the door of the actual *pastelaria* where all this had been arranged. 'It's better here,' Zu had told me. 'To stop people from talking. Or for me to have to give any explanations. It will draw less attention…'

Having said that, she drew quite a bit of attention to herself by turning up at ten past two, wearing a relatively loose blouse and rather tight trousers in flaming tones of shocking-pink, running all the way up from the depths of Palminha's chrome-sparkling grotto.

'You will forgive me, won't you? A last-minute client …'

'Don't worry. Get your breath back. I have only just got here myself.' (That wasn't quite true: I'd been there since before two o'clock.)

'Oh, it's so annoying! I'd even asked senhor Palma to let me off ten minutes earlier. It's the only way I could have had a sandwich and a coffee in there.' She pointed to the *pastelaria*. She had come straight into the car. 'And you, Mestre? Have you had lunch?'

'More or less. But I'd be delighted to keep you company while you have something.'

A cloud seemed to fall over her narrow, slanted eyes.

'No, no. There's no need,' she answered, almost in a sulk. Then, at once, with her eyes all clear again, she added: 'May I ask you something? Why won't you use the *tu* form when you speak to me, Mestre? That's what you used to do…'

'The *tu* form, no less? If it's convenient, we'll see later.'

'Whatever next! It'll be convenient enough if you give it a try… But I can tell you don't really want to, Mestre. See if you can say to me: "Come and have something to eat in my atelier", using the *tu* form.'

'Huh?'

'What a good idea.' Now, instead of being sulky, she was being flirtatiously coy. 'I know you always have some really nice things up there. I know full well you do! Perhaps you think I wouldn't know how to appreciate them properly… Or do you believe I'm not worth it?'

I'd already switched the engine on. I drove off down the Avenida, and all I said was:

'Don't be so daft, you.'

'See? See? You were incapable of using the *tu* form with me.' But this time her voice held the delighted tremolo of a small victory.

Fifteen minutes later we were both in the atelier, rummaging around the fridge and the larder, seeing what was there and setting aside what could still be eaten. I even found myself apologizing.

'There's hardly anything here. I haven't been here for a couple of weeks...'

'I thought as much...'

'What?'

'You're very lonely. It shows on your face. If you weren't, you wouldn't have agreed so easily to us coming here. It's the best time for me too. While my mother is still away on holidays.'

'How funny! I dreamt about her two nights ago.'

'About my mother?!' exclaimed Zu, somewhat taken aback, not to say horrified. 'I hardly ever dream. But I've never dreamt about her, that's for sure!'

She then talked about the inconvenience for her of having to take the coach back to Peniche every evening after seven; and having to come back into Lisbon again every day by coach, before seven in the morning.

'But that's the way I want it. And it's only because of the little girl. I don't even know why. In fact the only time I see her is when she's asleep. Not counting Saturdays and Sundays, of course.'

In the meantime we had come to the conclusion that the only things left that were fit to eat were two packets of cream crackers, four triangles of processed cheese, a packet of ham, one tin of pâté, one of foie-gras and a small jar of caviar. There was some left-over butter, but that had already gone rancid: into the bin with it. As for drinks, there were a few beers, some mineral water, a half-empty bottle of whisky and another bottle, luxury of luxuries, of genuine champagne, casually left more than a fortnight ago on the bottom shelf of the fridge.

'That's heaps!' concluded Zu. 'There's more than enough!'

But with great discernment, she chose the foie-gras to start with, spreading it liberally over one of the cream crackers.

'I've tried this once or twice before. It's nothing at all like pâté.'

Before each bite, on an exploratory mission, she stuck out her tongue, which was of a pink more shocking than anything she was wearing. She was a little more choosy when it came to drinks: whisky at that time of day, don't even think of it; beer, not ever, because she always felt it made her smell like a man ('It's all my husband ever drinks'); perhaps if there was some gin and tonic water... But as there wasn't any, not to worry! Unless I wouldn't mind opening the bottle of champagne...

'Of course not.' And while I was popping the cork, I asked: 'By the way, what does your husband do?'

'Sometimes he drives me crazy.'

'No, I don't mean that... What work does he do?'

'I know what you meant... Didn't you know he's in the Navy? He works in Alfeite, in the officers' mess. But I just can't get him to bring me back the sort of things he knows full well I like best. He's always so scared... As though the others don't all help themselves! Starting with the officers... And as if I need him to know what's good!' Then, with a loud smack of her tongue, she added: 'This champagne is really something else! This is what I like! This, or even our own sparkling wine!... But don't go thinking I'm being greedy or anything. Or even less that I'm some kind of pig. I like nice things, that's all. And I believe I have a right to... Washing heads day in, day out! Most of them are quite disgusting... Sometimes I feel like getting my hands stuck right in, giving those brains a good lathering and reducing them to pulp!'

What a fascinating insight into the secret thoughts of a geisha! But all I mentioned was my confusion in having thought at first that she worked at Palminha's as a manicurist.

'I wish! It's cleaner work, if nothing else... And I don't mean to boast, but I'm really quite good at it. Only there isn't a vacancy right now.' She let go of her glass of champagne, she let go of her (third) cream cracker, liberally spread with foie-gras and, full of professional interest, she took hold of my hands: 'Ah, if you like, I'll start taking care of these nails for you myself. Only I couldn't do it at work... But I could come here whenever you needed me. The other day, I didn't like seeing such fine fingers as yours in the hands of that old woman.'

'Rucha? But she's younger than me.'

'Younger? If you say so! But there's no comparison! Women always grow old earlier. And besides... Here, this is one of the things my mother taught me: she said that artists were ageless!' She was still holding on to my hand. 'See? Look at the state that fool Rucha left this nail in!...If we don't have a file, we'll just have to do it like this...' She took my finger in her mouth, moistened it slightly with her tongue, then set to efficiently rubbing the base of my nail between her front teeth: 'Is it or is it not better than it was before? See, as if the old woman could have done that!...'

'How about you...'

'Great! There you go using the *vous* form again.'

'How old are you?'

'How old do you think?'

'I have no idea.'

'I'm twenty-four. But sometimes I think I'm two hundred years old, other times I feel not a day more than ten!'

She proffered these last words with such powerfully captivating conviction that I felt the urge to go and look out of a window to see if she was out there, in her ankle socks, skipping, one foot over the other, following the edge between the pavement and one of the flower-beds on the Praça. Straight after, aged not quite two hundred but at least well into her forties, she mischievously asked me what I was waiting for to open the tub of caviar... Or did I mind?

'It's not that I like it that much... But this doesn't happen every day, and a person has to make the most of it. Afterwards, I'll have just a little piece of cheese. See? It doesn't take much to make me happy... As long as it tastes nice. Oh, this champagne! Do you know, I'm already feeling tiddly?'

A little later, I had to call her to order:

'Right. Let's get this over with so we can get down to work.'

Then I showed her the stool she was to sit on, and asked her to assume a position in which she would be comfortable.

'Like this? Or like this?' She tried half a dozen different poses, then, almost pouting, with her eyes if anything even more tightly closed than before she asked me: 'Could I possibly have another couple of fingers of champagne? One finger...? A thimbleful...?'

'That's up to you,' I said using the *vous* form. She reprimanded me from afar, opening her eyes as wide as possible. I corrected myself: 'You decide [*tu* form]. You're the one who knows what you'll be getting up to with your clients' brains.'

All I heard was the gurgle of the champagne being poured into the glass: she must have filled it to the brim again. With her back to me, she threw it down her throat with relish. Then, sitting back on her stool, she said:

'Do you really want me like this? Wouldn't you prefer the whole trunk?'

Without waiting for an answer, she pulled off her blouse without disturbing a single hair on her head; and she had nothing on between her blouse and her skin. Her two small, firm breasts with their pale areolae and nipples pointing pertly towards the ceiling, were like tiny prows of miniature ships thrusting against minuscule waves.

On the other hand, they were also a curious blend between the rounded bulkiness of two small apples and the fleshy petulance of two juicy pears. They were more odd than pretty; less attractive than provocative; in any case, they were probably more excited than exciting. They vibrated slightly, intermittently, as though activated by a small, autonomous engine, while the rest of her trunk remained motionless.

While she was taking off her blouse, she'd asked me:

'This is what all models do, isn't it?'

'It is,' I replied. Then I added: 'More or less. Now keep still. Keep still and be quiet. Let's see what I can do.'

I couldn't do anything. Not a thing.

A few sheets of paper from the first pad that came to hand ended up in the bin. Then I tried a few sheets of pasteboard: they ended up in the same place. In the end, all I drew, just for fun, but with great technical accuracy, were two small apples topped with a pair of impudent pears.

'You come and see…'

'You're bad. Always using the *vous* form!' Then, seeing the end result of my strenuous effort, she added: 'You're awful! You've been making fun of me all this time.'

'Not at all. I'm just having one of my off-days. We'll have to leave it for some other time.' Ignoring her protests, I tore up what I'd done.

'Oh, dear! That still would have been better than nothing… Some other time? When? Let's make a date now.'

'We shall do no such thing… One of these days, I'll phone you at the shop.' I corrected myself: 'At the salon.'

'Are you sure? Do you promise?'

'I promise.'

'Well, then, the sooner the better. While my mother is still away on holidays.'

I then had to remind her that it was already a quarter to four; that she really ought to hurry up (yes, I'd drop her off by car) if she didn't want to get a dressing-down by Palminha. We were already in the car when she said:

'Do you think I didn't notice? You didn't take me to that other part of your atelier on purpose… to that little nook where you usually entertain your admirers. But I don't care. Rome wasn't built in a day.'

When we took leave of each other between the *pastelaria* and the car showroom, she gave me two kisses that just happened to be aimed at my lips; but, without doubting their likely sweetness, I managed just in time to deflect them onto each of my cheeks instead. As a form of compensation, I put two fingers on her chin in a paternal gesture:

'Behave!'

'Of course I will. I can actually behave quite well even when I'm misbehaving… And, as for being with you, I feel as safe as I would with my own father.'

Shameless hussy! I at once imagined myself, stammering, stuttering and with slanted eyes, selling ties in the street.

After this, I popped into the Lisbon house as usual to see if there was any post; in terms of the unexpected or the unusual, there was a brief letter, written by a semi-illiterate woman living in Rua da Alegria, informing me of the recent demise (why tell me?) of a certain senhor Joaquim Maria dos Santos and asking me to come to see her as soon as possible, at the address she'd written down, as she had something very important to tell me.

Back in Monte Estoril, I was going to ask my wife if she had the faintest idea who this senhor Santos could be, but the matter completely escaped my mind when, as soon as I got in, my wife gave me this other message:

'There was a call for you from London.'

'From London? For me? Ah! Steiner… Was it Steiner? Was it from him? What did he have to say?'

'No. It didn't sound like Steiner. Or else his voice is very weak. He was quite unrecognizable. But, if it was Steiner, he left a message saying he would ring back tomorrow morning after two. I even told him it was all right to phone in the morning.' She took off her glasses, closed the file she had on the table and rose heavily from her chair. 'By the way: I also have to go to Lisbon early tomorrow morning.'

XXXVI

'I can actually behave quite well even when I'm misbehaving.'

I wake up suddenly hearing these words. But it isn't Zu saying them: it's you, all wrapped up in your friend's embrace, posing for posterity. You're both standing next to a moderately dilapidated palace, with an impressive spiralling stairway abutting its façade. I know this palace is in Venice although I can't place it right now, nor can I can I remember its name.

Then, wide awake, I remember other words spoken by Zu during our encounter the day before. The funny thing is, I'm incapable of recalling her face very well: it's you I see, with her voice, wearing her shocking-pink clothes. And suddenly you pull her blouse off over your head and your breasts are blatantly hers. The face I see, however, is still yours.

I put the light on. I am astonished to realize that I can only have been asleep for twenty minutes at the most: it's now four or five minutes to one; it had just gone half past midnight last time I looked at my watch. But my whole body is throbbing with such an urge to stay awake that I know I'm doomed not to get a wink of sleep all night. I do not often suffer from insomnia, but every few months or so, always after a few minutes' sleep, I am overcome with such an appalling and overwhelming inability to sleep that it feels as though I will never be able to sleep again.

Sleep has turned its back on me, but I still try to plead with it, to talk it into not going too far away from me, to come back and tarry a while. I put my bedside light out again. I try to think of nothing at all, of no one, trying to silence and banish into darkness the image of you in Zu's clothes – clothed in Zu's words and blouse, in Zu's semi-nudity. It isn't hard to dispel that image; the trouble is that, in its place, emerges the figure of Y herself, with the consistency of a golden stone covered in foam.

I realize that the prospect of Y's forthcoming phone-call has left me in such a state that I will not be able to go back to sleep tonight. I capitulate to the forces of insomnia. I switch the light back on, as though waving the white flag of surrender.

Soon after, when I put my slippers on (why just then?), I have the strange feeling that it's not me but someone I know, who is actually going through the motions; or at least forcing me to go through them in just this way, at just this speed. I drag my feet across the floor in a manner that has nothing to do with the way I usually walk. I dig into the pocket of my linen jacket, looking for a packet of cigarettes; but my fingers first stumble across the letter from the unknown, semi-illiterate woman living in Rua da Alegria; it is at that precise moment that it comes to me in a flash – perhaps this is what has stopped me from sleeping – that the letter refers to Nyasa: that Nyasa is dead.

Joaquim Maria dos Santos? J. Nyasa was the signature he always scrawled on his scenery, his caricatures, his sketches and his 'serious' paintings with 'more substance'. But who, starting with me, knew for sure whether that J. stood for Joaquim, Jorge, José, Jacinto or João? Hold on a minute: not so fast! There must have been a time when I did actually know his name was Joaquim... Otherwise 'Nyasa, Joaquim Nyasa' would not have sprung to mind so easily a little over a week ago when I introduced myself under a false name to that awful creature, Y's husband's secretary.

But why Rua da Alegria? Nyasa had indeed always lived very near there, in part of a house in Rua da Conceição da Glória where he never invited anyone in. Unless it was from someone he knew... Perhaps from the last good sport or show-off to have been his patron saint of late?

But when I read the letter again, I at once ruled out that possibility: the writing belonged to quite an old person. The brief letter, no more than a note, really, could not have been more awkward or insignificant, apart from a single detail that I only now saw as poignant:

Dear sir:

It is my duty to enform you that Snr. Joaquim Maria dos Santos died two days ago and he was berried yesterday. I have been crying so much, only I know how much.

Please come to this adress as soon as possable. I have a very important messedge for you.

Your's truely,

Laurentina dos Santos Serodio

This was followed by the address.

Who would be able to confirm Nyasa's death at that time of night?

As though I needed confirmation! What I did need was to speak to someone about him. But who on earth could that someone be?

Then I remembered that Press 2 knew him very well: and that Nyasa had vaguely wanted her, some twelve or fifteen years previously, before reaching the conclusion that he'd never be able to classify her, seeing that Press 2 was too much of a good sport to be a good sport, and in no way showed-off enough to be considered a show-off

But I couldn't find Press 2's phone number; I didn't even know if she was working now for the radio, a newspaper or for some other agency. As for Press 1, on the other hand, I could be almost certain of her whereabouts: from what I'd gathered from the all the gossip going around, not a night went by without her having too much to drink at the Manhattan Bar and mucking about with brainless teenagers of all sexes. I rang the place up and, minutes later, over the handset, in an euphoric but steady voice that did not yet betray an undue degree of intoxication, I heard her say:

'Yes, he died. Poor man! He was such a nice, genuine bloke! Allegedly, it happened last week. But it only appeared in the papers today. That's how I found out. Allegedly, it happened quite suddenly. Allegedly, he was fine when it happened. I hadn't seen him for over a year. Allegedly, he'd even gone on a diet and lost some weight...'

So much alleging: this is what the reliability of Press 1's information was reduced to; she then proceeded to inform me about other matters:

'What do you think about this other fiasco? The great currency trafficking fiasco...? Haven't you been following the news? There are quite a few members of government involved, allegedly. And allegedly, so are our Inca or Aztec friends, as you call them. Allegedly, the guy's in it right up to his neck.'

'If that's what they're alleging, then they're probably right. But they were wrong when they told you about Nyasa. He wasn't fine, nor did he even look fine. He'd known for a few months that he had cancer of the lungs.'

'Really? But according to them, it happened suddenly.'

'They were right to a certain extent. People always die suddenly. Even when they've been dying for a while.'

You must be laughing at the seriously pompous tone of my answer to that fatuous Press 1.

How unimaginative, that epitaph she gave you: 'He was such a nice, genuine bloke!' At that point too, you must have released, from under the ground, one of your unmistakable belly laughs.

I would have preferred a thousand times the 'He was berried yesterday', with its awesome and revealing spelling mistake, whereby *bury* is confused with *berry*, and through which death appears to carry the promise of life.

There I go, being pompous again. Forgive me, Nyasa.

Forgive me, too, for this whisky of doubtful origin and even more dubious authenticity, with which I'm toasting your memory throughout the night. But I couldn't find the least drip of *ginjinha* or drop of *genebra* in the house with which to toast you properly.

With you disappears the only person in my dwindling circle of acquaintances who can still remember Diana cigarettes, coffee at eight tostões[37] a cup, the first hot dogs at the Petit Suisse, and then at Gambrinus's (or was it the other way round?), the tea-room of the Padaria Inglesa for furtive encounters of the 'serious' kind and the basement of the Café Cristal, half way down the Avenida, for less selective pick-ups. And with you, other things disappear which I cannot even remember. You needed only to mention them for them to become real again before my eyes. But not any more; this will never happen again.

Every morning, you would pull from your pocket a portable moon that you kept with you during the day; every evening, a small, rusty sun that you'd only wind up for the night.

And you loved to laugh. And you loved to love.

You were never jealous either of my most insignificant or of my most notable successes. You never rubbed your hands with glee at my failures, large or small. You never once cheated me. You never once saw me as a competitor, a rival, much less an adversary. Even in this you were unique: you were always so Portuguese, so much part of Lisbon, in so many ways except in this.

Sometimes you would sigh: 'What do you expect? This is the only country where you'd find this kind of country.'

What's it like now, Nyasa? What's it like where you are now? It is my turn to raise my hands a little above my shoulders and wave them in two symmetrical question marks either side of me.

I spent all morning and part of the afternoon indoors, my head nodding with tiredness, but unable to go to sleep or to move very far in case that phone call from London should come through. I had searched the directory in vain for the phone number of senhora Serôdio from Rua da Alegria; I had even phoned directory enquiries to ask for her number, giving her name and address as the subscriber: but there was no phone at that address.

The phone call from London came at around four o'clock.

'I'm sorry if there was a problem. It was your wife I spoke to yesterday, wasn't it? But I simply had to talk to you. If you had a phone in your atelier, I would have phoned there. I don't know why, but I felt sure that… Have you been going to the atelier much?'

'As it so happens, I was there yesterday.'

'Ah!' There was a pause. Then: 'I knew it.'

The clarity of the connection was perfect and could in no way be compared to the one the day before. But neither of us seemed to be able to make the most of this technical improvement.

'I'm feeling very depressed, you know. Nyasa died.'

I had occasionally mentioned Nyasa to her, although she never showed much understanding or interest in the stories I told her about him; my news was followed by another silent pause. I heard her take a deep breath, then she coughed to clear her voice:

'Vicky's godfather died too.'

It would have been ridiculous for us to start exchanging commiserations. It was my turn to fall contritely silent. I did however manage to say 'I'm sorry' which Y probably didn't even hear, because at the same time, as though delivering a message, she started telling me that she wouldn't be able to see me the next day, Thursday, after all, but only towards the end of the following week; and that she'd ring me a week Thursday, probably at the same time, not before, as it would be quite impossible. Impossible? Impossible why?

'I'll tell you all about it later.'

She was about to hang up. But I tried to keep the conversation going a little longer:

'At least tell me you've missed me!'

'You tell me that. You tell me that first.'

'Of course I have. I've missed you so much! You can't begin to know how much!'

But just then we were cut off. I waited absurdly for over an hour for Y to call back, seeing that I couldn't ring her back myself, either this time, or the day before, as I hadn't even got round to asking her where she was, where she was phoning me from and where I could reach her in an emergency.

Finally I went out onto the veranda. The wind had started to blow; it was one of those cutting, blustery winds that blow around these parts during the last two weeks of August, bringing a foretaste of the rigours of autumn. In the stretch of sea that the municipality of Cascais still allowed me to see, I watched the blue of the sea swiftly turn dark green, then grey.

It was already half past five when I left for Lisbon; or, to be more precise, towards Rua da Alegria.

XXXVII

It was a ground floor flat, right at the top of the street, a bit beyond the bend that goes round the Mãe d'Água, almost opposite an hotel that was sufficiently modern to be looking sufficiently outdated by now. At my first ring on the doorbell, the thick lenses of an old-fashioned pair of glasses peered out of one of the windows, belonging to the almost bald, wispy-tufted head of an elderly, seventy-year-old woman. I asked her for dona Laurentina, gave her my name and mentioned the letter I'd received. The lenses were not only thick, they were impenetrable: it was as though the lenses also had trouble hearing and trouble understanding. I repeated what I'd said before, in a louder voice. She answered, somewhat peevishly, as though to prove she wasn't deaf:

'I see, I see. One moment...'

But she left me in the street for a good five minutes, without deigning to come and open the door for me. I was just about to ring again when I heard a bolt being drawn and, in the semi-darkness of the hall, I caught sight of either another woman, or the same woman, but without her glasses on and sporting a hastily thrown on blonde wig, the shade of sun-baked wheat:

'Come in, come in. Sorry for the delay.'

The voice was the same. I concluded that so was the woman.

She led me down a corridor where she'd left the light on, and I thought her way of walking was strangely familiar to me, with one shoulder leaning forwards and her neck slightly twisted, in a gesture of reproof or gentle encouragement, over the poor shoulder that always lagged behind.

The electric lights were on not only in the corridor, but also in two rooms that overlooked the street and where the late afternoon light should have been enough. But she entered a squalid inner room where the light was also on, pointed to an upright wooden chair for me, and hastened to occupy the other deeper and lower chair, also made of wood.

That's when I suddenly associated the person's first name on the letter (I hadn't thought of it before) and her way of walking – that had long been lost and buried in my memory – and in a flash I realized who it was.

Luckily, my name appeared not to have rung a bell with her, either when she wrote me her letter, or when she'd heard it a few moments earlier; it would have been highly unlikely for her to have recognized my face as, deprived of their thick lenses, her eyes had something vitreous and spongy about them, and all her movements since she had sat down (but, curiously, not when she'd been standing) where those of a blind person or of someone about to plunge into total blindness. Apart from the globular emptiness of her eyes, there still remained a few traces of the attractive woman she had once been.

'Yes, that's her.' Yes, that was her.

As though this amazing twist of fortune, meeting up with her thirty-three years later, were not enough, there was another question to add to this mystery: what was her connection with Nyasa?

Can you believe the remarkable workings of this dark and twisted brain of mine? However strange it may seem, my thoughts (you may well qualify them as petulant or improper!) did not turn towards Nyasa at that point, but towards none other than your friend. That's right: your friend! Suddenly, I *saw* him, with his inseparable pipe, and it was as if he'd been faced with this unlikely coincidence, not me. How would your friend react? Would he be brave enough, afterwards, to use an event like this in one of his books, to actually insert in one of his books such an incredibly fortuitous reunion, under circumstances such as these, with the almost bald and almost blind, ex-platinum-blonde-Lídia-alias-Laurentina? In his capacity as critic and essayist, or even as a teacher of literature, would he be uncomfortable with accepting this kind of situation in a novel?

The strangest thing was that, for the first time in many years, I was able to *see* your friend without feeling any kind of animosity towards him. I was even ready to forgive him his pipe; I would even forgive him for other things too. Perhaps your escapade to Venice had a little to do with my goodwill.

On the other hand – during ex-Lídia-now-Laurentina's monologue which I was finding hard to follow – I soon realized that your friend would indeed have been able to accept this unbelievable coincidence as naturally as I was doing right then. And also, in terms of life and fiction (where does one start and the other end?), we probably shared the same kind of inherent receptiveness.

Who would have believed it? Perhaps we were destined to be friends one day after all.

'...That's right: I also did some theatre... Mainly in Africa and in the provinces. Not for very long. And I was no child then. Even so, I went in straightaway as lead chorus girl, I played "Night" and "Yearning" in the same revue, not to mention other smaller parts. I must admit I never went beyond lead chorus girl. But I always had a lot of success in Angola, they all liked me very much... That's where I met my second husband. Maybe you've heard of him: Serôdio, Américo Serôdio, from Customs... We got on so well! Unfortunately it didn't last long. I married him when I was forty-one and by the time I was forty-three, I was already a widow. As for my first husband... It's best not to talk about him, I only get upset! That's destiny for you: Joaquim, who did all he could to stop me going into the theatre, Joaquim's the one who's stood by me all through these last few years. That's always the way: anything worthwhile that comes my way always arrives far too late and ends far too soon. But Joaquim, as I was saying... Perhaps you're not interested in all these things I'm telling you. It's just so that you can understand the rest. And why I sent you that letter. Don't worry, I haven't forgotten. To tell the truth, it wasn't me who wrote that letter. I asked my neighbour to write that one and three others for me. With the state my eyes are in, I couldn't be expected to do it myself! You see, Joaquim had begged me so much, he'd left me the four names and the four addresses, and I don't think his soul will ever rest in peace unless I fulfil his wishes. Poor man! Do you know, over the last few months, he had even got a little better. He just couldn't bring himself to believe he had cancer... But deep down, he knew. And in the end, he died of a heart attack. Oh, the number of times he said to me: "Here are four names, four addresses... If anything happens to me (he never mentioned dying), let these people know there's a painting here for each one of them"! Up until now (yesterday morning, it was), only one out of the four people, a lady, has come to fetch the painting he'd left for her. Don't ask me her name, I can't remember. I'm no good at all with names. So, as I was saying: Joaquim stood by me these last few years. His excuse was that there was too much noise at home (there was a non-stop coming and going of ladies from the local bars in his block of flats), and he used that excuse to rent a room from me here, and whenever he could, especially once he was out of hospital, he would come over and paint some of his more serious stuff, as he called it. I have no idea if the paintings he did were serious or not, I do know they were small, but with the state of my eyes, I only wish I could see the scenery he used to paint. And he never once brought one of his trollops here, that I can assure you. And, poor man, he did all he could to make sure I got some kind of retirement pension. When I was younger… he wasn't at all understanding then. He never forgave me for leaving my first husband. But I had my reasons. It's just that I realized, before our first week of marriage was up, that he wasn't the man for me. Even so, I put up with him for three years. And of course, I made mistakes too. That's when I most needed Joaquim to help me. And it wasn't just the battle he put up to try and stop me going on stage, that was not the only thing that caused all the doors to be slammed in my face, so to speak… He was always so worried that people might find out we were brother and sister. Different mothers, I know. But we shared the same father. Only towards the end did he stop minding. For a long time, that was the hardest bit. He of all people, who was always so good to everyone, so ready to understand everyone else's problems! Anyway, what's done is done… All I want now is for his soul to rest in peace. Forgive me for blubbering like this. It's something my doctor says I shouldn't do, because of the state of my eyes. No, don't get up. I'm just going to the other room to get the painting he left you.'

Five minutes later, if not less, I heard her screaming frantically for me:

'Senhor! Senhor! I'm sorry I can't remember your name, but for the love of God hurry up!'

In the corridor, the clouds of smoke billowing out of one of the front rooms at once gave away Laurentina's whereabouts. I found her engulfed in smoke, with a snuffed out candle in one hand, while with her other hand, she was aimlessly hitting the divan where the smoke seemed to be coming from. I noticed at once that one of the edges of the counterpane was already on fire: I yanked it off, began stamping on it on the floor, then ran to open the window.

'I kept all the paintings underneath here… I only lit a candle to see which one is yours… And then this had to happen! Please, for goodness sake, go inside for me and get a jug of water! The bathroom is just down the end…'

Foolishly, off I went. When I got back, not only had the counterpane burst into flames again, but two or three thick coils of smoke had started to rise from the divan. And, worst of all, without the woman realizing it, a tongue of fire was crackling on the top of her wig,

'Take that off your head – now!'

'What?'

'This!' Without further ado, I whipped it off myself. She stared at me, bewildered and incensed, as though I had tried to assault her.

As for me, after furiously beating the wig against the wall and finally giving it back to her (although I wasn't altogether sure it wouldn't flare up again), only then did I get round to looking for the paintings under the bed. But the blazing fire that my fingers encountered and the scalding blast that scorched my face made me give up the idea for the time being.

In the meantime, in the street, just under the window, several interested onlookers had gathered round. We could hear the growing murmur of their voices. There was also loud thumping on the front door.

'We need to call the fire brigade!' I decided. But then I remembered there was no phone. I rushed to the window-sill, shouting out: 'We need to call the fire brigade!'

'Someone's already gone. They're calling from the hotel over there.' This information was eagerly given to me by an unprepossessing, yet still relatively handsome man in his fifties, who looked rather like a retired pimp. He added: 'I'm the one who sent them to call the fire brigade. With all that smoke pouring out, I saw at once that this was a matter for the fire brigade.' And he stood there, with folded arms, on the edge of the pavement, making sure that no one mistook him for a fool.

A young woman in her dressing-gown and with curlers in her hair, and who must have rushed out of some nearby block of flats, hurled abuse at me from the middle of the street:

'Just get the old woman out of there before she chokes to death!'

'That's right! No one ever thinks of old people!' whined a kind of mummified crone all trussed up in black, who was standing nearby and looking at me spitefully as though I were some kind of pyromaniac.

But who could possibly convince Laurentina to leave? With her head covered in bald patches and brittle tufts of ravaged hair, she had already gone to fetch two more jugfuls of water, and at least put out the fire on the counterpane, which now lay in a sodden heap in the middle of the floor and, so doing, she had also reduced her wig to a limp, soggy mass. However, the billowing smoke had not abated, and a slender, sprightly flame had leapt out of the divan, and was almost touching the ceiling, spitting black soot into the corner between two walls.

'Oh, what a disaster! This would have to happen to me! But there's no way I'm going out into the street looking like this!' She was still clutching the snuffed out candle in her left hand, as though it were all important to hold onto evidence that this was all an accident.

'Just go and get a scarf, a shawl... anything!'

My eyes were burning, my throat was on fire: I was the one almost choking to death, but as for her, she was amazingly unaffected, and merely gave a little cough every now and then.

'That's funny! Your voice sounds strangely familiar... I've been trying to rack my brains...'

That's all we needed: the peripeteia of a reunion where the ending goes up in flames!

'Would you just go and get a scarf!'

I repeated this order with such a voice that she must have thought I was a hawker or a member of the riot police. As soon as she left the room, I thrust my hands under the bed again. I could barely go in as far as my wrists: that was where the heart of the fire was. Nevertheless, I was still able to remove a piece of carbonized canvas that stuck to my fingers; I nearly burnt the skin right off my left thumb and index finger. As soon as I got up, I saw a white shawl next to me (it was actually light grey) that Laurentina had wrapped around herself. Then (how efficient!) we heard the clanging of the fire-engines. My fingers were hurting, my eyes streaming, my throat in agony.

'Let's just get out of here!'

I pushed Laurentina ahead of me, we hurried down the smoke-filled corridor. In the street, from among the people who immediately surrounded us, rose the shrill voice of the mummified crone:

'Were you assaulted?'

'What do you mean assaulted?' exclaimed an indignant Laurentina. 'If it wasn't for this gentleman, I don't know what would have happened to me!' Instinctively, she pulled the shawl more tightly round her head.

In the eyes of the mummy, from suspected criminal, I was suddenly promoted to local hero:

'You poor man! Your fingers are all burnt!'

From outside, the fire seemed much more threatening than it had from inside. Two firemen, brandishing their axes, had already gone into the building. In the street, others were unrolling a long hose-pipe. In the hotel opposite, several guests, obviously of foreign extraction, were leaning out of half a dozen windows and taking great interest in what was happening, as though the show was included in their hotel rates or was an unexpected treat from the Secretary of State for Tourism.

That's when someone, calling me by my first name, touched me gently on the arm:

'What's all this about?'

Ah! It was Press 2. I quickly told her what had been going on, while she pulled out of her haversack a letter identical to the one I'd received, with its 'he was *berried* yesterday' and all the other absurd, carbon copy mistakes.

'Right,' she remarks. 'We know who two of the paintings were for...'

'Who they are not for. At least one was taken yesterday morning. By a lady. That's what Nyasa's sister told me.'

'Oh! Did he have a sister?'

'He did. Forget it.'

'I've forgotten already. Just don't you forget to get that hand of yours seen to.'

Half an hour later, in a nursing station bang in the middle of Praça da Alegria, and after watching the basic treatment I was given, Press 2 started talking to me, either to distract me or because the subject was indeed the order of the day, about the matter of the currency trafficking. But her version was the complete opposite of Press 1's: our Amerindian friend was innocent after all; other foreigners who don't even belong to the diplomatic corps abused his honesty and trust but then, on the other hand, there was indeed no shortage of important personalities in the highest ranks of government who were deeply implicated.

'It's like I said,' she concluded. 'The country has turned into such a sea of shit and corruption that all that comes to the surface is the purest tip of the iceberg.' She added: 'The newspaper has already scrapped a sentence of mine similar to that. Even though I'd been careful not to write the word shit. Then, looking at my two bandaged fingers, she said:

'Just as well it was your left hand. At least like that you'll still be able to work.'

'That's something I haven't done for a few months now. Yet now, strange it may seem, I actually feel like buckling down.'

XXXVIII

There were three more days to go until Y's phone call.

I went up to Rua da Alegria several times, always with Press 2. It soon became obvious that not a single brushstroke had been saved from however much Nyasa had done during the last few months of his life. As for any other damage caused by the flames and the water, the room in which the fire had actually started was a write-off. But of course, there was no insurance. Strong solidarity was soon shown towards Nyasa's sister: firstly, from the local neighbourhood and a large number of people from the Parque Mayer; then – as Press 2 proudly pointed out – from artists, journalists and writers who had little, if anything, to do with Parque Mayer, among whom she quickly organized a collection. She put my name at the top of her list, with a generous figure next to it, in an attempt to attract donations of a similar value. She succeeded. One of them – I want you to know this – was from your friend. (His donation matched mine exactly: not enough for the two of you spend another day in Venice, but enough for him to give up the idea of buying a new pipe.)

Once these matters had been more or less settled, I spent the whole of the weekend cooped up in the atelier. The two injured fingers of my left hand did not stop me from moulding out of clay and covering in plaster a cylindrical shape of extreme simplicity (although I'd imagined it made of the pink marble of Vila Viçosa). You have no idea what pleasure it gave me to make it. For me, it will always be my secret homage to the memory of Nyasa. If anyone saw it, they would probably start complaining that I was falling into the most execrable form of minimalism; unless I were to give it a trendy and pretentious name such as *The Dialects of Desire*, *Nuclear Explosion*, *A Message to Freud*, *Subterranean Soliloquy*, *Class War*, *Zero Orgy*, *Matter and Antimatter*, *Alberto Caeiro's Apology*, *Alienated Conscience*, *The Nightmare of Shapes* – or perhaps, for want of imagination, *Composition*, or even *Object*. (While we're at it, why not *Holyject*?) As it comprised an abundance of showing-off, stylized pears rising from the middle – or, more accurately, the bosom – of sportingly good, stylized apples, another name I fancied for it was *Pomoniassa*. But I shall not fall into that trap, lest they steal it for some new brand of washing-powder.

On Monday morning, although there were still three days to go until Y's phone call, I thought the time was right to replenish the empty fridge and bare larder shelves in the atelier. It's a chore that I usually take an almost sensual delight in, going to the well-stocked *charcutaria* near the Largo do Rato where, especially for clandestine encounters, I have taken my custom since the mid-1970s. And it was either because of the relative proximity of Palminha's salon or the sight of those gastronomic delicacies that Zu had enjoyed so much, but I began to feel guilty about the promise I'd made to her and that I hadn't kept yet, of sketching her and giving her the end result (but how would she justify such a gift to her family?): a good likeness of her mysterious, slanted eyes, her salient, high cheekbones, her turned-up nose and her mouth that could apparently only behave when it wasn't eating or gossiping.

That was it: I didn't so much want to see her again, as hear her again... As though hearing her again would reassure me that a part of Lisbon that was hard to find nowadays had not completely disappeared with Nyasa's death.

Enough excuses: I phoned her from the *charcutaria* itself. Would she like me to come and fetch her, same place as last time, at around two o'clock?

'All right, then...' There wasn't the slightest hint of enthusiasm in her voice. I almost regretted having spoken to her.

'It's just that there were people around... Apart from senhor Palma, there was also a really sticky client who had already asked me out to lunch. I had to say it was my father on the phone. So there we are, what a shame, nothing I could do, but I had to go with him to see an aunt of mine who was ill. It was the first thing that came to my mind. You wouldn't believe the story I made up about Aunt Esmeralda, whom we don't get on with anyway! Then I went to Palmiped (I'm sorry, but that's what we call him behind his back) to ask if he minded if I came back at around twenty past or half past four... So you see, we've even got a bit more time like this. But please don't look at me like that... Let me see your hand... Don't worry, I'm not going to eat it. Oh! What on earth is that? Where have you been putting those fingers of yours? And such fine fingers at that! It was either these or that misery guts who wanted so much to have lunch with me... Lunch with him! I should have made up some other excuse. But it's not as though my tummy wasn't actually beginning to feel a bit hollow. Yesterday all I had was tea and toast because of some mussels I ate on Saturday. That's my clever husband for you: he expects me to believe he bought them at the fish auction in Peniche when in fact it was probably some cheap shop or other that palmed them off on him. And that fool's on holiday, he spends all day on his back while I'm here washing hair, and he can't even buy mussels properly. They tasted funny to me straightaway, but he kept saying to me, "Eat up, eat up, don't be so fussy", and my mother joined in – "If it doesn't kill you, it must be good for you" – and in the end, I'm the one who came up in a rash and spent all night being sick. But at least I'm better now. I'm just really pleased to be having lunch with you today. At last you're looking a bit happier now, don't bother trying to hide it, I saw you smiling just then...'

She spent the rest of the journey talking nineteen to the dozen ('I just can't seem to stop today!'), one minute gossiping about Palmiped ('Whenever some minister or other important bod turns up there, he makes such a fuss and waddles about just like a duck, which is why I gave him his nickname.'), the next minute telling me her latest anecdotes about her 'young lady' ('Swimming in the sea is something she really doesn't like! Would you believe what she says? She says that sea water is dirty because it's all over the floor and full of sand!'). But when we reached the atelier and she saw the two big bags of shopping that I'd brought from the *charcutaria*, she was completely overwhelmed and stunned into silence. Only after a few moments was she able to exclaim:

'Gee, Heavenly Father! With so many things on your mind, how did you ever manage to come up with all these tidbits?'

That afternoon, she did honour most particularly to some diaphanous slices of smoked swordfish and a delicate galantine of veal – patriotically washed down this time with an Alvarinho of a good year, but its temperature wasn't to our satisfaction, so it spent its time backwards and forwards from the freezer to our glasses, from our glasses to the freezer.

Finally, it was three o'clock in the afternoon when I issued an ultimatum:

'Now, then, let's see... If you still want the drawing, it has to be done now. Now or never.'

'Right now, Mestre! You're the boss, Mestre... I'll even go back to calling you Mestre from now on, with all due respect.' She at once went off to the middle of the studio to fetch the little stool she'd sat on the time before. Then, in the twinkling of an eye, she bared her breasts, unbuttoning at a lightning speed the blue shirt she was wearing that day (but without removing it completely).

'What the hell!' I exclaimed. 'Don't tell me you always go around like that!'

'Like what?'

'Without a bra or anything...'

'Do you think I need one?'

'That's not what I mean.'

'What do you mean then?'

'Nothing. I was just wondering.'

Two minutes later, she was already starting on me:

'Today's the day. Today you really must show me the little nook you keep for your admirers.'

'What do you mean, my little nook?'

'Oh! So you think I don't know about it? That little room full of mirrors... With a large divan in it that's as wide as it's long... See how I know everything?'

'Well, if you already know about it, you don't need to see it.'

'Of course I do. Or are you afraid? Don't worry, I'm not really checking to see if it's more fantasy than fact!' As I remained silent, she went on: 'Don't tell me you're angry... I was only joking. And I'm not like everybody else. Everybody, starting with my mother, thinks I'm some kind of moron... But it's different when I'm with you. Or are you angry because I won't stop talking?'

'No, feel free. As long as you keep still.'

Perhaps she was being contrary, but that's all it took to induce her to the most silent sobriety. I worked on, in the meantime, with an ease both scholarly and embarrassing (perhaps Y is right and this is what I'm good at), as though I'd been miraculously transported back to my mythical time at the Belas Artes, faced with one of those moody models of the day.

I caught the expression in Zu's eyes with an accuracy that the layman would qualify as photographic but that had nothing to do with the tricks or flukes of photography; the impudence of her nose and cheekbones was in marked contrast with the hypocrisy of her lips that were pretending to be well-behaved; and I had decided that, since she enjoyed displaying them so much, I would also draw the good-sport impertinence and show-off modesty of her uncovered breasts, gleefully thinking about what she would do with this sketch that was so unsuitable to be shown in the bosom (not again!) of Floripes's family. Then, as though reading my mind, Zu broke her ten minute long silence:

'Feel free to paint my chest if you like...'

'Draw,' I corrected.

'That, even. But you can do whatever you like... But I won't be taking that portrait to my mother's home... It's to give to someone I owe lots of favours to.'

'Ah!'

'Don't start getting the wrong idea. It's for my daughter's doctor.'

I tried to give my second 'Ah!' a new intonation, not quite so full of innuendo. Without any transition, she went on to say:

'Do you know what? That dress was ruined.'

'What dress?'

'The yellow one. The one that got covered in ice-cream. The stains never did come out, you know. There's nothing they can do with it. That's what they told me at the dry-cleaners'.'

I uttered a third 'Ah!' which was, naturally, even more neutral.

'Can I ask you something? I know you'll start telling me to behave...'

'Well then, don't ask.'

'I'll behave, don't worry! But what I'd really like is for you to do my portrait one day... You know how?... In the nude...' She pretended to shiver; but I'm sure it had nothing to do with being cold.

'Would you give that to your daughter's doctor too?'

'Maybe...' Her eyes became two mocking slits. 'Or maybe not... Don't tell me you're jealous!' When she saw no reaction from me, she paused meaningfully for a moment, then added: 'Well let me tell you...What I'd like would be for the portrait to stay here. But on display. So that I can be sure your eyes see it even if you don't want to.'

'You do come out with the strangest things! And you tell me you know how to behave... But I can assure you that such a portrait will never exist.'

'I wouldn't be quite so sure, if I were you... What about this one? Can I see it yet?

'It still needs a touch, but if you like...'

She left the stool and came running, her little breast-activating engine revving excitedly:

'That's amazing! That's really me!' The engine was still revving. 'Right then, now I can tell you the truth... Obviously I can't take this home. What would I tell my mother? My husband's the least of my worries. And as for my father, poor man, he doesn't even count. That's why I'd like you to keep that drawing here. Until some day, would that be all right? Until I have my very own home, can you understand?' Walking backwards, or almost, and staring at the picture, she went up to the table to drain her glass of white wine. 'I know full well I won't be spending the rest of my life at my mother's. And I won't spend the rest of my life holding onto that man I happened to marry... I felt sorry for him, that was all, he was still young, my best friend's widower, and to make things worse, he was left with a baby girl.' She had come back towards me, and was doing her shirt up again.: 'What I said to you just now about the doctor was just to annoy you... I owe him some favours, that's true enough. But he also owes me.' She went into raptures again over the portrait: 'Oh! It's turned out really well... that's me to a T! How did you manage to get that expression on my mouth? And my eyes, my nose, even my boobs...!' She stepped back to stand next to the easel, on which I'd placed the drawing: 'Tell me the truth... I'm not that bad, am I?'

'If you don't hurry up, it's Palmiped who'll throw you out. It's already ten past four.'

Before leaving, Zu glanced over the left-over galantine and smoked swordfish, and stopped to consider certain practicalities:

'Don't you think all this might go off... even in the fridge? There's enough here for another meal... You wouldn't need to fork out any more... Tell me: shall we come back tomorrow?... It seems to me that tomorrow will still be a good day for you... For me too: my mother will be back from holidays in a couple of days time. Go on... Say yes.'

I must have nodded imperceptibly. And I was unable to stop her from flinging herself round my neck. But I was able, once again, to avoid her mouth crushing mine at a dangerous angle.

To be honest, I'm not sure I was actually proud of the speed of my reflexes.

XXXIX

It's you again, with Zu's face and with Zu's body. But the voice is yours; the cigarettes are yours; so are the jeans.

We are in a rectangular or perhaps trapezoidal brick room; three walls are covered in bookcases, and the fourth – which seems to be the largest of all – consists of a huge, single window-pane. There is complete darkness outside; as though outside it's the bottom of the sea. Only the inside of the room is brightly lit. In front of us is a portrait much like the one I did of Zu that afternoon: the face, however, is Y's.

'With eyes like that, it had to happen…' you say, trying to make me feel better, looking very much like someone who is presenting their condolences. 'But you can count on me. You can recount everything to me.'

How amusing: count and recount.

You persist:

'You have to count on me. You have to recount everything to me. Because she counts a lot to you!'

How very amusing: it's all a matter of counting.

I am about to speak these words, but my wife is standing next to us, all dressed in black; she's lost an incredible amount of weight, and she informs us with a matter-of-fact airiness that suits her very well:

'My aunts died today. All three of them, all at once.' Then, turning to you, she says: 'Oh, but your husband worked tirelessly… Do thank him for me.'

Y's portrait has disappeared; you no longer look like Zu.

'See?' I mutter, touching my wife's shoulder. 'Now you must think of yourself first.'

I wake up bathed in perspiration, with the light still on, and the uncomfortable feeling of having a crushing weight on my chest.

To count on you; to recount everything to you; it's all a matter of counting… These odd variations are what intrigue me most at the moment.

I try to raise my hand against the weight on my chest; but my arm is asleep and seems not to want to obey me. Almost in desperation, I try to move my trunk – and the book I'd brought to bed, but had barely been able to look through before falling asleep, drops to the floor. Ah! It's a copy of *La Chartreuse de Parme*... Why *La Chartreuse*? I've already read it three or four times before.

There are many other novels that I like quite a lot more; but this is the only one that can make me enter a state of grace or fall into a state of adoration. When I was in my twenties, it was this book that made me fall madly in love with Italy; it was an Italy that had the advantage of not having much to do with my mother and, as I discovered later, of not being much like Italy at all.

However, this would never be the novel that I wished I'd written, even if I'd been able to, even if I'd known how to. But it is in every way one of the books that makes me dream the most about how wonderful it must be to write a book: an invention of memory; a memory of invention; the sweeping cavalcade of a great escape, the prodigal offspring of a mysterious and impetuous polygamy with the multitude of womanlike words: words that surrender, words that slip away; words that need to be coaxed, seduced or deceived; and finally those that allow themselves to be captured, fondled, undressed, penetrated and retained, thus affording, before they vanish, the lasting heights of a successful love affair. There is no matter more physically non-existent; none more readily fertilized by love.

What other way is there of understanding ancient commonplaces such as having a child, planting a tree or writing a book? In all cases, they must be the result of great, inescapable acts of love: with Woman, with Earth or with Language. But there will never be a shortage of people capable of planting trees and having children. And also of destroying trees; and spoiling children, too. A book, however, a living book that multiplies over the years or over the centuries, then dies quietly, without anyone noticing, but never entirely, until it is either buried with the utmost discretion or suddenly reawakened, unexpectedly resurrected, a book with this kind of destiny – brilliant however obscure, obscure however brilliant – this is what has always been my fascination. Sculpture? My objects? Poor solitary shapes of metal or stone that will never have the gift of ubiquity.

But that night I had picked up *La Chartreuse* specifically to find those words that had for years and years been for me a creed, a motto, a guide, an ex-libris, an inner mandate. Ah! There they were... They were right at the beginning of the second chapter, a remark made by Pietranera, the future Sanseverina, on the banks of Lake Como:

La vie s'enfuit, ne te montre point si difficile envers le bonheur qui se présente, hâte-toi de jouir.

Now what? Why had I stopped listening to this message?

Before, even when some demigoddess occupied the place of honour in my erotic and emotional hearth, I would always find a way of keeping, in the cellar or in the attic, in the loft or in the foundations of the house, one or other transient, pilgrim woman who was only looking for temporary accommodation. How pleasant, entertaining and even stimulating it was whenever I left the stilted comfort and stuffy atmosphere of the *piano nobile* for the cosy retreat of one of the garrets! I even reached the conclusion that 'Nothing is equal, everything is equivalent.' Now, however...

I know, I know! As soon as Fabrice met Clélia, he at once stopped being interested in the Anikens, Mariettas and Faustas of this world... But it all started with his imprisonment. Which wasn't my case. Unless Y (here too the shape of her initial would be appropriate) had become my own tower of Farnese.

Do you see? When your friend and I grow close one day (which is highly likely), you will be able to tell him that I not only have the desire to write, but I am also a man of letters.

That night I persevered in my rereading of *La Chartreuse*, and it was dawn by the time I fell peacefully asleep, wrapped in the stifling intrigues of the court of Parma.

The next day, Zu turned up wearing a garish jump suit (or 'all-in-one', as she liked to call it) which couldn't help but remind me of the one that Y wore that afternoon I went to her *quinta*. The brownish material (an imitation linen) was indeed slightly reminiscent of veined marble.

After lunch, Zu waited until I had my back turned to her, putting the leftovers in the fridge, to sneak off into the other corner of the atelier. It was only when I heard the soft, crinkly whisper of her clothes slithering down her body that I turned to look back. There could be no doubt: she had slipped off her jump suit; and the 'all-in-one' was nothing more than a limp, shapeless lump round her ankles.

'Well?' she asked. 'Do you or do you not want to draw me in the nude?'

My attention was immediately drawn to her pubis, which

displayed an inviting if somewhat daunting exuberance between her lean thighs. It looked like the single remnant of a luxurious fur coat that might once have covered her whole body and that had shrunk or been ripped off. It had something of the jungle about it, a primitive, archaic and antediluvian quality, yet at the same time, its flawless, triangular outline pointed to the intervention of more modern procedures; it hid what it was meant to hide with such luxuriance that all it did was draw attention to what it was hiding. But, like her unbelievably knobbly knees, her legs were nothing much, a little short and almost skinny, especially when compared with the longer and more harmonious fullness of her thighs.

I had not moved an inch from the fridge. Realizing that Zu would not be able to move either, with her feet caught by her ankles in the second-rate marble from which her whole body emerged, it took me a good few seconds before muttering from where I was, in the tone of voice one uses reluctantly to reprimand a child for committing some mischief that is actually quite amusing, but in need of curbing:

'Put that back on.'

Zu bent over without embarrassment and extracted from the brownish marble that held her to the floor, a minute pair of white panties which, with a lack of haste that was more impish than impudent, she pulled up her legs, over her knees and along her thighs, and then adjusted, with a wiggle of her buttocks, in the duskiness of her groin and around her boyish thighs.

'I knew all along,' she explained, 'that there wouldn't be time today... It was just to see, Mestre...' (she stressed this word with sarcasm, and then repeated it) 'to see, Mestre, if you might change your mind...'

We were still about five yards away from each other, as though obeying the strict pointers of an invisible choreographer. She stood for a moment in just her see-through panties that made her look even more naked. Then, bending over again with the same lack of embarrassment as before, and with the same lack of haste as before, she put her 'all-in-one' back on. As though obeying that same invisible choreographer, we moved away from the positions we had been frozen in, moving around the studio from then on with the ease and informality with which one walks across the stage when the show is over.

During lunch, there had been nothing to make me suspect that Zu was about to give me that little display for my dessert. She had been far less chatty than when we'd been together the day before, with a veil of relative composure demurely covering her face, from the roots of her hair down to her chin, and as we hadn't started on the swordfish or the galantine yet, her whole attention had been focused on the brands and the quality of the various bits and pieces from the *charcutaria*. She even went as far as asking me if, some other time, I would write down the names of these 'delicious eats' on a piece of paper, to see if her husband ('I have to do all his cooking!') could bring it back from the mess.

Just as we were leaving ('I mustn't be late today!'), she suddenly held me back by my arm:

'Seriously now: do you think I'd make a good model? Or even a catwalk model? I've got no hang-ups, have I? I'm not inhibited either, am I?' In an almost mystical trance, as though the salvation of her soul depended on it, she said: 'Oh! It's what I'd really like to do most of all in life!... And whenever I can...'

'Hmm... So you have already "poised", as you say, have you...?'

She closed her eyes tighter, as though trying to add a little more mystery to her words:

'Something like that... Yes and no... Never for an artist like this. I'll tell you all about it sometime.'

She told me all about in the car on the way back to Palmiped's.

'Go on then! See if you can guess who it is I've poised for...'

'I haven't the slightest idea.'

'Well, it isn't quite poising... But it's the same thing as far as I'm concerned. Can't you guess?...'

'I've already said I couldn't.'

'Well, you'll soon realize who it is: it was for a doctor...'

'Ah!'

'For that doctor I told you about. My daughter's doctor.'

'Ah...!'

'No, no, it's not what you're thinking. He's never touched me. On my life. At the end of the day, it's a little like the poising I did for you yesterday. Or just now, even... If you must know, I don't even know how it all started. He confided in me one day, he said he had lots of problems...'

'Problems? What kind of problems?

'Well, he implied... I mean: this is exactly what he said. He said that at home, with his wife, either it's all over in a second, or else, however hard he tries, he never gets anywhere. So he asked me, he begged me to help him...'

'To help him? To help him how?'

'What do you think? To control himself... That's how he puts it. At the end of the day, it's actually quite easy. Once or twice a week, I go to his surgery, always at lunchtime, and those are the days I only have croissants or sandwiches for lunch, and then, that's it, it's always the same kind of thing.'

'But the same kind of what?'

'Now don't go and think ill of me, because there's no harm whatsoever in it. I swear on my daughter's good health and on my own happiness. He's always very polite, almost over-the-top... He starts off by showing me some photographs... You wouldn't believe the photographs he has! But they're always of individual girls, they're never in pairs or in groups or anything like that. Then there's nothing to it. All I do is get undressed, he even puts a pillowcase over my head so that I don't feel embarrassed, and then he wants me to do what I saw in the photographs. But he also wants me to walk around, to sit down, to lie down on the carpet, to get up, to pretend, well, this and that...'

'I see...'

'Mind you, he never moves from behind his desk, he never touches me, I swear, and all I hear is him breathing, breathing in a particular way, sometimes it's more than breathing, but I pay no attention and he doesn't say anything, but of course I know what's going on, and in the end I don't know if I pity him or if I'm actually pleased to be helping him out like that.'

'What does he do... in exchange?'

'He helps me too. He never charges for seeing my daughter, he gives me medicines, sometimes even some clothes... They happen to be my best ones, too.'

'The yellow dress, for instance?'

'How do you know?'

'You mentioned your yellow dress yesterday, right after you mentioned him, that doctor.'

'Ah! Just as I always say... there's a lot to be said for intelligence. Which is one of the reasons, apart from the fact that I trust you, that I'm telling you these things that I've never told anybody else. I just wish you trusted me as much as I trust you. But you will. I have a feeling it might become more difficult for us to meet from now on, but I'm lucky that way, I know how to bide my time. For a start, I know you won't think ill of me. All it takes is a bit of intelligence to realize this is no life for someone like me (what the hell, I'm not that bad, am I?), washing people's heads, some of them dirty on the outside, others dirty on the inside, and not even being able to dress the way I want. What does it matter if I take my clothes off so that I can dress better? Aren't there loads other women doing just that? But in other ways... I don't want to do it their way. I couldn't. I'm no saint, mind you. Even after I got married, I've had my moments, I even had an all-consuming passion, but never for gain, thank God! Not that I refused small gifts, of course, but whenever I can, I too give a little gift in return...'

In the meantime, we had arrived within sight of Palma's barbershop and the entrance to the car showroom, where another group of local Fittipaldis – or was it the same one? – were hanging about. I stopped the car a little further up. Unexpectedly, Zu removed a small package wrapped in tissue paper from her bag. Then, instead of trying to kiss me on the cheek as usual, she merely placed one of her gentle and fleeting geisha kisses on my wrist; and, almost furtively, she put the little package in the palm of that same hand. Swiftly, she opened the door and got out. Once on the pavement, she leaned through the window and said breathlessly:

'It's nothing much, I'm sorry. It's just that I noticed your one was worn out.'

It was a leather key-ring. It looked like quite a good quality one, too: the only thing was, it had the artless pretension of imitation snake skin.

It was only two days later, when Y phoned me, that I suddenly realized that we'd exchanged very few presents up until then: on her birthday and on mine, that was about it. It was as though our love was above such trivialities, above the ritual of such demonstrations. Besides, what could I possibly give her, if she wanted for nothing, if everything seemed superfluous and if it might make her husband and daughter suspicious? Whatever my present might have been to her, how worthless it would have been compared with the magnificence of her eyes, the availability of her time and body, the alternating shadow and light that marked her every gesture, or even, as had happened that afternoon, the agitated state that the merest hint of her voice left me in?

'Do you know what?' she had whispered straightaway. 'I'm back in Lisbon. That's right, in Lisbon... In a hotel. But it's best if I don't tell you which one right now. I've only got Vicky with me... She's just next door, having a shower. No, I can't talk any louder. But I miss you so, so much! I miss everything! Yes, tomorrow… At twelve. Twelve sharp. Then, if you want, I can spend the whole afternoon with you.' After a brief pause when all I could hear was her breathing, she said: 'What a nightmare! You can't imagine what a nightmare these past few weeks have been!' There was another pause, but this time I couldn't even hear her breathing. 'I'm sorry! I have to hang up… I'll tell you all about it tomorrow.'

XL

'Don't ask.'

She had started off by throwing her arms around my neck: as though she was about to drown; as though she had also given up any hope of being rescued, as though she even wanted to drag me down to the bottom with her. Then, gently but firmly, she released herself from our embrace, grasped my shoulders with both her hands and, taking a step back, she questioned me with her eyes in a long and silent stare, until finally, she cried out:

'Don't ask.'

Dropping her arms to her sides, she came straight in here and dropped onto that armchair:

'Please! Stay where you are. Don't come near me. I'll be better soon.'

She sat there sobbing, her eyes crying tiny, uncontrollable tears. Her left arm was stretched out towards me, her hand open, her fingers stiff, trying to keep me at bay. I was stunned by this gesture – it was in no way theatrical, if anything, it was magical and hypnotic – and I felt I had to obey her so as not to prolong the state she was in. I remained standing by the door.

The greeny-blue of her eyes, streaked now with red, seemed more green than blue, then more blue than green, which made them almost frighteningly beautiful, and I didn't know whether to feel elated or heartbroken.

Suddenly, she closed her eyes, placed her hands flat on her knees, rested the back of her neck on the back of the armchair, and started to breathe with forced regularity. Speaking as though from somewhere else far from here and taking part in a hypnosis session where she was both hypnotized and hypnotizer, she said:

'See? I'm nearly better.'

But I was probably the one who was hypnotized, by the impressive outline of her eyelids, the clear lines of her finely chiselled features, a perfection that was almost out of this world. Who is it who once said that beauty is the beginning of awe? Someone said it; I can't remember who; but they were right.

A few moments later, she opened her eyes, which were by then quite dry; she looked around, a little dazed, and said in a matter-of-fact voice:

'It's all very tidy in here.' She got up. With housewifely concern, she wiped a cautious finger along the top of the dresser and in the corners of the mirror: 'There's no dust… Has the cleaning-lady come back from holidays?'

'Who? Floripes? I think so. I mean: of course she has. She came a little earlier today to freshen things up, and I noticed everything was fine…'

'Ah, this morning, was it… Do you mean you haven't been coming here…?'

It didn't sound like a question; I wanted to make the most of her apparent willingness to talk, so I went up to her, touched her forehead with my fingertips and lightly stroked her hair. But as soon as I tried to reach the back of her neck, she stiffened and avoided my hand:

'Not now. If you want to be kind… I feel like a cool drink. Gin would do nicely… Vodka or gin and tonic… Would that be all right?'

'Of course it would. I stocked up *our* bar recently.'

'So you have been coming here?'

'Not in here as such. I've been through there, in what you call the workshop.' I told her of the piece I had sculpted in Nyasa's honour. 'Would you like to see it?'

'Later. Not now. Bring me my gin, if you wouldn't mind.'

I stood there, without touching her, just watching her: she was standing, with her back to the mirror; I thought she had lost a little weight, there were wrinkles in the corner of each eye, an embittered twist to the corners of her mouth, an almost imperceptible trembling of her chin. She was wearing a blue and white cotton dress, I couldn't tell if it was dark blue with a white design or the other way round, as the somewhat intricate pattern allowed both interpretations. When I half closed my eyes, the blue, which was very dark in itself, became almost black; and this made it look like a retriever's coat. Her very low-heeled shoes were also dark blue with a white trim. She had not taken them off.

'Are you going to let me to die of thirst?'

'Oh, if only you knew all the things I have to tell you! How I ran around looking for you!…'

'You can tell me afterwards.' The tone of her voice was drier than the voice of someone who's just thirsty.

When I returned with the duly prepared gin and tonic, I found her leaning over the divan in the unmistakable posture of someone straightening out the cover; and I even felt as though she had not only been inspecting it, but almost sniffing to discover what was hiding beneath the cover. Caught by surprise, my beautiful retriever straightened up and declared, perplexed:

'The linen has actually been changed.'

'Of course it has! After all this time...!'

I handed her the glass which she grasped immediately, but she didn't appear to be in any hurry to drink it; indeed, she placed it on top of the dresser after walking round the divan. Then, in a manner that was probably intended to appear purely mechanical, she opened the first drawer a little, then the second, and from it she pulled out her snowy white nightdress:

'It must need washing.' She took it up to her nose, but then she put it back where it was.

I couldn't contain myself any longer. Raising my voice a little, I almost shouted at her:

'What on earth is the matter with you? What are you looking for? What's going on?'

'Please! I don't like being spoken to like that. And I've already asked you not to ask me any questions.'

'But yesterday, you said that today you'd tell me everything.'

'That was yesterday.' She looked away; lowering her voice, she said: 'Can't you see you're being very selfish?'

'Oh! I'm the one being selfish, am I?... You're the one who disappeared three weeks ago, exactly three weeks ago, you went off to London, you only rang me ten days later, you've only spoken to me twice since then and now you've come here, pulling that face, behaving like this, with a...'

'Well maybe I shouldn't have come. Maybe I'd better never come back here again. It's what you want.'

She picked up the little bag she had dropped by the side of the armchair (it was not her Hermès bag) and walked towards the door. But I barred her way:

'That is not what I said. I'm sorry if I got carried away. Sit down again and let's talk.'

'Talk? What for? With someone who disappeared three weeks ago? With someone who has been so rude to you? The way you're carrying on, it's as though I never left you a note telling you... You wouldn't believe what I had to go through to get here that morning! You're the one who didn't ring me afterwards.'

'But I did ring you. Lots of times. But I couldn't get hold of you. And there was a fault on the line. So it was only the next day that I got hold of the maid. You're the one who has no idea what I went through that day and every day since… I went to the Algarve, I went to the Alentejo, to your husband's factory, I even went to the Aztecs' house… By the way, your house is in Vale do Lobo, isn't it?' Taken aback, she nodded yes, and I continued: 'Well let me tell you that no one was able to confirm that.'

'Don't you believe me? What exactly is it you don't believe?'

'Nothing. I'm just telling you what happened.'

'What name did you ask for? That house is in Vicky's godfather's name. Along with a number of other things. It seemed like a good idea eight or nine years ago, with the *Verão Quente*[38]… Now he's died… Now I'm not so sure it was for the best.'

She proffered these last few words as though they were no more than a charade for her too. During the brief conversation that had preceded them, she had put her bag back on the floor, but she still remained standing. In the meantime, I had sat down sideways on one of the arms of the chair. I suddenly felt exhausted by the tone and content of our exchange, as though drained by the realization that it was all falling apart, that everything was becoming absurd and petty, and it was probably all my fault.

I wished it was winter; instead of the heat that had been steadily rising over the past few days, I wished it was a crispy cold day outside; the wind would be howling, I would have remembered to light the heater in readiness and would now be wrapping the white shawl around her shoulders.

I suddenly grasped her hands; she did not pull them away – but did not exactly surrender them to me either – as she was probably disconcerted by the speed and spontaneity of my gesture.

'Why must we persist,' I asked her, 'in making accusations that are leading nowhere? We need to tackle what really matters. Then we can see exactly where we stand.'

'I don't understand. I don't know what you're talking about.'

'Yes, you do. You understand perfectly well. Do you or do you not want to live with me?'

'Oh, you think it's as easy as that, do you?' She freed one of her hands, not angrily, and raised it to her eyes which were damp again. 'My mother left my father when I was Vicky's age. Do you think it was easy?'

'At least your mother did it.'

'What about me?' She removed her other hand; she went to the other side of the room and stopped by the bookcase. I was almost shaking in fear at the thought that she might want to see the portfolios where I keep my sketches: in one of them, half an hour earlier, I had placed my portrait of Zu. But, with her back to the bookcase, she continued: 'What about me when it happened? What do you think it was like for me? And what would it be like for Vicky?'

'Have you spoken to her about it?'

'Me? Of course not. The way things are? No way!'

She went back to the dresser: she finally took a sip of her gin and tonic. 'Did you know I've been in London with my mother? I hadn't seen her for nearly five years. She was fine, she's still going strong. She looks amazing! No one would guess she's my mother. I don't understand why she seems so happy. Her husband is old, getting madder every day. But he's still having affairs. Everybody knows he is. If I were her… *Quelle bêtise*! I know very well I'm not like her.' She took a deep breath: and unexpectedly threw her arms round my neck again: 'But I want to! I want to! I want so much to live with you! And I want so much to have your child! It would mean so much to me. Trouble is, it's one thing to want something…'

Before my very eyes, her mouth gaped and twisted as though she were in pain, leaving no doubt about her pressing desire. In a few seconds we were both undressed. But when I pulled the covers back, she almost screamed:

'Not there! I'd rather here.' Trembling all over, she lay back on the carpet. However, she immediately brought her legs together and bent them up over her chest: 'No, no. I'm sorry… I can't do it today.' She leapt up onto her feet again, scurried over to a corner of the room clutching her pants and bra in one hand, and her dress in the other.: 'Please! Please get dressed too. I can't see you like that… All you feel is desire. It could be me or any other woman.'

Over the next two hours, this scene was re-enacted twice, with few encouraging variations.

'I really must go now.'

She had just got dressed again for the third time. So had I. Apart from feeling extremely frustrated, the ludicrous situation made me feel quite despondent; but I was also full of pity for both of us. Not to mention, more prosaically, as Zu would say, that my tummy was beginning to feel a bit hollow.

Without a word, I went to the larder to get some cream crackers and petit-fours, to the fridge to get some pies that I'd bought earlier that morning, and one of the tins of foie-gras that had been there since Monday. I made two fresh gin and tonics: I had drunk most of the one I had given her before. On our empty stomachs made worse by all that unnecessary emotion, we had to steer away from dangerous mixtures.

As soon as she saw me arrive with the tray, she attempted a smile that could only be described as poignant:

'I see you haven't lost your knack...'

'For what?'

'For organizing this kind of meal.' She started to nibble at one of the pies, and ate a couple of petit-fours. When she finished, she remarked: 'These are a bit dry. Or am I imagining it?'

'You're imagining it. I bought them this morning.'

'I'm sorry. I'm sorry for what happened today as well...'

I was about to retort with: 'For what didn't happen today'; but when I saw her walking towards the door, I merely asked, with an almost total lack of feeling that quite appalled me:

'Well, when shall I see you again?'

She looked surprised:

'You want to see me again? You're not angry with me?'

'When shall I see you again?' I repeated in the same tone of voice.

'I'm the one who's most to blame. You must think I'm mad. What I wanted most of all was to be with you. But I couldn't do it.'

'See you when?'

'So many things have happened. I'd so much like to tell you about them! But I can't. You don't mind if I ask you... not to ask me any questions?'

'No, no, I don't mind. All I want to know is, when am I going to see you again?'

'Can we make it tomorrow?'

'That's fine by me.'

'Let's make it tomorrow, then. At twelve again. I hope I'll be a bit more calm tomorrow. Now stay where you are. Don't take me to the door. Let me leave on my own.'

Less than twenty minutes later, there was loud, impatient banging on the door.

How could the heat, at two o'clock in the afternoon, have

disfigured her features so much in such a short time, making her hair limp, her big eyes protrude and her chin quiver more than before. She seemed to be in a state of shock, not even daring to come inside:

'I've been walking around all this time looking for a taxi. There was a man in a Fiat who kept following me. He wouldn't leave me alone. But he looked as though he was only trying to frighten me. So I rushed back here.' She suddenly clutched my arm, pulling me outside: 'Look! That's him! That's the car.' I went up to the end of the pavement with her, but I was blinded by the sun and didn't see any car. She added: 'It went round the corner. Just now. You can't see it anymore.'

'Calm down.'

I took her gently by the wrists, led her back inside here and put an arm round her shoulders; I closed the door with my other hand, kissed her hair, kissed her forehead, kissed her eyelids. This time, she at once took off her shoes.

She came back the next day, she came back on Sunday, she came back on Monday.

As though wanting to exhaust in a matter of hours the contained turbulence of a subterranean sea. As though wanting to exhaust herself. As though wanting to exhaust me.

Her hands: one minute, they were all over me, the next they were gone. Her mouth: one minute, all-embracing, the next, withdrawn. Her eyes: always the same, never the same.

Instead of conversations, there were words, though not many; there were long periods of silence. Nothing was mentioned: not even the name of the hotel where she and Vicky were staying.

Every now and then she would be overcome by tiredness and suddenly have a little sleep. But she never surrendered to one of these naps without first holding onto one of my wrists beforehand. She would wake up as suddenly as she had fallen asleep.

On Saturday and Sunday she allowed me to drive her to the corner of Avenida Infante Santo in order to catch a taxi. On Monday, it was a little after six o'clock in the afternoon when we were about to leave: just then, there was the sound of keys in the lock, and there before us stood Floripes.

'Well I say, Mestre! What a sight for sore eyes!' But she interrupts herself when she sees I'm not alone and am bodily trying to hide the person I'm with. 'If you prefer, Mestre, I can come back later…'

But it is Y herself, stepping out of the shadow I wanted to keep her in, who goes up to Floripes, smiling, saying, not at all, of course she could come in, we were just about to leave.

'Very well, madam! Well, if you'll excuse me...' By the tone of her voice when she said those words, I knew at once that Floripes was delighted.

In the car, Y made this request:

'Please don't ask any questions. But today you don't have to take me to the Infante Santo. You can drop me off over there, by the trams. Or even here would be fine. Look, there, would you mind calling that taxi for me?'

I hooted, I waved, I overtook the taxi and pulled up in front of it. Just as she was getting out of the car, she said:

'Oh, I was forgetting... I can only come back on Friday now. I have to go to the Alentejo. With Vicky. At least you won't get sick of me.'

XLI

'Oh, Mestre, what a beautiful lady! What you might call a real picture! And those eyes of hers, they're something else! I knew it, I knew it all along: all the fuss you've been making these past months, Mestre, always checking to see if I'd changed the linen, changed the flower water, done the dusting, remembered to put water in the ice-tray... There had to be something really special behind all that, oh, you don't have to tell me, somebody really special, and not one of those women who like to pretend they're artists, or pretend they're models, as though you're one of those, Mestre, who need models to turn into clay or whatever it is they do, all covered in make-up and all looking the same, as though they'd just been to have their photograph taken! After all, I do know what real artists are all about, working all these years in these ateliers, and I also know that what you like, Mestre, God preserve us, is to find all you need inside your head, isn't that right...?

'Models, I say to myself, that's what the craziest ones call themselves as an excuse to take off all their clothes. There was even one, so help me God, who once left behind a bra with such filthy straps, I didn't even know what to do with the thing, of course after a few days I just threw it away, because no one would claim it as it would only point the finger at them!

'This doesn't mean, so it doesn't, that it wasn't mostly ladies who came here before, I could always tell by the smell they left behind of their perfume and how clean the sheets were afterwards, some folded the little hand-towels after themselves and threw their tissues into the basket, some were even so fussy that they wouldn't even use the little hand-towels, that was my idea, those little hand-towels, years ago, I don't know if you still remember, Mestre, and a damned fool I was too, because all I was doing was making a rod for my own back, it's just more work for me to do, how was I to know then that they'd be bringing in things as nice as those Kleenexes and stuff.

'Oh, what if that great mirror there was a picture, with little miniature portraits of all the ladies who've been here...? I know all about them, not that I've ever seen them, but there were many times when there'd be three or four in the same week, first this one, then the other, and they must have all been pretty classy, so they must, but I could tell them apart at once by their perfume, because this nose of mine, it never lets me down. That's not to mention those that came two by two at the same time, I wish I had a thousand escudos for every time that happened, and with you too, Mestre, because you'd never pass up the chance of a couple of dishes like that, which is like, Mestre, oh, I must be quiet, having two helpings of pudding in the same bowl.

'Now there's something you can see straightaway in your lady, so bashful and trying not to show it, even if you asked her, Mestre, I'm sure she wouldn't do such a thing. She's so beautiful, so lovely, she even looks like some saint or movie star, and when I say saint, I don't mean just any old saint, and when I say movie star, I don't mean just any old movie star, because there are saints who are really not very beautiful at all and stars who are actually quite ghastly. What I would have liked, and that's what I thought of straightaway, was for my daughter to have been able to see her, if only to stop her, whenever I tell her all about what you get up to, Mestre, from saying that I'm exaggerating and probably making it all up.

'Oh, yes, that's right, I was told you've met her already and you asked about me, and that you were a darling, as she says, which is just like you, and that this time round she found you a little less down in the mouth, still a bit low, perhaps, but you know what girls are like at that age, Mestre, anyone over fifty is lucky to still be alive and is fit for nothing except for the rubbish heap. She should have seen this lady, and I would have told her: "Look here, girl, not everyone needs such a big dustbin as you!"

'What am I going on about, saints and movie stars, a queen is what she is, and with such a manner about her that she goes straight to people's hearts, you can tell straightaway that she must be kind, even a little bit simple, and, poor woman, who can help this kind of thing, she's definitely fallen in love with you, Mestre, and she even led me to believe she has.

'Oh, silly me, what a fool, what a great big ninny I am, what's got into me to let on like this! Oh, Mestre, for the love of God, on your good health, on your mother's life, don't ever tell the lady anything about what I've just been talking about, she begged so much for me not to say anything, but deep down I wouldn't have rested easy if I hadn't told you. After all, poor woman, she meant no harm, she thought she had left her hairbrush here, that's why she came back, but her brush was in her bag after all and then, that was it, she stayed here all innocent and friendly, so she did, chatting to me for a while.

'Now, now, why should I hold anything back? Of course she also wanted to see what she could worm out of me, but with such good manners that you wouldn't have believed it, so kind, so polite, and such a bird-like voice in such a tall woman! And who could hold it against her, when you could really tell that all that's the matter with her is that she's jealous. But you can be sure, Mestre, that I put her mind at rest as much as I could about all the things she wanted to know about, the poor woman kept on asking me questions, all the time pretending she didn't want to know about anything.

'Well, why shouldn't I put her mind at rest? It was no skin off my nose! Even if I'd had to lie, I would have put her mind at rest. But luckily, I didn't have to, so I didn't, and that's why I swore to her, I even swore on my daughter's happiness, on my grand-daughter's good health, that you hadn't brought anyone here for ages, oh, yes! I was sure of that, so I was, sure as sure can be, because, thank God, this nose of mine never lets me down!

'I was also telling her about other things, and not just to put her mind at rest, because after all I was just telling her a few undeniable truths. For instance, that you had never, Mestre, in all these years, taken so much care over little things, making all this fuss about having flowers in the vases, not to mention, as far as I can remember, unless with that lady-friend of yours from some embassy or other, who never made it a secret and even left her car right outside the door, all this extravagance with the champagne and those little black ball things that cost the earth and stink to high heaven.

'That's when she asked me, like someone who doesn't really want to know, but please, Mestre, over your dead body, don't ever tell the lady what I'm telling you now, if I had ever noticed if someone had been here, here in the bedroom or even in the other room, if anyone had been here during the last few weeks of last month. No way, I told her, what a silly idea, with this nose that God gave me, even if it had been a whole month ago, I would have noticed it!

'Then, poor woman, she even had tears in her eyes, she started telling me she was really worried, that she had no one she could talk things over with, that nothing like this had ever happened to her. And she didn't want me to think that she was one of those women who go around doing this kind of thing, those weren't her exact words, but I know that's what she meant. And that her husband was a fine man, she didn't want for anything at all, but she did have loads and loads of problems, and that she had a young daughter at home, getting quite big now, and all she wanted was to be a good example to her.

'So I said to her straight: "Lady, as if I don't know all about these things! Take my daughter, I trust her totally, yet she has never found out, nor will she ever find out, about the huge mistake I made once!" Of course, I only said that to the lady to cheer her up, and so that she wouldn't feel so alone, but the truth is I never made a huge mistake at all. I did nearly, once, so I did; I nearly gave in, but I didn't... It just came out of my mouth, just like that, when I was talking to her, just one of those silly things you say just to be friendly. But you, Mestre, you have known me all these years, you know very well that I'm not lying now. Why would I need to, you tell me?

'So there we are: we chatted away for ages... And in the end, as I'd told her I really liked the perfume she wears, she took out a little bottle from her bag, still quite full, so it was, and she really wanted me to have it. But I said no, thank you very much, but no thanks, I'm too old for that sort of stuff, unless I took it for my daughter. And even when she knew it wasn't for me, she still didn't give up until I accepted it. And she stayed so polite, always so kind, not at all proud even being so beautiful, you can actually tell that she's a bit foreign, I knew straightaway from her accent, because our own ladies, those who are just from Portugal, would never be able, I think, to be so beautiful and at the same time so simple, so they wouldn't.

'Then, when we were saying goodbye, she kept thanking me, she even wanted to stuff a large note into my pocket, she kept asking me not to say anything to you, as if she need to worry, as if I'm not able to keep a secret!

'Hey, hey, you can't go doing that! Now you're troubling yourself too, Mestre... What's this for? I might even be offended if it wasn't you, Mestre... And those are two notes of the biggest sort, too! No, no... I'll take one if only to take care of that little rise that I was going to ask you for. The holidays were awful, what with my daughter coming and going every day, and everything being so expensive, we had a burst pipe, we had to foot the bill, my son-in-law can't deal with that kind of stuff, all my husband wanted to do was rest, my granddaughter broke two lamps, a tureen and four glasses, and that was another huge expense… So, when it comes to holidays, no more rented houses ever again, you'll never catch me having that kind of holiday again! Next year, if all goes well, we'll go to a little *pensão*… But I'll have to start saving straightaway, because if I don't think of these things, no one else will. Otherwise I wouldn't even accept it. But it will come in handy, so it will, especially with the other note the lady gave me.

'And such a beautiful lady, so friendly, so kind! She's enough to make your heart go all gooey… She's so much in love, so very much in love, more than in love, I can tell these things! She's just the kind of lady you need, Mestre, I know exactly what artists are like, they can burst with sadness if they don't have someone beautiful like that with them… Oh, Mestre, Mestre! May the Lord our God keep the two of you together for a very, very long time!'

XLII

Do not feel sorry for me: Floripes's discreet indiscretions hurt me less than you might fear.

What did it matter that Y had come down a few steps from the pedestal on which I had placed her? Come to think of it, it was a slip that only made her more human.

For too long I had been attracted (perhaps awed as well?) by the thought of loving a goddess, so that it was high time now that I should see, in her place, an ordinary woman whose weaknesses I found unexpectedly disappointing yet endearing at the same time.

The worst was not to be able to tell her this – at least not straightaway.

What first came to my mind while Floripes was talking, was a frequent saying of Xô's, which she repeated so often that it must almost have become ingrained in the tables and chairs on certain esplanades in Rome: 'Oh, how I long for my blue soul!' Then she would stretch herself. But it was a phrase she would only utter under two specific circumstances: either to get over the slight disappointment (she always used the definite article, too) or else to dispel a profound nostalgia. Only under these circumstances: the slight disappointment or a profound nostalgia.

There was another frequent saying of Xô's (but this one I invariably associate, I don't know why, with a small restaurant in the Campo de' Fiori, where we would often have lunch on the *terrazza*), which would erupt furiously, laden with vindictive bitterness: 'Fortunately, I can manage my losses!' She used this one mainly when she was depressed: especially when she received bad news from Brazil, either regarding her Texan ex-husband's wiles and 'freshness', or regarding her father's stubborn refusal to loosen the strings of his immense purse. But the more she was unable to 'manage' said losses, the more she would say these words. The only thing for sure was that, just by saying them, she would feel better.

Floripes went on and on talking, and all I wished for was this one absurd thing: that her infallible nose had not discovered, nor would come to discover, that after her talk with Y, Y had never been back here.

Ten days had gone by since that Friday when she was supposed to turn up and never did. But every morning and most afternoons, I still took refuge in here. And every now and then I went beyond carefully setting the stage by leaving dirty dishes in the sink, and convincingly messing up the divan: I would also sprinkle the sheets and pillow-cases with a few drops of 'Y'; namely: a few drops of *one* of the toilet waters that Y used. Floripes's nose hadn't, after all, noticed this inconsistency when it came to the perfumes Y used.

Not that I'd bought a bottle specifically for that purpose: it had simply occurred to me, that Friday, to make her a little 'gift'.

It had in no way crossed my mind that Y and Floripes might have had a chat here that afternoon. But I was strangely displeased that Floripes, having seen Y with me once, should so quickly be aware of the fact that she'd gone. Now, after ten days of drenching myself alternately with antidepressants and whisky, it was actually quite refreshing to have someone talk to me about Y. Just in the same way as it must have been good therapy for Y to have someone to confide in.

But every time I reached into my pocket, every time I touched some scrunched-up sheets of paper inside it, my fingers touched either fire or ice. This letter I couldn't bring myself to read again, this letter that had been waiting here for me that Friday morning, which was it, fire or ice?

Nor would I dare to transcribe it here now. It was a bewildering, breathless, impetuous, confused, chaotic letter. Apart from the postscript, there were seven short paragraphs in Portuguese; the other two were much longer and written in English; all were interspersed with a great number of French expressions.

There was one refrain: *I cannot say a word.* But every now and then, from the halting Portuguese, emerged pure gushing sentimentality of an irritating yet touching immaturity. Only one conclusion could be drawn from what was better articulated in an almost torrential English: *My husband needs me.*

It would be too painful to transcribe it all here. The postscript will suffice: especially as I know it off by heart. Strangely (what would Freud have to say about this?), each one of its short clauses is a negative sentence:

You do not know how hard this is for me. I do not want to say Adieu. I do not know if I can say Au revoir. Do not chase for (sic) *me. Do not forget of* (sic) *me. You cannot imagine how happy you made me. I do not know when I am coming back. I do not know if I am coming back. Do not believe of* (sic) *me when I said I prefer drawings. I do not know for* (sic) *why I am so jellous* (sic) *of the sculptures. I cannot live without you. You cannot imagine what these months.*

This was followed by two or three words that had been violently crossed out and were completely illegible. But in this postscript, and only in connection with the sculptures, the word 'jealous' only appeared once. Misspelt.

How my inner barometer kept moving during those ten days: knowing I would never forget her; wanting to forget her; fearful of forgetting her, being certain I would forget her and that I will never ever forget her.

It was hard to find, in either a near or distant past, situations that I could profitably use now as models for how to cope. Before, it had almost always been the case that my hearth was inhabited not only by the chatelaine of the *piano nobile*, but also by one of those transient, pilgrim women; and it was only a matter of installing one of them temporarily, or at least pretending to, in one of the spare suites. There were even some who knew intuitively that the time had come for a stormy occupation. But these were seldom the ones who would get to enjoy the whole *enfilade de salons.*

The by now distant situation with Xô (how strange: at that time there were no transient, pilgrim women in the attic or in the basement, either) was no use as a point of reference, because then it was I who sang the discordant swansong of our separation. And I did with most of the others, too, though perhaps with them I was not quite so out of key. In the last few years, it was just with Ursula von W. that things didn't happen quite like this. In the same way as Y was doing now, but over weeks on end and with no dramatic effects, she too had intoned the consecrated aria of *my husband needs me.* Except that in Ursula's case, the aria was justified by the natural vicissitudes of her husband's career or, to be more precise, by his forthcoming transfer to a new post.

But how was I to make comparisons, or even draw parallels, when the relationship between Ursula's diplomatic *corps* and my own body, so little inclined towards diplomacy, had always been so epidermal? Even so, many months after having got completely over her, I could still feel my heart miss a beat whenever I spotted the number-plate on a Volvo bearing those fateful red letters, CD.

And that's not all: that's where my incurable allergy to all forms of entertainment at embassies or diplomatic residences stems from.

No. There are no patterns. There are no antecedents. And I will find nothing but caricatures of the hard, implacable design – to forget or not to forget – that only Time will determine, and has started to already.

'The white shawl is her unfailing attire during our intimate ritual on winter days.'

As though undergoing some kind of rite of exorcism, I have scribbled these words down time and again, right here on the dresser, after reading Y's letter again and again.

How much would I have preferred her to have left her shawl behind, in that drawer, instead of that nightdress that never took on the shape of her body!

Oh, that dresser! Now that vaguely Venetian, vaguely genuine eighteenth-century incommodious commode appeared quite hateful to me. Around twelve years ago, I had the brilliant idea of forking out a fortune to buy the thing, from a *bottega* in the Via del Pellegrino, in Rome, not realizing for one minute the bureaucratic bedlam it would take to move it to Lisbon.

Xô's flat was situated between the Via del Pellegrino and the Via Giulia (but that had been eight years earlier). How desperately annoying to keep thinking of Xô all the time!

With Y, everything was perfect. At least with her, for a whole winter and a whole spring, I did indeed experience a successful love affair.

When Y comes back, if she comes back, nothing will be the same again. But perhaps then I might, somehow, be able to tell myself again that nothing is equal, everything is equivalent.

In the meantime, I shall never stop being grateful. On paper, in clay, in iron, in marble: an act of grace, a *Te Deum*, a celebration.

XLIII

It was a Saturday. I was parking my car in one of the spaces on the Praça, and there was Vana, parking right next to me:

'You big bad boy! You never did come to see my tapestries!' Then, raising four fingers of one hand to the two-finger breadth of her forehead, she exclaimed: 'Oh, no! I forgot to bring the *Expresso*... Have you read it? There's a very good review in it. My husband went out and bought several copies, first thing this morning, and I so wanted to bring one with me! At least one. I don't have to tell you who for... Do you know the beast is still on holiday? Oh, it's been so peaceful... Well, depends on what you mean by peaceful, doesn't it?... And how about you? You don't need to say anything; the shadows under your eyes say it all... You're mad! You will never learn... But you and that green-eyed tigress?! And knowing what you're like... I can imagine, I can just imagine!' She threw all this at me without getting out of the car, while switching her engine off and putting on the handbrake. I was already out of my car, leaning over the window on which she was resting her elbow, and I stood there, listening with a bemused patience that must really have surprised her. She made the most of it, looking at her wristwatch and twittering a few notes of thoughtful indecision: 'Come to think of it, there is still a little time... Are you in a great rush? Well, then, get in. Come with me, won't you. I'm just going down to Belém to look for a paper.'

Why not? It was three o'clock in the afternoon. In the atelier, there were only the same ghosts of other ghosts waiting, who came with me even when I was away from the atelier. To listen to Vana, to go off with Vana: a way as good as any other of keeping in touch with the vanities of the world.

From the four copies of the *Expresso* she managed to find in a kiosk ('You never know... there may be other interested people'), she at once chose one to reward me for my stupid and devout patience.

It took fifteen minutes to go there and back, if that. But when we returned and Vana parked her car again in the same place, I at once noticed that there was another one of those repellent pieces of paper under my windscreen-wiper. It had been so long since I'd last seen one! I rushed over to remove it and stuff it into my pocket, without even stopping to read it.

'Ah!' she exclaimed. 'A little billet-doux from your sweetheart?' Then, looking all around and not seeing a likely car in the immediate vicinity and with a little furrow of concern on her insignificant forehead, she added: 'Don't tell me she was angry at not having found you... Or that she saw the two of us together and got jealous...'

'No. Don't worry. Fortunately, she's above such things.'

'Oh, that's all right then. I haven't seen her for ages. How is she?'

'She's fine.'

'How about your mother? I never did see her again either.'

'She's fine, too. Equally fine. Everything's fine.'

This brief conversation took place on the way to the door of my atelier, where she at long last released me, with two twittering kisses on my cheeks, preceded by a no less twittering 'May I?'

'Thank you for the newspaper,' I managed to add. 'I'll read the review straightaway.'

What I did do first, however, was to read the vile piece of paper. It held two brief lines, and I seem to recall that neither of them had any punctuation. The first line said: 'You disgusting old man'. The second said: 'It won't be long now before the bomb goes off'. Or perhaps only: 'The bomb will soon go off'. I cannot be much more precise, as it was the only piece of paper that I threw into the waste-paper basket straightaway. It was only because I'd left my wallet at home that day that it didn't go the same way as all the others I'd received. Because of the way this last one had turned up, Vana was completely exonerated from the vague suspicions I'd had until then, though without paying them too much attention. And I was relieved to revert to the theory that, unless they were stupid jokes by an out-of-season Carnival prankster, there was a mistake and these bits of paper were not really destined for me.

Then, leafing through the newspaper, I idly searched for that 'very good review'. 'In the reviews section,' Vana had told me. It wasn't a review after all; and it was neither very good nor very bad: a mere seven or eight lines in a light-hearted register (Vana's full name alone took up a line a half) in a kind of brief account under the misleading heading of 'Summer Exhibitions...'

But my attention was drawn, on some other pages of the weekly tabloid, to no less than two articles on the scandal, which was apparently still quite serious and gaining notoriety, of the so-called currency trafficking. According to the author of one of the texts – the one labelled 'analysis' – the case had complex and mysterious political implications, covering up a confusing tale of arms trafficking; whereas for the author of the other piece – this was a straightforward report – there could be no doubt that it was no more than a financial stroke of such genius that it fell outside the reaches of the law. Yet both were unanimous in believing that certain rumours concerning the possible involvement of accredited members of the diplomatic corps in Lisbon had been somewhat premature. 'Except that' (both columnists happened to use the same expression) the main suspects or people implicated in the case were all foreigners; and some of them had indeed been living a long time among us. Although cautiously, the report even went so far as to mention names of at least four people alleged to have 'spontaneously' abandoned their homes on Portuguese territory. The second one of those four names was Y's husband's; but it was so distorted by fortunate misprints as to be hardly recognizable by anyone.

Do I need to add that this was no great news to me? And the tolerant tone of the report reassured me: Y would be back.

The rest of September dragged past in a sequence of threatening thunder, light showers, morning mists, temperatures falling at night, and one or two afternoons of skies brightly streaked with blue.

At the beginning of the following month, the weather returned to a deceptive *beau fixe*, and I was filled with nostalgia for the foggier August days at Foz do Arelho forty years ago.

I felt unkempt, sluggish, and quite uncouth; and the day before a public holiday I returned to Palmiped's competent shearing hands. But I didn't see Zu. I was told she was 'off sick' until next week.

A few days later, I again called on my mother. The maid who answered the door was quite reluctant to let me see her; in the end, she suggested that I should keep my visit as short as possible. My mother was sitting on the *chaise longue*, a white silk shawl tucked around her shoulders, and she didn't recognize me at first. Then, in a cold, bitter voice – twice calling me by my father's name – she asked me if I didn't feel any *rimorsi* at never having been to see her there before. I only bumped into dona Mercês on my way out: she congratulated me on my mother's good recovery from her mild stroke ('Luckily, it was nothing very much'); she also thanked me for not having turned up during the first few days ('She gets so excited when she sees you!'), in the same way as she'd asked my sister not to. I do believe she never realized that my sister (my half-sister) had never said a single word about any of it to me.

That night, it dawned on me that my wife was probably aware of what was going on: 'You've been so low, lately... Especially since Nyasa's death. I thought it was best not to worry you too soon. And your mother will get better. She's tougher than both of us put together.'

October was coming to an end and we had returned to our house in Lisbon, when we received a very sober invitation from the Aztecs to attend their farewell cocktail party. After consulting Press 2, it was clear that the proper response was indeed to accept, and to attend. But my wife couldn't go: she had to go to Oporto that day to argue a doctoral thesis.

A dozen pallbearers were there already. In Portuguese, we call them 'dripping-cats'. And all meanings of the word were appropriate here: it had been raining non-stop since morning and all the guests were more or less dripping wet when they arrived; and indeed, we all looked as though we were at a funeral, or calling to give our condolences to the master and mistress of the household. But our hosts were the ones who most succeeded at appearing relatively at ease: they must have felt as though we were compassionately coming to the wake of some monstrous son begotten through them by the Devil, and only because it had started to whimper was their stay in Lisbon being cut short, forcing their precipitated departure. That was it: the wake of the child Rumour. With our being there, they could keep up for a bit longer the illusion that the little monster had indeed kicked the bucket.

This time, there was no show of allegories, nor trumpeting parade of the famous and newsworthy: only a few unhappy people who were there just as themselves, who weren't even particularly intimate, men and women with the contrite, puzzled look of people who fear they've entered the wrong chapel of rest, other men and women with the competent air of those old concierges who never miss a funeral or seventh-day mass,[39] not only for the tenants of their own block, but at least those in the next-door block as well. The first group included the daft Music, once again overawed by the ghastly pseudo-Inca and pseudo-Aztec objects, visibly baffled by the fact that she must have seen them before in a different setting, which was that of a plain fourth-floor flat in Estrela and not in this pretentious villa in the Restelo. The second group, on the other hand, appeared to include the insipid, fat-bottomed wife of some flaccid member of our unctuous coalition government – precisely the one who, three months previously, had taken the opportunity of consulting my wife for free under a sunshade. It was quite easy to see that she wasn't there because her husband had sent her; and that her good deed on this rainy afternoon had merely been an impulse from the bottom of her magnanimous heart, which was probably even larger and no less heavy than her own wretched buttocks. But it was clear that Music was not there as a representative of Music; that Press 2 had turned up not in her capacity as an informant; that I was nothing to do with sculpture, and even less with Art with a capital A in general; and that the extremely official wife of the extremely official governor was not officiating at this funerary emergency in any official or even officious capacity. As for the rest of the mourning guests, I soon realized that, apart from the ambassador himself, they comprised mainly downcast, self-conscious embassy officials.

Fortunately, the pseudo-canvases of the pseudo-disciples of Klee and Kandinsky had already been packed. Through a crack in a window-pane, I saw that my stone and concrete Monstrosity was stoically bearing up in the rain; it would probably remain there, having probably been profitably fobbed off onto the future tenants of this frightful villa. But it was the first time that I had ever walked around its interior; in my fingertips, I carried a glass of whisky that was being topped up every ten minutes or so, and I suddenly wanted to find those two armchairs in which Y and I had sat, where nearly a year before, the glow from her sunburnt knees, beneath their dark blue stockings had seemed to replicate the glow in her eyes. I did not find them: they too were probably already on their way to the Amerindians' country of origin, unless they had never come down from that fourth-floor flat in Estrela where they might have been on loan or even hired.

The whole house, actually, was reduced to the bare essentials, especially the hall and the three reception rooms on the ground floor. There was nevertheless something beautifully melancholic in the relative bareness of the rooms: instead of depressing me even further, I found it almost comforting. With the help of the whisky I was conscientiously imbibing, I remained ensconced in the corner of a settee from where I could hear Music without listening to her and look at an angle into the hall, which was rapidly becoming the way out rather than the way in. Wrong! Someone had just arrived, the doorbell had just gone.

There are always people who turn up late, if only to say they're not coming after all, as Y and her husband had done, towards the end of July, right here, during the swimming-pool party.

One of the hired waiters (who had probably been in the kitchen counting his money or filling his doggy bag) came along only after the third ring, crossing my field of vision of the hall. Then he crossed it again in the opposite direction, carrying a raincoat that looked thoroughly wet. In the meantime, the hosts had rushed into the hall through another door to meet the latecomer or latecomers. But all that could be overheard was the shrill pseudo-Castilian prattle of *mi caro consejero y su señora*. Whoever the caller was, he or she was talking very quietly.

Just then, Press 2 came and sat down on the settee, between Music and me, to ask me if I was thinking of leaving yet and could I give her a lift.

But, very kindly, Music immediately offered to take her as soon as she realized that they both lived in the Benfica area. The trouble was that they both stood up at the same time, blocking my line of vision just at the moment when our hosts entered the room with someone new. Because of the whisky, I didn't have the lightning response of standing up as well, and the three of them slipped into the next room.

The idea was quite absurd, the likelihood so remote and so unreal… You can believe me when I say that I wasn't even too disappointed.

It was a man after all. The lady of the house had already put a glass in one of his hands, and was trying to put a sausage roll into his other hand, while he clumsily wondered what to do with the smouldering pipe that he still clung on to with his few remaining free fingers.

Although he didn't appear any slimmer, rather the opposite (that belly of his, bulging through his jacket!), I didn't think your friend looked too good. I could have sworn that his first reaction was to pretend that he hadn't seen me. Or maybe I reacted first, by pretending that I hadn't recognized him at once.

What I do know is that we spent the next twenty minutes or so in a strange game of blindman's buff, in a ridiculous game of poker, where we took turns in avoiding each other, alternately looking up and looking away. Then we found ourselves coincidentally face to face (or did we subconsciously engineer it?) before our hosts, making our goodbyes. Then he made the first move and, ever so casually, we exchanged the following greetings:

'Hello, Fernão.'

'Hello, David.'

XLIV

It had stopped raining.

'What? You don't have a car?'

'Well, yes, I do. But I don't drive. I've never learnt to drive.'

'That must be inconvenient. Or perhaps quite convenient too. So let me take you wherever you want to go. Where are you going?'

'Nowhere.'

'That's funny. That's where I'm going too. Let's go together so it looks as though there's lots of us.'

'Aren't there already? I think there's about ten million of us.'

I looked at him more carefully: as Floripes would say, he really did look a bit 'down in the dumps'. Either I was very much mistaken, or the two of you must have fallen out. But what was meant to start off as a dig at our country for not getting anywhere stuck in my throat: as soon as I got the chance, I would have a go at him about his share, however small, of the blame. After all, according to the imbecilic and trite expression, hadn't he 'held a few governmental responsibilities'? I well remembered, for instance, having seen and heard the people from the world of theatre, and perhaps also from the world of cinema, clamouring against some of the 'measures' he had taken whilst Secretary of State. So you took 'measures', my boy, you took 'measures', as though there were no metaphysics left in this world ('Look, all the religions put together teach us nothing more than clothes-making': this is wrong, but that's on purpose), and now you dare to complain about the nation's destiny! Just you wait, I'll bend your ear at the first opportunity.

But at first bend (literally speaking), on turning into the motorway, coming from the Avenida das Descobertas, the car skidded and two brilliant specimens of our national *intelligentzia* almost met their end. Your friend pressed his feet down on the mat as though trying to brake.

'You may not drive,' I said to him once I'd regained control of the car, 'but those reflexes of yours are not bad at all. Nor are mine, even though I have been drinking a little.'

'"Do not drink and drive." We've just passed two posters saying that...'

'That just goes to show how useless posters are. And the places they put them. It's back in the Aztecs' house that there should be a poster warning, "Do not drink and drive".'

We kept quiet until we reached the brow of the hill from where the city lights can first be seen.

'To think how I used to love Lisbon!... And nowadays...' he mumbled. But I said not a word.

Without slowing down at all, I had begun to concentrate on the unpredictability of my own driving. When we left the viaduct, there was only a slight swerve which I was able to control. I then set off towards the Marquês de Pombal, going through one or two irrelevant red lights, aware that there would be no great danger involved. We were going down the Avenida da Liberdade when I said to him:

'It's nearly half past nine. Do you feel like dinner? I don't think you used to go to the Parque Mayer very much, in which case...'

'In fact, I did at one point.'

'But it's deteriorated so much now that you probably cannot even trust the fried whitebait anymore.'

Then, just as we were driving past the entrance to the Parque, your friend started discussing Nyasa. He had been talking with Press 2 and found out about what had happened to the three paintings hidden under the settee in Rua da Alegria.

'One of them was for me,' he explained.

'Oh, really?' I was dismayed to hear an involuntary hint of grudging resentment colouring my voice.

'I also received,' he continued, 'a letter like the one he sent you and the others. But I only went round there two days after the fire.'

'I didn't realize you knew each other so well... He never said anything to me. He never mentioned you to me.'

'That's probably because he knew you didn't particularly like me... There's at least one other person who has never mentioned me to you for the same reason.'

I was dumbfounded. And yet I knew full well that your friend would go no further than vague allusions of this kind when referring to you. It was better that way: when we got near the Parque Mayer, I couldn't help remembering that, in some flea-pit in that small village in the heart of town, we had exchanged our one and only kiss.

In the meantime, I drove the car into the underground car park of the Restauradores.

'How about having something at Gambrinus's?' I suggested.

'Only if we eat at the counter. Something light. I don't really feel like having dinner.'

'Nor do I. I'll go along with you on that one.'

Some nibbles, a couple of beers. Suddenly your friend remembered:

'It was with Nyasa, about forty year ago, that at this very bar, I had the first hot dogs that arrived in Lisbon.'

'With Nyasa? Me too. Right here.'

'In those days they were still called *hot-dogs*...'

'So they were. It wasn't nearly as much fun once they started calling them *cachorros*.'[40]

'Nyasa went through a phase,' he recalled, 'when he wouldn't eat anything else.'

'That was before the phase when he'd only eat prawn rissoles.'

'Not before. After.'

We stuck to our guns for a while – before, after, after, before – then we took turns in recalling the images of other famous eccentrics of our times, though all of them lacked Nyasa's gift for genius. Thus, for a few moments, in Gambrinus's bar, some of the characters we had both known in our youth lived again: there was Anastácio, whom we called Spent Light-Bulb (by antonomasia) or Beaches' Delight (by antiphrasis), a fearsome miniaturist and calligrapher, who spent years and years copying the whole of the first canto of *Os Lusíadas* onto a postcard; there was the deaf-mute, Maró-Maró, who was arrested three times by the *Pide*[41] for his habit of continually spreading rumours of great scandals and imminent revolutions, albeit by gestures alone; there was Nito, also known as The Cadge, who drank dozens of *bicas*[42] a day at our expense, and who turned up one afternoon in the Café Chiado, without even so much as glancing our way, looking rather grand, with an ageing blonde on his arm, and with whom he feasted on two enormous steaks in succession, only to go round from table to table the next day, admonishing us: 'Hey, you lot! Did you see me around yesterday with a made-up, peroxide blonde, who's still quite good for her age? You probably thought she was a tart or something, didn't you? And that I'd become a pimp? Just you watch it! None of your jokes: that was my mother!' But your friend couldn't remember someone we used to call Gummy and who claimed he knew how to burp in several languages. Nor could I remember at all someone he mentioned – Chang-Kai-Chek – who was a student at the Instituto Industrial, whose father was probably one of those Chinese men selling ties, and who was expeditiously and devastatingly successful with the more modest class of females in Lisbon, simply by using the cunning device of convincing them all that he was a descendant of the Emperor of China. Who knows if it wasn't him, years later, who became Zu's actual progenitor?

Towards the end of my second beer, I couldn't hold back any more and I asked your friend straight out:

'Would you mind... Would you mind if we used the *tu* form now? Haven't we used it before when speaking to each other?'

'We've had phases. Like the moon. Like Nyasa's hot dogs and rissoles.'

'And like the good sports and the show-offs.'

'And the *ginjinhas* and the *genebras*.'

'No, not like those,' I amended. 'Those were always... How can I put it? Not quite simultaneous... Con-... Concomitant.' I found it hard to say this word. 'Well, a *genebra* would go down nicely!'

'Right then! One coffee and one *genebra*.'

'Mind you, come to think of it, we have known each other for a good number of years! At least since the end of the war...'

'Since before then, if you don't mind... If you don't mind, I can remember you from Foz do Arelho.'

'Foz do Arelho? Well, I really cannot remember seeing you from Foz do Arelho. You must have kept some pretty bad company.'

The coffee cleared our minds a little. We left and went on a silent pilgrimage to gaze in awe at the door of the wine bar, 'Ginjinha do Largo de S. Domingos', with its colourful doggerel about Dona Fedúncia da Costa, the wretched Mateus, the reverend father's nanny... I have always found these verses sublime. A masterpiece, as Nyasa would have said.

I agree that it wasn't the best time, at that point, to say to your friend:

'Although poetry is not my forte, I have read some of your verses. Only the odd poem, I must admit, the odd poem, here and there... For instance, I remember some verses about an ambulance. About what you feel and what you think when you hear an ambulance siren... You must have been feeling really threatened when you wrote them. I can remember some other verses... Damn! I can't recall them right now...'

'Don't bother trying.'

'Wait, wait... I know! They're verses in which you compare Europe to a half-crazed girl who is both in one city and in another.

They're yours, aren't they?

'I think so.'

'But when it comes to hearing your poetry, you wouldn't believe it! When I was twenty or so, I knew a girl who wasn't all there in the head, I can't even remember her name, I think she was one of your students… And she had this thing about reading your poetry to me! In between you-know-what. It was rather strange… Our privacy went straight out the window.'

'I can imagine. It must have been very irritating.'

'And you've also got a book of short stories. See how I know? I read most of that one. But then it won a prize, and that was enough for me to not to trust it any more. Now… as for novels, you've never written a proper novel, have you?'

'I've started several. But I've never finished one.'

'Ah, too lazy, were you, you skiver? Well, as sure as I'm standing here now, I am not departing this world for the next without first writing one myself! People like you say that it's a genre that'll die out, or that is already dead… One more reason for me to go to its funeral, at least to its seventh-day mass. As you see, I've been contaminated by the atmosphere in the Amerindians' house (let's hope that's all it is). But coming back to the novel… I too have started several, and half way through, I too became too lazy.'

'Now I remember… You used to write!'

'I did and I still do. Or is that not allowed?'

'We even collaborated on a newspaper towards the end of the forties…'

'Not quite! I was one of the editors. You're the one who collaborated.'

'Forgive my inaccuracy!'

'I don't think I need anyone's permission to write as well. Michelangelo didn't…'

'Nor did Almada.'

'Nor did Alberto Savinio. But he…'

'He was also a composer and a musician, apart from being a sculptor and a writer. And his essays are quite something else.'

At this, I was quite taken aback:

'You know Savinio's work?'

'As it so happens, I do. Most of it.'

'Hey! Let's shake on this. You're the first Portuguese person I've ever met who knows about Savinio. Some man, hey? As a creator, I don't think he has anything to do with me, and certainly nothing to do with you… But his essays, as you say, they're such an uplifting tonic!'

'Like the *ginjinha* we had in the Largo São Domingos: "a pectoral and digestive drink"…'

'It ought to be administered by dropper, on medical prescription, to all our rubbishy politicians.'

'What? *Ginjinha*?'

'No. The works of Savinio. What turns my stomach the most is that there are so many crappers (that's what I call them) around, that the more crap there is, the more seriously they take themselves!'

'Do you remember what Savinio said about the State?'

'Do I remember! In his *Nuova Enciclopedia*…'

'And especially in his little book called *Sorte dell'Europa*.'

'You're quite right: especially in that book. What I don't understand is how you can like Savinio and yet you've still been involved with the official rabble of this land.'

'I was weak… I'm no longer involved with them, nor shall I ever be again.'

'I hope not. You have to leave the easy stuff to people who are "easy". Apart from a few exceptions, what the politicians will never forgive us for is our being able to do the things they do, but without their being able to do the things we do. Deep down, they hate us.'

'You're exaggerating.'

'No, I'm not, and you know it! We know quite a few of them from old. Some have frustrated killer instincts, others have such complexes about their son-of-a-bitch origins that they'll never rest until they've got rid of us. The worst are those who set themselves up as cults. Before, the anti-cults used to be after our hides. Now it's the turn of the pseudo-cults to be after our balls.'

'Isn't this persecution mania?'

'I wish it were! What most of them want is for those who spatter surfaces or create grotesque objects, especially those who think, not to fulfil one of their greatest obligations: that of reminding them at all times that they are no more than the drudges of the people, the servants of the despicable masses, and that if we elect them and pay them (not much we can do about that!), it is certainly not so that they can go around giving themselves airs and graces, blatantly getting rich, behaving like *nouveaux riches*, thinking they can burp in several languages, like that Gummy did…'

'Goodness! You're being eloquent… Even epic! But I've already told you I will never again be involved in anything "official".'

'Do you promise?'

'I promise.'

'Then let's shake on it again!'

I don't know if we were being ridiculous or pitiable, holding forth in the middle of the Rossio, surrounded by puddles of rainwater glistening on the paving stones, under a threatening canopy of black clouds that seemed to be awaiting an electoral decision as to whether or not to send down more rain, standing right next to that opulent marble candlestick on whose tip, as dark as the clouds, D. Pedro IV did not know if he was in fact Emperor Maximillian, unless he had always been Maximillian not knowing if he was D. Pedro IV. Further up ahead, still in the skies, the ruins of the Carmo discoursed in a quiet voice with the top of the Santa Justa lift on the fleetingness of styles in matters artistic and the swiftly unhurried passage of time.

Then, walking slowly up the Chiado, we reached some fascinating conclusions. Although we were as different as two drops of water – one drop of sea water, one drop of fresh water – that didn't stop us from having other tastes in common apart from being keen on Savinio: Italy, all of it, or nearly all, a country that was absolute, embracing, abusive, brazen yet mysterious, extravagant, surprising and exacting; women that did and women that didn't; those, for instance, who when they take off their shoes in a certain way (there're not many of them, they're even quite rare), are at once more naked than if they were totally undressed; but also those whose nudity can only move us once they are completely undressed; the music of Vivaldi, Mozart and Brahms; the aphrodisiac tranquillity of some luxury hotels during the low season; the Alentejo, the Alentejo and again the Alentejo; parts of Spain that are the prolongation and amplification of the Alentejo; parts of France that are the opposite; films by Visconti and Bergman, some by Fellini, two or three by Truffaut; London taxis, far more suitable for almost everything than the gondolas of Venice; the trees in Buçaco, the beaches of the North-East of Brazil, a few on the Ionian Sea, some others on the Aegean, the cliffs of Marvão; certain islands and certain lakes; two canvases by a 1920s artist from Trieste, called Piero Marussig; the complete works of Stendhal (no: not all of them); one or other corner of the Algarve coast that was not yet polluted by the new class of political dogs and crass technocrats; Giacometti's sculptures; those bookshops in Greenwich Village that stay open all night; meaty prose such as Fernão Lopes's and pointed prose such as Rabelais's; Foz do Arelho as it was forty years ago; a Lisbon that no longer exists, either; and a Portugal that never did; and a Europe that never will.

Arguing in great dialogues and monologues, stopping, backtracking, and setting off again, we were like two teenagers meeting up again, telling each other what they'd experienced and discovered during the summer holidays.

Around us, the shabbiness of Rua do Carmo and Rua Garrett seemed to us less depressing than usual. And it took us over two hours to walk up less than two hundred yards.

In the fado restaurant in the Bairro Alto where we ended up, only very few of the customers were in any way reminiscent of those coarse-looking, frustrated, would-be *Marialvas*[43] who are now managing directors, drug-pushers, parliamentary representatives or heads of security for some political party or other; the fado singers were drowsy and ungainly, barely interested, if at all, in touching up their make-up, smoothing their tights or untangling the fringes of their shawls; the guitar players were practising together, softly, discreetly rehearsing new variations for a show in the Coliseu in two weeks' time and which might be shown on television; the waiters and waitresses, dressed according to tradition as herdsmen and fishwives, were finding it hard to detach themselves from the doorways, as though the doorways, without them, might be sadly deprived of precious decorations. Although the place was no longer busy, we had to wait a good twenty minutes for them to bring us a jug of red wine.

Leaning back in his chair and removing his pipe from his mouth, your friend looked at me straight in the eyes, and said:

'Tell me about your novel… I'm sure you're writing *one*. Or should I say: *the* novel? If you weren't, you wouldn't have said what you did.'

'You're wrong: I am not. But I will soon, perhaps…'

'Well, I may as well let you know that I have an idea for a novel, based on someone, and that someone is you, more or less. To be precise, it would be a novel where you would be the narrator. In fact, it would be a novel about you and narrated by you.'

'That sounds rather complicated,' I grunted.

'A little. But it's feasible. Totally feasible.'

I drained my glass: what ghastly wine! I filled it up again straightaway, in case my first impression was wrong. I asked him:

'What if I'm already writing that novel?'

'Better still,' he replied. 'It may be necessary for you to want to write it so that I can write mine. What can the poor writer do when faced with the powers and whims of the narrator?'

'Stop playing games. Try that one on your students.'

'I mean it.'

'So do I. Now just imagine that this is really happening.' I drank another gulp: my worst impression remained unchanged. Then I continued: 'Just imagine that I too put you in the novel in question, simply as an extra, as quite a minor character, as that's all you deserve.'

'Fascinating.'

'Don't get too excited. I might very well find myself treating you rather badly.'

'I have no doubt.'

'And I might even make up some compromising stuff about you.'

'Some of it, people won't believe. If they do, there will always be facts to disprove it.'

'I could, for example, turn your life upside down, and you might not be able to cope with it.'

'We shall see,' he threatened.

'Indeed we shall. Just don't complain afterwards.'

Lighting up his pipe again, he added boldly:

'You've given me an idea... As you like imagining things so much, just imagine that I am indeed going to write that novel, the one where you are both main character and narrator, and I'm the one who'll have you speaking about me as quite a minor extra...'

'What are you on about? Do you know what? I think we're both a bit drunk.'

'I would even say: very drunk. Which, besides, is unforgivable in people our age.'

'Hell! Don't you start going on about age as well. I've been feeling eighteen years old this evening... And only I know how my tricycle has been letting me down these past few months.'

'Your what?'

'My tricycle: heart, head and sex.'

'Ah!'

'But I'm not saying this just for someone to give me a new tricycle. That happened when I was a kid, and I didn't like it then... I always preferred the tricycle I had before.'

In the meantime, a couple (so to speak) had come in, whose irreproachable vulgarity could not have allowed them to go unnoticed: he was short, average-looking and stocky, and he greeted us both with a kind of intimate, yet restrained deference. I hadn't the slightest idea who the blighter could be. But your friend explained that it was someone he'd given French lessons to a long time ago (the restraint had therefore been because of me) and who had then switched to economics, becoming today a respected bank manager: over the last few years, going along with a succession of governments to which he proved himself indispensable, he had moved around from bank to bank (on the board of directors, of course) to such an extent that he has been nicknamed the Mountebank. As for her, she gave off many signals that indicated that she was not in fact his wife: she was vivacious and smart, very much a lady, incapable of being over-generous with her favours and of being accountable to more than two managers at a time. She was wholesomely attractive.

'Notice,' your friend remarked, 'how privileged you are in being chosen as my narrator. I could have chosen the Mountebank over there. The world of today, as seen through the eyes of the Mountebank, must be quite something: especially these new people, this new society, whose murky waters this toadfish inhabits. As for her, she would only be a bit-player...'

'Like you...'

Your friend ignored my barb and continued:

'But I cannot come to terms with having to talk like the Mountebank. Can you imagine how limited that oaf's vocabulary probably is, or must be? You, at least, have a few letters, you have your lights, you have a certain world, and in your own way, if nothing else, you're an entertaining bloke. Because of you, I refuse to "paint" these so-called "new people".'

'Can I tell you something?' I asked. 'You can't pull the wool over my eyes. Do you want my advice? I've got quite a lot to give you... Write about Savinio, write about Stendhal: they're worth it. Carry on working at the Gulbenkian: the Gulbenkian is worth it. Carry on teaching, carry on giving talks: the students and the audience are worth it. Carry on writing pretty, emotional poetry for emotional young girls to force on the men they take to bed, and which will then make those same men get mad at you: that's what you deserve... But when it comes to the novel, leave it to me. I'll manage somehow.'

I was foolish enough then to give him a brief description of my main female character. I nevertheless had the common sense to tell him that I'd made her up, that she corresponded to no living person:

'Her eyes are greener than green, bluer than blue... Yes, she's foreign... or at least half-foreign... The embodiment of Beauty.'

And off I went, putting scenes together, conveying details, outlining the character's behaviour. At one point, your friend let out an insulting guffaw:

'But who on earth do you think you're going to "sell" such a character to? From what you're saying, either you have to show her crudely as a psychotic or at least neurotic woman, or no one will believe in such an incredible character... You make it worse: I can tell by the way you describe her that you would never be capable of being so crude. You spoke of her with too much emotion...' And resting his fingertips on my arm, he added: 'Forgive me for laughing like that just now.'

The guitarists were thankfully concluding the frenzied variations that introduced what was certainly going to be the last round of fados: this was more than likely in honour of the Mountebank and his companion, who both seemed very well acquainted with the in-house artists. As for us, it would have been incorrect to carry on talking. Silence, therefore: the fado was about to be sung.

At the end of the round – no points scored – the Mountebank's companion got up from the Mountebank's table to go and whisper a few words to the players, then she asked the singer, who had just finished, for her black shawl. Then, turning specifically towards our table, she informed the small audience that she was going to attempt to sing a fado that belonged to the repertoire of the great Amália (and if the great Amália were to find out, she begged her forgiveness!), the lyrics of which had been written by someone here present; she then named, and pointed to, your friend, to whom I just about managed to whisper:

'You don't even have to become a bank manager... You're so lucky!'

Then, in a domestically keening voice which is probably delightful to listen to when the Hoover's been switched off, or even the hairdryer, the first few lines arose, more languid than vibrant, more sluggish than languid:

I went to the beach and saw our lives
Entangled in the seaweed...
Oh, my love, if we ran away,
No one would ever know!

With my prosaic mind, I pondered these words; at the end of the fado, when your friend came back from thanking the amateur *chanteuse*, when he even went so far as to kiss her hand (but she did plant two kisses on his cheeks), slightly overdoing the congratulatory smiles towards the enthralled Mountebank, I couldn't refrain from saying:

'You're telling me that if they run away no one will find out about anything? That's poetic freedom for you! If they do run away, that's when everyone will find out...'

Your friend attempted a plausible explanation:

'Not at the time I wrote the lyrics... That was over thirty years ago. Who knew about me then?'

'In any case,' I replied, 'this is what you call fame: people knowing your poetry off by heart...'

'... and singing it rather badly...

'... in front of a few lost souls.'

'You're right: fame at last.'

'So why do you need to write a novel?'

'You don't either. Least of all you. You've got your fair share of fame.'

'I know. It's not fame I'm after... Seriously now: do you realize that, for me, writing is, how shall I put it, something much more fulfilling than sculpture itself? I don't know if it's the same with you... But for me, above all, writing means making love with words, and then...'

'Not for me, it doesn't: I make love with sentences. Words are no more than parts of the body: they are the knees, the shoulders, the chest... I'm not a fetishist to that extent.'

'That's what I was trying to say. But that's not the only thing that gives me pleasure when I write... There is another aspect. You're the one who interrupted me just now... For I think that writing is also a means of saying no to the State, no to the Establishment...'

'Some people maintain the opposite... That writing is precisely...'

'What do I care about people who think differently! All I know is that when I write, I am denying what the State wants to achieve when it writes. Or what the State writes when it thinks it's achieving. I cannot explain it any better than that.'

I was befuddled by all the alcohol I'd been drinking over the past few hours. I'm not even sure if this part of our conversation took place in the fado restaurant or once we were already outside, on our way to the Largo da Biblioteca, automatically retracing the final walk I went on when I saw Nyasa for the last time.

It had been raining again; but only while we'd been indoors. The weather was being our ally and accomplice throughout this night. The roads were now muddy and slippery and, through a kind of pedestrian gymkhana, we were repeatedly forced to walk round the largest and more evident puddles. We even warned each other of the treacherous puddles that only became visible at the very last minute. But I had the feeling that, deep inside both of us, our dormant love-hate relationship was reawakening.

When we reached the Largo, an inexperienced or drunken driver raced past us at full speed, liberally spraying our shoes, our trousers and our raincoats with mud.

'Any other plans?' I asked. 'Apart from the novel that you're not going to write?'

'Many, but nothing specific. I don't feel like spending the second half of these wretched 1980s in Portugal. If my predictions are correct, the second half is going to be even more vile than the first. I feel greatly in need of a change of air, of changing my skin. A few months ago, I actually received an invitation to go to Recife to teach literature. I have several good friends over there, and one good friend in particular. I could lecture two or three afternoons a week and spend the rest of my time reading and writing by the coconut-trees and the waves on Boa Viagem beach.' Suddenly, putting his hand in the inside pocket of his raincoat, he exclaimed: 'Oh! That's right… *Someone asked me…* I'm meant to put this in the post. It's for you. It doesn't matter if I give it to you by hand anyway… I already know you know.'

He handed me an unsealed envelope and I immediately recognized your handwriting.

'You'll even save on postage…' I commented. 'May I open it?'

'As you wish… Of course you can.'

Inside were some ten sheets of unsigned, typewritten pages. The title had been written by hand: *Seven Disclosures (Of a confidential nature)*.

'Would you rather I read them later?'

He hesitated for a moment; then he replied:

'I would.'

I dared to ask:

'Well, is everything all right between you two?'

'Yes, between us it is.'

'I see... As Sartre said, in the days when we were still fascinated by him, hell is other people.'

'That's right.' He cleared his throat; then, in a vaguely lecturing tone, he stated: 'When you read it, you'll see that she's trying hard to free herself from certain influences. Perhaps mine, to start with. I think she'll succeed. She's got what it takes.' These last words were proffered in the chuffed voice of the proud father of a child prodigy.

'I've told you already that poetry is not my forte...'

'Now it's my turn to say: stop playing games.' And he hailed a passing taxi, apologizing with some embarrassment for not taking me as far as the Restauradores. After giving an address to the taxi driver, he added: 'The car park will more than likely be closed.'

The bastard! So that's how the good-for-nothing was going to make his getaway! Our evening had been enjoyable to a degree; but the conversation was, for the most part, forgettable. Especially what he'd said about the potential star of my potential novel.

I walked back up the Rua Ivens, with the envelope dangling from one hand. Seven disclosures, then? Seven, no less?

XLV

How sad is Lisbon
on days when love is alive!

Take Aznavour's record
off the record player.

Love affairs are better dead
than stifled

between seething walls
and begrudging people.

Tear up the photographs
you took in Venice.

Better still: throw them on the fire,
to be licked by the flames

until they are all
the colour of a gondola's hull.

Especially the picture
where the two of us are

standing by a well,
so open, so alive.

If only our love
had died out there!

★

While this town tightens its siege,
pointing its finger at us
day after day,
and day after day

making note of our footsteps,
through the streets,
on our shoulders,
we carry a gondola.

We brought it back easily, in all innocence,
right under the nose of Customs,
without even knowing the gondola
was in with our baggage.

We are travellers returned from an ephemeral heaven,
where anyway we only stayed for a week,
as though we'd gone to the cinema on the corner
of Europe
to watch a film that was far too short.

We cannot mention
the name of that film, nor that heaven.
Only in here, to and with one another.
But this room can no longer bear
our calling it Venice:
it has started to shrink out of spite,
becoming so restrictive and confined
that we have to go out in the evenings
with the gondola on our backs.

Now the whole town is shrunken as well.
The gondola now fits nowhere,
no road, no avenue, no square,
even the Tagus has become the size
of a zinc bowl
overflowing with dirty water.

We are travellers returned with no right to asylum.
We shall soon be accused
of being smugglers,
of obstructing the highway,
of destroying our architectural
heritage,
of disturbing the peace,
of endangering public health,

not to mention being a hazard to morality.
The formal indictment will comprise
365 paragraphs a year.

One day we shall be able
to feel sorry for ourselves.

★

This is what is called love:
to drink stolen hours,
amidst the constant fear
that they might be discovered
(how to get a criminal record!);
to hurriedly bite into
the pulp of minutes,
without drinking their juice,
without peeling their skin
(how to get stomach ulcers!);
to know how to briskly
swallow up seconds,
as though capsules
full of barbiturates
(how to die, sometimes!).
The culprit: this dog
we're holding so securely,
tied to our wrists,
and whose name is Time.
(Who always whimpers with fear.)

★

Do not speak to me now of other lands,
other skies, another roof, another bed.
Keep on counting my orgasms,
as this arithmetic delights you;
with canticles, keep filling three caves,
and sail each one in a gondola;
keep on pledging that no, not ever
like this, not even almost like this,
with no one else ever again.

You are born and you die, you die and are born again:
how will you ever remember so many lives?

I do want, I don't want, I do not know if I want
those tropical fruits, that hot
country you tell me about. It is so sad
the way you say maybe.

★

Before you place me
in the handcuffs of litotes,
I can soar just as high
on the wings of a metaphor.

In another age, you are the one
who taught me about litotes and metaphor.

Why should you impose on me
this excessive number of litotes?
Just leave me my wings,
lest I should fall from even higher up!
You are the one who taught me
so badly and so well
about litotes and metaphor.

★

And we are walking together in the evening
on a long tropical beach.
With your head to the side, like the trees
in the wind, you are walking by my side.
You are now a very old man.
You were made doctor honoris causa
by the vaguest, least known
of all universities in these parts.
We arrived nearly twenty years ago.
Your children and married grandchildren
came when you were made emeritus:
those not able to come sent telegrams.
Apart from them and a few others,

no one remembers you in Portugal.
Time has passed me by as well.
I dye my white hair now
so as not to see in your eyes
a possible horror, perhaps nothing but pity.

★

You could die, of course, in a few days' time;
or could even be dead right now.
Only over the radio, only by chance,
would I be told of your death.

Others you have loved, because it was before,
having reached a respectable status,
will have been told, en passant,
not only in good time, but even by someone
in your family.

Mine will be mourning's most secret, most unrewarding
task:
to walk anonymously past your coffin,
silently grieving that it's not a gondola;
to be nothing more than some past student
among so many others.

And that's when I'll rebel
at having been so indifferent, or worse, so sensible
when faced with the madness of your more impetuous
projects,
and not having experienced what you call the Escape,
and not having transplanted, for the duration,
our summer days to another hemisphere.

Of course, you might have died
on the way, on the journey.
At least then I would have been at your side.

XLVI

It seemed impossible, it was becoming almost unreal: the days were growing shorter (as they say) and so much was happening during them.

I began to write from notes I'd made over the past few months: will this turn out to be a novel? (Or an opera? Or an operetta?)

My mother was getting better, then she got worse again: a second stroke; this one was much more severe. She is now thirteen or fourteen, she calls me Daddy each time I go and see her; she asks me and pleads with me to let her leave Bergamo, to allow her to go to Milan to perfect her singing. She addresses dona Mercês either as Vincenzina or Donna Giuliana. (Who are they? Who were they? Who might they have been?) Sometimes, in a pleading tone that can swiftly become resentful, she calls out to my wife: *Mamma*! She only speaks Italian: an appalling, guttural Italian that bubbles up from her insides through one side of her mouth, as though her throat had sunk into her stomach. She is paralysed on the right side, but her left eye shines with an adolescent, at times almost childish, twinkle. One afternoon when both my sister and I were at her bedside, she became very excited: it seemed she was shouting for Tá, thinking my sister was Tá, and accusing Tá of trying to steal her son's affection. Then, repeatedly, she called my name, distorting it even more than usual. According to the doctors, she may remain in this state for one month or a year, one year or six years: her heart is strong, it is still in fine fettle.

On the afternoon she made those accusations against Tá, I left there feeling as though my chest had been wrapped in a light, even comfortable, woolly coat that was lined throughout with the tiniest of needles. Hours later, I came to and found myself wandering along the docks. In the meantime, night had fallen.

Two days later, a letter from Y was waiting for me in the atelier. Or rather: four lines scrawled in English; headed notepaper from a hotel in Copenhagen; a request not to write to her there or anywhere else. Apart from that, it was postmarked Zurich. She was telling me she might be able to come to Lisbon at the beginning of the new year. She'd let me know nearer the time. Until then, she wished me a Merry Christmas.

Palma's salon was by then already discreetly decorated with a few branches of holly. Zu made a great fuss of me; she was sorry she'd missed me the last couple of times I'd been there and that had coincided (bad luck) with two separate occasions when she'd been 'off sick': the first time she'd had flu, the second, a slight tummy upset. When I left, putting her tip in her apron pocket, she squeezed two of my fingers very hard; then she took hold of one of them and, very gently, traced down it: 'Will you be coming here again before Christmas?' she asked, closing her eyes. While washing my hair, she'd found a way to whisper in my ear: 'Well, are we ever going to have lunch again?...' and then, in the other ear: 'I've been waiting...' But this last gesture of hers, so furtively explicit and performed so expertly right under old Palmiped's feet, disturbed me a little more than might have been expected: there, before my very eyes (there she is, removing her thimble), were the fleshy fingers of Mrs Zolda, seamstress.

The following week, I finally gave up my dismal performance of leaving washing-up in the sink, and sprinkling the bed linen on the divan with toilet water; the little bottle of 'Y' was more than half empty.

I was tempted on several occasions to phone up Zu: if she came with that eau-de-Cologne Y had given her (which was not necessarily 'Y'), it would be a good test for Floripe's nose. But whenever I thought of ringing her, these words of Xô's (Amalfi, July or August, 1963 or 1964), which I had not remembered for over twenty years, kept springing to my mind: 'It's absurd to only want a man as a pillow in bed. But it is also absurd for a man to only want a woman in bed as a mattress with blinking eyes. It becomes quite tiresome.' This was another way of her letting me know that, ever since she'd known me, it hadn't even crossed her mind to go to bed, in Rome, with A, B, C or D or any other letter of the alphabet.

Xô, Y, Zu: if only they were the only unknown quantities I'd come across in my life! It is not inevitably on top of a mattress or under a blanket that unknown quantities can be determined.

I continued to write.

Then one night came the bombshell: it was not quite the one foretold in the latest scrap of paper.

I arrived home at around eight o'clock and found my wife in a state of such aggressively subdued tension as I'd never seen her before.

'What's the matter?'

'Nothing. It's nothing. Nothing's happened. I have some papers to go through.'

She shut herself in the study, turning the key. I ate alone. After that, I went twice to knock on the study door; both times, her harsh and exhausted voice answered me from within: she was dealing with an extremely urgent file; she wouldn't be finished for ages yet.

So I stretched out on my bed, I tried to read a book and I dozed off. When I woke up, I knocked once again on the study door; I had just thought of something:

'Has something happened to my mother?'

'No. It's nothing to do with your mother. Just me.' But her voice seemed calmer.

That's when I wished you were at home and that I could speak to you over the phone: I hadn't yet said anything to you about your poetry, and I'd received it nearly a month before; I just didn't know what to say about my meeting with your friend. Besides it would be difficult, even impossible, to broach certain subjects with your paediatrician standing guard. But if it was he who came to the phone, I could always ask him if anything was wrong at the hospital or at College, and try to find out a possible cause for my wife's tension.

But when I looked at my watch, I realized it was already coming up to midnight: I hadn't really dozed off after all, I'd slept for over two hours, and obviously more deeply than I'd thought at first. Nevertheless, I dialled your number, I let the phone ring three times, I hung up and dialled again: no one was answering.

When I went back to my room, I heard my wife calling me:

'Would you mind coming in here?' She had unlocked the study door; she was still sitting at the desk; she insisted I should settle down in one of the leather easy chairs and, turning her chair, she rested her arm on one of the shelves behind her: 'I thought I'd better tell you. So you might be forewarned.' She then started talking about your husband: 'You know how highly I think of him... How much I even respected him. He's intelligent, hard-working... But for a while now there have been certain rumours among us, then they were no longer rumours, and complaints have been made within the profession. Complaints that have unfortunately been validated. At least in part. Matters of a deontological nature. Quite serious ones. I cannot tell you what exactly, nor would you think of asking me. Last week I had a long chat with him, it was quite unpleasant for both of us, but I told him straight out that he was not to count on me and that there was still time to change direction and find another career. He seemed to understand. Some accusations he didn't deny, others he did, but he swore he would reform, that he would make sure that certain things would never happen again. And would I give him a chance... Would I, if need be, testify in his favour, purely on a professional basis. I said I would. There was however one point on which I refused to budge: he would have to chose another speciality, and I would not go back on the decision I'd made not to support his application for a grant to go to the United States. Even that he seemed to understand. But today when I saw him, he was completely and utterly devastated. He might even have been drinking. I've never seen him so upset. I would never have thought him capable of behaving the way he did. At first, I didn't even understand...' Then, after a pause, looking straight into my eyes, she said: 'But you probably know already, don't you?'

'Me? What do I know?'

'That his wife has left home. Because of that man who's a writer, the one with the pipe, the one who used to be on telly... You even know him. I always thought you didn't even like him very much. Only I didn't quite understand if she left home because of him or if they've actually gone off to live together.'

'That's the least important.'

'It certainly doesn't matter in the least to me.'

'Get back to your assistant... It's beginning to sound as if the girl was right to drop him!'

'That's where things become complicated. He assures me that it's all your fault. No more, no less: you're the one at fault. That you may have had a relationship with her, before... I didn't say yes or no to that. And that you then "passed her on to the next", that was the elegant expression he used, and that "you even gave your blessing" (she quoted him again) "to all this sordid carry-on". This too: he said that you even had the audacity to insinuate to him that you lent them your atelier. That in the summer, you spent a whole afternoon laughing at his expense, but that he only realized it later. That when you met in a bookshop, you even went to the extent of shoving the other man's picture right under his nose, just to show him that you were no longer with his wife and that you had definitely "passed her on to the next"... Anyway, it's all such a muddle, I cannot even explain it properly!'

'What a bastard! The man's insane, he's a fool, he's vile.'

'He's not a fool. Not usually. But he was today. Because all that talk was just so that he could blackmail me: either I would continue to support him and second his grant application, or else he'd go to everyone, including the newspapers, the radio, he even mentioned the television, saying what "kind of a person" you are (the "kind of a person" was also his expression, and at that point I had to put an end to it!), knowing full well, as he added, that my reputation would also be jeopardized by it all. I had to grab him by the arm and throw him out of my consulting room. And, of course, I told him loud and clear that I didn't believe a single word of the accusations he was making against you. As to whether or not you did have an affair with his wife, I said nothing.'

'You were too cautious. You could have said something. But I understand... And thank you for everything!'

Bending the truth slightly, I then told her about the fatuous conversation I'd had with him a few months earlier, in that bar in the shopping centre, when I'd quite simply, and only to shock him, made up this friend of mine who, and so on and so forth...

'But why did you have to...?' She didn't finish her sentence; she raised one of her hands to her left shoulder blade, breathed in deeply, and merely added: 'Always such a clown!'

Although this exclamation was accompanied by only the faintest of smiles, I went up to her:

'Don't you feel too well?'

'I'm all right. The worst is over. It was worse this afternoon.' She lifted two fingers up to my chin, without quite touching me. 'That's enough emotion for one day. I'm going to bed.' She brushed my forehead with a fleeting kiss.

Less than one hour later: I was already undressed, but still awake, with something going round my head that I seemed to have just worked out, when my wife appeared at the bedroom door, wearing the same dress she'd had on before, with her shabby fur coat over her shoulders.

'I didn't wake you up, did I? I'm sorry... I just need to check something... Your watch has a second hand, doesn't it? It's just that mine is being mended, and all the others we have here...' She leaned against the door-way; she tried to breathe; she was ashen. 'Don't be afraid. I'm not having a heart attack. I'm so antiquated that it's plain old angina pectoris...'

'What a bastard! That bastard knew all along!... And still he...'

I was completely stunned: I don't know how I handed her the watch, how I watched like a moron while she took her own pulse, staring intently at my watch in her hand.

'Don't worry...' she repeated. 'But if you want to put your mind at rest, you could call me a taxi, so I can go over to the Santa Maria's casualty department...'

'What do you mean, call a taxi! I'll take you there myself. Right this minute!'

I put on my flannels straight over my pyjama trousers, flung on a polo-neck jumper and my duffle-coat.

During the journey, I kept on asking: 'How are you feeling? How are you feeling?', interspersing my questions with always the same exclamation: 'What a bastard!'

Be strong, don't give in, hold on to life, show them what a great woman you've always been. Don't give in, think of me. 'How are you feeling? How are you feeling?' Why did you just close your eyes? Try just a little bit longer, we're almost there, 'What a bastard!' That's it, that's it, squeeze my hand, look how many people would miss you, starting and ending with me. I swear, I swear that if this all blows over, I don't know what to swear by, but I swear I'll never be so selfish again, nor shall ever I neglect you again. We'll go to Italy, shall we? You'd like that! How about Rome? 'How are you feeling? How are you feeling?' We're almost there, they won't find anything wrong, 'That bloody bastard!' Look how happy we've been in our own way, how we've even had what can be considered a successful relationship.

In casualty, they immediately did an ECG on her when we arrived. And they thought it best, as a precaution, they said, to take her at once to Intensive Care. I was to calm down, leave, there was nothing to be alarmed about, it was more a matter of being able to run more thorough tests.

Leave? Where to? It was three o'clock in the morning! And I shot off towards that bastard's house. I rang the doorbell for fifteen minutes, I woke up the caretaker, I woke up a neighbour and both of them grumpy and barely awake informed me that the people in 5F, both the doctor and his wife, must have gone away, for no one had seen them since last weekend.

'Do forgive me, won't you? I'm sorry I woke you up. But I am not exaggerating. This really is a matter of life and death!'

XLVII

Some forty or fifty pairs of boots and shoes splashing in the puddles of water; some twenty umbrellas dripping heartless fat raindrops on the shoulders of those who held them and on the heads of those standing nearby; and between the water that came from above and the water that was gathering below, there were eighty, ninety, perhaps even one hundred indifferently or hypocritically mournful eyes – at best, mournful, if not quite mourning – and not a single tear, however small, appeared on a single one of those thousands of eyelashes. That's what first brought a lump to my throat

They had just closed the door of the tomb. After the relative care with which the first wreaths and bouquets had been placed on and around the urn, the last ones were thrown in pell-mell and higgledy-piggledy. In the flurry to close the door before the contained torrent of petals and muddy leaves should overflow, a white carnation had been trapped by the neck – the stem inside, the bloom outside – as though in a last salute to life and a final farewell to the world.

Wearing a light raincoat and a grey astrakhan hat, Vana was the first person to give me a hug and deposit a heartfelt kiss on either side of my mouth: even under these circumstances, she couldn't help twittering. On my right, my sister was immediately given another two – although she didn't know who by – but much less noisy ones. Elvira de V. e S. (oh, it had been so long!), presumably just woken up from sleep therapy and not yet got round to dyeing her hair (what a stringy white tangle!), simply squeezed both my hands with comatose affection. The landlord of our block of flats in Lisbon (who was also our neighbour from the floor below ours), putting aside our old differences on the matter of plumbing, made a point of hoisting his short, fat arms above his metre and a half of adiposity up to my shoulders, surprising everyone – including me – with what close friends we were. Isabelinha P. M. de B. gave me a gentle but matey pinch with her finger-tips, just under my cheek-bone: her hair was shorter than the frayed hems of her jeans; and she seemed a little uneasy under the watchful eye of a no less androgynous, rather ugly woman with hard eyes, who didn't even come up to us, as though she was only there to stop Isabelinha from straying. And then came dona Mercês, with her solid homeliness of well-born spinsters, who mumbled while vigorously shaking my hand: 'I'm so sorry, I'm so sorry.'

Although it was Christmas Eve, many more people had turned up than could possibly have been expected; in the meantime, some people had already fled from the rain. Of my wife's three aunts, only the brigadier's widow was missing (she had always been the frailest), in bed now with her second bout of pneumonia this season; and the other two had just been recognized by dona Mercês, whose deceased mother had also belonged, as she was explaining, both to the Mother's Guild and the Concert Society. Press 2, not having gone to the church service, had been waiting for me at the entrance to the cemetery: without leaving her inadequate shelter under a cypress-tree, she had waved at me in a discreet and friendly manner; then she had disappeared

I had not even thought of bringing an umbrella. Continuous trickles of water fell from the spikes of my sister's umbrella, soaking my hair, then dripping down the back of my neck: some drops went beyond the boundary of my collar, setting off boldly between my shoulder blades. Each incursion made me shiver lightly; but more than anything, they were shivers of pathos.

Poor Vana, she was so full of nothing yet always willing to give of herself, so eager to give away the actual nothingness she was made of: those who give away what they don't have can do no more. My poor landlord, who is both his own landlord and his own tenant. Poor Elvira, for only occasionally being Elvira, and even then so dormantly; poor Isabelinha who can only just have discovered the deep-rooted cause for her being at odds with the world. Poor dona Mercês who, with prudent foresight and of her own free-will, lives in exile in the nebulous land of Senior Citizenship, where rather than just cultivating the pretence of being useful, she can create the illusion of remaining young. And my poor little sister (why keep referring to her as my half-sister?), who is so frustrated, so bitter, so much her father and my stepfather's little girl, so much her husband's little woman, who would never dare send her spouse's obvious genital incompetence to hell, being so used to only having with him orgasms of dollar signs and credit notes, flats in Lisbon and plots of land in the Algarve.

The main reason for the coolness of our relationship (that had not even been lukewarm before) now, at long last, no longer existed. I had certainly never been agreeable to my stepfather's body being placed, some twenty years earlier, in my father's family vault, especially as the family, apart from those in the vault, consisted now entirely of me. It is also true to say that I never openly opposed the decision to do so. But it seemed aberrant to me that those two men who had never met should lie there together, as they say, for all eternity. Well, from now on, my mother was in there too – sorry: I meant our mother – and she could at long last introduce them to each other.

Without even thinking about such trivia, my nervous tension was beginning to ease, and that's when the first tears welled in my eyes. Oh, how I had loved, how I had worshipped, at least until I was around six years old, that which since the day before was nothing more than a coffin-full of heaped bones, black silk and black leather, hair, skin and lifeless sinews! But it was mainly for myself that I was crying, overwhelmed with wretched grief for the pain I must have felt long ago, feeling and believing myself, rightly or wrongly, to have been abandoned and betrayed by my very first woman.

Maybe I wasn't even crying: maybe it was a more personal, simple way of raining too, of getting myself in tune with the cold inclemency of that rainy morning.

But my wife, who from the start had been standing a little behind me to my left, tenderly squeezed my arm, ran her fingers down to my wrist and pulled me away from there. Yes: it was best we should leave. Especially because of her.

I had tried in vain to convince her not to come. Ten days earlier, we'd had that scare: but she hadn't even been admitted to Intensive Care. After I'd been told to go home, a doctor who'd been a student of hers had turned up, looked over all the test results again, and concluded that it was not a slight myocardial ischaemia, even less a serious infarct, but just a new and bothersome manifestation of the already diagnosed angina pectoris. At least, that's what I understood. And that's all my wife needed to hear before going straight back home, but only after giving her solemn word that she would get some rest. She didn't. Nor did I.

Earlier that morning, I had phoned Zu.

'Are you free at lunchtime? Can I come and fetch you?'

'Ah, yes, lunchtime...!' she mumbled on the other end of the line, with a radiant ellipsis in her voice, followed by a veiled exclamation mark.

'Two o'clock, then. In the entrance to the *pastelaria.*'

But half an hour later, I rang her again.

'Would you mind? There's a slight change of plan: what would suit me best, actually, would be for you to go straight to the atelier. By taxi. Catch a taxi. We'll settle up afterwards.'

'Not to worry… OK. See you later.'

As soon as I arrived, after a hasty lunch, I at once began removing all the clutter off the top of the dresser; I replaced it with much more modest, not to say entirely trashy, objects which were now displayed in all their glory. The end result looked like a shoddy attempt at an exhibition of schoolchildren's handiwork.

Nevertheless, when Zu came in, I guided her towards the workshop end of the atelier where I had always entertained her. To be more precise: towards the corner where the fridge, the larder and the small Formica-covered table were to be found. And I at once handed her a one thousand escudo note to cover the expense of the taxi.

'But this is too much,' she protested.

'It will do for going back. I'll not be able to take you back either.'

A shadow of surprise or suspicion clouded the slits of her eyes.

'Are we really just having lunch?' she asked, then audacious and provocative, she went on : 'Just lunch…?'

'Perhaps not. We'll see later.'

That day, beneath the red coat which she quickly removed, she was wearing dark blue corduroy trousers and a low-cut, saggy white woollen jumper, underneath which the volume of sportingly good apples could be made out, rather than show-off perkiness of pears. The whole of her smelt good, though in no way of 'Y', let alone of Y.

I took a tin of foie gras and a jar of caviar from the fridge.

'You can start off by making a note of these brand names… Isn't that what you wanted?'

'Hey, what's the matter with you? Are you angry with me?'

'Me? Is there any reason why I should be?… It's just that there may not be time afterwards.' And I pointed to the top of the table where I had placed a note-pad and a felt-tipped pen for this very purpose.

I settled her on a stool. In an attempt to dispel the wariness that still lingered in her eyes, I placed a hand on her shoulder and drew two fingers, just the two – the tips of my middle and index fingers – along to the shadowy place where her downy hair grew at the back of her neck.

'Mmm… That's nice. But it's cold here. Is today the day you're going to show me that little nook?'

'It would seem so.'

With great diligence, as though doing some homework she'd brought home, she started to write in large, rounded letters, with her capital letters the same size as all the others. That's all I needed; but I let her finish copying down the two labels. Then, grabbing her by the arm, as though leading her off to the promised playground, and clutching in my other hand the sheet of paper she had just scrawled all over, I merely said:

'Now come here.'

Standing in front of the dresser, I at once compared the lines on that sheet of paper with those on the scraps of paper that littered the dresser-top, and at the same time confronted Zu with them:

'Just you try and deny this. Was it or was it not you who wrote this filth?'

'What? Me? Well, yes it was... It was me, yes. But why did ...? How did...?'

She seemed to be more surprised than actually worried.

'And it was your daughter's shitty wanker of a doctor who told you to write all this, wasn't it?'

'Poor man! Don't call him such names...'

'Was it him or wasn't it?'

'Yes, it was. What's the big deal? He told me it was just a joke, a joke that he and some of his colleagues were playing...'

'On me? Did you know they were playing it on me?'

'What do you mean, on you? He never so much as mentioned your name. How was I to know you even knew each other? He spoke about a boring old hospital employee who was getting on a bit and who was almost geriatric having it off with a servant. It was only a bit of fun.'

'And was it also for their entertainment that you phoned me at home? Leaving little messages like this...?'

'At home? I never phoned you at home.'

'Oh, yes you did! Just you try and remember!' I tightened my grasp on her wrist. Now she was looking almost terrified, and I found her flushed face and panting breath made her strangely arousing.

'Let go of me... How was I supposed to know it was your house! There were some times, yes, there were, when he dialled a number and then asked me to say those things... We would even laugh about it afterwards. I swear that's all there was to it.'

'Oh, you hussy, you shameless hussy!'

She was struggling and wriggling without too much conviction, as though she too were slightly aroused by my rough behaviour. Or perhaps it was me, finding her more exciting like this than on the other two occasions when she had bared her breasts at me, or even that time she got completely undressed. Suddenly, she quietened down and told me:

'I don't like to hear names like that. Unless doing something else...'

I dropped her wrist. But I immediately exploded again:

'And that arsehole? That son-of-a-bitch? Where is he? Where is he hiding? I've looked for him at home, I've already phoned him at his consulting rooms, I've already phoned the hospital...'

'How do you expect me to know? I went to his rooms yesterday, because it was my day for going there, and they told me he had gone away. That he would definitely not be back before the New Year...'

That was the same as what I'd been told. And perhaps it was because I wanted to discharge the emotions of the last few hours, or because I'd been abstinent for the past few months, but all I wanted was to see Zu's face light up again, not with the teasing fire of attempted seduction, nor with the flickering flame of premeditated abandon, but with the sparking intensity of someone surrendering, or pretending to surrender, in an almost complete state of panic. Brutishly, I grasped both her wrists even more roughly than before:

'Hussy! My hussy! My shameless hussy!'

That was a mistake: Zu can only have interpreted all this as moronic aggression on my behalf, when I was actually responding to the pressure of my unbearably pent-up lust. She freed one of her wrists with an arrogant tug, rearing up like a filly tired of being docile:

'What do you mean, "hussy"? I'd like to know which one of us is the bigger hustler! Do you think I haven't noticed how hungry you've been ever since you saw what I showed you? But then you chose to go all funny about it... You didn't want to, but you couldn't help wanting me. Why? Is it because I'm Floripes's daughter? Or were you too yellow-bellied? Did you think I threw myself at you and that I'm like that with everyone? You're wrong... I haven't been with many men, anyway. Only those I want to. And only when I want to.'

I was still holding on to her wrist, but so lightly that she could easily have pulled away: maybe she didn't so that I could actually feel the current of her indignation flowing through her fingers. And she carried on, with her eyes tightly closed, looking like someone who was taking the final plunge:

'You're funny, you men! Very funny and very stupid. When you think we're not grand enough for you, what you all like is to throw yourselves on us like animals, or else you just go along with whatever a girl would have you believe. Like those who say you're the first or you're the one and only. Those who say they have a husband at home who never touches them anymore.'

'Shut your mouth.'

'I will not. I am not one of those. I am not ashamed to say that my husband jumps on me whenever he can. But then he only jumps whenever I let him. And sometimes it's nice, others it's not. Most times it's neither good nor bad, neither hot nor cold... And what's so wrong with me wanting to know what it's like with other men every now and then? Don't proper ladies do the same anyway?'

I had finally let go of her wrist. She went over to the dresser and furiously bunched up all those scraps of paper into a ball that she clutched tightly in her clenched fist:

'Still, I'd like to know... If I was someone else, if I was that other woman, would you still have thought that I'd written these things, knowing they were for you? And that I'd been deceiving you all this time? Well let me tell you this: I don't even deceive my husband! Being unfaithful is one thing, deceiving someone is something else all together! But I did deceive myself about my husband, I must say. And about you too.' She could no longer hold back the tears that had been choking her voice for the past few moments and that wanted to escape her slanted eyes. 'In time, you could have had anything you wanted from me. But what with you going around full of yellow-bellied hunger, and me making it so clear that you could eat and didn't need to be afraid, you had to bring me here under false pretexts just to be unkind to me, to accuse me of something I did just for fun, just because someone asked me to, even if I didn't know who to... this is something I'll never be able to forgive you for!' Noisily, she sniffed up the tears that had managed to collect even at the back of her nose. 'In time, you could have had anything you wanted... and now? Now you couldn't, even if you went down on bended knees! Not even if you covered me in gold-dust from head to toe!' She'd made her way to the door. Her hand was resting on the latch: she was getting ready to leave. But, stamping her foot three times on the ground, like someone throwing a meaningless tantrum were it not for the tears falling from her eyes, she screamed: 'You see? You see? You see how you can't even get down on your knees for me?' Then, lowering her voice, suddenly overwhelmed with tiredness, she mumbled: 'I couldn't have given a damn about the gold-dust...' She took off, slamming the door behind her.

She'd forgotten her handbag and coat. I went inside and grabbed them, ran back, opened the door and spotted her up ahead, near one of the flower-beds, looking quite lost and bemused, one foot on the pavement, the other on the little wall of the flowerbed.

'Zu! Zu! Your handbag, your coat.' I handed them to her, my arm outstretched, keeping my distance.

'It wouldn't have mattered if they'd stayed behind,' she stated, without even looking at me. 'It wouldn't have mattered at all. My mother would have found them. And I could have told her my side of things.'

At the gate to the cemetery, there was Floripes. Checking it had stopped raining, she closed her umbrella, shook it vigorously and stood there waiting for us. From a distance, it was impossible to tell whether the expression on her face was sorrowful or downright unfriendly.

XLVIII

As I was climbing up the steep paths and alleys lined with pretentious family vaults that reminded me of the Aztecs' ex-villa in the Restelo in miniature, with my wife by my side (with two of her aunts following a little behind, assisted by dona Mercês), it wasn't just Zu that I'd been thinking of. I had also been thinking of you. I had also been thinking of your friend.

What can have happened to the two of you? There is no way of getting through on his home phone number; and even if there were, it would probably not be the best place to get news from right now. I phoned the Gulbenkian three times; three times the same friendly female voice told me he was out: the first time, he hadn't said where he was going; the second time, he'd gone to Brazil; the third time, she didn't know how long for.

I'm certain he will not be in Portugal for the second half – or even for the end of the first half – of what he called these wretched and vile 1980s. And you? Are you with him or not? It serves you right if you are; I even cast this spell on you with this: that both of you be quite unbearable at all times. Besides, who isn't, unless they live by a relaxed agreement such as the one my wife and I have come to? My greatest mistake with Y was to have dreamt foolishly of an idyllic future together: from then on, everything started falling to pieces.

I do hope you two are living together: there can be no greater punishment for your fear of embarking on yet another extra-marital affair. Your sins will catch up with you someday.

In any case, I need to find out your whereabouts. I have to account to you for all this: all this that I have started to recount only because I can count on you.

I did have news of your ex-husband recently. Through Press 1. It may need to be discounted. But not even a week ago, having found out, I don't know how, about our past association, she did tell me that the man is somewhere in the Douro region, in his family home, and that he intends to launch himself into the world of politics, as a parliamentary candidate during the coming elections. I almost said something along the lines of: 'What's one more bastard amongst so many?' But I feared that Press 1 might use this as a saying she'd claim to have invented, even worse, that she might start bandying it about indiscriminately. And after all, wasn't Christmas coming? And isn't it Christmas now? Peace on earth and in the heavens, not only to men of goodwill, but also to those who chose certain life-styles, because often, or at least sometimes, they cannot or know not how to do otherwise.

So many people! So many figures and figurines, actors and players surround us, be it in spirit or in the flesh, even when we think we're at our loneliest, even when we believe that the cards of our destiny can only be played with one other person! I wanted to call them all on stage, as though for the curtain-call of a show.

That's when I saw Floripes closing and shaking her umbrella.

As soon as we reached her, she made straight for my wife, especially as I'd fallen behind a little to chat to some people – including Vana – who would not have been happy to leave without reiterating their condolences. There were others who were only just arriving (because of the rain, the traffic, Christmas Eve, who'd have believed we were in the middle of a crisis!) or who perhaps did not like to step through the gateways of a cemetery, as a matter of principle or superstition. I didn't discover which of these categories Vana's husband belonged to; nor my neighbour from the atelier that Vana so often visited: they were both standing next to each other, wearing identical raincoats; and, side by side, rather like Thomson and Thompson, they came over to give two symmetrical half-embraces, which still allowed Vana – before she left, escorted by the two of them – the opportunity gratefully to deposit on my battered cheeks a third pair of twittering kisses. Only then did Floripes come up to me:

'What a shame, Mestre, that's your poor mother gone! God rest her soul, it was a blessing, really, she's been spared all that suffering! My daughter's only just phoned me to tell me the news, she found out in the salon, it was senhor Palma himself who read it in the newspaper, and my daughter thought I might like to know, that I might like to come, she even said, Mum, give my condolences to Mestre, I'm sorry I can't come, but it is Christmas Eve, so of course she couldn't come, but she doesn't realize how hard it was for me to catch a bus, everyone packed in like sardines, nothing but rude people carrying loads and loads of bags, which just makes them even worse! Your poor, dear mother, she's had a good innings, I must say, but mums are mums, and we all suffer, so we do, and I know all about it, when my mother died I spent a good two days half out of my mind!'

My wife was up ahead, standing between her two aunts (dona Mercês had disappeared), still waiting for me.

'You all go on to the car,' I said, handing her the keys, having realized that Floripes wouldn't be letting me go quite yet.

'Look, Mestre, I may as well tell you one more thing, but it's not really something we should be talking about here, let alone on a day like this…' She almost dragged me out of the cemetery; she then planted her feet on the edge of the pavement, having stepped definitely back into the world of the living. 'It's just that, since yesterday or perhaps even the day before yesterday, back at the atelier, there's been a letter for you from abroad, and maybe I'm imagining it, but I could swear it smells of that perfume that this nose of mine recognized at once… Now I've known all along that the lady hasn't been around, she's not completely Portuguese so she must have needed to go abroad, especially at this time of year, it being Christmas and all that, who wouldn't want to be with their loved ones? You see, I notice everything, I realize I shouldn't be talking about such things on a day like this, but how can I help it if I happened to notice last week, no, no, it was the week before, that you weren't able to contain yourself any more, Mestre, poor man, who can blame you, least of all me, I know full well what artists are like, so I do, but you did have another lady round, so you did, after this one had gone abroad, even if it was nothing serious, and it's not as though you didn't go to a lot of trouble to try and hide it from me, the divan was quite tidy, really, I don't know if you even lay down on it, the pair of you, the trouble was the perfume, it was another smell altogether, this nose of mine never lets me down! But what really got to me was that you took everything off the dresser that day, and I thought to myself, and I even discussed it with my daughter afterwards, don't tell me it was someone who likes it like that or maybe it's the fashion now, but even if it's called a dresser, it's got nothing to do with what you do when you're undressed, you must forgive me Mestre, but you do know what I mean, don't you? Talking of my daughter, do you know, she was really cut up about your mother's passing away and she begged me over the phone, oh, Mum, tell him, tell him, tell Mestre that I am so very, very sorry and tell him also, if he won't take offence, that I send him a great big hug. Of course he won't take offence, I told her, but how sad, how stupid, that on a day like this I cannot even wish you Merry Christmas, and I wanted to so much, but what I wish you most of all for tonight is a nice, quiet night with your lady wife, I've told her already, and that you may both keep in good health, which is the most important! Heavens, Mestre, always troubling yourself like this!… On my life, as if that's what I said Merry Christmas for!…'

Having dropped my wife and her aunts off at the house of the aunt who was ill, I arranged to meet them all back there in the late afternoon.

'We can make a little chicken soup,' said the Concert Society.

'I've got some turkey breast,' added the Mothers' Guild. 'And also some *fios de ovos*[44] that I ordered earlier.'

'Of course, this won't be a proper Christmas dinner, let alone a fancy meal,' explained the first.

'But only if you don't mind, maybe you'd prefer to be alone,' considered my wife. 'Unless you'd rather I went home and waited for you there.'

No. I didn't want that. No. I didn't mind. Everything they were planning to do was just fine by me. I kissed them all on the forehead as lovingly as possible, as though bestowing on them a reward for trying so thoughtfully to stop me feeling even more of an orphan than I ever had.

Then I went to the atelier. On the way over, I switched on the car radio. But all the stations were playing nothing but Jingle Bells and jingles, jingles and Jingle Bells. Until suddenly one particular French *ballade* got through to me: lyrics by Aragon, vocals by Léo Ferré. Oh, I knew it all right; I had the record at home. And yet, only now did two of its lines stand out from the whole convoluted tune, like two searchlights (that were really one) illuminating both my past and my present:

J'aimais déjà les étrangères
quand j'étais un petit enfant.

The letter was indeed from Y. I couldn't even bring myself to open it, although just the look of the envelope was comforting, made of excellent Wathman paper and bearing a much more self-confident handwriting than the previous two messages had. On top, where it said sender, were only her initials, followed by an address in Saint Moritz. It was postmarked Saint Moritz as well.

I sat on the edge of the divan, filled with an indescribable feeling of contentment just from touching the slightly rough paper. I lit the heater, after realizing that I'd been mistaken in thinking I'd lit it already.

Oh, my beautiful Cancer, with Scorpio in your ascendant, what a contradictory person I am compared to you, always swaying between the impetuosity of Taurus and the indecisiveness of Pisces! You, Water and Water: how fluid! Me, Earth and Water: how often I land in the mud!

I wonder if your friend is right: is Y neurotic? Or even psychotic? If so, is there any way I can love her less? Isn't Beauty itself psychotic? Or isn't it, rather, that the love of Beauty is psychotic? But it is only Beauty, or the love of Beauty, however psychotic it may be or outdated it may appear, that can actually thrill me and make me soar above the world.

On the last time she was here with me – that's right, a few hours before that conversation she had with Floripes – when our bodies were moving as one towards ecstasy, Y had suddenly exclaimed:

'Can you feel it? Can you? We have the same flow.'

And, soon afterwards, we lay on our backs, side by side, like two fallen statues. In her quiet voice, she referred again to that moment:

'I didn't mean flow. Not just the same flow... I meant the same blood as well.'

The prolonged contact with the envelope made me sure she'd be coming back. And maybe very soon: she'd come in, she'd lie down...

Sure? How could I be sure? The envelope could just as easily contain the promise of a fresh start or the farewell of a permanent break-up. I couldn't even decide which would be better to help keep alive the illusion of a successful love affair.

I remained like that for a good few minutes longer, holding the unopened letter in my hands.

Lisbon (and other places),
between 18 March 1982
and 31 August 1986.

Appendix

Oh church bell in my village
(*Ó sino da minha aldeia*)

Oh church bell in my village
Plaintive in the evening calm,
Your tolling ever calls awake
An echo in my soul.

So slow and lingering is your rhythm,
So sad, as if on life's account,
That the first stroke of the sequence
Has a sound already heard.

However near to me you ring
When I pass by, ever wandering,
You seem to me to be a dream,
In my soul a far-off echo.

At every sounding stroke of yours
Throbbing through the cloudless sky,
I feel the past is further off,
And longing ever nearer.

Ó sino da minha aldeia,
Dolente na tarde calma,
Cada tua badalada
Soa dentro da minha alma

E é tão lento o teu soar,
Tão como triste de vida,
Que já a primeira pancada
Tem o som de repetida.

Por mais que me tanjas perto
Quando passo, sempre errante,
És para mim como um sonho,
Soas-me na alma distante.

A cada pancada tua
Vibrante no céu aberto,
Sinto mais longe o passado,
Sinto a saudade mais perto.

(Fernando Pessoa, *Cancioneiro*; poem dated 1913.)

Fernando Pessoa, *Selected Poems*, edited and translated by Peter Rickard (Edinburgh University Press: Edinburgh, 1971).

Notes

1 A small, rural estate.
2 Twentieth-century Brazilian poet.
3 These are all regional dishes of Portugal; they correspond more or less to corn bread, fried pastries, a traditional fruit cake eaten at Epiphany, French toast, pumpkin pudding and a fish-shaped cake covered in egg-yolk filaments.
4 The Portuguese monetary unit translates literally as 'shield' (the same word as the French 'écu').
5 The Portuguese equivalent of a patisserie.
6 The Lisbon School of Art.
7 A dairy shop that also doubles up as a café and patisserie; a milk bar.
8 Fish cakes made of potato and salted cod.
9 Large landed property, somewhere between a farm and a cattle ranch.
10 The official school-leaving age in Portugal until 1974.
11 A traditional gift at Easter.
12 An 'industrial' school for girls in the street by the same name, preparing them to join the workforce, rather than university.
13 The specific term *Outra Banda* is used to refer to the south side of the river.
14 The following two lines have been omitted by the author: 'I half-rise, energetic, full of conviction, human, / And I decide to write these verses in which I say the opposite.'
15 'The Tobacconist's' ('A Tabacaria') is a poem by Álvaro de Campos, translation by Suzete Macedo (Calouste Gulbenkian Foundation: Lisbon, 1987). Álvaro de Campos is a pen name of Fernando Pessoa (1888–1935).
16 The coastal road from Lisbon to Cascais, passing through Estoril.
17 The *Jornal de Letras* is a literary review.
18 A bloodless revolution took place on 25 April 1974, when the government was overthrown by a group of Portuguese army officers, marking the true end of dictatorship and the end of Portugal's involvement in Africa.
19 A poem by the Spanish poet Luis Cernuda (1902–63): *A fixed term had / Our relationship and agreement, like everything else / In life, and one day, a day like any other, / For no apparent reason or pretext, / We stopped seeing each other. Did you sense it coming? / I did, because I had always known it would.*
20 Traditional hot red-pepper sauce.
21 A reference to the last two verses of Álvaro de Campos' poem 'The Tobacconist's': 'He waves a greeting, I shout "Hello, Esteves!" and

the universe / Falls into place for me again without ideal or hope, and the Tobacconist smiles.' Translation by Suzete Macedo (op. cit.).

22 The 'Ordem de Santiago da Espada' and the 'Ordem de Cristo' are decorations given to civilians by the Portuguese government.

23 Again, a quote from 'The Tobacconist's', glossing the anti-metaphysics of existence.

24 A huge earthquake hit Lisbon and the surrounding areas on 1 November 1755; widespread fires and large-scale destruction resulted in Lisbon being rebuilt by the Marquês de Pombal, with a modern approach to town-planning.

25 The Lisbon opera house.

26 A reference to a poem by Fernando Pessoa who was born in this area. See appendix.

27 A feature of Portuguese bullfighting is the *pega* (or 'tackle') whereby the bull is immobilized by eight *forcados* (or 'grapplers'), unarmed men who tackle the bull in fair combat.

28 A traditional form of cherry brandy, and a coarse form of gin.

29 The badge of the Portuguese Legion (Legião Portuguesa), a right-wing political organization during Salazar's regime.

30 This 'Public Library Square' has been renamed, as the library was moved from there to another part of Lisbon (Campo Grande).

31 A terrace or veranda that has been closed in with panes of glass.

32 The name of the sewing lady in the original text would translate literally as 'Miss Isolde'. As the woman is divorced and also a clairvoyant, the phonetically identical 'Mrs Zolda' seems more appropriate.

33 These are men who work the fields; *malteses* are casual labourers, contracted on the spot, and *ganhões* work for a period of time agreed beforehand with the contractor.

34 A diminutive of the name Palma (which does also mean 'palm-tree') indicating affection and slight condescension.

35 A *monte* is the main house of a large landed property in the Alentejo.

36 A paint as popular in Portugal as Dulux is in Britain.

37 One tostão is a tenth of an escudo.

38 Literally, 'hot summer'; this refers to the summer of 1968, when students in Paris rebelled against the authorities.

39 A memorial mass said seven days after a person's death.

40 The Portuguese word for hot dogs translates literally as 'puppies'; there was a conscious attempt to keep one more foreign word out of Portuguese.

41 Polícia de Informação e Defesa do Estao, the infamous security police under Salazar.

42 The equivalent of an espresso coffee.

43 The Portuguese version of a Don Juan.

44 Egg filament cakes.